Abigail is a comedy writer living
diet of three-shot coffee, bourbons
She was born and brought up in
blame for the sardonic humour
Abigail was the runner-up in 2019's Comedy
award for *The Lonely Fajita,* her first novel.

www.abigailemann.com

twitter.com/abigailemann
facebook.com/abigailmannauthor
instagram.com/abigailemann

Also by Abigail Mann

The Lonely Fajita

The Sister Surprise

THE WEDDING CRASHER

ABIGAIL MANN

One More Chapter
a division of HarperCollins*Publishers*
1 London Bridge Street
London SE1 9GF
www.harpercollins.co.uk

HarperCollins*Publishers*
1st Floor, Watermarque Building, Ringsend Road
Dublin 4, Ireland

This paperback edition 2022
1
First published in Great Britain in ebook format
by HarperCollins*Publishers* 2022

A catalogue record of this book is available from the British Library

ISBN: 978-0-00-848910-6

This novel is entirely a work of fiction. The names, characters and incidents
portrayed in it are the work of the author's imagination. Any resemblance to actual
persons, living or dead, events or localities is entirely coincidental.

Printed and bound in the UK using 100% Renewable Electricity
by CPI Group (UK) Ltd

To anyone who wondered if you made the
right choice.

Here you are.

Prologue

THE WEDDING DAY

'If you see her, don't let her come closer!' shouted Poppy, her foot sinking through a floorboard that lined the base of the dinghy.

'How am I supposed to do that?' asked Lola. 'Whack her with an oar?' She tucked her five-inch heels under her armpit and unwound the landing rope like a lasso, glancing up the zigzag path that led to the hotel. The wedding party could be heard, if not seen.

Will hovered on the jetty, eyes frantic, hands interlocked behind his neck. 'Poppy, are you sure?' he asked, a pained expression on his face.

'No, of course I'm not,' she said. 'But are *you* sure you want to stay?'

Lola gripped the wall and peeked around the corner of the pub. The silhouettes of a small crowd appeared on the cliff side, a hand pointing down towards the harbour. The fact that Poppy's best friend had colour-matched her hair to a Dairy Milk wrapper just before arriving on the island of Loxby didn't exactly help them blend in, but then again no one had anticipated that they might need to flee, let alone quickly, and definitely *not* with the groom in tow.

Poppy crawled to the other end of the dinghy, the hem of her dress damp.

'Will, look at me.' Poppy reached up, her hand outstretched. Will turned and took a steeling breath, his chest heaving. 'Decision time,' she said. Will nodded, but he didn't look sure.

'It'll be all right. It's not all right now. In fact, it's horribly, laughably shit. But would you rather make a bad decision now that'll take years to unpick, or a good decision that'll at least buy you some time to figure out what you want to do?'

Will didn't speak. Instead, he interlocked his fingers with Poppy's and jumped down into the dinghy beside her, sending it rocking from side to side.

'Lola!'

Lola groaned as she made her way down the jetty, her bottom lip stuck out as Will helped her into the dinghy. 'No offence Will, but if anyone else in your family gets married, I'd rather shave my teeth than take them on as a client. And no, you're not getting your deposit back. Or the origami swans I made – I didn't slice my fingers open on crafting card for nothing.'

Poppy gingerly made her way to the back of the boat, took Lola's face in her hands, and smacked a kiss on her forehead. 'You are an *excellent* wedding planner. Even though I'm jaded and difficult and made that situation'—Poppy gestured to the cliff-side path, where the tight-jawed bride descended towards them, armfuls of ivory lace gathered in her fists—'a lot worse than it should have been. Until then, can you help us coordinate a departure before Ottilie gets a chance to gouge out our eyes with the heel of her shoe?'

'I don't think she could. She's wearing ballet pumps,' said Will.

'I'd rather not split hairs over the details, Will. Quick, help me with the engine, will you?'

Will rolled onto his stomach and propped himself up on his elbows, which were submerged in a puddle marbled with leaking fuel. They gripped the starter cord together, his hand covering her fist.

Lola unhooked her earpiece and tugged the wire out from beneath her clothes, throwing it back onto the jetty. 'They can have the mic pack, but I'm not leaving this behind,' she said, slipping her iPad down the front of her dress.

With three of them at the rear, the nose of the dinghy tipped up like a playful dolphin, sending sea water up the dinghy's cushioned sides and over their feet.

'One, two, three!' said Poppy as she and Will tugged at the starter cord. The engine coughed, sending the propeller on one pathetic rotation before coming to a standstill again, accompanied by thick diesel fumes.

'Again. One, two, three!' In her haste to get moving, Poppy jerked backwards into Will, sending her elbow straight into his crotch. Will yelped and crumpled to the floor, eyes glossed with pain. He clutched the back of Poppy's leg, his expression caught between constipation and nausea.

'Now is not the time to be melodramatic, Will! Shit. Poppy, look!' cried Lola.

Ottilie had reached the harbour, her ivory veil trailing behind her as she ran past the family's flotilla of yachts.

'Does she look angry?' asked Will, his voice strained.

'Well, you just left her at the altar in front of two hundred people, so I'd be surprised to find her cup overfloweth with joy,' said Lola.

Will slid lower into the belly of the boat, his dark curls hidden below the line of the jetty.

'Harsh, but fair,' said Poppy, wiping her sweaty palms on

Will's shirt sleeve. 'Now, can someone *please* help me start this engine?'

The boat squeaked as Lola shuffled down from her perch. The three of them huddled together, their sodden clothes clinging to their bodies. Fist over fist, they gripped the cord.

'Pull!'

Chapter One

Poppy zigzagged between rogue chairs and wonky tables, a tray balanced on her hip.

'Miss, do you want help with that?' asked a student of Poppy's with the same *Peaky Blinders* haircut that every boy in Year Ten had as soon as they stepped into a barber's without their mum.

'Miss, don't buy it. Leo's sucking up to all the female teachers after Mr Lattimer's assembly on *empowering the women in our lives*,' his friend said, the last line rolling with sarcasm.

'Fuck off,' breathed Leo.

'Oi! Swearing!' said Poppy, glancing at the door to check that none of her colleagues were within earshot. She picked up a disposable camera from the desk. 'What was Mr Lattimer's assembly about?' she asked, trying her best to look disinterested as she pushed a chair under the table with her foot.

'Some women's rights thing. How we should be nice to girls because they have to sit in a sandbox whilst they're on their period. Wish my sister did that – she leaves tampon wrappers all over the bathroom. Proper nasty.'

'Leo, you're being incredibly misogynistic.'

5

'That's a big word, miss,' he replied. At this, his friend spluttered into the back of his hand. Sakima, unashamedly Poppy's favourite student, appeared beside her, twanging an elastic around a rope-thick braid that ended at her waist.

'It's actually not, Leo. You need to read more.'

'I read,' said Leo, his neck mottled pink. He shouldered a drawstring JD Sports bag and glanced at the clock, jerking his head backwards to flick his fringe out of his eyes.

'The back of a cereal box doesn't count.'

Leo gulped like a fish. 'You need to... to—'

'Message me when you think of something. Miss, I've collected the other cameras – they're on your desk.'

'Can we go?' said Leo, standing up.

'The bell hasn't rung yet—'

Before she finished her sentence, three sharp bleeps reverberated in the tiled corridor as her students dismissed themselves. Poppy sighed.

'Sakima, you're a star, thank you.'

'Shall I get a dustpan?' she said, gesturing to the floor where a broken camera had been knocked off a table.

'Please, it's—'

'By the sink, I know.'

'Yep.'

Sakima took the tray from her, leaving Poppy to scoop shards of broken camera casing into her palm, the film reel chopped into plastic confetti. She knew that photography was seen as glorified babysitting by her colleagues, which was why she was sent so many of their students who had 'do not give scissors' typed on their student reports.

'You should go. You have to catch the bus, don't you?' said Poppy.

'Nah, I'm walking. I've got an hour in the dark room at The Art House, but it doesn't start until five. I've been doing double exposures, but Dad's fed up of me photographing him watching *Pointless*, so I thought I should take my baby out and about, you know?' Sakima smiled and patted her rucksack, where her camera sat inside.

Poppy nodded, her head fuggy from Friday afternoon noise, too much instant coffee, and the delightful blend of Lynx Africa and body odour that hung heavy in the room. Eau de Teenage Boy at its finest.

The previous Easter, her teaching partner, Frances, had left school in the midst of a breathy tantrum, threatening to leave for good. In a waft of patchouli, overwhelmed tears, and – unbeknownst to Poppy – a ticket to Ibiza, she'd actually done it. Poppy's admiration outweighed any residual envy. According to Facebook, she'd changed her name to Celeste and now performed reiki healing to a crowd who appeared far more open to her claim that she could photograph guardian angels.

Poppy packed her tote bag with a class set of disposable cameras. It was going to cost her a fortune to have all these developed, but seeing as she'd had barely a week to prepare for an additional twenty students taking her subject and no school budget to give them decent cameras to use, it was either this or she had to let them use their phones, which was far riskier.

Cricklemead Academy was in the relegation zone of schools, always dancing between 'satisfactory' and 'requires improvement' when Ofsted came to visit. On the eve of their last inspection, Poppy's field trip request was dredged from the stack of previously rejected files and signed off for approval. Off she had gone to the local botanical gardens, which conveniently took the worst offenders away from the school for an entire day.

'I've always wondered...' said Sakima, hopping up to sit on a desk. 'What do teachers *actually* do in the summer holidays?'

'Well, some go on holiday to the south of France to eat Boursin and baguettes for six weeks, but in reality, most of us crawl under our desks, where our bodies turn wrinkly and hard like a walnut, then Shane the caretaker cracks us open with a pickaxe on September the first and we go through the whole rigmarole again.'

Sakima swung her legs, fiddling with the end of her braid. 'Last year I saw Mr Kane in the big Sainsbury's near my house. On a *Saturday*, right? He was buying a jar of pickled onions and said hello to me. *So* weird.'

'Weird that he was buying pickled onions or weird he said hello?'

'I don't know, both. Maybe because he was wearing shorts. *Really* short shorts. Like, *illegally* short shorts. Seriously though, miss, are you doing anything nice? No offence, but I think you could do with getting away for a bit. Some sunshine. Some *fun*.'

'Pfft, no. Well, I am. Sort of.' Poppy busied herself at the tap by the window and filled a paint-smeared yoghurt pot with water. She looked down at the school gates, the glass dirty with chalky water droplets. There was Josh – her husband – marching towards a group of boys who were taking it in turns to kick a half-drunk can of Relentless towards a steady stream of traffic. She'd found it hard to refer to him as Mr Lattimer when they'd both started at the school some six years before, but now she'd become well-adjusted to their compartmentalised lives since Easter. After nearly a decade together, a feeling had settled in Poppy's stomach like poured concrete, rock-hard and immovable. Did it count as an official separation if they still lived in the same house? Split chores? Ate each other's leftovers?

She dried her hands on a blue paper towel and unzipped a battered suitcase, carefully stacking old lenses, fixtures, and wobbly tripods inside. Poppy's Friday routine involved wheeling equipment back and forth to her attic at home, tinkering away with tiny screwdrivers and a four-finger-deep gin and tonic at her side. It hadn't helped the image that many of the Cricklewood students had of her, the slightly odd photography teacher who didn't eat lunch with the other staff, despite being married to one of them.

Back at her desk, Poppy pulled a copy of National Geographic out from under her keyboard and passed it to Sakima. She tapped the cover, a smile tickling her mouth.

'You're going for it?' said Sakima.

'I'm going for it,' said Poppy, running a hand through her hair. 'Thought I might try and practise what I preach for once. Get out there, just me and my birds. Settle in on a clifftop. Become at one with the puffin community. I can't keep telling you to enter competitions if I don't do the same myself.'

'Miss! I'm proud of you!'

'Thanks, Sakima,' said Poppy with a faux curtsy. Poppy *was* looking forward to a fortnight on the Devonshire coast. She craved solitude. When she was alone, she wanted to be *more* alone, if that was possible. A single pickle in a jar. If a stone cottage off the national grid with only seabirds for company didn't scratch the itch, she wasn't sure what would. Poppy had come to the conclusion that isolation was better when you brought it on yourself. Most of the time, anyway.

There were many examples she could point to over the past few years. Take last weekend: after a bout of silent treatment from Josh, she'd spent a solitary morning in her local Wetherspoons just so she could experience a normal burble of noise. It turned out that the grumbling of retirees working through pints of Fosters and a mixed grill at eleven o'clock in the morning was far more depressing than being stuck at home, so despite her avowal that she wouldn't be back for hours, Poppy caved and returned to Josh's smug face at the front door. Again.

'Will you show us your photos when you're back?' said Sakima, shouldering her rucksack.

'Sure,' said Poppy. The thought of a new term starting in barely seven weeks made Poppy's stomach tighten.

She waved goodbye to Sakima and clunked her suitcase down the stairs, pausing on the landing as the English department shut their classroom doors behind them, ties loose, tea-stained mugs and houseplants in hand. Between them, there was an inordinate amount of polka-dot print on display.

'Poppy! Last day of term! Coming to The Stag? Your fella is getting the first round, I heard.'

Poppy openly scoffed. She often forgot the golden rule that she and Josh had agreed on: their split was a secret until he'd decided on the right time for 'a clean break'.

'No, I don't think so.'

'Oh, come on,' said Mike, a middle-aged man who chaired the teaching union and could quote the entirety of *Animal Farm* by heart.

'I've got to pack, fix some equipment, you know? I've got a big trip to prepare for.'

'He got you doing his packing as well? Cheeky sod. Put a brick in his hand luggage.'

'He's not coming.'

'Oh?'

'Mmm.'

The group loitered with fixed smiles as Poppy tried to think of something else to say. She'd never been very good at making things up on the spot.

'Well, have a good one, Poppy.'

'You too.' Poppy nodded and walked in the other direction, where she stood behind a wall and waited until there was no chance she'd accidentally catch them up on the way out.

Now that she knew to expect an empty house, she wanted nothing more than to return to it. She'd never anticipated a kinship with Melania Trump, but as the last day of term swung around, she felt a similar need for large sunglasses to hide her swollen eyes when around her husband. At work, she forced a smile when her colleagues asked what she'd done at the weekend. Poppy's stories of homemade croissants and hiking in the dales were the stuff of fantasy. In reality, she lived like a dormouse, scurrying up to the attic where she slept on a rattan couch every night whilst Josh took their bedroom. She came downstairs after he'd left for his HIIT class at 6.30am, and walked to work nursing a coffee that made her eyelids twitch, then dashed up to the art classroom until the bell rang at 3.30pm.

Josh stalked the corridors in skinny suit trousers and a crisp shirt with the sleeves rolled up to the elbow, a look he claimed was 'approachable, yet authoritative'. Although it was petty, around six months ago Poppy had told him that he looked like a division two footballer about to read an affidavit, but he'd replied 'thank you' without a hint of irony and it was then Poppy realised they'd been running on different tracks for longer than she'd thought. Then again, had they ever been on the same track to begin with?

Chapter Two

'Why don't you come here instead, Pops?'

Poppy propped her phone up against a shoebox that housed loose butterfly screws and old canisters of film. The sound of wind blasting up the Cornish coastline distorted over FaceTime, making it hard to hear her dad. In the background, Poppy could see Reggie trotting to keep up on disproportionately stubby legs – the result of an ill-timed interlope between a dachshund and their family golden retriever. She'd never quite figured out the physics of that particular copulation.

'It's breeding season down on Orwell Island. I'm photographing the puffins.'

'We've got seabirds here,' said her dad, looking beyond the camera. 'There's one. There's another. Can't move for birds.'

Poppy let out an exasperated sigh and smiled.

'Haven't seen you do that in a while,' said her dad.

'What?'

'Smile.'

Poppy frowned and dragged a chair over to an old wardrobe that had once been in her childhood bedroom. She pulled her hiking rucksack down and shook it, loosening the straps to repack with the essentials for a successful solo trip: waterproof trousers, five bars of dark chocolate, and a hip flask of sloe gin. She unzipped the front pouch and found an old map of Budapest, biro marks circling the places she and Josh had visited on last year's summer holiday. There wasn't a nicer city for sitting in a hot stone square, cooling your sunburned chest with a cold glass of pilsner whilst your husband kept track of cricket scores on his phone.

Her dad whistled for the dog, the shrill sound cutting through the musty air of the attic room.

'How's Diana?' Poppy asked, pre-empting the answer.

'Diana? Ah, she's not around no more.'

'Oh, sorry Dad. What happened?'

'The usual,' he said, running his hand down his chin. 'Wanted to move in. Then said we never go out, which is a lie 'cos I took her down The Rat Catcher, Thursday last, for steak night.'

'Isn't Diana vegetarian?'

'Yeah, but there's chips, in't there?'

'Can't think what she was complaining about, in that case.'

Poppy looked towards the camera and laughed. She was astounded at her dad's ability to maintain relationships despite how incredibly low he set the bar. By all accounts, he hadn't let one month of singledom pass him by since he was fifteen. Down in Cornwall, his work as a part-time pottery tutor supplied a steady stream of divorced women who spent their evenings overscheduled with art classes and fantasies about Patrick Swayze squeezing clay through their fingers. How Tony Pascoe fit the brief was a mystery.

Poppy's jaw felt tight, like someone had twisted a key and locked her teeth together. She stuffed a raincoat into her rucksack, punching it into a gap beside the tripod she'd shoved inside. Downstairs, the bathroom door clicked shut. Poppy stood, head tilted in meerkat fashion.

'What the fuck's he doing back?' she hissed.

'Who? Oh, Poppy, you've got to be joking.'

'Dad, shh!'

'It's been over three months. What're you doing?'

'Trying to pack so I can get out of his way for a fortnight,' said Poppy, ducking under a side table to fetch her hiking boots.

'He should be getting out of *your* way, Pops. That house is more yours than his.'

She bridled and pointed a camping spork at her phone.

'Dad, I can't have this conversation now,' said Poppy, over-articulating each whispered word.

'Yeah, I'd agree if you hadn't fobbed me off with the same excuse every time I bring it up.'

'You don't need to get involved. It's sorting itself out.'

'You've put the house on the market, then?'

Poppy jabbed at her phone to turn the volume down. 'No, Josh needed some time to— Don't make that face, Dad.'

'I'm not doin' nothin'.'

'If you're worried about me recovering the deposit money, it's fine. I'll manage either way. I just want to get it done with as few battles as possible.'

'I'm just sayin' that house is the best asset you have. Don't assume he won't screw you over, love. Your mum left you that money for a reason. I'll be damned if your inheritance ends up in someone else's pocket.'

Poppy paused, a stack of chunky Regency-era romances tucked in the crook of her elbow. She tried to gauge his expression, but he looked beyond the screen, his skin bathed in the amber glow of a sunset Poppy couldn't see.

'I know, Dad.' She picked up her phone and sat back in a wicker loveseat pushed beneath the eaves. She tucked her knees under her chin and wrapped an arm around them. 'Hey, what if I come to see you when—'

'You know what I think about the situation. Look, I've got to go. I'm meeting Uncle Kev down the bowling green for a drink. You know where I am if you need to… yeah.' He trailed off, the offer dying on his lips.

Poppy waved, ended the call, and took a second to contemplate her movements.

Knowing Josh was downstairs made her fidgety. She'd planned for an evening hunched over an old stop-motion camera that she'd bought herself as a graduation gift and for which she had spent years sourcing replacement parts. After racking up three thousand posts on photography forums, a man named Bert in Massachusetts had sold her an antique chrome shutter that, upon fitting, would complete a project lasting longer than her seven-year marriage.

Since moving into their Victorian terrace, Poppy had seen a systematic migration of her possessions upstairs, where she settled like a magpie amongst shiny things salvaged from other people's garages. The room smelt like a scout hut, and was characterised by furniture riddled with woodworm, warm dust, and windows that wouldn't open.

Poppy and Josh tried to act 'normal' around each other, but what did that even mean when you'd spent most of your adult life together? South of the attic, Josh kept the house like an IKEA showroom. It was fifty shades of slate grey, the walls sporadically dotted with mass-produced art and a singular Billy bookshelf that held Josh's ever-growing collection of Jamie Oliver cookbooks.

When they decided to split, Poppy and Josh had tried to finish the Netflix series they were halfway through, but all their shared anecdotes tripped on her tongue and she'd grown numb from the effort to suppress it all. To fill the time, she'd started the unnecessarily laborious hobby of stop-motion film photography.

Over the past year, what had once endeared her to Josh now made her feel silly and self-conscious. He used to call her his 'little weirdo in the attic', which didn't sound affectionate when she thought about it now, but at the time she'd worn it as a badge of pride. Now, if she played Kate Bush records whilst she worked (which was most of the time), he trotted up the carpeted stairs and shut the door without saying a word.

Poppy poked her head into the corridor, listened, and crept down to the bedroom, unhooking her oversized dressing gown from a pair of decorative stag antlers. There was a packet of dehydrated noodles downstairs with her name on it and she only had to linger for as long as it took the kettle to boil. Food scientists didn't get the credit they deserved.

As she attempted to silently glide towards the kitchen, Josh opened the bathroom door, warm steam tumbling into the corridor. Head down, naked, he ruffled his hair dry with a towel as he crossed into their bedroom. Poppy stopped and looked at the ceiling.

'Jesus, Josh. Come on.'

Josh rocked onto his back foot and roughly dried his hair, his fringe falling into curtains.

'Don't be weird, Poppy. It's a human body. One you've seen many times before, I'll add.'

'I thought you were out.'

'I was. Do you want me to leave my location switched on in future? If you time it properly, you can hold the door open for me as I leave, no need to double-lock it.'

Poppy wondered if he had the stamina to sustain deep-set resentment or whether it would dictate the tone of all future interactions. The contrast of 'Josh at home' compared to 'Josh at work' had Jekyll and Hyde levels of duality. There, he demonstrated medieval acts of chivalry, making reference to her in front of the students as 'my *esteemed* colleague, Miss Pascoe.' Six years ago when they'd first applied for positions at the school, Josh warned her not to use her married name because of the apparently well-known fact that 'schools are honeytraps for newly married women looking for overly generous maternity leave.' The assumptions weren't worth dwelling on.

Josh finished drying his hair, the towel dangling in front of him. Poppy kept her eyes fixed on his face, but it was a big ask. He sunk hundreds of pounds every month into a niche gym located in an old dockyard, where he flipped tyres and used other participants as human weights. Annoyingly, his frustrations had been channelled into a sleek, muscular physique from which she could no longer benefit.

As much as they'd emotionally detached from one another, sex was something they'd continued until she'd moved into the attic room to sleep. This wasn't a conversation point so much as it seemed illogical to stop. Whenever she *really* thought about the things she still liked about Josh, the list was small but not insignificant. One: he chose good pizza toppings. Two: he liked beaches in winter. Three: he had a truly exceptional penis.

Josh walked into a room with an energy in his frame that pulled Poppy's gaze towards him. Over the years, they had perfected an activity of flipped bodies and articulate hands. Sex was the only time their communication felt uncomplicated, the aim clearly outlined, the pay-off easily achieved. Josh had never been one for pillow talk. Poppy would tiptoe back from a post-sex bathroom trip to find him scrolling through Sky Sports, his eyebrows furrowed in a frown. Eventually, the routine grew roots that were too deep to pull up.

Poppy hovered by the doorway to their bedroom, wanting to say something that felt suitably consequential. This trip felt different. She'd spent the last few months dragging her brain behind her. With bags packed, she wouldn't have to listen for floorboards creaking in the house, or passive-aggressive quips in the hall. Bliss.

'What time are you off?' asked Josh, the elastic on his boxer shorts thwacking against his stomach.

'Early Monday morning. I'll try not to wake you up.'

'I might not be here anyway,' said Josh. 'Night out, after all. Might be out all weekend.' He sprayed antiperspirant under each arm. Poppy coughed as it hit the back of her throat.

'Mmm, who knows where an evening with the PE department, Trish from reception, and whichever group of sixth formers have accidentally walked into the same pub as you will lead. Sounds like a great night out.'

'Oh, take a day off, Poppy. You're the one who wants to go on a Bear Grylls expedition to a random part of the country on your own. Don't blame me for going out to a pub that you were *also* invited to.'

Poppy opened her mouth, ready to correct him. She had been purposefully vague about where she was going. It would only freak him out if he knew.

'I'm hardly going to come along when you're such delightful company.'

'Like you were ever planning to...'

'I'm busy,' she said unconvincingly.

'Look, I'm just being honest with you. If I sleep with someone, I'll tell you. You know why? It's because I respect you. Don't do that thing with your eyes, Poppy. Is there a chance I'm going to sleep with someone tonight? Maybe? I don't predict these things. It would be kind of predatory for me to do that, don't you think?'

'I didn't ask for your weird manifesto about casual sex.'

'No, of course you didn't.' Josh pulled a comb through his hair. He parted it at the side, the lines perfectly straight. 'Do we have any toothpaste?'

Chapter Three

FIVE DAYS BEFORE THE WEDDING

Poppy looked down at her phone and tapped her fist against her lips. She'd slept on the early morning train to the south Devonshire coast, head tipped back, mouth hung open. Standing at the harbour, her back sticky from the rucksack she'd overpacked, Poppy shielded her eyes from the July sunshine and reread the name of the boat she was looking for. Surely not. *The Wet Dream*? There wasn't a chance she was going to ask someone where to find it. She'd spend the next hour walking up and down the marina if she had to.

The town had barely changed in the decade since she'd last visited. This part of the world held a captive market of discount pensioner coach trips and students who looked out of place without a surfboard propped beside them. An elderly woman in an elasticated skirt sat on a bleached bench, feet dangling above the ground as her husband handed her a Thermos of tea. From the marina, a handful of boats pin-balled between the islands that featured on postcards – buckets of chalky shells from Southeast Asia flanked by turnstile stands, plastic fishing nets, and crab lines.

Poppy glanced around uneasily. When she first came to Orwell Island, Josh had bought her a fist-sized puffin toy with a squashed beak and eyes sat too far apart on its head. Objectively, she was pretty sure that it was made for dogs to tear apart. Before they left on different trains, he'd tucked it under her bag strap, said 'I'll come back for it,' and kissed the underside of her jaw. In her late teens, such an act was on a level with Leonardo DiCaprio letting Kate Winslet climb on the door after the Titanic sank.

Poppy looked towards the horizon to the island where she and Josh had met for the first time. For weeks, she had been telling herself that he had nothing to do with her decision to come back. After all, it wasn't her fault that puffins were incredibly picky when it came to breeding grounds. Poppy didn't want Josh to think that she was doing a retrospective soon-to-be-divorced-loser tour of their relationship, which was why he thought she was in Wales. She hadn't come here for him.

Poppy was sick of not showing up for herself. Every year she told her friends that she was going to enter the National Geographic Wildlife Photographer of the Year Award, but when it came to clicking submit, she stopped. Why? Was it because she'd rather stuff her mouth full of cotton wool than talk about her own work? Or would a taste of success make her think too much about all the other things she'd turned down? Failing was bad, but it didn't hurt as much if *you* were the one who cast your fate in concrete.

Poppy unhooked her sunglasses from her top and looked at the time. Images of Josh danced at the periphery of her thoughts like an annoying twitch. Josh's attempt to offhandedly speculate as to whether or not he'd sleep with someone was far from his first attempt at bravado. The more he did it, the more embarrassment she felt for him. Seeing as they were still a couple according to everyone at work, the second-hand shame was just as bad.

She closed her eyes, the sunlight dappling on her eyelids in blooms of pink and orange. A weariness had settled into her bones now that the school year had ended, along with the relief that came with a temporary end to her daily verbal jousts with Josh. She'd agreed that he should be 'allowed the dignity' to stay in their home until he found somewhere else to live because it was easier than forming an argument as to why he shouldn't. As it turned out, he took this as a chance to flex against each and every boundary she tried to put between them, as well as outlining which feelings Poppy was and was not allowed to have.

Pasties finished, the elderly couple stood, the man leaning against his stick as he bent to brush dried seagull poo from the back of his wife's skirt. Poppy smiled at them, but her lips were tight.

She walked between crab pots, trying to keep out of the way as fishermen in grubby waders hauled buckets of winkles from their boats. Poppy blinked and lifted her hand to shield the sun from her eyes. Beyond bunting that flapped in the breeze, she spotted someone she knew.

Lola, her stupidly demure best friend, was standing at the end of a stone jetty, her fresh-from-the-bottle violet hair pinned into a neat chignon, her silhouette backlit by the morning sun. Lola used her body like Play-Doh, squeezing it into different shapes by constantly altering her clothes on an overworked sewing machine. Going by the bolero and waspish waist, Poppy guessed that Lola was having a 1950s renaissance.

Poppy waved at Lola. By the time she'd clambered up seaweed-streaked steps to meet her friend, Lola had trotted up to the banister, eyes wide with surprise.

'You! You're here! Aren't you going to Orwell Island? To photograph the puffins? We're not meeting until next week, are we? I'm trying to keep on top of everything but I'm working across five shared calendars at the minute,' said Lola, opening an app on her iPad.

'No, you're fine!' said Poppy. 'I'm just looking for my boat. Are you all right? You seem a bit... on edge.'

Lola pursed her red lips. 'Oh, just one expensive fuck up after the other. The photographer isn't here – Christian Withers. The family specifically requested him because he shot a royal wedding – not a big one, just a second cousin or something, but still – he's excellent with posh old people, which makes up the majority of the wedding party, but hey! He's just called to say he has norovirus and is stuck in Bristol Parkway overseeing the mass exodus of his insides. It'll be fine though,' said Lola, nodding frantically to herself.

'That sounds... stressful. In all honesty, you look quite terrifying, like you need to remind your eyes they've got a role to play in this whole smiling thing,' said Poppy.

'Yes, well it *has* to be fine because if not, I've sunk thousands of pounds into the biggest break of my career for nothing. Oh, fucking fuck fuck. There are more guests arriving. Their transport will be here in five minutes and the tide is coming in, so I can't wait any longer or they'll be stuck on the wrong side of the bloody channel. Apparently, there's only one person in a fifty-mile radius of Torquay who can operate the fucking sea tractor, which isn't wholly surprising considering I thought someone was having me on up until an hour ago when it chugged up onto the shore.'

'Okay, hang on...' said Poppy, taking the iPad gently from Lola's hands. 'Shall we dial back a little bit? Why do you need the photographer to be here now? Is the wedding tomorrow?'

'No, it's on Saturday, but there's five days of lead-up that apparently requires the same level of documentation as a royal tour of the Commonwealth. Everyone's had to sign an NDA, me included. To give you context, there's a press officer on the island.

And security. Lots of it.' Lola tapped her teeth, eyes speed reading the horizon.

A set of sleek cars pulled up by the marina, chrome wheel rims glinting in the sunshine. This was clearly not a 'rate your driver out of five stars' situation.

'Hey, Lola? Look at me.' Poppy stepped closer. 'Do you need me to make some calls whilst you're organising the guests? Have you got a list of back-up photographers?'

'There's no time. Oh, hi!' Lola cooed, adjusting her posture. 'Mr Wilson, I knew it was you. Looking sharp! We're not expecting Mrs Wilson until Friday, are we? Let Terry take your suit bag, okay? We'll just be a minute.'

The man touched the rim of his white trilby hat, a playful grin on his face.

'Isn't he—'

'A cabinet minister, yes.' Lola spoke in her throat through a smile, the ventriloquist and puppet in one.

'What the hell is that?' said Poppy, turning towards the noise of an engine bubbling underwater. From the shallows, a platform emerged, like a garden marquee on tractor wheels, drawing level with the jetty.

'Sorry I'm a few minutes late, love. I had to top it up with diesel,' called the driver, wiping his forehead.

'Not to worry!' said Lola, leaning back to give him a wave. She lowered her voice. 'I've got about four minutes before I have to head to the island on that thing, which means I've got eighteen minutes until I walk into the snake pit without a photographer. I might pull out my own intestines and string them from a flagpole: a warning to all ye who step afoot Loxby Island without five good ways the wedding can feature in a *Vanity Fair* article.'

'Who *is* this wedding for? Is it, like, someone famous?'

'Not famous as such. Loaded, money-wise. God, I wish I could tell you. You wouldn't believe it.'

'If they're loaded, why are they using a sea tractor as transport? A *sea tractor*?'

'Yep, it's quaint, but that's part of the vibe. There's a finger buffet tonight that contains crab sticks as a centrepiece, except these ones contain actual shellfish pulled off the boats a few hours ago.'

'I hope there's a bowl of mixed flavour crisps for you to dig into,' said Poppy. 'Then it's a real party.' She bumped Lola's elbow, but her friend was too preoccupied to notice.

Lola clutched Poppy's arm and blinked, as though she'd realised something important.

'Poppy...'

'What?'

Lola interlocked her fingers in a prayer stance and looked at Poppy with spaniel eyes.

'No... Lola, *no* way. I've got plans for the next few days that involve pelagic birds and nothing else. Surely you have someone else who can help?'

'I don't. I'm not just saying this to convince you, but there's a really, *really* good reason why you should at least consider coming to Loxby.'

'Why?'

'I can't say.'

'Lola!'

'I know, I know, I know. But, A, I wouldn't ask if I wasn't desperate, and B, I think you'll enjoy yourself, just a tiny bit, if you agree to come,' she said. 'The bathroom toiletries are worth the trip alone. This is not a Radox and After Eight on the fucking pillow hotel. I *wanted* a back-up photographer, but they wouldn't let me book anyone else in order to keep the details out of circulation. You know me. I never leave things to chance. Don't you remember the night-out bag I used to pack?'

'Plasters, two paracetamol, fold-up pumps, and a pre-paid taxi? Of course, it's the only reason I was ever tempted into a bar.'

'Exactly. What am I supposed to do now?'

'If they're picky about who they book, they *definitely* won't want me. I'm not a professional photographer, for one.'

'Has anyone ever paid for one of your prints?' said Lola, smoothing down her dress.

'You know the answer to that.'

'Well?'

'That was different. I'm a photography teacher now. I specialise in empty car parks and abandoned shopping trollies. The very obvious metaphors that kids base whole projects around. A wedding is all... doe-eyed family and close-ups of miniature food.'

'You wouldn't have to shoot the actual wedding, that's not until the weekend. But if you could cover the run-up until Christian Withers is back on the scene, you'd save my neck. You'd be saving my career, actually. I'll invent something to make it seem plausible. You have a degree in photography and I did an online course in musical theatre, so there's no reason why we can't pull this off.'

'Why, are you planning to distract them by doing the "Cell Block Tango"?'

'Don't tempt me. You know I love an audience.' Lola smiled, knowing she'd gone into battle and won.

'This isn't why I came here,' said Poppy, stalling. She rubbed the back of her neck, the July heat prickling as the sun pushed higher in the sky. She'd rather take baby portraits in a suburban supermarket than photograph a wedding, especially considering her current aporia for anything promising domestic bliss.

'I'll give you a proportion of my fee,' said Lola. 'As soon as the official photographer is here, you'll be on that island with your birds. I promise. Although, I've got to say, it's a weird rebound. Staying alone on the island where you met Josh? Sheesh, you're a sucker for punishment, aren't you?'

'It's facing the dragon head-on, which will be ten times harder now. How am I supposed to recover from my failed relationship when I'm taking pictures of a bride about to make the worst decision of her life?'

'Um, a tad judgmental, but I'll allow it. Like I said, I *promise* you if you delay your little bird trip for a couple of days, you won't regret it. In thirty minutes, you'll find out why. After you've signed your soul over in the form of an NDA.' Lola shielded her eyes from the sun and gave Poppy a simpering smile.

From the end of the jetty, the tractor driver shouted. 'That's us ready to go, lovely!'

'All right, just a minute,' said Lola, pretending to log something on her iPad as the sea tractor's exhaust coughed grey fumes between the passengers on the dock, who spluttered into handkerchiefs and pocket squares.

'I've got to get her moving or this lot will be coughing smog into their pillows,' he said in a West Country burr.

'Yep, we're coming, Terry!'

'We're coming?' said Poppy.

Lola sighed, nails pinching her waist. 'Sorry. I'm projecting my panic onto you, which isn't fair. You don't have to come. I know we've been waiting to catch up about Josh, but if you think that being around someone else's wedding is too much, maybe it's best you stay here, even if you're turning down the best catering this side of Monaco. I'll... figure something out, but you'll kick yourself when I tell you whose wedding this is next week.'

Poppy hesitated. 'Perhaps Terry knows his way around a DSLR?' she offered.

They both looked at the sea tractor as Terry screwed a jerry can of fuel shut, a rolled cigarette hanging from his lip.

Poppy scraped her hair into a messy bun and disguised her reluctance by tucking it behind a smile. 'Two days,' said Poppy. 'That's how long you've got me. Then I'm off to join my puffins.'

Chapter Four

JUNE 15TH, 2008

'Can we go down there?' asked Etienne, pointing to a rocky shelf that sat below a ten-foot sheer drop.

'No,' said Lola, flicking the ash from the end of her cigarette.

'Why not?'

'Because you'll die. *Morte.* Death. A horrible one.'

Etienne kicked a stone into the sea and tugged on the straps of the yellow rucksack that all the teenagers had been given when Lola and Poppy had greeted them as they left their coach in Dover. Five days around the south coast and their penultimate night was an 'authentic camping experience' on a small island off the coast of Devon most famous for the puffin population and not a whole lot else. Unsurprisingly, the group of French teenagers that they had been assigned to look after weren't enthused by the lack of electricity, but she and Lola were off-duty tonight and thus sweetly deprived of parachute games and tent allocation. Poppy was at the tail end of two near-sleepless night shifts spent in the hostels of Eastbourne and Lyme Regis, or 'saliva duty' as the camp leaders had termed it, because it largely consisted of breaking up incredibly tame games of Spin the Bottle. Tonight, she had a plan to drink cheap vodka and watch the sunset with Lola, no head counts involved.

'Sam is going to roast some marshmallows round the campfire with you later. That'll be good, won't it?' said Poppy, unconvinced by the faux enthusiasm in her own voice.

Etienne smiled at her in a way that implied he felt sorry for how incredibly stupid she was. *'Y'a rien à faire sur cette putain d'île,'* he said, swinging his arms in dejection as he walked away.

'Oi! I can lip-read French, mate!' said Lola, shouting after him.

'Can you?'

'Absolutely not.'

'He said "There's nothing to do on this fucking island",' said a voice from behind them. They turned. Two men of a similar age stood in tracksuit bottoms and fleece-lined hoodies branded with a familiar navy and gold that Poppy had seen before. These two lacked the swagger that she had become accustomed to on campus, where sports teams self-aggrandised to the point where they truly believed they were about to be selected for the Olympics.

'Such an attitude for one so young,' said Lola, tugging her uniform polo shirt to lower the neckline.

'I don't know, I was pretty bad when I was that age. I'm Josh,' he said, holding out a hand. Poppy had never had cause for a handshake before and this seemed wildly mature for a twenty-something-year-old.

'Poppy.' She gripped it, noticing his husky-blue eyes and a jawline that most boys didn't seem to develop until well past graduation. Poppy didn't know what to say next, because looking at him seemed to render all other modes of communication useless, like a fuse had blown at the back of her head. He moved to Lola, his cheeks pink.

'And there was me thinking we were stranded with a bunch of French teenagers, some of whom I'd quite like to dropkick into the sea.' Lola didn't shake his hand but allowed him to hold hers like a medieval knight. 'Charmed.'

'Sounds like a different kind of trip than the one we're on. I'm Dan,' said Josh's friend, grinning from beneath a sparse beard. He had the two features that Lola rated above all else: a thick neck and good thighs. It was a preference that ensured they never clashed over boys.

'So you guys go to Bath?' said Poppy, pointing to the crest embroidered on their kit. 'So do I. Lola doesn't, but she's there visiting me pretty much every weekend.'

'Yeah, we're down here for training. Athletics, but like… hardcore,' said Dan.

'Calling a triathlon *hardcore* doesn't make it cool. We're on a lonely boys' holiday ahead of the season kicking in when we head back to uni,' said Josh.

'Oh, I wouldn't worry. There's no way you can convince me that sports of any kind are cool, but I appreciate the effort,' said Poppy, holding up a hand as three pre-teens approached them from behind a corrugated iron hut. Lola groaned.

'Not now, Etienne!'

'We found a mouse. It looks like, er… broken?' Etienne lowered his cupped hands to show them from a distance.

'Lovely!' said Lola, giving them a thumbs up. 'There's literally nothing I can do about that. Leave it for a fox.'

Etienne and his friends retreated, looking over their shoulders at Lola as though she was a psychopath.

'Brutal,' said Poppy.

'Well, come on. I'm not going to perform CPR with my little fingers, am I?'

'An excellent point. Personally, I see strawberry cider and a packet of smoky bacon crisps in my near future. We've gone above and beyond the call of duty with these kids. Lola, how long have we got until we can clock off?'

'Four minutes,' she said, checking her watch. 'Time to catch the sunset.'

'Do you want to come?' said Poppy, turning to Josh and Dan. She was surprised at how breezy she sounded, as though she regularly invited strangers to hang out with her and Lola.

'Where? I didn't know there was anything here,' said Josh, shrugging his shoulders up to his ears as a gust of wind sent chill sea spray into the air.

'The speakeasy. And by speakeasy, I mean a mini-fridge and a few foldout tables at the back of the convenience shop,' said Lola.

'You get great views,' Poppy added. 'The puffins dive-bomb off the cliffs at this time of day.'

'You sound like a local,' said Josh.

'Just a bird enthusiast.' Poppy caught herself, hyperaware of how lame she sounded.

'I'm up for it. Josh?' said Dan, his eyes fixed on Lola.

'I don't know, mate. We've got a swim at four in the morning and twenty kilometres to lay down on the bike before lunch.'

'That all sounds incredibly boring,' said Lola, ducking slightly as a seagull rode a slipstream of wind above their heads.

'Come hang out with us. If nothing else, think of the children. We've been stuck with them for a week,' said Poppy.

Josh pouted and tilted his head at Dan, his flop of chestnut hair ruffled by the wind. He looked like he would smell good, in a branded shampoo and regularly-changed-bedsheets way. She wanted to tuck herself under his arm like a baby bird. She wanted to put her finger on his bottom lip to see if he'd bite it.

'Okay. We're in. We were only going to eat a pot noodle and map our route for tomorrow, which does sound dry now I think about it.'

'In that case, you're welcome. Here, this way.'

They walked ahead of Josh and Dan, conscious of the way they looked from behind. Lola swung her pendulum hips and

Poppy tried to appear aloof and mysterious by looking out to sea.

Lola interlocked her fingers with Poppy's and pinched her thumb, a signal that wingwoman mode had been initiated. 'Your banter was on fire there, Pops. Hilarious, but decidedly cool. I'd fancy you,' whispered Lola. 'How are my boobs? I can stuff some tissue in my bra if need be.'

'No, the girls are great. Can you see my spot?'

'Only if you look at it from below. Ay-oo, *someone* might be looking up at you from below. He's staring at you. Those eyes! Thank God I like men who look like hairy potatoes. Josh is too intense for me – you can have him.'

'Excellent. Hey, if the mood takes you, you're welcome to the room.'

'You know I never keep them long enough for it to be a problem. He'll be out within the hour. I'll put down a towel on the floor so the bed isn't contaminated.'

'Your kindness has no bounds.'

'I am nothing if not a conscientious shagger,' she said, a doorbell chiming with a polyphonic rendition of Vivaldi's 'Four Seasons' as they stepped inside a roughly clad shop, the noise of a generator whirring in the background and the faint smell of petrol in the air. A door at the back led to a veranda that wrapped around the building, framing a view of the bay as sunlight jostled on shifting waves.

'This beats marshmallows,' said Poppy, taken by the view and half wishing she could enjoy it without the pressure of keeping conversation going with people she didn't know.

'Mm, we'll see…' said Lola, distracted.

'I'll get these,' said Josh, fishing a six-pack of beer out from a cooler box that sat beneath a shelf of cellophane-wrapped tea and tiny bottles of fairy liquid.

'You see? It just gets better and better,' said Lola.

'I'm not saying women can't run, I'm saying that it's not discrimination if they get less funding. Money follows elite sport, so when you look at it on paper, running a hundred metres in nine seconds is more impressive than running it in ten. If people don't want to tune in to watch second-rate sport, you can't blame "the system". Surely that's stating the obvious?'

'Yeah, that you're obviously ignorant,' said Poppy, sitting back in her aluminium chair. She swigged her bottle of cider with a flourish, having passed on the cheap beer that Josh had offered round. 'Just out of curiosity, have you tried to get tickets for the Olympics?'

'Yeah, course I have.'

'Which sport?'

'Women's volleyball.'

Lola, Josh, and Poppy burst into laughter.

'You walked right into that one,' said Josh, his skin bathed in golden light from the low-angled sun.

Dan shrugged. 'Just playing devil's advocate,' He stood up and stretched, knocking a half-drunk can of beer onto the plastic table. 'Whoops. I need a piss.'

'Toilet's over there,' said Lola, pointing to the cliff edge. 'Make sure you know which way the wind is blowing first.'

Dan retreated, not quite far enough to hide his wide-legged stance from view.

They fell into comfortable silence, punctuated only by Lola shaking each can that littered the table. She drank the remnants of Dan's beer, pinched Poppy's thumb under the table, and winked at her with a nod towards Josh. Poppy subtly shook her head, trying not to draw attention to herself.

'Dan's too macho to admit he's struggling to keep pace with you, but I'm not,' said Josh, nursing his beer. He shuffled in his seat, chair legs scraping against the patio slab as he inched closer to Poppy. Her knee hummed with a current that urged her to close the gap between them.

'What can I say, I'm a heavyweight,' said Lola, her words trotting into each other. When it came to drinking, Lola always led the charge, but Poppy couldn't imagine anything more painful than sitting on a coach for five hours tomorrow whilst sugar-fuelled children sang all the way back to Dover. For some reason, hangovers didn't seem to affect Lola in the same way they did everyone else.

'So, let's play fastball. Your mate, Dan. Got a girlfriend?' said Lola.

'Nope. He broke up with someone from home at Christmas. I'm not sure he's looking, to be honest.'

'Excellent, neither am I.'

Dan vaulted over the veranda railing and slumped back in his seat. 'Don't worry, I wiped my hands on the grass,' he said. 'Joking, obviously.'

'Don't get comfy, I need you to help me with something,' said Lola, tapping him on the shoulder.

'Oh, right.'

'It's funny, I can't remember where our cabin is,' said Lola, her lips pouted to one side in homage to a 1950s pin-up girl.

'Isn't this island, like, half a mile wide?' said Dan, failing to pick up on her very obvious cues.

'It's very easy to get lost, isn't it Poppy?'

'Oh, yeah. You can walk straight off a cliff if you're not careful.'

'You better look out for her, mate.' Josh grinned, joining Poppy's façade.

Dan nodded to himself, realisation slowly dawning on him. He slapped his knee and scooped his beard through his fingers as he stood up. 'Now I think on it, I'm a natural navigator. Josh, mate, I'll see you back at the tent.'

'I won't wait up.'

They left, leaving Poppy and Josh alone. She crossed her legs and twisted to face him, sleeves pulled over her fingers to keep out the cold.

'She's forthright,' said Josh.

'Lola knows what she wants and doesn't hang about. I wish I was half as decisive as her.' Poppy propped her chin on her fist and smiled at the seat Lola had occupied.

'You don't strike me as the kind of person who holds back their opinion, if that conversation earlier is anything to go on.'

Poppy raised her eyebrows. 'Don't tell me you agree with him.'

'Me? No way. I've actually been volunteering on a scheme with a buddy on my course about ways to keep girls in sports teams throughout secondary school.'

Poppy relaxed, slumping back in her chair. 'Really? That's amazing.'

'Yeah, we had to come up with a public health campaign as part of a project, but a few local schools were interested so we're going to keep going with it.' Josh ran a hand down his thigh, his former bravado replaced with a bashfulness that Poppy found endearing. 'I know it's, like… weird for a guy to say, but I see myself as a feminist.'

Poppy tilted her head back, assessing him. 'You're right. Not many guys would say that. Although *seeing* yourself as a feminist and *being* one aren't the same.' She intended it as a friendly jibe, but they weren't on that level yet.

Josh looked surprised, then impressed, as though no one had ever questioned this response before. Poppy laughed, worried that she'd let an awkwardness creep between them. The air was charged, the atmosphere taut. Josh stood up.

Poppy apologised, but she wasn't sure what for. 'Sorry, I didn't mean to accuse you of anything, I just—'

Josh clutched the arms of her chair and lowered his head inch by inch, his nose brushing hers as she tilted her head to meet him. Before she closed the gap, she knew that every time she smelt jasmine washing powder and the deeper, earthier scent of damp rain on a woodland floor, she'd be brought straight back here, straight back to Orwell Island.

Chapter Five

FIVE DAYS BEFORE THE WEDDING

Loxby was a little closer to shore than Orwell Island, which hole-punched the horizon as a mist-shrouded lump of rock to the east. In the distance, she looked for the characterful silhouette of a puffin diving into deep water for herring. In contrast, Loxby was a glamorous cousin you wouldn't want to stand next to in a family photo. A clean-lined, Art Deco hotel followed the curve of the island, whitewashed walls gleaming in the sunshine. An emerald golf course lined the cliff, below which a stone pub sat beside the harbour, where a collection of boats bobbed in the breeze, their masts swaying like metronomes.

'So, I'll run through the headlines,' said Lola, her cat-eye sunglasses pushed down the bridge of her nose. She lowered her voice so as not be overheard. 'The island is owned by the Mountgraves. Ordinarily, it's open to day-trip tourists and punters for the hotel, but this week it's just wedding guests and a few people here on business, both of which sink a lot of wine. There's a pub in the little harbour and it's still in use, but only as a staffroom. There's a one-to-one staff to guest ratio and it's not the kind of place you can smoke hanging out of a window, if you know what I mean. If you want good chips, head down there, but once you sign this, I think you'll find this whole set-up a little more welcoming.'

Lola tapped her iPad and brought up a document. 'Here's your NDA. Be quick. We're pulling in and I need to pretend that you coming here was all part of a slick plan.'

'Shouldn't I read it?'

'It's all common sense. Don't sell any stories to the press, don't tell anyone you're here, and if you overhear any dodgy business talk, look the other way.' Lola scrolled to the bottom of the small print and turned the screen around to face Poppy. She signed with a finger, but her maiden name looked clunky and unfamiliar on the screen, like she'd found an old school report and couldn't recognise the person being described.

'So can you tell me whose wedding it is now?' said Poppy, flicking a smile back onto her face.

'You're going to be so gassed,' said Lola, locking the tablet. She glanced at the guests and mouthed her words with barely more than a whisper. 'Wait until we've got a moment away from this lot,' she said, jerking her head down the aisle of the sea tractor.

Over the noise of the engine came the sound of distant laughter from a group of men in light chinos and dark suit jackets practising golfing swings on a precipice above them.

'Oh, isn't this something,' said a woman beside Poppy, clutching her floppy hat to shield the sun as she looked up at the cliff. 'It looks like somewhere F. Scott Fitzgerald would come on holiday. Still, could be a degree or two warmer.'

'I think they have a few hotels, so I'm sure we'll see the portfolio in due course,' said her husband, who checked the most enormous wristwatch Poppy had ever seen. 'I can't wait to get off this bloody thing. I didn't give up cigarettes in the noughties to die from emphysema.'

'How do you know the couple?' said the woman, noticing Poppy.

Lola jerked her head up from the iPad on her lap and patted Poppy's shoulder. 'Paul, Nicola, didn't see you there! Poppy, these are the bride's parents, Mr and Mrs Spruce. Poppy is our photographer. She's very hard to pin down, so I'm thrilled we managed to book her,' garbled Lola. 'She's got quite the reputation in the South West.'

'I have?' said Poppy, her pulse thrumming.

'She doesn't read reviews,' said Lola by way of explanation. 'It interrupts her creative flow.'

The woman nodded. 'I understand. You've got to be tough to stick with the artistic path. I studied Fine Art, so I understand, sweetheart. It's how I met Paul, actually. He bought my showpiece when I graduated from Christchurch.'

'Oh, Christ, that thing. Yes. Thank God she changed career.'

Paul pulled a silk pocket square from his linen jacket and wiped the corners of his mouth. Compared to the others, Paul and Nicola wore clothes that were a little louder than the sea of sand and stone-coloured linen elsewhere. 'Now, Poppy,' he said, as though the syllables contained gunpowder, 'had any gallery interest? I've got a mate who loves this sort of thing,' he said, gesturing to the landscape as if he were lazily swatting a fly.

'Here we go. Always a businessman, is Paul. Hobby art-dealer,' she said, adding a conspiratorial eyeroll.

Lola turned to Poppy and waited for an answer, her lips parted mischievously.

'I'm more into… experimental photography.'

'Oh, I bet Colin will *love* that,' said Nicola, pushing down her Dolce & Gabbana sunglasses.

'Who's Colin?' said Poppy.

'Father of the groom,' said Lola through a smile. 'I'll explain later.'

'No offence, but your style sounds a little left field for this bunch, but weddings are a pantomime. Anything goes. It's all we've heard about from our daughter. Thank Christ we're not paying for it.'

'*Paul,*' hissed his wife.

'Ah, looks like we're here,' said Lola, slipping her iPad into a grass-woven handbag.

Despite the fact that the sea tractor could feature as runner-up in an episode of *Scrapheap Challenge*, they pulled up to Loxby's stone jetty in a graceful arc, arriving at well-worn stone steps beside a tiny pub flanked by picnic benches and canvas parasols. Beside this, a shingle beach ran to the base of a path that trailed up the rock face, the hotel hidden from where they stood.

As Poppy stepped down, her heartbeat thrummed in her throat. She felt like a crow trying to blend in amongst a flock of opalescent doves.

'I never understood who the target market was for deck shoes... until now,' said Poppy, leaning in to whisper in Lola's ear as she supervised their disembarkation.

They hung back as the guests slowly made their way up the cliff-side path to the hotel entrance. 'It helps to own a deck. Like, a boat deck, not, you know... decking bashed together on a bank holiday weekend.'

Poppy swung her rucksack on her back and tagged onto the end of the group as they started on the steps, pausing as older couples turned to admire the toy-like sailboats gliding across a shallow sandbank that hadn't been visible an hour before. Each step she took, a knot tightened in her stomach. There would be people here. People that she'd have to make small talk with. How was she going to get through a week of someone else's happy wedding haze when she was trying her best to forget her own marriage?

'I knew I shouldn't have worn boning in heat like this,' said

Lola, a hand placed delicately on the flat plane of her corset. 'I'm sweating in places you wouldn't believe.'

'I'd say the look is more... sexy lobster,' said Poppy, gesturing to Lola's cinched waist and the panels of red and cerise that exaggerated the curve of her hips. 'So... please can you tell me who the couple are before I give myself a hernia?'

Lola clapped her hand to her temple, fumbled with the clasp of her bag, and flicked open her iPad.

'Oh my God. You've just reminded me. Lobsters. What's the time? I can't see a thing – it's too bright.' Lola squatted to the floor and held the screen close to her chest.

'Ten-thirty.'

'Are you serious? *Shit*. The caterers should have unloaded at the service marina by now and I will *not* see a crate of live crabs crawling their way back into the sea because no one came down to pick them up. Poppy, I need to run but I'll catch up with you in a bit, all right?'

'Wait, don't you need to check me in? I can't blag to a receptionist – you know how pathetic I am when it involves lying to someone with a name badge.'

Lola tapped a message out on the screen and repinned her sweeping fringe above the ear.

'Say you're staff and have a wander. There's a welcome luncheon later—'

'Luncheon?'

'It's like a beige buffet, but they cut the crusts off sarnies.'

'Weird.'

'I know. Right, I'll see you on the other side. This island is tiny, but there's about two hundred stairs up and another two hundred down to the service marina. Not ideal in a pencil skirt, but I've literally stitched myself into this thing, so that's that. I'll be back with you as quick as I can. Ciao!'

Lola took her heels off, tucked them under her arm, and leapt from one step to another, dropping down onto a smuggler's path that Poppy wouldn't have noticed if not for her friend's violet chignon bobbing up and down as she disappeared from sight.

By the time she reached the hotel, Poppy's legs were sticky from the heat. She hadn't performed her usual anti-chafing trick of spraying deodorant between her thighs and thought it might be indelicate to do so whilst standing on a highly polished marble floor.

She un-shouldered her rucksack, which crumpled on the tiles like a half-filled bin bag. Beside it, a concierge stacked luggage on a stand as another weaved between the guests, taking monogrammed suitcases from raised hands without so much as a glance from the person holding it. Poppy pulled a carrier bag out of a side pocket, unlaced her hiking boots, and swapped them for a pair of cheap flip-flops that she'd planned on wearing to use the outdoor shower on Orwell Island.

Chatter burbled around her. If the purpose of small talk was to act as a social leveller, the scale was not tipped in her direction. As she stepped beneath the atrium's stained-glass dome, she had the unsettling feeling that she had wandered onto the set of a murder mystery, but no one had given her a character to play. The room echoed with voices that Poppy associated with antiques, Barbour, and Latin as a core subject. She'd rather be mucking in with Lola, like they had done as hosts for French youths during a long university summer. One of them would butter forty-five cheese sandwiches whilst the other attempted a scavenger hunt in broken French to occupy a moody brood of Parisian pre-teens on a rainy Tuesday in Broadstairs.

Lola had disappeared before giving her solid details about the couple getting married on Saturday, but reading the room, she guessed at someone older, on their second or third wife. Groom in his late fifties? A ski-goggle tan line? Wife-to-be found via Guardian Soulmates? She lingered, surveying those nearest to ascertain the chances of finding a conversation she could slot herself into.

'We missed you at Henley this year,' said a woman with a blunt honey-coloured fringe. 'It was a scorcher. Brought out all the riff-raff, of course, but you couldn't hear the chanting so long as you stayed in the old boys' paddock.'

A man opposite undid a button hidden in the folds of his chin, his wide mouth downturned. 'Oh, it's not what it once was. Jonathon was in the Isis boat – I don't suppose you saw him.'

Poppy stepped forward. 'Isis? Really? That's awful. I'm so sorry,' said Poppy. It wasn't the conversational stepping stone she'd thought she'd have, but she'd take what she could.

He made a noise that sounded like a colicky horse trying to clear its throat. 'Humph! Can't tell you how much money we've spent trying to get him out.'

'You can't trust people in those situations, especially when it comes to money. The exploitation that goes on is awful. Oh, I'm Poppy, by the way. Nice to meet you.' Poppy offered a hand. The man shook it at an awkward angle, his thumb holding hers down until his nail went white. 'I'm sure there are human rights lawyers who specialise in this kind of thing,' she continued.

'Too bloody right. Ha! That's what we need. Let's just say that a master's degree in Water Management didn't exist *before* I offered to pay for an extension to the boathouse, so how he's not pulling for the blue boat really does make the mind fucking boggle. You a rower in your time?'

'Oh, I shouldn't think so,' said a woman next to him, slotting her sunglasses into a patent handbag. 'Look at the size of her. More of a coxswain.'

Poppy felt her neck flush. She had the horrible feeling of being stuck on the other side of a glass wall; she could see mouths moving but couldn't understand what was coming out of them.

'Bit early to be talking about cocks, isn't it?' said Poppy.

The couple exchanged a look.

'Oh, you're a breath of fresh air. Who are you here for again? Bride or groom?'

Seeing as she still didn't know who the bride and groom were, Poppy played it safe.

'Neither. I'm the photographer. For now, anyway.'

'Ding *dong*. Excellent. Not much like the Mountgraves to break from convention. Don't they use that stuffy chap? With the cravat? Births, deaths, christenings, crisis management press conferences…'

'Richard, stop it.'

Poppy lifted a finger as though she'd just remembered something important. 'Ah, I've got somewhere I need to be. Would you mind? Thanks, I'll just…'

She inched back towards the perimeter of the room and looked for a way out. She felt like a laser dot had been trained on her from a distance. Any second, she'd be shot with a dart gun and stashed in the kitchen with everyone else who laid out complicated cutlery but didn't know how to eat with it.

Poppy headed towards a sign that read 'To the terrace', a kaleidoscope of colour passing across her skin as the sun pierced through a stained-glass ceiling. She cradled her bag as it dangled by her hip, her valuables hastily stashed inside – phone, purse, keys, and most importantly, camera. It was a habit she couldn't seem to shake.

As newlyweds, Poppy and Josh had a routine that complemented each other. The nickname 'little cricket' had emerged over time, taken from the noise of her shutter clicking and whirring on hikes, Josh wrapping her close to his chest with his raincoat held wide as she tried to change film in the darkness. It took a couple of years before he started to complain about how long it took them to get anywhere. Poppy always stopped to watch and wait for a creature to crawl into shot. Josh wore trail shoes, entered ultra-marathons, and ran ahead, looping back to meet her by the car once his mileage was complete. They started and ended their journey in the same place, always orbiting each other's interests, never quite aligning. Poppy saw her life as a pie chart and always allowed him the biggest slice.

What parts of her world had she shrunk to make room for his? With distance, Poppy was starting to notice exactly how much she'd given up.

Chapter Six

To call it a 'terrace' would be akin to calling Versailles 'quaint'. The back of the building had doors that were designed for throwing open during a raucous party; each set off a long dining hall with a parquet floor and chandeliers that tinkled in the breeze. The hotel was Art Deco, a style recreated on DIY programmes with cheap vinyl and dark paint. Here, the English Riviera formed an azure backdrop set against a stone balcony, the cliff dramatically falling away to frame two long dining tables with crisp tablecloths that fluttered in the breeze.

Poppy instinctively reached for her camera, a breath caught in her throat. Strips of hessian sack bound cutlery together, two-foot tall lemon trees forming centrepieces between ruler-straight rows of crystal glasses, fish forks, and place settings. Poppy picked one up. The name 'Zaffia' was written in green ink above a printed logo that featured an insignia inside a coat of arms, two swords crossed behind it. 'The Mountgrave Foundation'. The name rang a bell. Poppy thought back to the photography darkroom at Cricklewood Academy. It had long been used as a store cupboard for collapsible tables in lieu of having actual camera film to develop. Outside, a chrome plate was screwed into the door: 'Provided thanks to a generous donation from The Mountgrave Foundation'. Poppy was sure of it.

'I was looking for her.'

Poppy looked up from the place name in her hands. A man with a flop of blonde hair stood at her right shoulder. Poppy could see inside his shirt thanks to the fact he had not one, but three buttons undone. He pushed a pair of aviators onto his head and nodded towards the closest dining chair. 'All right, you can have Zaffia, but the pay-off is you have to take Daniel or Sanjit.' He held up two more place names between his first and second finger. Poppy laughed and looked down the table.

'I'm not here for this. Actually, I suppose I am, in a way. I mean, I'm not here as a guest. I'm helping my friend. I'm a photographer. Sort of.'

'I'm a part of this,' said the man. He reached over her to tap the same logo stitched onto each cotton napkin and smirked. He smelt of things that shouldn't have scents, yet are branded as though they do: sea salt and spiced oak with a hint of brushed leather.

'Are you working here too?' said Poppy.

'An excellent question.' He plucked the place card from Poppy's hand, swapped it with another, and continued down the table. 'Sort of.' He glanced back at her and smiled, his eyebrow arched.

'You might know my friend, Lola. She's the wedding planner.'

'Eurgh, I don't envy her. Do you take pictures, or just carry that around for moral support?' said the man gesturing to the bag bundled in Poppy's arms. She hadn't realised she'd been holding it to her chest like a baby since leaving the atrium.

'Not a huge amount happening, is there?' said Poppy. 'I thought I'd let everyone get settled in. It's a long lead-up to the wedding, isn't it?' She didn't know how honest to be about her credentials, so decided to skirt around the details. Weddings were the last thing she wanted to photograph, and it wasn't just because they reminded her of the very thing she was trying to avoid thinking about. It was the prospect of portraits, directing sloshed uncles, and attempting to coordinate sixty people to hold sparklers in a 'tunnel of love' without the bride's hairspray going up in flames.

'I didn't catch your name,' said Poppy.

The man reached the furthest corner of the table and turned the place card around. He pointed to it with a little finger. 'Lawrence. That's me.' He shook his head. 'God, they've really scraped the barrel with this end of the table. A brave move – placing me next to the family accountant – but luckily you've taken David off my hands so Rachael and Zaffia can tap in,' he said, placing their cards down on either side of his own. 'David once excused himself from a Sunday roast because the horseradish "made his nose tickle". Look out for that one. Absolute nutter.'

'I'll have to take your word for it,' said Poppy, placing David's card beside a lemon that had been split open to resemble an oyster, the pips rearranged inside like pearls. What was the theme here? Could fruit not be left to look like fruit?

'I'm more than happy eating a bag of peanuts for dinner,' said Poppy, her stomach hollow. She had packed a tub of high-calorie fruit and nut bars but they weren't much help to her now. 'Besides, I'm not officially on duty. I don't know what the brief is yet, so probably best not to point a camera at people when they're trying to eat their...' Poppy leant in to read a menu card, which had been printed onto a slate tile and propped against a miniature lemon tree. '...cider-cured brill with tomato sea foam.'

'Oh, it'll be the usual. Don't take pictures of the over-fifties before 11am, smiling is good, but not too much or it'll seem out of character, and if you can get more than three family members in the same shot, you'll take home some John Lewis vouchers as a special bonus.'

Poppy laughed. 'I think I've still got some of those left over from *my* wedding.'

'Your wedding? Dammit. You were about to be my third musketeer,' Lawrence said, gesturing to the reshuffled places beside him. 'Anyway, you'll be given an information pack or something,' he said, scratching the back of his neck. 'I know that because I was in charge of picking them up from the printer's before I left London and didn't manage to fuck it up, so I've earned day release until tomorrow. Huzzah.' Lawrence bit his lip, but it was more awkward than coy. He opened a silver case lined with filters and tobacco, rolled one, and licked along the seal, far slower than Poppy thought necessary.

'Where are my manners. Want one?'

'No, thanks. They make me feel sick.'

'Cor, you and David are going to get on.'

Poppy wasn't lying. The smell of nicotine reminded her of the house she grew up in, of her parents chain-smoking and the stale cigarette butts that she tipped out of overflowing ashtrays after her mum left. She'd filled her bedside drawer with half-used lighters like a pyrotechnic magpie, having plucked them out of her dad's pockets before she took herself to bed. As a ten-year-old, Poppy had worried that he would set himself alight from dangling lit roll-ups above a carpet sticky with cider. Nowadays, the smell of cigarettes made her feel oddly nostalgic and slightly anxious.

From behind, a parade of waiters brought bread baskets, silverware, and glasses to the table, inspecting each flute for smears. Lawrence jerked his head towards the balustrade beside him. Poppy followed.

'Best step out of their way. Fuck, there's a lot of staff here. I feel like we've stamped on an ant's nest. So much... scurrying.'

He looked at her and grinned. 'You can laugh, you know. I won't tell the boss.' Lawrence tapped his nose and flicked his sunglasses down. He spoke as though he was rolling a fat olive under his tongue. Poppy had to tune in to catch every word.

'Do you know the family?' she asked.

'Mmm. Some more than others. By their standards, this counts as a "modest" wedding. I expect you've met the happy couple?'

'No, not yet. Only the bride's parents.'

'Lucky you.'

'I have met some of the other guests.'

'Sorry, you mispronounced "leeches",' said Lawrence. He took a drag of his cigarette. 'But they have got deep pockets, so it's all swings and roundabouts really.'

Poppy knew this was a big gig for Lola. She'd started up as a freelance wedding coordinator after her seventh run as maid of honour. When a twice-removed cousin asked Lola to put the shoes on again, it was clear that news of her hyper-organisation and comprehensive knowledge of bunting suppliers had reached far and wide. She started charging and that was that. Goodbye temping as a legal receptionist, hello wedding planner.

Poppy hadn't made time for Lola as much as she should have in the past year. Between Lola's demanding job and the demise of Poppy's own marriage, they'd been too busy. A Friday night cheese platter couldn't eat itself, could it?

Poppy looked up at the hotel and sighed. 'It's a bit much, isn't it? A *week-long* wedding?'

'A six day lead-up to a day that defines the rest of your adult life? Yeah, I can't think what the fuss is about. Oh, was there an Alan on your side?' He stubbed his cigarette out in a plant pot. 'I need to put him on the other side of Rachael. He's nearly as dull as David, so she'll have no choice but to talk to me.'

This man was exceptionally difficult to read. Poppy didn't know whether he was laughing at her or at the people who had hired a whole island to plump up a ceremony that took ten minutes and a signature to complete.

'Bit ironic, isn't it?' he asked. 'A wedding photographer who hates weddings?'

Poppy laughed and shook her head. She didn't feel like being honest. For one, she wanted to get through the next few days with her head down, which necessitated staying out of the drama for which weddings were a catalyst. *Never elaborate on a lie* – wasn't that the golden rule? Although she was covering for Lola, Poppy didn't want to add detail to her invented biography as the West Country's most exciting new photographer. Would that class as fraud? Anonymity was the name of the game, not just here, but to be half-decent behind the camera too. She'd said it to her students just last week. She'd also said, 'Don't give up on your art for anyone,' but it was always easier to say than do.

Poppy looked on in disbelief as a heaving silver platter wobbled onto the terrace held by two waiters with pink faces and strained necks. On it, a seafood medley was arranged, complete with a whole octopus, its tentacles wrapped around oysters and clams the size of fists.

'All right, it's a bit gauche. But I don't know these people. Who am I to decide what they spend their money on? Even if it is a monstrosity like that,' she said, nodding towards the platter. 'Nothing says true love like slightly warm seafood.' Poppy was surprised at the cutting sarcasm in her voice.

A woman in a neat suit dress stepped out onto the terrace and spotted Lawrence beside Poppy. 'Mr Mountgrave?'

Poppy's gaze snapped towards him. *'You're* a Mountgrave? Oh, God. I wish you'd said. I wouldn't have been so rude about the—'

'Slightly festering by-catch?'

'Not the words I'd use.'

'Oh, it was "monstrosity", wasn't it?' Lawrence smirked, but it wasn't sinister. If anything, his interest was piqued. 'We can all be duplicitous, Miss Pascoe.'

'I... don't think I told you my name.'

Lawrence pointed at Poppy's bag, where a rectangular sticker sat at an angle, her teaching name scribbled across it in black marker pen.

'Oh, yep. I should have taken that off. It's from a school trip. I'm a teacher.' Poppy bit her lip. So far, her attempts to be enigmatic were not going to plan.

'I love teachers. And wedding photographers, for that matter.' Lawrence put on a suit jacket that hung from the back of a chair and slipped his cigarette case into its silk-lined pocket. 'Don't worry, I won't tell my brother what you said.'

'Your brother?'

'The groom.'

'Oh, shit. That's even worse. I'm sorry, I didn't realise.'

'Look sharp. Here comes the sergeant,' said Lawrence, nodding towards Lola, who strode along the terrace towards them, eyes fixed on her iPad. 'We've fallen out already. If she says anything about the table arrangement, I'm blaming you.'

Poppy's neck flushed with heat, but before she could think of anything to say, Lola was at her side, eyes wide. She clapped a hand to her waist, swooping towards Lawrence as he quick-stepped inside. 'What in the *shitting* hell is this?'

Chapter Seven

'I asked for sea-themed, not *dregs from the arse end of a Japanese trawler*. How long has it been sitting here?'

'Only a few minutes, although it's clearly been sitting somewhere else for longer...'

A fat bluebottle landed on a waxy tentacle as it sank further into its rapidly melting ice bath.

'I was so clear with the caterer; I may as well have written it in permanent marker across his forehead. If it's above twenty-three degrees in the day, we put the seafood on ice for the evening.' Lola consulted a mini-thermometer that she'd looped through the handle of her bag. 'Twenty-five and climbing. Brilliant. How's my lipstick?'

Poppy leant in to check, angling around Lola's face like a dentist inspecting hard-to-reach molars. 'Flawless.'

'Good. I can't shout at someone with a smudge; it loses impact.' Lola dumped her bag by Poppy's feet and headed inside with a purposeful stride. Poppy had seen it employed many times before, most often in bars. Lola's hips could divide a crowd like Moses parting the Red Sea.

They had spent their early adulthood in neighbouring cities, Lola working in Bristol, Poppy at university in Bath. Weekends had involved pinballing between train stations with discount tickets and Evian bottles full of pre-mixed vodka cranberry juice, their collective friends pulled into a constantly metamorphosing group through Lola's efforts as self-appointed social secretary and Poppy's reluctance to organise anything herself. It was why they worked. It was also what made Poppy feel so guilty about hiding from Lola for the past six months. She had burrowed herself like a mole, digging deeper the closer anyone came.

Poppy avoided confrontation by pretending it wasn't happening, but she was sure Lola thrived on a healthy dose of chaos. Even now, Poppy felt a sharp ache in her stomach as though she'd distilled her discomfort, drank it, and allowed it to harden into emotional gallstones. Given the chance, Lola would pull a surgical light overhead and pluck them out for closer inspection. Knowing this, Poppy had slipped into a habit of rejecting calls and leaving messages unread. After six months, the energy it took to pretend she was fine had run dry.

Lola didn't need any additional strain, so Poppy didn't mention the sabotaged seating arrangement. She still couldn't fathom how week-long wedding celebrations necessitated stuffy lunches with company-monogrammed napkins. Was this a conference, a party, or some strange amalgamation of both? The guests she'd met so far were a mixture of Cluedo characters and a corporate accounts team. She couldn't begin to picture what the couple getting married might be like.

Lola returned, followed by the same waiters who had brought out the seafood platter. They hovered by the table, throwing nervous glances in Lola's direction.

'What's the matter?'

'Where do you want us to dump it?'

Lola blinked slowly. 'It's not like you can release them back into the sea, is it? Take it home in some Tupperware, feed it to a basking shark, I don't know, just get it off the terrace before people come through.'

The two waiters nodded and gingerly walked the platter back towards the kitchen. One of them staggered, water sloshing down the front of his waistcoat. As he gagged with the melodrama of a child trying broccoli for the first time, Lola took a slow, deliberate breath. 'Breathe in love, breathe out love… breathe in love, breathe out love,' she whispered.

'Have you ever considered becoming a teacher? The quality of your sarcasm has the power to wither a teenager's self-esteem in seconds.'

'Nah, one big career change is enough for me. Oh! I need to give you something. It'll get pretty busy round here in about… ninety seconds, so unless you want to schmooze with the guests about the quality of Burgundy grapes this year, duck out now. I'll meet you by the grotto.'

Poppy headed down a set of wide stone steps and walked around a lawn that was hidden from view by a huge rhododendron, the branches heavy with pink and purple flowers. She kicked her flip-flops off and tentatively stepped onto the grass, ignoring the 'lawn games only' sign staked into the shingle beside her. The ground was spongy and damp underfoot. It reminded her of long shoeless summers, of the days spent playing rounders in the road, of clambering down coves, and getting fed by whichever neighbour offered to make jam sandwiches for the kids at their end of the estate. She had avoided her own home as a child. She avoided it now.

At the lawn's edge, a man-made cave had been sculpted into an overhang, pockmarked by flint, seashells, and broken masonry. A low rectangular window framed the horizon. As the sun dipped low, the sea blushed pink, the two on the cusp of kissing.

She should message Josh. Nothing weird. Just to say she'd

arrived safely. Poppy reached for her phone, but something stopped her from going any further. He hadn't asked her to. She hadn't said she would. This was how it was going to be. Instead, she flicked her phone camera on and lifted it to take a picture, the horizon flooded with colour that never translated accurately on screen.

'Put it away, quick!' said Lola, appearing at her side. She waved her hand as though Poppy had pulled a cling-film-wrapped rock of heroin from her knickers. Poppy glanced at Lola.

'What?'

'Your phone! Shove it somewhere it won't be seen.'

Poppy did as she was told. 'Why, what's up?'

'There's a social media ban on the island. All the guests have to hand over their devices on arrival and they get locked in a safe behind reception. I know, it's massively OTT. Nothing shouts "fun" like a list of rules as long as the Bayeux Tapestry.'

'But professional photography is okay?'

'Oh, yeah. The family can approve those photos; they can't approve what Uncle Lesley puts online when he's self-medicating with oysters and Crémant. Honestly, boomers should never have been given access to Facebook.'

'No phones, got it.'

'Not within sight anyway, or I'll be in the shitter. I'm surprised you managed to slip through without a heavy frisking. I quite enjoyed mine, but don't tell anyone. Bad feminist moment. If it's an emergency, you can make a call at reception, but there's a steroid-fuelled security guy called Big Steve who hovers beside you the whole time. Quite intimidating, but I'm weirdly into it.'

'It sounds a bit... overcautious? What are they expecting to happen?' asked Poppy.

'It's complicated, but there's a big business announcement happening this week, or that's what I've gathered. I've noticed that when you're working at a place like this, a lot of the really rich people will quite literally pretend you don't exist, which means eavesdropping is a piece of piss. Needless to say, there are a lot of whispers about The Mountgrave Foundation and it's not speculation about what the first dance song choice will be.'

'Now you've said that, I haven't got a *clue* who this couple might be.'

'You'll know when you see the groom, I'll just say that…'

'If it's Orlando Bloom, you're *not* allowed to tell him that I got off with his poster so often as a teenager that his mouth quite literally disintegrated.'

Lola laughed and leant against the balustrade, chin tilted to catch the sunlight. 'Not quite. I'd had three months of meetings with a publicist before I knew who the bride and groom were. I think they might have been sussing me out before a contract was signed. This?' she said, gesturing to the hotel. 'Is a *way* bigger job than I thought I was signing up for. You know me. I'm all about the *event*. I wanted to step up to this scale eventually, but I thought it might be three years down the line. I took it on as a favour. You know what Will is like. Kicking a puppy wouldn't feel half as bad as saying no to him. I didn't *quite* put two and two together at the time, but when someone says "my family like to get involved", you think "mother-in-law has a penchant for lavender", not "my family members occupy three spaces on the annual Forbes Rich List".'

'Hang on, Will? Will *who*? Is Will the groom?'

'Will!' said Lola, rolling her head in a semi-circle to stretch her neck, her eyes heavy with fatigue. 'You know, Will.'

'I don't know a Will Mountgrave.'

'He wasn't called that when you knew him at uni.'

Poppy slipped her flip-flops back on and paced from one end of the grotto to another. 'No… not *that* Will.'

'Yes, *that* Will. He's never used his full name. No wonder. Imagine if we'd known he had all *this* at his fingertips,' said Lola, winking. 'This is why I knew you'd want to come – I just couldn't *say* anything.'

Poppy felt her pulse thrumming at her wrists. 'Hang on, this makes no sense. If he chose his name, why did he go for one that makes him sound like a Dickensian undertaker?'

Lola folded her arms and smirked playfully at Poppy. 'So, let me get this straight. You find out that Will Graves is from a family wealthier than the Murdochs and it's his fake last name that shocks you the most?'

'Well, yeah. You don't *assume* people are rich, do you?'

'Babe, some people do. I can guarantee that ninety-nine per cent of the guests here have no idea who's paying for what.'

Poppy laughed to give her face something to do, but inside she panicked. The last time she'd seen Will, they hadn't exactly left on good terms.

'I thought you'd be made up. You were good mates, weren't you?'

'We drifted apart in second year, so...' Poppy shook her head. 'Won't he find it weird that I'm here? Are you sure we're talking about the same Will?'

Lola's eyes widened and her nostrils flared. 'Will used to bulk buy packet mac 'n' cheese and eat it from the saucepan. I'll admit, that doesn't exactly scream "rich kid", but yes, it's him.'

'Do you want to check first?'

'Check what?'

'That he's okay with me being here—'

From the grotto door, Poppy heard a voice.

'I ate multiple saucepans of cheap macaroni back in the day and I only glow in the dark at weekends. Powdered cheese is the best kind, right?'

Lola directed a Colgate smile at Poppy, clapping her hands in girlish glee as she turned to look at the man who had joined them in the grotto. Poppy's cheeks flushed with embarrassment. When he saw her, Will's frog-like grin glitched. It was him. Will who had slept on the other side of a shared wall in their dingy, third-floor halls. Will who she'd saved from rugby initiations when he was paralytic in a disabled toilet wearing just his socks and a stripy tie. Will who had brought her a doughnut every Saturday after his weekend shift at Sainsbury's.

'Pops?' he said, his cheeks flushed pink. 'What are you doing here?'

Chapter Eight

MAY 7TH, 2008

'When's your deadline?'

'9am.'

'That's in eight hours.'

'I know. Loads of time,' said Will. Poppy sat on the edge of his single bed drinking water from a chipped mug. He slumped beside her, his bony hip padded by the cushion he had duct taped around his torso. They had settled on panda costumes for the Noah's Ark themed club night that took place in a refectory on campus, both in black t-shirts with a round patch of white fur safety pinned to their bellies. The overall look was more adorable than spooky, but Poppy had enjoyed watching Will's fluffy ears bobbing above the crowd as he returned with a round of drinks.

Will pulled a red ethernet cable from the side of his mattress and tugged it over to his desk. 'Do you think your essay will be better or worse after half a crate of Stella?' asked Poppy.

'Better. I scraped a third on my last one and I actually tried. I've got three cans of Red Bull in the fridge to help me transition out of party mode,' said Will.

'And into cardiac arrest?'

'If Red Bull was bad for you, why would they sponsor so many sports teams?' said Will. He tried to plug the cable into his laptop, but the wire folded back on itself, his coordination clumsy.

Poppy yawned and rubbed her eyes. When she looked at her hand, it was smeared with black face paint. 'Oh, shit. I forgot I was wearing this.' She stood up and pulled open Will's wardrobe.

'Where's your mirror gone?' she said, looking at the back of the door.

'It's behind my dressing gown. The Jedi one.'

'And the reason you have two dressing gowns is?'

Will turned around, as though this was a debate he'd been looking forward to having. 'You see, this is something people don't understand. There are varying tiers of cosiness depending on the occasion. Winter and summer have their own requirements. If anything, I'd have a third dressing gown for sprinter.'

'Huh?'

'March to June. Nine to fifteen degrees is a tough nut to crack. If you think you can shove your blankets to the back of the wardrobe you've got another thing coming, I'm telling you straight.'

Poppy laughed and shook her head. 'It's no wonder you never got on with the rugby club.'

'Bunch of tossers. Can't see the appeal of drinking someone else's piss for banter.'

Poppy went to their shared kitchen, soaked a paper towelette, and returned to Will's room to scrub at her skin. When she was finished, she took another one and tossed it to Will. It landed on his cheek with a wet splat, his head jerking upwards from the first sagging stages of sleep.

'In the nicest way possible, I have no hope that you're going to finish that essay.'

Will held his finger on the 'x' key and threw a goofy grin in her direction.

'Here's a better idea. I have a streaming link for *Point Break* and a bag of chicken nuggets in the freezer. If we load it up now, it will have buffered by the time they're cooked.'

'But... my essay?'

'Get up early and do it then.'

'I can't. I'm going to yoga with Gabriella at seven.'

Poppy shut Will's wardrobe door. She left his room, took some baby wipes from her washbag in the communal bathroom, and continued scrubbing her neck. She had removed the worst of her panda make-up, but now looked like she'd been through an emotionally turbulent break-up.

'Why would you agree to yoga that early? Are you mad?' said Poppy. 'Who even *does* yoga at 7am other than weirdos and show-offs?'

'Gabriella does. She teaches it.'

'You are a walking cliché.'

'She's really into intense breathing. Too much sometimes. It's like having sex with Darth Vader.'

Poppy shook her head and covered her ears. 'I don't want to hear any more.'

'You know, out of everyone in the flat, you're the only one who goes pinker than the Pope when sex is mentioned.'

'That's because *everyone* lies about it,' she said, skirting over the fact that she'd never done it herself and hadn't corrected those that assumed otherwise. 'Harry told us last week that he shagged Swedish twins on his sixth-form hockey tour.'

'I think he did,' said Will earnestly.

'Of course he fucking didn't. His mum still buys his pants. So, are we having a nugget party or not?' Poppy said. She wiggled the panda ears that she'd attached to an old Alice band. 'Also, you should text Gabriella and cancel yoga. If you fail first year and get kicked out, who am I going to convince to leave clubs early with me? Just go yoga-ing another time.'

Poppy dropped her grey baby wipe in the bin, removed the safety pins from her T-shirt, and walked to the kitchen. Will followed her, his panda eyes smudged like he'd attempted to contour with black paint and given up halfway.

'I want her to think I'm a cool early-morning smoothie-drinking yogi.'

'You're not though.'

'Yeah, but she *thinks* I am and that's what I'm concentrating on for now.'

Poppy tore the bag of nuggets open and inspected a baking tray that one of their flatmates had left on the side. In the corners were the blackened remnants of another meal along with a layer of sausage grease. Poppy covered it with a sheet of tin foil, slid the tray of nuggets into the oven, and stood against the door to warm the backs of her legs.

Will took a carton of orange juice out of the fridge, his T-shirt riding up as he unscrewed the lid and drank. Poppy squinted at his stomach. 'Have you shaved your belly?'

'No.'

'You have!'

Poppy ran to the other side of the room and lunged for Will. He tossed the empty carton towards a Jenga tower of recycling and lowered his elbow to protect himself.

'Let me see!' she said, pulling at the hem of his shirt as he tried to push her away in mock annoyance.

'No, no, ah! I'm ticklish! It's a trick of the light!'

'Liar!' she said, grappling with Will. They bumped into the fridge, which showered them with Domino's coupons.

'If I go down, I'm taking you with me,' said Will, wrapping his long leg around the back of Poppy's knee.

'I have the strength of a thousand wolves!' said Poppy, holding him up for a moment before they lost balance and tumbled to the floor.

Will made a gagging noise and shook his head from side to side. 'I always suspected that Sam clipped his nails in here and now I know for sure.'

Poppy extracted her leg from underneath Will and sat on him, one knee either side of his lap.

'One peek,' she said.

'No way.'

'One peek and I promise not to mention it to anyone. I'm supplying you with nuggets and I paid for your club entry tonight.'

'This is exploitation.'

'Shut up and show me.'

Will pressed his lips together and looked down uneasily before slowly interlocking his hands behind his head. Poppy lifted his shirt and gasped.

'Will! No!'

'What?' he said with blameless intonation. 'Come on, girls don't like hairy bellies.'

'Bollocks! I've never thought this was something I had to have an opinion on until right now.'

'So you shouldn't care that I tidied myself up.'

'I don't, but you should only do that for you, not because someone you're sleeping with told you to.'

'That is a very quick assumption to make,' said Will, pushing himself up onto his forearms. Poppy felt his hip bones press into her thighs.

'Tell me it's not true then,' she said, folding her arms.

Will lifted his chin and blinked at her coolly. 'It's not true.' She inched her fingers towards his ribs. Will wriggled beneath her. 'Okay, okay, it's true! But why does that have to be a negative thing?'

'Because you're not being yourself around her.'

'Maybe this *is* the new version of me. As Dickens once said, "we contain multitudes".'

'That was Shakespeare.'

'Excuse me, I've read *Far From the Madding Crowd*. And watched the film. I'm obliged to; it's Mum's birthday tradition.'

'That's Thomas Hardy.'

'We've all read books, Poppy, no need to boast about it.' His attempt to be serious was hijacked by a cautious smile. Poppy rolled her eyes.

Will sat up, his eyes almost level with hers. Neither of them moved, as though doing so would break the momentary ease between them. A fluorescent bulb flickered overhead and the fridge hummed beside them, but still, she didn't move. His expression changed into something she hadn't seen before – eyes soft, lips slightly parted. He put his hand on her knee and moved his thumb in a cautious circle, the weight of it heavy and iron-hot through her eighty denier tights. Will raised his chin. Poppy leant down.

The oven beeped. Will bit his lip and let his hand fall to the floor as Poppy sat upright, the warmth that had pooled in her stomach now taut with tension. The timer continued to sound in an off-key pitch, but neither of them knew what to say.

'I should turn that off.'

'Mm-hmm,' muttered Will, rubbing his chin.

'You know what Mini Hitler will do if she hears it,' said Poppy, internally screaming at herself for cracking their eggshell moment by drawing attention to their hermit flatmate who had a low tolerance for noise and had bought her own whiteboard to detail each resident's decibel readings past eleven o'clock.

Poppy stood up, inched her skirt down, and pulled the tray out of the oven with a twice-folded tea towel. She scooped nuggets into a dish with a fish slice, her face hot with a feeling that sat somewhere between embarrassment and dissipating lust.

When she turned around, Will was still on the floor staring straight up at the ceiling, his fingers interlocked at his chest.

She slid down the fridge door and slipped her feet under the small of Will's back. It wasn't quite clear what had passed between them, but she wanted to offset the lingering awkwardness between them. Poppy balanced her bowl in the soft curve of Will's stomach, fished out a nugget, and smeared it with ketchup.

'This was an excellent choice,' she said, her voice far more upbeat than she felt.

Will stared at a polystyrene tile in the ceiling.

'Hey. Food,' she said, nudging him.

'Do you think it's possible to find a girlfriend who's happy with everything about you?' he said.

Poppy sighed. 'Probably not. "Everything" seems unreasonable. But on the other hand, no one should feel like they're underperforming just by being themselves. Take my grandparents – absolutely adorable – held hands when they walked to the corner shop and everything, but even then, they only liked, maybe... seventy per cent of the stuff the other one did? Beyond a shared appreciation for garlic bread and conspiracy theories about Princess Diana, it was the person they loved. Everything else was surplus to requirement.'

'What about your parents?' he said, inspecting a nugget in the light.

'Way more complicated. They split when I was about ten but couldn't pay for a divorce, so Mum moved out and Dad's been unsuccessfully trying to replace her ever since.'

'Were they happy when they were together?'

'No.'

'Quick response.'

'I've collected a decent evidence bank over the years. They got married when Mum got pregnant with me and Dad thought it was "the right thing to do" even though it was 1988 and everyone was pretty much cool with cohabitation by then. I would say it's because he's old school, but to be honest I think he saw it as a really good deal. He laboured on building sites, Mum worked as a classroom assistant and then did another full shift when she got home keeping us both fed and happy. Basically, she emptied her tank to fill ours. Proposing to Mum is where Dad's measure of effort came to an end. Cue a decade of talking at cross purposes, growing resentment, and all without ever really bothering to figure out how the other one ticks.'

'I thought you got on with your dad?' said Will, cushioning his head with his hands.

'I do, but it's not been straightforward. Mum left and moved to Jersey with a landscaper called Rick, or Mick, or some other local-radio-sounding name. Then three years later, she died and Dad lost his job, so, yeah... complicated.'

Will blinked and raised his head an inch higher.

'What? I never knew that. About your mum.'

Poppy shrugged. She felt her throat spike with the threat of tears. She was seeing a counsellor for the first time who encouraged her not to shut down conversations about her mum, but in reality, it felt like asking someone to stamp on her foot. The pain was inevitable.

Will put his hand on her knee, his touch cautious, his palm soft. Poppy pushed hair out of her face.

'Don't hug me because I'll cry and I never know when it'll stop. I like to plan for it,' she said, her voice catching. 'At least if it coincides with my PMS I can get away with locking myself in my room without being questioned.'

'I just thought you had a traumatic, you know... monthly girl thing.'

'Monthly girl thing? You're a nineteen-year-old man living independently and you can't say period?' said Poppy, laughing.

'You've been adding Galaxy Ripples into my Tesco order every month since September. I thought that made me an ally for the female cause.'

'Yeah, sorry about that. It's always been dead-mum chocolate. That carries more weight than period chocolate, so kudos to you.'

Will gave Poppy a sad smile and patted her arm. The warmth she felt in the base of her stomach peaked like a shard of ice.

'You see, this is why I don't mention it. It brings everyone down,' she said.

'You could have told me before.'

'Nah. Mum likes to surprise me. It's like pass-the-parcel, but the prize is childhood trauma.'

'And your dad coped badly, did he?'

'Oh, it was pretty much as bad as it gets. I kept us both alive for years and he rewarded me by turning my bedroom into an electrical workshop. He buys broken appliances from charity shops to fix up and sell, but he's blown the fuses in the house more times than I can count and I'm not a hundred per cent sure what he's doing is legal. We get on a lot better now that I've moved out, but I just want him to find a good enough reason to look after himself without having to rely on me all the time.'

'What are you going to do this summer when we have to leave halls?'

'I don't know. Find a job. It's not like I *can't* stay with him, but I don't really want to go back home for longer than a weekend if I can help it.'

'Nah, come and hang out with me!' said Will. 'My dad has planned a family thing in Italy, but me, Isaac, and Faith are meeting in Croatia afterwards. Haven't booked anything yet, but y'know. Plans are in the early stages.' Will sat up, his expression less pinched with worry than before. It must be nice to forget so easily.

'I can't. If I don't earn some money, I'll be eating potatoes for the rest of the year.'

'I'll cover you.'

'I won't let you.'

'It's not a big deal.'

'Says the person who won't go to the cinema unless there's a two-for-one voucher going,' said Poppy.

'Yeah, but this is different. This is you.'

'Honestly, that's really sweet, but I'm fine. Summer holidays were always a bit of a dodgy time for me. A lot of hours and not a lot to do except rattle around at home picking up after Dad, which, as appealing as it sounds, loses its shine after a while. If I get a job with Lola, at least we'll have a laugh. I like working.'

'You love a routine.'

'Exactly! And I can do shoots in my downtime, especially if Lola's with me to interview people. She has the mouth; I have the camera. The other alternative is getting my job back at Shoe Zone, but I'd rather shoot my toes off than fit school plimsoles for ten hours a day.'

'You sound set on it,' said Will.

'Mm-hmm. Anyway, what's with the parental relationship quizzing?'

'I'm trying to widen my data pool of happy couples to learn from.'

'Well, strike mine off for starters. What about yours?'

'Mum's boyfriends are always obsessed with the fact she used to be a model. They wear T-shirts that are too small for them. Instant write-off. Dad has been married twice since Mum and the most recent one answers questions at least two minutes after you asked them. She's on a different planet. Or a lot of Xanax. I can't figure out which.'

Poppy felt a swathe of tiredness settle across her brow. She rested her head on her knees, yawned, and looked at Will. 'Don't change for anyone. You're too good as you are.'

'Doesn't seem like it.' He sighed. 'I want to die on a single bed having lost my marbles with a wife I've had for sixty years.'

'We've had this discussion before. If you use *The Notebook* as the gold standard for relationships, you're going to be disappointed.'

'He built her a house. I want to build someone a house.'

'You will. Just not Gabriella. She sounds terrible.'

'She is terrible,' said Will, threading his fingers between hers. Poppy's brain slipped into rapid response mode. They'd held hands before, but then it had been ironic. This time, it felt like they'd closed a circuit of electricity that flowed up her arm, down her spine, and back to Will at the point her toes made contact with his body.

'Oi, oi!'

Harry walked into the kitchen cradling a polystyrene tray, a strip of grey kebab meat dangling from his mouth. 'What are you two twats doing here? I had a suspicion you'd slipped out early. Wink wink,' he said, smirking at Poppy.

'Yeah, what happened to the Brightside rule?' said Laura, elbowing him out of the way. 'Repeat after me: no bailing until "Mr Brightside". Louder at the back! No bailing until "Mr Brightside"!' She kicked her heels under the table as someone plugged a portable speaker in. It didn't take long for the rest of them to join, a menagerie of drunken animals, chips squashed underfoot as they belted the opening lyrics until it sounded like a football chant.

Poppy left her bowl on the side, helped Will up, and slipped out into the corridor, allowing the fire door to close behind them.

'I better do that essay,' he said.

'Right.' Poppy hovered at the threshold to her bedroom and looked down the corridor at Will. He gripped the door frame, back arched as though he were about to skydive from an open-sided plane.

'Hey, Will?'

'Mmm?'

'I think I left something in your room.'

Chapter Nine

FIVE DAYS BEFORE THE WEDDING

Three chefs sat behind a row of potted olive trees, plates of mixed leftovers balanced on their knees. They both ate with one hand and smoked with the other, tapping ash into a chipped gravy boat propped on an upturned crate. Will nodded to them, parted a chain-link curtain, and stepped aside to let Poppy and Lola into a basement kitchen. Poppy hung back. She wanted to refamiliarize herself with Will's movements, his sloped shoulders, his hairline, the way he walked with his head slightly bowed, as if conscious of his height. A decade ago, she'd be able to locate him in seconds from the balcony of a heaving club, a WKD in each hand, arm dangling across a friend as he jumped out of time with the music. He'd stopped wearing T-shirts with stretched necklines, but his dopey smile was the same.

Inside, a sous-chef called over to them by the sink, elbow deep in soap suds. 'Will, mate. There's a leftover terrine in the fridge. Help yourself. Good with a bit of sourdough. It's Tamiko's recipe, so you know it's shit-hot.'

'Cheers. I'm starving,' said Will. He opened the fridge, pulled out a weighty rectangular plate, and set it down on a stainless-steel worktop alongside half a loaf of bread. Lola hovered by the door, clutching her bag in front of her with both hands.

'You hungry?' asked Will.

'No, I'm fine...' said Lola, angling her wrist to check the time.

'She isn't,' said Poppy. 'Lola, when was the last time you ate?'

'I had a Diet Coke earlier,' she said.

'When?'

'This morning. With a boiled egg.'

Will held Lola at arm's length. 'Lola, you've been amazing today. Let Dad get on with his schmoozing. Chill out for a bit, come on. Free terrine!' He spoke quickly, but Poppy couldn't tell if it was awkwardness, excitement, or both. There was an atmosphere between them, but was that because Poppy was looking for one? The last time they spoke, it wasn't on the best of terms.

Will released Lola with a look of friendly reproach, cut a slice of terrine, and spread it on a thick wedge of bread, finishing it off with a slug of olive oil and a twist of pepper. Was there any recollection in his eyes? Any memory of the last time they spoke?

'I should probably add a bit of context to this,' said Lola, waving her hand in Poppy's direction.

Poppy panicked, unsure how honest she should be about the reason why she and Will were awkwardly fidgeting, hyper-conscious of their body language like extras on a daytime soap. 'I'm not a stripper,' said Poppy, warmth flooding her cheeks. 'In case that's what you thought.'

'It's... not what I thought,' said Will.

Lola smarted. 'Steady on, babe.'

'I just thought... wedding... my surprise appearance, etcetera, etcetera...' Poppy rubbed the back of her neck, her skin radiating heat. 'Obviously, why would you think I was a stripper? That was a proper brain fart. I would have prepared a more elaborate entrance if I *was* a stripper. Jumped out of a cake or something.'

Poppy laughed at herself, wishing she could self-detonate from shame. Will gave her a confused smile. Lola shook her head in disbelief.

'Glad we cleared that up. Also, quite glad Ottilie wasn't here to hear it,' he said, running a hand inside his buttoned collar.

'Ottilie is Will's fiancée,' added Lola. 'You met her parents on the boat. Is she around?'

'She's down at the fisherman's hut, charging her crystals.' He shrugged. 'I can't pretend to understand it. Still, she always comes back bubbly as anything.'

At this, Lola pursed her lip to the side, recalculating her decision. 'In that case, I think I can spare fifteen minutes... She's staying there overnight?'

'Yeah, I think so.'

Lola hung her bag by a rack of chef's whites, pulled her heels off, and audibly sighed as her bare feet touched the cold tiles. 'Oh, good God, that's nice. The last time I wore these shoes was when I dressed up as Frank-N-Furter at that *Rocky Horror* party I organised when you guys were at university.'

Will scratched his chin and blinked. 'My first time in fishnets. I forgot about that. What would that have been, nine years ago?'

'Ten,' said Poppy.

'Ten, *wow*. Hey, we've got some catching up to do, right? I've got so many questions. But first of all, can I give you a hug?'

Poppy smiled. He was right. Ten years *was* a long time – long enough to forget about something that happened so long ago, back when they were highly strung and naïve with youth. She swayed on the spot in faux hesitation, her worry easing. 'Go on then.'

Will wrapped his arms around her, his chest pressed against her ear. When he spoke, Poppy could hear a murmur through his ribcage. 'How come you're on the island? I mean, it's great, but... unexpected. Lola, is this your doing?'

'No, no. Not me. Actually, that's not true. Poppy *is* here because of me, but she wasn't intended as a surprise guest. I needed a photographer. Poppy is one. Thus, Poppy is here!' Lola smiled, skittish with nervous energy. Back when they were baby adults living in each other's pockets, Lola had been introduced to Will through their mutual friendship with Poppy. Although Lola didn't go to their university, her frequent visits to Poppy's campus gave her the experience without the debt, a fact she was incredibly proud of. The three of them would watch films together on Poppy's single bed, backs against the wall, legs dangling above a faint vomit stain that the previous year's tenant had left behind. They were close as a trio, but Lola didn't know everything. When Lola went home, Will was there.

'Oh, that's great. What, er… I'm just asking because Ottilie will want to know, but what happened to the original photographer, Christian?'

'Christian had an unexpected emergency. He called me earlier, head halfway down a bog, going by the echo. Norovirus. He didn't give details, but the phrase "out both ends" was used.'

'Say no more. Bad timing. I don't suppose you took Princess Eugenie's engagement photos, Pops? You used to be good with portraits. Do you still run that photoblog? What was it called again?'

'*The World's Eye*? No, 'fraid not. Only kingfishers and lapwings of late.'

Will bit into his bread and picked up a napkin, attempting to catch crumbs. Hearing her old nickname alleviated a tension that wound between her ribs and pulled her up short. She reached for the butter knife, her stomach aching with hunger.

'Poppy, can you cut me a slice?' asked Lola, waggling her bright-red acrylic nails. 'I can't get a grip on the knife with these.' Poppy cut a doorstep wedge of bread and slid the plate over to Lola. 'Thanks, you're a dream.'

'This could be fate,' said Will. 'I know you spent months trying to book Christian and my dad is a fan, but... I don't know, Christian's pretty old school. Takes pictures from a stepladder, teeth too big for his mouth, you know?' Will scooped at the terrine with a dessert spoon.

Lola nibbled her crust, careful not to displace her lipstick. 'He does have a good track record of getting six-page spreads in *Hello* magazine...' said Lola.

'Exactly. Dodged a bullet there,' said Will, grimacing. 'Although I don't want to be the one to break it to Ottie.'

'I'll give him a couple of days and check in to see how he's doing,' said Lola. 'There's no need to mention it to Ottilie now.'

'You know what this needs?' said Will, his tongue pressed against the inside of his cheek. 'Maldon salt.'

Poppy watched Will as he navigated the kitchen as though it were his own, plucking condiments and cutlery from the drawers until they had a Tudor feast before them. She struggled to assimilate this Will with the one she'd known from halls, back when he'd worn T-shirts featuring Che Guevara and thought Ultimate Frisbee was cool. His hair was buzzed at the sides, curls sleek and springy on top. From this, Poppy inferred that he now paid money to a barber rather than allowed a drunk friend to wield a shaver with no instructions. Another change. Once shy, he now took up space without apologising for it. It suited him.

'So, you're a Mountgrave?' said Poppy.

'Mmm.'

'And this is all for you? Married, eh? Big deal,' said Poppy, trying her best to maintain a neutral interaction.

Will swallowed a clod of ballotine and thumped his chest. 'I'm trying to be cool and composed about everything. Lola keeps saying I'll burn out before Saturday if I keep buzzing around the island like an excited bee. *Married.*' Will shook his head as though he couldn't believe his own luck. 'Mad, right? Still feel weird saying it. Weird, but amazing. Got any advice?' He looked at Poppy, his eye contact unwavering for the first time.

'Huh?'

'About marriage. Last thing I heard, you and Josh got hitched sometime after graduation. Any advice? You must be a veteran by now.'

Poppy presented her hand in mock imitation of the many engagement announcements she'd seen on social media over the past couple of years, except this time her ring finger was bare.

Will leant forward. She still had a slight indentation where her wedding band had once been. The day after they had decided to separate, Josh had had the audacity to ask if she was planning to give her engagement ring back. Of course she wasn't. Her dad advised her to put it towards a good divorce solicitor, but that cycle of expenditure was too depressing to contemplate.

'Oh... Pops. I didn't realise. I shouldn't have said anything,' said Will.

'Hey, why would you know? It would be worse if you assumed I'd be divorced by now.' Poppy laughed. Will didn't reciprocate. 'Anyway, you were always too cool to have social media and I wasn't keen on announcing my new relationship status. But, back to your question. In short, I'm the last person you want to ask for marriage advice, because I'd say don't do it.'

Will's smile faltered as he looked from Poppy to Lola. 'Oh. You're serious,' he said. 'Shit. Was it messy?'

Lola pulled her chair in, sat tall, and pointed at Will with a lacquered nail. 'Hey. Your marriage is going to be a bloody triumph. It'll last your whole life. People will write screenplays inspired by the Will and Ottilie origin story,' said Lola, nodding. 'Stop laughing, it's true. Richard Curtis will be banging down your door for the rights to it. Who do you want to be played by?' Lola gave Poppy's hand a warning squeeze under the countertop.

Poppy had spent months thinking about how she'd let people

know that she and Josh were separated. She couldn't say 'single', not when they still co-owned furniture and a National Trust membership. She'd entertained ideas of wearing bright lipstick, doing a pottery course, and buying a dachshund. Her fantasy single life was suave, straightforward, and full of purpose; the kind that her friends in long-term relationships would mute her on Instagram for. In reality, would *anyone* covet the hours she spent creating surreal stop-motion animations in the attic? Envy her for sleeping on a wicker couch beneath a skylight smeared by greasy pigeon wings? Her throat prickled with tightly coiled anger. A stranger had slipped beneath her skin, a meaner, pithier, withered version of Poppy. Right now, she didn't like herself at all.

'It was a messy break-up, yeah,' said Poppy. 'But what break-up isn't?' Poppy thought about her use of the past tense and felt like a fraud. 'Do I really think that getting married is a bad idea?' Lola lifted her chin, another warning for Poppy. This was not the right audience for the speech she had in mind. 'No. I'm just jaded.'

'I can understand that,' said Will. 'It must have been difficult.' Poppy's jaw tightened. She wasn't going to burden herself or anyone else, not today.

'Sorry, Will. You have to ignore me. I'm old.'

'We're literally the same age.'

'Okay, I'm bitter.'

'So is Aperol, for that matter. Want one?' Will squatted down by a corner cupboard, emerging with a half-full bottle of orange liquid. 'Chef's supply. Lola?' He took some tumblers from a shelf and unscrewed the cap.

'Not me, thanks.'

'Come on. Seeing as it's my wedding and you've worked on it for, what, a year? I insist you have a drink with us.'

'Alcohol doesn't agree with me at the best of times,' said Lola, pinching a black olive between her nails. She popped it in her mouth and shrugged.

Will cocked his head to one side. 'Hang on, this feels like a role reversal. I remember multiple occasions when you came to visit Poppy in Bath and pulled her out of bed for a night out. You had that hip flask. You kept it—'

'In my knickers? Yep. The signs were there, Will. Spilling booze in your handbag is funny when you're nineteen, not when you're hosting a breakfast meeting and the croissants are soaked with vodka. One year, four months sober, and counting.' Lola lifted her bag onto the kitchen island, grinned, and gave herself a literal pat on the back. Poppy smiled, in awe at her ability to instantly deactivate conversational landmines.

'Hey, congratulations,' said Will.

'Thank you. It's the thing I'm most proud of, other than the excellent quartet I've booked for Wednesday night.'

'Ottie will be made-up. And they're going to play our song? It's still a surprise?'

'Of course. You know me, I don't promise something I can't deliver. Except for photographers with norovirus. Oh, I meant to give you this, Poppy,' said Lola, pulling a folder from her bag. 'It's the contact sheet of everyone in attendance this week. There's a brief on page five for the next couple of days: who to photograph where, doing what, with whom, etcetera.'

Will put his head in his hands and groaned. 'Did my dad give you a ton more work? I did tell him that you're here to coordinate the wedding, not his business dealings.'

'No, this time it was his publicist. They want pictures for an announcement at the end of the week, although I expect you know more about that than I do. But don't worry, it's all under control... it's my job to deal with things so you don't have to, remember? You and Ottilie are my number one priority. Unless there's a landslide and the hotel disappears into the sea, I won't bother you with anything unnecessary.' Whilst Lola spoke, her eyes ran over an email on her phone. 'Poppy, you're fine to stay in

Christian's room until he arrives. Reception knows. All right, duty calls. Will, family brunch tomorrow morning at eleven, followed by a couple of remote press interviews. I've given them a list of questions in advance, so there shouldn't be any surprises. I think they want the whole "united front" narrative: Mountgraves and Spruces, joining forces for world domination. Will Ottilie be recharged by then?'

'Should be. Her chakras take around twenty-four hours to realign.'

'Of course they do. Thanks for the bread.' Lola balanced against a shelf stacked with baking trays as she tried to wriggle her shoes back on. 'I knew I shouldn't have taken these off. It looks like I've swapped my feet for ham hocks. Nope. Not happening.' She tucked her heels under her arm, handed Poppy a door key, and left via the service stairs, leaving sweaty footprints on the tiles.

Without Lola acting as a buffer, awkwardness crept between Will and Poppy.

'I'm sorry to hear about you and Josh. Genuinely. I can imagine this is the last place you want to be,' said Will.

'I don't know, the surface of Mars is high on my list. Without a helmet, my skull would concave within three minutes, which is appealing. I have googled that, so I'm ninety-nine per cent sure it's true.' Poppy snorted and shook her head. 'Honestly, it's fine. I won't suck up your joy like a parched dementor. I'm really happy for you. Truly.'

Will swallowed before he spoke. 'Thanks, that means a lot. Selfishly, it's really cool that you're here. I didn't have a huge say over the guest list—'

'You don't need to explain anything,' said Poppy. 'I've been meaning to drop you a message for years, but, well, life. It has a habit of getting in the way. You haven't changed your profile picture since 2012, so I figured you weren't really online.'

'You looked me up?'

'Of course. This is the way our generation keeps tabs on each other, right? Why, haven't you looked me up?' asked Poppy, only half joking.

'I keep myself pretty sparse online,' he said. Poppy nodded, noticing that he hadn't answered her question. 'Either way, it's nice to see an old face that's not *literally* old. Most of our family friends could qualify for a bus pass. Not that they'd be caught dead using one.'

Poppy laughed. 'I did wonder where your mates were hiding.'

'Haha, yep. I'm still a closet loser,' said Will, his hands raised in admission.

'That's flat-out untrue. Although, remind me, did your Sea Monkeys ever survive graduation?' said Poppy, feigning a straight face.

A chef pulled back the chain-link curtain as half a dozen waiters stepped inside, smeared plates balanced between fingers and forearms. 'Heads-up, it's about to get busy in here.'

Will gave Poppy a slow nod, a small dimple in his cheek as he tried to suppress a smile. 'All right, all right. Let's keep the Sea Monkey thing between us.'

Chapter Ten

FOUR DAYS BEFORE THE WEDDING

One particularly strained Christmas in 2001, Poppy spent three days completing a one-thousand-piece puzzle that solely featured baked beans. Whilst her parents made increasingly petty comments about how thin the gravy was, she painstakingly pieced together every near-identical puzzle piece and tried hard to concentrate on a rerun of *Home Alone*, which featured a far more glamourous kind of family chaos. Now, looking down at the spectrum of interchangeable white middle-aged men in the booklet Lola had given her, she was having an acute sense of déjà vu.

From her hiding place behind a column, Poppy looked out at a long table which had been set up for brunch on the terrace outside. The crowd was differentiated only by wine paunches and tactically combed hair, their varying appearances too subtle to register with real certainty. Are they wearing red trousers? Yes. Do they have wiry eyebrows? Yes. Is their skin pink and loose, like the neck of an uncooked chicken? Yes. According to her list, this could account for Richard Murphy, Nigel Millican, or Oscar Van Guttenburg. How the hell was she supposed to know which three men to photograph together without asking for responses to a verbal register?

'All right?' said a voice behind her.

Poppy turned around to see Lawrence licking the paper of a roll-up. When he was finished, he slipped it behind his left ear. 'I wondered if we'd opened the circus yet, but that's my question answered,' he said, nodding towards the group outside. 'I thought we might have a straight twenty-four hours before one of these spin-off "definitely not a board meeting" meetings occurred. Still, when the albatross shits caviar, you know where to point the gun, as they say.'

Poppy couldn't conjure a context that might explain Lawrence's statement, so she answered with a vacant smile, her eyes back on the booklet. 'Not mixing up the table plan today?' she said.

'Nah, no point. This is an old boys' gathering. Totally different agenda. What you see before you is a human centipede of nepotism. Essentially, they'll all reminisce about the glory days when business trips involved bribing cabin crew to reallocate the most attractive women to first class so they could target their sexual harassment with more efficiency. I'm not condoning it, just stating facts. Look, you see Oscar? Second on the left, with the chest hair? He and my father have been suing each other for the best part of thirty years. For banter. That tells you everything you need to know.'

'What a world...' said Poppy.

'Dad is going for an angle with Ottilie's parents, can't you tell?' said Lawrence. He leant over her shoulder and pointed to an image of Nicola Spruce in her booklet, albeit a younger version set against a marbled backdrop. He read the line printed in bold underneath. '"Requirements: Lord Mountgrave and Mrs Spruce shaking hands with enthusiasm." Interesting! Seems like Dad's expanding the empire.'

'Your family's publicist has been... very specific,' said Poppy.

'Oh, *Julia*. Of course. This is all highly orchestrated. Dad's given me lines to perform, but the problem is, I'm not very good at remembering them. I'll say the wrong thing, and bam! Two dollars per share are whipped off overnight.'

'And what about Will?' asked Poppy.

'Oh, Will doesn't have a business brain, so to speak, but he has helped polish up the ol' Mountgrave reputation. He's the "dead cat" of the family. You know, whack him on the table at an opportune moment to create a distraction? No, scratch that, he's more of a six-month-old cockapoo. Will wanders into a room of Dad's associates, rolls onto his back, gets a few belly rubs and... Bob's your uncle. We're no longer corporate monsters.'

Although they had actively stepped away from each other over the past few years, Poppy still felt protective over Will. He'd never been interested in the hyper-masculine, chest bumping, heavy drinking culture of the uni rugby club, which had seen so many of their peers slide seamlessly into the hierarchical world of corporate finance. What role did he play in the family business?

'So, your dad is a *lord*. Are you and Will both in line for a title?' asked Poppy, stepping outside to check the light levels on her camera. Lawrence scraped muck out from beneath his fingernails. 'Or is it one you can buy off the internet by owning a bit of land the size of a postage stamp? My dad made his last girlfriend a "Lady", but when she looked up the coordinates of her land, it was one-eighth of a parking bay in the Great Yarmouth branch of Lidl. She was underwhelmed, to say the least.'

'Yeah, ours is the old-fashioned kind, but if you ask me, I'd bet Nicola is keen for a recommendation to the House of Lords. Me? I won't be titled until Dad has checked out, so we've got a way to go. I can't wait, to be frank. Not for the death part, obviously, but I've noticed that people congratulate you for doing totally ordinary things when you've got a title, like driving your own car, or eating at Bella Italia. Fucking brilliant.'

Poppy balked. She couldn't remember Will being as tactless about privilege as Lawrence. In fact, she couldn't remember Will demonstrating his family's wealth at all. 'Sorry if I'm missing something, but why are you telling me this?' said Poppy.

Lawrence rolled his tongue around the inside of his cheek. 'Good question. I'm bored?'

'Well, I'm not here as entertainment. I'm working,' she said.

'Are you though?'

Poppy took her camera down and cocked her head to the side. Lawrence spoke like he was part way through a push-up, all lazy tones and elongated vowels. How on earth was Will related to this man? They didn't look alike, speak alike, or act alike. As far as she could remember, Will had never mentioned him by name *or* that his father was a lord.

'I've got an itinerary, a brief, and somewhere to be after this,' said Poppy.

'You sure? Because it looks like you're playing a backbench version of *Guess Who* going by the number of times you've flicked through portraits in that booklet,' he said.

'I'm fine, thanks. I'll figure it out.'

'Do you need my help?' said Lawrence, his voice smug. 'You've got about five minutes before I'm duty-bound to discuss last year's ski season in Val Thorens with Ottilie's father. You're better off asking me than Dad, I'll say it now.'

Poppy totted up the list of photographs she was expected to produce over the next hour and bit her lip, a conflicted panic settling in her chest. She wanted to be alone. She wanted to use her telescopic lens to shoot puffins building their nests in rock crevasses, not hover over someone's shoulder as they ate oak-smoked salmon and spilt champagne. Then again, Poppy owed it to Lola. When she had faltered on the precipice of making her split with Josh final, Lola had been there for her. She should be there for her friend in return.

Lawrence beckoned her towards the terrace stairs, where the sun inched across the manicured lawn. 'So...?'

Poppy tipped her head back and looked at the sky, her eyes screwed up. 'I'm just a bit...' She dropped her voice. 'Confused by the vibe, I guess? These descriptions are more "annual business report" than "wedding album",' said Poppy, gesturing to the booklet. 'Should I be asking people to sit up and smile? I need to ask Lola, but she's MIA.'

Lawrence put his thumbs through his belt loops. 'Yes, yes, and yes.'

'What do you mean?'

'I could explain, but it'll be more *entertaining* to watch you figure it out. Personal preference, of course. Right. There's a kipper over there that's got my name on it. Good luck.' As he walked away, Poppy took three quick strides to face him square on.

'Hang on. I promise I'm not trying to be thick on purpose. Your brother is an old friend, so if I'm here, I want to do a good job for him,' said Poppy.

'Oh, Will would be happy if we sketched each other with wax crayons and wrote our age in the corner. He's very much pincered in the headlock of love, so everything else is surplus to requirements. Portia is Dad's fourth wife, so why he's choosing to rebrand our happy family image using a wedding is outside of my fucking remit. I'm sure it'll be *fine*. Just point and shoot, eh?'

'Lawrence?' A man with silver hair and a pink chest approached them from the terrace. He squeezed Lawrence's shoulder in the way you might test an avocado for ripeness. 'Ah, hello. Friend of Will's? Or Ottilie?'

Lawrence coughed and ran a thumb across his lower lip. 'Dad, this is Poppy. An excellent photographer from Bath. Very up and coming.'

'Ah, yes,' said the man. 'Lola did mention something. Great girl. However, you are... not Christian.' He spoke with his chin lowered, eye contact maintained from beneath thick, wiry eyebrows.

'No, but I went to a Church of England school if that helps.'

'Ah! I meant Christian Fowler.'

'No, alas! I'm handy with a camera and *physically* here, which gives me the edge, I think?'

'Hmm. Does Ottilie know?' asked Lord Mountgrave

'I'm not sure. I haven't met her yet.'

'Well,'—he inhaled deeply, nostrils flared—'I guess you'll have to do. You might get on, you never know. Has my publicist given you—'

'Yep, I've got the booklet.'

'Good, good. Lawrence, get over there and see what Henry's scheming about, will you? His daughter has quit Columbia and followed her yoga teacher back to India. He's devastated. Bring it up, will you?'

Poppy's stomach flipped when she heard the name of that university. Columbia. A lifetime ago she had turned down a scholarship to go there.

Lawrence gave his father an Air Force salute and turned towards the table.

Lord Mountgrave rocked back and forth on his heels. 'I didn't want to put it in the... what-do-you-ma'thingy,' he said, gesturing to the booklet, 'but it's very important that you catch some good angles of Ottilie's parents and me together.'

'Nicola. Yes. Nicola and Paul...'

'Spruce.'

Poppy nodded, feigning confidence. 'Lawrence mentioned you're keen to show good relations? I can take some candid shots.

Keep it on the right side of serious?' Poppy tried to sound more confident than she felt. When she'd studied photography, conversations hadn't been a part of her work, not on this side of the camera. In her early twenties, she'd gained a reputation for capturing urban life through street photography: a sea of placards boasting political slogans, two pigeons tearing the same chicken bone, bug-eyed chihuahuas in open-top prams. Poppy only found stories in her photographs *after* she'd taken them. For this job, she'd have to do it all in reverse.

'Lawrence didn't fill you in on everything, and quite right too,' said Lord Mountgrave. 'The Spruces and I need to build an image of... how shall I say it? Trust. Fortitude. Longevity...' Poppy could have sworn that he was brainstorming team names on *The Apprentice*, but not so. 'As many pictures as you can. I'm planning an announcement at the end of the week and the papers will want visuals.'

'Of the wedding?'

'What? No. Of Will, Ottilie, the Spruces and me. Do you catch my drift?'

'So, you and the Spruces...' Poppy drew a star next to the picture of Ottilie's parents in her booklet. Lord Mountgrave stepped closer as she tucked her purple biro back inside her camera case.

'*Christ.* Don't make it bloody obvious.'

'Sorry, I just don't want to forget.'

'Well, do your job properly and you won't have to, eh?'

Poppy was surprised he hadn't rounded it off by patting her on the head and slapping her rear like she was his favourite heifer. Lord Mountgrave walked away, a sticker on the bottom of his shoe visible with each step he took.

If Lawrence spoke the truth about Will and his indifference to being a passenger in Mountgrave business affairs, how did his fiancée navigate the same strange dynamics?

'Hiya, stranger,' said Will, appearing beside her in a crumpled shirt, a soft smile on his face.

'Hey, you.'

'Hot, isn't it?'

'Sweltering.'

'I hope it calms down before Saturday. Ottilie gets flustered in the heat. Four days. I can't believe I'll be a married man by then. With a *wife*.'

'Mmm. Crazy,' she replied in monotone.

'Sorry, just tell me if I'm being insensitive,' said Will, misinterpreting her reaction.

'Not at all! It's the sun, it's giving me a headache. I'm pathetic. I react to climate like a Victorian aristocrat. Too hot, too humid, standing up too fast… all legitimate reasons to feel faint,' she said.

'In that case, I insist you come and sit down. I won't let you leave until you've drunk two glasses of water.' Poppy fell into step beside Will. 'Is that how it works with you? You'll only do something if it's an instruction?' He laughed, but the statement soon died on his lips when Poppy slowed down. She rubbed her neck where the camera strap chafed against her sweaty skin.

'Was that… angled at me for a particular reason?'

'No, no, I—'

'Will! Look who's here!'

Poppy and Will looked over to a striking older woman on the terrace. She wore single-pleat straight-legged trousers, an untucked shirt, and trainers. Her blunt bob was swept in a deep side-parting, her eyes covered by aviator sunglasses. Lord Mountgrave was the only person who hadn't stood in greeting. Instead, he stared, his mouth like the opening of a letterbox.

'Is that? No… I think it is,' said Will.

'What?'

'That's my Aunt Josie.'

Chapter Eleven

During drunk conversations in their student kitchen, lips purple with cider and blackcurrant juice, Will had made it clear that he wanted to be a husband in the same way that others wanted to be musicians, teachers, or marine biologists. In his room, they would talk about the future until the clubs shut and the corridor silence was broken with the loud, slurred voices of their flatmates. Poppy found Will's sentimentality touching, but ultimately, outdated. He saw being someone's husband as a role he could rehearse for, whereas Poppy danced between a number of contradicting thoughts about marriage, some of them negative, but most of them clunky, half-formed, and contradictory.

It wasn't that Poppy hadn't *believed* in marriage, but for her parents it had been akin to a doctor finishing open heart surgery with a *Peppa Pig* plaster. The idea that it might fix any underlying problems was laughable. She put this forward to Will back at university, but he would dismiss her with a smile that made her feel like he knew different, somehow. During their first year, Poppy had watched as he jumped from one intense, short-lived relationship to the next, spending money she didn't think he had on girlfriends who at some point made the decision to carefully extract themselves from his tentacle grasp. By the time Will booked a Valentine's date in Paris for girlfriend number six, Poppy had started seeing Josh, which led to her retreating from her friendship group and getting married a year after graduation. In short, she had fallen pretty heavily on her sword.

Here, on an island that blinked back at the Devonshire coast, Will was happy. He had made it work.

Will jogged over to the brunch table like a performer returning to the stage for an encore. When he reached them, a cheer erupted.

'Surprised to see me, kid?' said his aunt, speaking across the table. Those already seated went quiet when she spoke, her accent a melodic American that Poppy associated with straight roads, long shadows, and jugs of filter coffee.

'I am, but in a *really* good way.'

'I got a feeling your dad doesn't feel the same, but hey, this is your time, right?' said Josie. She hooked her thumb in a pocket and held her other arm out as Will approached her, pulling him into a side hug. Over her shoulder, she winked at Lord Mountgrave.

'Are you staying for the wedding?' said Will.

'Of course. This is a serendipitous stopover. It beats having my accountant bore over numbers with me in London. I've been in Sao Paulo with Marcia, but she's gone ahead to Cannes for the festival. Her movie is getting played out there, so I'm joining her next week.'

'We've got you for nearly a week?' said Will, ignorant of the vein pulsating in his father's temple. This moment definitely wasn't in the booklet of candid shots Lola had requested from her. Still, the photographer in Poppy was itching to raise the viewfinder to her eye.

Along the table, Josie's appearance triggered a spectrum of responses. Lord Mountgrave looked like he was in the process of passing a sharp-edged bladder stone, going by the sheen of sweat forming rapidly on his top lip; Paul Spruce fiddled with his watch, and at the far end, Lawrence reclined, decidedly amused.

'I don't think I've ever seen you in the same place for more than a few days, Josephine,' said Lord Mountgrave.

'Exceptional circumstances, big brother,' said Josie. 'All right, what have I missed?'

Josie was the most effortlessly suave woman Poppy had ever seen. She stood at the centre of her own gravitational field, her crisp, oversized shirt so bright in the sun that Poppy was at real risk of retina damage if she stared at her for much longer. Josie didn't bend to people; they stood to greet her. She reminded Poppy of a late-80s Sigourney Weaver. If Poppy had to call it, she'd say Josie's self-assurance came from years of queue jumping through airport terminals with a heavily stamped passport as opposed to exterminating aliens, but it wasn't beyond belief. All she'd have to do is step into military boots.

'Richard, how are you? Steven still in college? Oscar, is that the same shirt from our weekend in Maine? Christ, that feels like a lifetime ago. Nicola, Paul doing all right? You must be so pleased for Ottilie. Terrific.'

As she worked the table like a charismatic politician, Will came to stand by Poppy. 'That's unexpected,' he said. 'Your arrival was maybe a four out of ten in terms of surprise factor, but Josie is a solid nine.'

'I have two questions. One: did they model the Statue of Liberty on your aunt? And two: how is she related to your dad when he speaks like an Old Etonian and she could do voiceovers for Cadillac commercials?'

'Ha! Good question. She's younger than Dad and they've got different mums, you know? Josie grew up Stateside, but Dad was raised here.'

'Like *The Parent Trap*?'

'Kind of, but they didn't go to camp together and *definitely* didn't make up a secret handshake.'

'I'm surprised you caught that reference.'

'It's when Lindsey Lohan peaked as an actress.'

'Hard agree.'

'I never met my grandfather. I've seen a few pictures, but he was ancient when Dad was born. There's a family joke that the Mountgrave men father children in the territories they want to expand their company in.'

'Is that an approved strategy of the Harvard Business School?'

'I think it's on their master's programme,' joked Will. 'It was the same for Lawrence and me. He went to boarding school in Austria and I stayed in London, but I'm not jealous.'

'Where did your parents meet?'

'Lewisham.'

'Bit different...'

'Yeah. She was staying at one of his hotels.'

Poppy nodded, and silently fizzed at the phrase 'one of his hotels'. Her parents had met at a campsite that her dad managed in the summer holidays, so, not all that different. 'And Lawrence?'

'Right, so his mum has something to do with fashion retail. She lives in Milan. Or Madrid. The Buzz Lightyear jawline has made its way to both of us, so we've got that in common. But, Josie? She's a bit of an enigma. She's on the board of directors, but I heard about her more than I saw her growing up.'

'I thought *my* family history was confusing and sad, but now I realise it's just sad,' said Poppy.

As Josie got closer, Poppy felt a little starstruck. Will beamed as his aunt rested a hand on the back of his neck.

'So, this must be Ottilie, right?' said Josie.

'No, no, no. This is Poppy, the photographer. We knew each other a bit at uni. Old friends, sort of.'

'Just friends... Hey, I got away with that excuse for years until your grandfather wised up and stopped giving my girlfriends an invite to our summer house in the Hamptons.' Josie's eyes were bright and mischievous.

'I really am the photographer,' said Poppy in an attempt to match Will's haste. They were *sort of* friends, were they? Poppy knew they hadn't spoken in a long time, but his hurried clarification felt unnecessarily curt. 'His fiancée is—'

'Joining us soon,' said Will.

'Ah, right, right,' said Josie, her accent softening the consonants. 'Of course. She's blonde, right? You sent me a picture at Christmas. How's your mom?'

'Yeah, good. Working too much. She retrained as a midwife last year and takes on all the hours she can. She's coming on Saturday, just for the wedding.' Poppy leant away from the conversation, half-curious, half-self-conscious about being party to delicate discussions about a family that wasn't her own. She hawk-eyed a waiter who carried a tray lined with glasses of fresh orange juice, a bowl of ice, and silver tongs. Poppy turned on her heel and swiped a tumbler as he bobbed past, swigging the juice for something to do.

'It's nice to be back on the island, but... it can get intense. I see your father has developed a new twitch.'

'That one has only cropped up today.'

'What a coincidence,' said Josie, exaggerating her shrug with a wry smile. She winked at Will, who shuffled from one foot to the other. 'I hope your girl is sat near me. I'd like to meet her properly.'

'I... don't know where she is, actually. She's been doing a lot of meditation in preparation for the ceremony.'

'What is she, a monk?'

'No, but she did study Eastern Philosophy, now you mention it.'

'Religious family?'

'Not particularly. Ottilie would describe herself as "spiritual" over anything else,' said Will.

'Sheesh. Good luck to you. I'm kidding. Come on, let's rinse your Pa. Are you sitting down, Poppy-who-is-definitely-the-photographer?'

'My stomach is rumbling like a drain, but I'm supposed to be working at this brunch,' she said.

'Will, friend or not, you can't let this girl stand here taking pictures of the old folks at brunch like we're an advertisement for an over-fifties vineyard tour.'

Will looked at Poppy side-on, unsure whether he should speak for her. Before he could make up his mind, Josie had slipped her arm through the crook of Poppy's elbow and led her to the table.

'I love creatives. It's what attracted me to Marcia, actually. She observes the world before making a comment on it. There's something beautiful about that. You'd love her films, I just know it. I hope everyone does, because I paid the production costs and it's killing me, let me tell you. Here, let's bump you in between Paul and me...'

'I think this is more of a business brunch—' said Poppy.

'In that case, it shouldn't be. This is a celebration, right? Hey, you guys, budge down, will you?'

When Poppy was a teenager, she'd helped her dad at his weekend job, working as a beater during shoots in the countryside. It wasn't dignified, but then, first jobs never are. She'd whacked the hedgerow with a stick to scare the pheasants out, their boggle-eyed heads quivering as they ran directly towards a line of rifles. Although majestic, they were far too stupid to justify their own existence. As Poppy glanced down the table, the similarity was striking. These people didn't 'just budge down'. Watching their brash coordination of chair shuffling was physically painful.

'Got cold feet yet, mate? Mine still haven't warmed up and it's been fifteen years,' said a man Poppy recognised from the booklet. Hair the colour of unpasteurised milk. Lips like raw bacon. Must be Steven Fortescue: owner of a mine and fan of trophy hunting in Zimbabwe. Will tittered, but he kept his eyes down. 'Where's Ottilie then? She *does* exist, doesn't she?'

'Oh, she exists,' said Lawrence from the other side of the table.

'Marriage is the best thing you can do, the *best* thing,' the man continued. 'Sorted me out. Bit of a party boy in the 90s, but it a takes a good woman, doesn't it? A real good woman. Or two.' The older members of the party erupted into guffaws. Josie looked on with cold eyes.

'Your wife still fucking her personal trainer, Steven?' said Josie, silence swathing the terrace. 'I'm kidding, of course. Poppy, sit. Will, you're head of the table,' said Josie, hands in her pockets.

'Hang on a minute, this isn't a free-for-all,' said Lord Mountgrave, half standing in his seat. 'She's got a job to do.'

'She does?' said Josie, pretending to look surprised. 'That's a rarity around here.'

A flush of embarrassment crept up her neck.

'Ignore them,' said Will. 'Stay for breakfast, please.'

'Breakfast? I thought this was brunch? Can't have changed my watch from Spanish time.' Paul Spruce squinted at his wrist.

'Hold on a second. Josie, you've— This isn't a— We've got an agenda,' said Lord Mountgrave, adding depth to the colour in his cheeks.

'Okay, good to know. Proceed, please.' She took a slice of bread from the table, bit into it, and clapped the flour from her hands.

'I'm going to go...' said Poppy, pushing her chair back from the table.

'Oh, please don't leave on account of us,' said Josie, looking at her brother. 'You *are* a guest, right?'

'She's the bloody photographer!' said Lord Mountgrave, his

fingers scratching the tablecloth. 'Have I gone mad or has everyone completely lost their sense of normality?'

Poppy stepped back, humiliation shifting from her throat to her chest where it bloomed into anger.

'I clearly have,' she said. 'Still, if it's all the same to you, I'll take some of this to go.' She tried her best to smile without gritting her teeth, unfolded a linen napkin on the table, and loaded it with three golden croissants.

'As you were,' she said, licking a flake of pastry off her little finger. Poppy stepped out from under the awning. The sun beat down onto the terracotta tiles, but her skin felt clammy and cold. By the time she reached the atrium, Will had caught up with her.

'I'm so sorry about that. It's all bravado; you get used to it. There's no malice behind it,' he said.

Poppy didn't have the energy to come up with anything intelligent to say. After months of swallowing sarcasm and bracing herself for verbal jabs from Josh, she was bruised to the bone.

'I'm fine. Need a coffee, that's all.'

'I'll come with you—'

'No, you stay. Catch you later,' she said, tucking her croissants under her arm as she shouldered her camera and left.

Chapter Twelve

'Hi, hi, hi, thanks for coming early, guys. You all right? Need anything?' said Lola, a clipboard in one hand, a manual tally counter in the other. As part of her first guest club night in Bath, Lola had bribed Poppy and Josh to "make the place look popular", which saw them arrive at eight o'clock with a group of friends who took advantage of the empty bar and the grandeur that came with a private booth. Lola had gifted Josh temporary VIP status on account of it being his birthday, but he was at dangerous risk of pushing that privilege to breaking point.

'Any chance we could get a bottle with a fizzy sparkler on the end?' asked Josh.

'I've got a party popper, some Sellotape, and a £12 bottle of cava. That's top of the range – a birthday special.'

He grimaced. 'Just the cava, thanks.'

Since Josh had started his teacher training, being out together was a rarity. Although they shared a bedroom in a shared house, they were most often found crouched over different desks in the same room, Josh marking exercise books, Poppy batch editing hundreds of photos, a handful of which would be uploaded onto her photoblog to an increasingly engaged audience of clickers and commenters. Tonight, she had promised the evening to him. Most of it, at least.

Poppy went to the bar and returned with a wooden paddle of shot glasses filled with flavoured vodka that seemed explicitly designed to transition teenagers from the pick 'n' mix binges of their youth to a hard-line cocktail of sugar and booze. As she passed the entrance, she grinned at Lola stamping the hands of the recently arrived netball team. Although Lola had been quietly unsure about tonight's success, Poppy had never doubted it. If one thing was true, it was that wherever Lola was, a party followed.

Poppy reached their booth and slid the shots onto the table.

'Steady on Poppy! I don't want to have to take you home before the night's even started,' said Josh, dropping his voice to avoid being overheard.

'They're not *for* me. Your mates asked if I was going to the bar, I was, so I've been landed with a thirty-five quid tab and whatever this is,' said Poppy, lifting the luminescent vodka to eye level like a mad scientist. 'Can you make sure they pay me back? Rent comes out tomorrow.'

Josh undid a button of his shirt and scratched his neck with irritation. 'I'm not going to go round with my hand out begging for money. Just ask for a drink off them later.'

'I'm only having one or two tonight. I'm covering the student protest in London tomorrow and I'm up super early. Remember?'

'Hardly my fault that you decided to book an early train the morning after my birthday.'

'It's hardly my fault that our government failed to protect student fees from escalating.'

'I forgot how much fun you are,' he said, nodding in greeting to someone over Poppy's left shoulder.

Poppy stepped away from the throng of people that had squeezed into the booth. 'Josh. Come on. This is important to me.'

'And I'm not?'

'It's not like those two things are mutually exclusive.' Poppy felt a twist of anxiety. She didn't want to be an uptight girlfriend or the reason they'd fallen out on his birthday.

'Come here, you,' he said, slipping behind her to hook his arms around her waist. He kissed her neck. It sent a warm current down her spine, tingling in the base of her stomach.

'I'll square up with you later,' he said. 'You know what the boys are like.' Poppy nodded, but she knew it wouldn't happen. She'd have to bring up money another day when Josh was post-hangover and more likely to listen.

Josh's friends each took a shot glass, leaving her with an empty plank of wood and feeling all the more stupid for it.

An hour later, Poppy's right foot was sore from the number of times it had been stood on now that they were sitting on the edge of a bulging dance floor.

'Weeeeeee like to drink with Josh because Josh is our mate! We like to drink with Josh because he gets it down in eight, seven, six, five...' Poppy stifled a yawn as Josh drained his glass with a grimace. He tipped it upside down, placed it on his head, and stuck his tongue out to catch a dribble of liquid as it ran down his cheek. As Dan ducked beneath the table to top up the empty pitcher of cocktail with shop-bought vodka, Josh draped his arm lazily across Poppy's shoulders. 'You look really fit tonight,' he said.

'Thanks.'

He dropped his voice an octave lower. 'Can't wait to get you home.'

Poppy didn't say anything. He must have forgotten that she wasn't going back to theirs tonight, but it didn't seem worth bringing up. She slipped out from the booth, her shoulder warm from where his armpit had been. The boys drummed a beat into the table.

'Weeeeeee like to drink with Poppy, 'cos Poppy is our mate! We like to drink with—'

'No, no, not me!' said Poppy, grinning apologetically.

'Oh, here comes the fun police,' said Dan. 'Why did you come if you're not going to get battered with your boyfriend on his birthday?'

'Who else is going to fetch things from the bar?' said Josh.

The table erupted with laughter. Poppy looked down at Josh, her chin wound tight.

'Excuse me?' said Poppy.

'I'm joking!'

'He's joking, Poppy,' said Dan, his eyes watery from a laugh he could barely contain.

'Dan, I say this with love, but isn't it about time you stopped buying your shirts from the children's section of H&M?' She smiled through gritted teeth.

'You know your West Country accent gets stronger when you're angry?' said Josh with a look of pride. Poppy picked up her handbag from underneath the table.

'I need to head off,' she said.

'What?' said Dan, biting his lip in an unconvincing performance of regret. 'No, sorry Poppy, I'm being a dick. Ignore me. I've had too much Red Bull.'

'Dan, you do realise your heart is going to explode one day, don't you? Thanks for the open admission, but don't take it personally. I'm doing a shoot tomorrow. The protest.'

Out of the corner of her eye, she saw Josh roll his eyes.

'What was that for?'

Josh blinked. 'Nothing, babe.'

'Seriously?'

Josh stretched his arms along the booth and tilted his head to the side. 'Well, it's not like anyone is forcing you to go, is it?'

'What difference does that make?'

'You keep talking about it like you're going to let someone down if you don't show up.'

Poppy crossed her arms and gripped her elbows, nails digging into her skin. 'I don't know if you've heard about this thing called being self-employed?'

'Don't you have to earn money to be classed as self-employed?' said Josh.

Dan snorted into his drink whilst the others fell quiet and fiddled with soggy coasters. Realising he had pencil-dived into a problem of his own making, Josh rocked forward, the bravado pulled from beneath him.

'That came out wrong,' said Josh.

'You think?'

Josh slid out of the booth and walked Poppy into an alcove beside the men's toilets. 'Hey, forget that. Poppy? Look at me. I think what you're doing is really cool. You know you're a good photographer; you hardly need me to tell you that. Just… everyone knows I had to retake my final exams over summer and when you inevitably go on about how many followers your blog has, it doesn't make me feel great, does it?'

'I didn't even bring it up! I've maybe mentioned it… once?'

Josh's eyes glazed over. She couldn't tell if it was alcohol that softened the edges of his otherwise sharp observations or if he had managed to successfully detach from anything she said that was remotely accusatory.

'I feel like I'm doing something wrong,' said Poppy, anxiety crawling up her throat. 'I don't know why, but I get the impression your friends think I'm a boring bitch.'

'No, no, no. They don't. They're just bantering you. If anything, it means the opposite. You're three times as intelligent as all of them put together. Fuck, you're way cleverer than me.' Josh smiled and swept Poppy's French braid over her shoulder.

A woman stumbled out of a disabled toilet, one hand slapping the wall to keep herself from falling over. She tugged at the fly of her skinny jeans, hair a curtain of curls as she squinted at Josh.

'There you are!' she said 'Happy fucking birthday! Sorry we're late, Katie got us kicked out of the cab for spilling a bottle of Zinfandel in the footwell.' She took Josh's chin in her manicured hand and planted a pink rimmed kiss on his cheek. *Fran.* She always appeared in a cloud of Nina Ricci perfume, like the banished genie of an understaffed TK Maxx.

Josh loosened his grip on Poppy, grinning as a shimmering gaggle of Fran's friends dragged him back to the booth. Poppy went on her tiptoes to tell Josh she was leaving, but stopped when she heard her name from behind.

'Poppy?'

She turned, her heel sticking to the floor. Holding a trifecta of plastic cups, his wallet clamped between his teeth, stood her first-year housemate, Will.

'Will? Oh my God, hey! It's been an age.'

He nodded, wallet flapping like a duck's bill. Behind her, he balanced his cups on a thin rail that ran along the back wall and pulled her into a hug.

'Shit, I can't believe it. Poppy! She's real! I've seen your stuff online. You're basically famous.'

'Pfft, hardly.'

'What? You're being modest. How many followers has your blog got now? The one with all the portraits and interviews? *The World's Eye?*'

Poppy pretended to look modest. 'Three hundred thousand.'

'See! Famous,' said Will, bumping her with his hip. Buoyed by his enthusiasm, she elaborated. 'I'm going to London tomorrow to cover the march.'

'Of course you are, big shot.' Will grinned, his eyes bright. 'Lola still your sidekick?'

'I think I'm more her sidekick, actually. She does all the talking,

I do the clicking. The whole concept came together when we started interviewing people alongside the pictures. Teamwork makes the dream work and all that.'

'I saw her at the door. She seems a bit frantic.'

'It's her imposter syndrome shining through, but I don't know what she's worried about. She was basically a club promoter when she wasn't getting paid to do it.'

'Lola was always quite persuasive, wasn't she? I remember missing at least half of my nine o'clock lectures in first year because of her impromptu nights out. She'd be a very successful cult leader. In a good way.'

'Is there any good way to be a cult leader?'

'I don't know. Jesus seemed all right.'

'Controversial.'

Will laughed. Poppy couldn't help but mirror him. Her time on social media was largely spent uploading her photoblog, but when she did look him up, Will only featured in posts others had tagged him in. Some people made a statement about having no digital footprint, but Will didn't exist online because he was busy existing in real life.

Will clicked his fingers to fill the silence that had opened up between the bass that thrummed from subwoofers.

'How's Josh?' he said, gesturing to the booth.

'Yeah, good, good. It's his birthday,' said Poppy.

'Twenty-two?'

'Yep, twenty-two. He stayed on to do a PGCE. Our wardrobe is now full of shirts. He's who I live with. We live together, I mean.'

Will nodded, the threat of a broader conversation tucked behind his dark eyes.

Poppy bit her lip hard. 'I was actually just about to leave—'

'Do you want to come outside?' asked Will. 'Smoking area? Bit quieter?'

Poppy glanced back at Josh, surrounded by friends and empty shot glasses. She nodded.

Will shimmied through a growing crowd on the dance floor. Down a corridor lined with indie tour posters and imitation Banksys, they reached a fire door that opened out onto a concrete courtyard, fake ivy wound through gaps in mesh fencing that flanked them on three sides. Will spluttered into the crook of his elbow as a woman exhaled a cloud of smoke over her shoulder. Poppy wafted the space between them.

'How're you?' asked Poppy.

Will looked back towards the club, his jaw tight. 'Yeah, good. Bit stressed. Too many deadlines. You?'

'Same. The joys of third year, eh? How's Lily?'

'Ah. Another stressful subject.'

'Did something happen?' said Poppy, recalling the long-legged, red-haired girl she had last seen hooked on his shoulder at a house party.

'I took her to Paris for our six-month anniversary. In short, she liked it so much she applied to do a year abroad and left me for a French guy called Julien who wears a lot of black and never smiles.'

'How annoyingly cool of him,' said Poppy.

'I *know*. Hey, sounds like you're nailing the photography. I can't believe my degree is nearly finished and I still haven't got a clue what to do. I took one of those online career tests in an act of desperation and it's not looking good for me.'

'Why, what did you get?'

'Dog groomer, choreographer, or paediatric nurse. How is that a natural career path after a geography degree?' He shook his head and leant against the wall. 'I might volunteer for a while. At least then I'm doing some good. What's going on with you? Other than being the world's next best photojournalist.'

'Ha, well. I don't think there's much else to report. I don't really know what's happening next year either. I've entered a few competitions and applied for a couple of scholarships, but there's such a slim chance that anything will come from it. I've got to earn some money, so if you need any promotional shots for your interpretive-dog-dancing-children's-hospital entertainment business, hit me up.'

Will pretended to consider it, nodding sagely. 'It's niche, but I think we can make it work.'

They tucked closer, Poppy's back arched as a group of students pushed past. Will glanced at the door again. 'Do you think you and Josh will live together after graduation?'

'Ah, well. That's a conversation we're yet to have.'

'Just tell me to mind my own business if you want.'

'No, it's fine.' Poppy pondered the question. Since Josh had started ironing his clothes on a Sunday evening and setting an early alarm, Poppy had the keen sense that adulthood was just around the corner, rather than the bouncy-castle version of it she currently experienced. It excited and terrified her in equal measure, not that she'd ever admit it. When she contemplated her future aloud, Poppy could viscerally see the panic rise behind Josh's eyes, as though she might ask him to give up his fledgling teaching career to spend a year trekking across Mongolia.

Will gave her time to think. Poppy pulled at the hem of her bandeau skirt and folded her arms.

'I *do* want to live together, obviously. We do now, but there are three other housemates. Six if you count girlfriends and boyfriends, but they change semi-frequently. Apparently, it's *inappropriate* to ask them to contribute towards bills, even though I know Lauren and her girlfriend frequently empty the hot water tank to fuel their inclination for shower sex.' Poppy bit her thumbnail and waited to see if Will would laugh. He didn't. 'I don't know. I guess I'm a bit torn. I feel like there's two angry cats inside me swiping and hissing at each other. One wants to settle down and buy sofa throws; the other wants to climb the garden wall and go on a mad adventure. Josh knows what he wants, and he knows where I fit into that. I can't say the same.'

Will smiled, but he stared down at the ground.

'Why did we stop hanging out?' he said, blinking. Poppy had seen this look before. It usually happened after he'd chewed something over that didn't sit right.

'I don't know,' she said, her words measured. If she was honest with herself, the closer she and Will became as flatmates, the more confused her feelings had got. Eighteen months ago, they danced around the edge of a friendship that had verged on something else, but Poppy had never been able to line up with the gaps between Will's sporadic relationships. Lola always said that everything happened for a reason, but Poppy didn't believe in fate. If it existed, Will would have noticed her to begin with. In reality, he hadn't. Josh had. How could she explain all that now?

'One of those things, isn't it?' said Poppy. 'You went off to Croatia when term finished and by the time you got back, we were moving in different circles.'

'You'd started seeing Josh,' said Will, his tone accusatory.

'*You* were abroad a lot,' said Poppy, matching him.

'I catch up with our old housemates. They say you don't go out anymore.'

'It's true. I don't. Between my dad, work, and photography assignments, there hasn't been space for much else.'

'Is he okay?'

'Josh?'

'No, your dad. I remember you saying he doesn't cope well on his own.'

'He's got a job, so at least he opens the curtains now. Most days.' Poppy scratched the back of her neck, irritated. 'I should get going. I've still got to prepare for tomorrow and—'

'Our timing was off, wasn't it?' said Will, his warm hand reaching out to rest gently on her forearm.

Poppy closed her eyes and smiled in disbelief. '*Timing*,' she repeated. For a moment, she stopped scrolling through her list of worries: how likeable she was around Josh's friends; how much it would cost to repair her broken camera lens; whether her dad was eating properly.

She put her hand over his knuckles, ignoring the shrieks of shouted conversation behind her. Will tipped his head back and looked skyward.

'Why are you with him?' he said.

Poppy pushed his hand off her arm. 'I'm sorry... what?'

'Why are you with him?' he repeated, his voice stronger this time.

'I heard you before. I was giving you a chance to think about what you just asked.'

'I don't want to.'

'What did you anticipate I would say now? Would you like a list of his attributes? Because if this is a question that's actually about you and me, it's a weird entry point.'

'I heard how he was talking to you.'

'It's his birthday, Will. He's drunk and he's acting macho around his mates. So what? I don't care.' Poppy folded her arms and scuffed the floor with the toe of her boot. 'The point is, why do *you* care? And why now? We've been together for well over a year. If it's timing you're on about—'

'I might be wrong,' said Will, holding his hands up, 'but we weren't exactly strangers in first year, were we? Do you think things would have been different if we'd given it a go? Properly?'

Poppy exhaled sharply. 'Why are you asking me this?' she said, desperation slipping into her voice.

'Because I care about you!' said Will. His eyes darted across her face, looking for proof that she felt the same way.

Feelings that Poppy had almost forgotten about rippled in her chest like they were floating on an underground stream. No sooner had they appeared, frustration followed. 'It's taken you this long to realise, has it?' she said.

'What? No. I did before, but I never knew if you were on the same page.'

'Is that why you always came to me for advice on your girlfriends? For pep talks when things were rough? Correct me if I'm wrong, but that doesn't sound like an efficient way to tell someone you like them.'

'What? When was that obvious? You have to admit that you're a closed book when it comes to what's going on up here,' said Will, tapping his temple.

'That's a cop-out and you know it. What was I supposed to do? Barge in on your dates to confess my feelings and risk living next door to someone who rejected me in favour of bendy fucking Gabriella? I'm not a homewrecker. I'm not that person and I never will be.'

'I wouldn't have rejected you,' said Will, quietly.

'You *did*. You might not have said so explicitly, but it wasn't just days we spent together, was it? There were nights too, followed by sporadic weeks where you barely spoke to me.'

'You've never brought this up before,' said Will.

'Snap! Don't blame me for not moving at the same speed as you. Did I have a timeframe? Tell you how I feel within ten minutes of a break-up, otherwise, whoosh! Will is gone, onto the next one.'

'We could have made it work. We *still* could.'

'You're too late.' Poppy shrugged. She tried to appear detached, but seeing how hurt Will looked made her feel a bit sick. 'I wasn't going to wait around for you. Josh keeps his word and he loves me, without question. Whatever *we* had doesn't have oxygen. Not anymore.'

Will rubbed his face with the heel of his hand, realisation dawning on him. 'I'm an idiot.'

'Don't use this as an excuse to be mean to yourself. To use a massively clichéd phrase: it is what it is. I can move past it. I have. But I still want you in my life.'

Will groaned. 'As friends?' Poppy nodded. 'If it means being close to you but not being with you, I can't,' said Will, avoiding eye contact. 'I know you need consistency, but you and Josh? You're playing it safe.'

'I need safe. I like safe. If it means keeping a friendship with you, safe sounds fine to me.'

'I don't think I can do it,' said Will, his voice quiet.

'You're not willing to try?' said Poppy, hoping he would give the answer she didn't want to hear.

Will shook his head.

Poppy folded her arms and bit her lip until the tightness in her throat relaxed. 'Timing, eh?'

'Timing,' Will repeated, his chest rising with a deep breath.

Will hugged her so delicately it made her wonder if the underwire of her bra was sticking out at a strange angle.

When they released, Will held her gaze, eyes hard, chin high. Poppy stepped back without saying a word. In fairness, she didn't think she could.

Inside, the dance floor had doubled in size as more students trickled in. Poppy squeezed behind a group of women who screamed S Club Seven lyrics at each other in a circle, lips tacky from syrup-laced drinks and the remnants of lip gloss applied at a more coordinated hour.

She exchanged her cloakroom ticket, shrugged her jacket on, and glanced out of the window, her eyes hot with tears that blurred the lit headlights of taxis idling outside. As she flicked her hood up, Josh pushed through the swing door from inside.

'Oh, hey,' she said. Poppy wiped her eyes with the back of her hand and performed a smile.

'You not coming to Po Na Na's?' he said.

'No. I'd only be there for half an hour and they charge a fiver entry on Friday nights.'

Josh blinked and opened his eyes wide as though she'd said something outrageous.

'Oh, a *fiver*, that changes everything.'

'It's how much the taxi home costs, so yeah, it does, actually.' Irritation prickled at the back of her neck as she pulled out her phone. She was at capacity in every sense of the word. Lola had emailed her a list of interview questions that she desperately wanted to go through before tomorrow, but it was Will's crestfallen face that flooded her mind. The quicker she got home, the less time she'd have to dwell on their conversation. Tomorrow's protest was the biggest event she had covered so far. If they came in from the students' perspective and found a café to upload the series as quickly as possible, she'd have the chance of a credit in one of the broadsheets. With something like this, if you were too late, you may as well not have bothered. Funny how frequently that theory rang true.

Josh pulled her to his chest, squashing her hands awkwardly between them. 'You could wait and come home with me,' he said, his breath hot and sweet from sugary shots. She kissed his jaw and pulled away.

'You won't leave until the club shuts and I can't stay that long. I'm not having a dig, honestly. This was always the plan. I'll be back tomorrow night, okay? Happy birthday. I'm sorry. I love you.'

Josh pushed the door open for her, his mouth a thin line of dissatisfaction. She felt torn between a need to stand and explain herself and a deep-rooted panic that pulsed at the base of her neck.

'Fine. Whatever.'

'Aren't you going to say good luck?'

'You don't need it,' said Josh.

Poppy nodded, her mouth pouted to one side. Just once, she wanted to hear him say it first.

Chapter Thirteen

FOUR DAYS BEFORE THE WEDDING

'Psssst.'

Poppy turned around, her flips-flops squeaking on the polished marble. Other than a tinkle of laughter from the terrace, the atrium was deserted except for the five different versions of herself reflected in Art Deco mirrors. Her chest was pink, her skin hot, and the pomade she'd used to fill in her eyebrows was now smudged across the bridge of her nose, giving her the look of a frazzled Frida Kahlo. She leant towards a mirror, licked her thumb, and wiped it clean, cross-eyed with concentration.

'Psssssssst! Pops!'

From behind a pillar that flanked the gilded doors to the dining room, Poppy saw Lola's violet hair disappear from view. A finger jutted out at waist level, beckoning her over.

'Lola?'

At this, the finger became more frantic. Poppy squeaked across the atrium, her flip-flops slapping against the floor. Lola surveyed the staircase and clutched Poppy's wrist to pull her into a side room. A rack on the wall held twine, florists' scissors, and strips of hessian sacking, below which were three crates of jam jars and a box of tealights. At the other end, a half-open stable door led onto a stone courtyard brimming with buckets of gypsophila, hollyhocks, and eucalyptus. She could visualise the Pinterest board it came from: sage palettes, French linen, and golden-hour photography. She'd done the same thing almost a decade ago. The thought made her uncomfortable.

'I hope you're getting paid well by the Mountgraves. Will's family are walking subjects for psychoanalysis. How he's made it to adulthood without driving a Rolls Royce into a lamppost is a total mystery. I'd have burnt my money and moved to Alaska by now. What? Why are you giving me that look?' Poppy scanned her friend's frantic expression.

'Has something happened? I've been stuck in here checking the flower delivery but at least five members of staff have rushed past the window in the past twenty minutes and they look increasingly sweaty. I don't want to go out without having gauged the situation. I hate being on the back foot.' Lola leant against the door and traced her teeth with her tongue.

Poppy spoke with caution. 'From my position of near ignorance, it *doesn't* seem like this "very intimate wedding week" is part of a wider manifesto that all the Mountgraves signed up to. I've got welts from all the dirty laundry they're whipping out there. Did you know about the aunt?'

Lola thrust her chin forward. 'Oh, shit a brick. What aunt?'

'Will's aunt. About sixty. American. Very angular. I can't figure out if it's *her* I fancy or her ability to wear monochrome without looking like she's on the way to a criminal hearing.'

'What?! No... not Josie. Is it Josie?' Poppy nodded. Lola shut her eyes tight, walked to the open stable door, and gripped the florists' rack for support. She picked up a wilted gerbera from the scrubbed bench and plucked the petals with the sharp edge of her nail. 'This complicates things,' said Lola.

'How come?'

'You know the phrase, *they like to rock the boat*? Well, consider Josie a meteor crashing into a canoe and you've got a good measure of the impact she has on Mountgrave family dynamics. It could be exaggeration, of course. I've only heard it from one side. What was the reaction when she turned up?'

'Everyone seemed... quite surprised. Will too. I thought his dad might actually use his pocket square to mop his neck, but no. They really are just for show.' Lola swallowed, her face increasingly pink despite the thick foundation she wore. 'Are you all right?' asked Poppy.

Lola nodded with her eyes closed, her fingers green from the massacred flower stem. When she spoke, her voice was slow and melodic. 'I'm fine. Everything is absolutely fine. And by *fine* I mean teetering on a precipice of shit.'

'Because of Josie?' said Poppy.

'No. Although that is the glitter sprinkled on top of the shit.'

Poppy was at a loss for how to help. Wedding planning was difficult enough without having to negotiate family drama in the midst of buttonholes and ill-timed canapé deliveries. When the family in question features on the Forbes Rich List, the problems don't go away, they just get more expensive.

Poppy grappled for something useful to say. 'I've had a flick through that booklet you gave me and Josie isn't in it.'

'There's a reason for that. She's a major shareholder in the company, but according to Lord Mountgrave, Josie only ever pops up with the sole intention of making him look like a tit. He didn't use those words, obviously. He makes a weird noise whenever she's mentioned – like a goose being stamped on. In short, Josie wasn't invited. I don't think Will knows her that well.'

'How did she know when to turn up?'

'The family owns the island, so she's still got her finger on the pulse. The Mountgraves have had this place for centuries. It sounds mad, but I read somewhere that it was a prize from Henry

VIII, back when rich fuckers got drunk on mead and chopped up their land to pay off gambling debts.'

'I won a flip-phone from a 2p machine in Torquay when I was nine and even that skewed my sense of privilege. The case was hollow and it only functioned as a calculator. Can't think what I'd do if I won an island.'

'Barricade yourself away from your family?' said Lola, angling across the butler's sink to look outside. 'Blow it up? Hey, was anyone… whispering?'

'A few comments when Josie turned up, but nothing more. I was *supposed* to be taking pictures, but the musical chairs around the table made that tricky.'

'Good. No other surprise guests?'

'Not that I can think of.'

'Okay, fab. Ottilie is requesting so many last-minute changes that I'm having to fast-track security clearance. Everyone who steps foot on the island has to sign the same NDA you did and I had background checks done on the contracted staff who are working all week. Deliveries are coming so often that I've had to send boats out into the bay to collect packages.'

'Like Pablo Escobar, but with a different kind of confetti,' said Poppy. Lola pouted and looked out of the window, as though she were solving a complex equation in her head. 'You're being *really* sketchy. Are you actually a wedding planner or is this a front?' said Poppy in an attempt to lighten the mood. 'It's getting very… espionage-y.'

Lola let down a Roman blind and dropped her voice. 'There's been a leak. A reporter was lingering in a mackerel boat by the dock this morning and next thing I know, I'm getting asked to comment on the business announcement happening this week, which is really, really bad. I'm supposed to be building rapturous anticipation for Will and Ottilie's wedding,' said Lola, biting her lip with concern. 'I know the Mountgrave shareholders are all here, but I'm working on the principle of "ask no questions, tell no lies". It's a bit fucking stressful.' Lola forced a breath out through a narrow gap in her lips. 'I'm getting the feeling that I've bitten off more than I can chew, babe. There are plates spinning on every finger and toe.'

'Woah, let's break this down for a minute. Josie *did* rattle the cage this morning so it's obvious that Will's dad wasn't expecting her. In this family, I get the impression that changing plans last minute is only ever a problem for the chauffeurs.'

'You know, I actually feel nostalgic for *your* wedding. What I wouldn't give for a hotel conference room and a sugared almond. Sorry to bring it up, but as a punter it was fucking glorious. That business with your Uncle Mike and the urinal was better than anything featured on a season finale of *Married at First Sight*.'

Poppy allowed it. 'How about you remind them that you're the wedding planner, *not* a life manager?'

'Ha. Good one. Before you got here, Lord Mountgrave gave me a quiet word about "maintaining expectations" because I hadn't telepathically noted that he preferred supper at eight, not nine o'clock.'

'What even *is* supper?' asked Poppy.

'I think it's what Nigella Lawson does when she sneaks down to snaffle leftovers from the fridge in her nightie.'

Poppy pushed a bucket of daisies to one side and sat on the draining board. 'For a wedding, don't you think Lord Mountgrave is a little overinvolved?'

'Keep your voice down,' hissed Lola, pulling on a cord to lower the blinds further. 'There are ears everywhere.'

'Sorry,' whispered Poppy.

'Every time I change a plan on Ottilie's request, I have to pass it second-hand through Julia – the Foundation's publicist – who refuses most of them for incredibly pedantic reasons. It hasn't been so bad until now because Julia is based in New York, thank

God. She was so persistent last month that I started sleeping on East Coast time so I wouldn't have to get up in the night to take phone calls. She's like a caffeinated chipmunk. I'm walking a mental tightrope every waking minute of the day, wondering how I can possibly manage a happy equilibrium between the couple *and* Lord Mountgrave. It's just not aligning.'

'It sounds like bad calendar coordination to me. Why plan a business announcement the day after your son's wedding?' said Poppy, shaking her head.

'The world loves a wedding. Especially one that showcases a blissful union between two families who would have comfortably earnt their own decapitation in revolutionary France. Take weddings on their own – you know how highly strung people get. Your cousin Kerry was a bridesmaid even though you've hated her ever since—'

'—she scratched my Enrique Iglesias CD with her tweezers. I know. Where do Will and Ottilie fit into this? Are they happy with the way the week is panning out?'

'Lord Mountgrave has the run of things until Wednesday afternoon, then wedding stuff properly kicks in. Everything up until then is relationship management,' said Lola.

'For who? Will and Ottilie, or the family business?'

'If I lay out the details, I'll give myself analysis paralysis. I'm on a knife-edge as it is. It's going to be fine, isn't it? Because if I fuck this up, there's no way I'll recover the money I've ploughed into contractors,' said Lola.

'It'll be fine. You can't control everything. If not, we'll run away,' said Poppy, taking Lola's hands in her own with a grin. Lola shook her off.

'Seriously, Poppy. If everything goes well, I'll get recommended to their friends, all of whom are extortionately rich and happy to throw money at ideas of mine that are more ambitious. I have *no* shame, you know that. When I met the

Mountgraves a year ago, they said they needed someone reliable and asked for my fee, so I thought, *Here we go, boys. Call me Money McGee!* I pitched *way* too high –thinking they'd say no – and they said yes straight away. I was like… what the fuck? My last testimonial is from Auntie Alison and I sort of… tweaked her wedding pictures to disguise the off-motorway garden centre she used as a venue. It wasn't Petersham Nurseries, let me tell you. Who wants to say their vows in front of a garden rope and chains display?'

'I don't know, were they into S&M?'

'Yeah, that's my point. Keep it behind closed doors, please and fucking thank you.' Lola lifted the blind to peer out. She sniffed, her breath ragged. 'I don't want anyone to see me like this.' Lola only cried at two things: dogs in sweaters and compilations of clips from *Grey's Anatomy*. Anything approaching a rational response to stress was a real cause for concern.

'Look, what can I do to help? Anything,' said Poppy.

'I've already asked you to do too much,' said Lola, in between sniffs.

'Don't thank me yet – I haven't taken a single photograph.'

'Will is keeping his head down and Ottilie is meditating herself into a different dimension. At this rate, when Julia the PR nightmare does eventually curate their magazine spread, all they'll have to choose from are phone pictures I took of the embroidered golf slacks Will's dad ordered. If any details are leaked to the press early, I won't get the rest of my fee. Or any work in the future. I know you think Will is easy-going, but he's not the real client here, if you know what I mean.'

'You are not going to lose your career over the playground squabbles of rich people.'

Lola laughed and blew her nose on a scrap of taffeta. 'Could you stall Ottilie for a bit until I've sorted out the mess from brunch? Stop her from coming up to the hotel? She'll be down by the cove. I need an hour to speak with Big Steve on security. I'll get us lunch at The Drunken Prawn on Wednesday afternoon to say thanks. I could do with some time away from the guests. It might actually mean I get a chance to eat something, too. I've got a window between...' Lola bit her lip and scrolled through an itinerary on her phone. 'Three forty and five o'clock.'

Poppy hesitated. If ever Lola had a right to cash in a favour, it was now. But the thought of enmeshing herself further within the family didn't light her up from within. One of the things she liked best about photography was how necessary it was to stand at the periphery of a scene, but never imprint herself on it.

In a way, had that been her problem all along?

Chapter Fourteen

Poppy ran up the stairs two at a time, her toes like talons in her flip-flops to keep them on her feet. After Lola had cooled down by slipping an ice cube down her cleavage, she'd perked up dramatically. She wasn't sure it was the method Boudicca had used before she went into battle, but it worked for Lola, who sashayed onto the terrace with a tray of crystal flutes to break the lingering tension brought on by Josie's arrival.

Hotels were not a frequent feature in Poppy's life. She'd stayed in one for a singular night after a particularly horrible Sunday lunch with Josh's family, during which his mother had placed a hand on her abdomen as she poured gravy onto her plate. 'You know, darling, conception is a little trickier if you're carrying a tum.' The sum total of Josh's defence had been to cough and change the subject. Poppy had eaten so many roast potatoes in retaliation that she'd had to google 'what happens when heart palpitations turn sinister'.

The corridor that led to her bedroom was lined with a carpet so thick Poppy barely made a noise as she scanned the doors for a room number that matched her key card. When she reached it,

Poppy pushed the door open to the room and squinted, confused. Her once tightly packed rucksack was draped across the end of the bed, her possessions unpacked into an antique wardrobe that could have passed for the entrance to Narnia. If only.

A summer spent sleeping in a grubby Slovenian youth hostel had given her a harsh lesson in the consequences of leaving her camera unattended, so she swapped it into her worn padded carry-case, accompanied by a collection of lenses that she strapped around her waist like a 90s dad at Disney World. Poppy slipped out of the dress that she only just noticed was streaked with coffee stains, plaited her hair, and looked for a pair of cotton trousers that she hadn't planned to wear until her cottage break with Lola. When she opened a drawer lined with her tank tops, she paused. A necklace lay on top of the pile, a familiar pendant catching the light. She picked it up, the chain coiling in the palm of her hand, a dried poppy that had once sat in her wedding bouquet trapped inside cast resin. Before their split, Poppy had worn this necklace every day for almost seven years. Ever since, it had been stuffed at the back of her underwear drawer. She hadn't packed it, which meant that Josh almost certainly had. What was he hoping to achieve? Poppy closed her fingers around the necklace and dropped it back in the drawer, kicking it shut with her foot.

Her rushed arrival at Loxby had ensured she'd avoided the mobile phone amnesty at reception, but if Lola was instructing security to tighten surveillance around the island, she didn't want to be caught with hers. Taking it out of a zipped pocket, she unlocked the screen and bit her lip. Josh's name flashed up alongside an email. Poppy didn't want to open it. It wasn't so much him, but the effect of him that she didn't trust. The wall of awkwardness he had built in their own home stung, but without it she was afraid of how easily he could pull her back again. Who was she when she wasn't with him?

When she initiated the separation, Poppy had thought she

would return to the person she had been before she'd met him. Poppy had spent her twenties entangling her life with his, swapping each facet of herself until she couldn't tell where he ended and she began. Her evenings in the attic with metal cutting scissors and an Edwardian film camera had sprung from a fear of long evenings and attempts to make them pass quickly. Whilst he brazenly continued with the routines they'd wrought together, Poppy realised that they weren't shared routines at all; she had been pulled into *his* world. How much of her tapped on the sides of *his* skull? Josh had thrown her independence back at her like a stack of dirty laundry he no longer wanted to touch and now she didn't know what to do with it.

After running a cold flannel over her neck and swallowing the pillow chocolate like a shucked oyster, Poppy headed back outside. She walked along the terrace as waves slapped the cliff side and passed through a well-kept rose garden. Spotting a sign for Mermaid's Cove painted on a stone wall in front of her, she descended a stepped path that bent between palm trees and artfully arranged succulents. At the bottom, she paused. The cove was nestled between high-sided cliffs, the sun pooling on the water as though concentrated through a magnifying glass. In the middle, a woman lay on a wooden platform, propped on her elbows, salt-licked hair falling in waves between her shoulder blades. She looked in Poppy's direction, pulled up the straps of her bikini, and lifted a finger to indicate that she'd be a minute.

Poppy scuffed the foam of her flip-flops against the decking. This must be her. Ottilie. The woman curled her feet over the edge of the platform and dove into the water, resurfacing an arm's length away from a metal ladder on the decking nearby.

'Sorry to intrude,' said Poppy, fiddling with her bag strap. I'm—'

'Poppy?' said Ottilie, dimples appearing on her cheeks as she wrung water from her hair.

'Yes,' said Poppy, surprised. 'I thought I'd introduce myself.'

'No need. Will told me about you. You're helping us out, right?'

'Right.'

Ottilie gave her a side smile.

'What a peach. Thank you, seriously,' she said, leaving damp footprints on the boards as she walked over. Before she could react, Ottilie pulled her into a hug, her fingers spread wide against her back. When relinquished, Poppy's breasts were imprinted with two damp outlines of Ottilie's own. 'Oh, I'm sorry. I've been in and out of the water so often the past couple of days, I hardly know the difference. Are you heading back to the hotel? I'll walk with you.'

'No!' exclaimed Poppy, remembering her instructions from Lola. 'I was actually... wanting to check in with you. About... light levels.' She held her camera up as evidence.

'Oh, wedding talk? If we're going to do that I'll have to sit down with a drink. My head is swimming with plans. We have this wedding coordinator...' said Ottilie, pinching her mouth into an ironic grimace. 'She's... great. She really is. Lovely person. But a little much, you know?'

Poppy resisted an urge to push Ottilie back in the pool. Sure, Lola had loud clothes, a loud laugh, and an all-round loud personality, but it was what made her so good at her job. She lent her loud to other people when it mattered most.

'Don't get me wrong, she's been working *so* hard. I'm worried it's making her a little frantic. I'm trying to be careful about the energy I invite towards me right now, you know?' Poppy did not know. 'Will's father, have you met him? He's got her doing double time for some corporate this-or-that, poor thing. Wait here, I'll be back.'

Ottilie pulled on a kaftan and walked towards a staircase that led to a small fisherman's hut painted in teal tones to match the water. The delicate sound of fizz escaping from a bottle and tinkling ice preceded Ottilie's return. She gestured to the decking and sat down far closer to Poppy than she was expecting, two cold drinks by her side.

'It's matcha lemonade. All natural, don't worry.'

'I did wonder why it was so… green.'

'Cheers,' said Ottilie, handing Poppy a glass. Poppy took it, clinked glasses, and grimaced as she took a sip. Yum. A delicious glass of mildew. 'I don't like the whole contractor–client divide,' continued Ottilie. 'This wedding is *so* important to us and I only wanted to share it with those who have been real pillars in mine and Will's life. I don't know you, but Will said you both had a connection at university and that was a really transitional time for him. This must be fate, right?' Ottilie hooked her straw into her mouth and smiled at Poppy, squinting in the sunshine. 'Can I be honest with you?'

'Sure.'

'I've burrowed down here to keep away from all *that*,' said Ottilie, nodding up towards the hotel. Poppy could sympathise. She'd planned a retreat of her own to get away from a reality she couldn't control on a smaller island just visible through a gap in the rocks. 'I have *so* much to be grateful for. Will's family are incredibly generous – always have been – but I sometimes feel like a spare part, like our wedding is good publicity first and the authenticity of it comes second.'

'Isn't that what most weddings are like?'

'Oh, you're married too?' said Ottilie, brightening.

'No. Not anymore. On paper, I technically have a husband. It's complicated. We still split the cost of milk and bicker about who forgot to cancel the craft beer subscription, but that's another story.' Ottilie nodded slowly, unsure how to take Poppy's candour. 'I guess what I'm trying to say is that weddings can spiral pretty quickly. They're not just for you, they're for your friends, your family – even the ones you don't like very much. The silver lining is that you can bugger off pretty sharply when it's all over.' Poppy crossed her arms. 'Although, saying that, my husband took us to Greece and trained for an Iron Man competition for six hours a day whilst we were there. I've never seen so little of him. Or drank so many margaritas, for that matter.'

'He sounds very driven,' said Ottilie.

'He'd like that assessment.' Poppy clapped to signify a change of subject. 'So, with your pictures, are you looking for traditional, or a little more unique?'

Ottilie wrapped her arms around her knees, vulnerable and childlike. 'I know you and Will didn't know each other well at university, but if he trusts you, I trust you. As an outsider, I can be honest with you. Would that be fair?'

Poppy blinked to disguise the hurt she felt at hearing Will's description of her. Sure, ever since they agreed to break off contact, they had been strangers to each other. But before that? It was another story entirely. She understood the need to omit some details, but it had been years. They were both over that, weren't they?

Poppy sucked on her metal straw and tried to swallow without tasting anything. She'd stick to the instructions Lola gave her. If Will wanted to cherry pick the details of their shared history, that was his prerogative. 'You can trust me. If it's honesty we're doing, I should say that I know my way around a camera – really well, in fact – but if you looked at my CV, it would say "photography teacher". I don't want you to feel misled.'

Ottilie placed her hand gently over Poppy's, the band from her engagement ring clinking against Poppy's mood ring that she had worn since she was thirteen years old. 'I value honesty above everything else. Thank you.' Poppy smirked, but Ottilie's tone was sincere, which made it worse. Poppy rearranged her expression and nodded.

Ottilie interlocked her fingers in her lap. 'If it's universal truthdom we're seeking, I'll share something too. My yoga degree is fake. It got signed by a bohemian guy at Burning Man a few years ago – beautiful soul, but overfamiliar with women. Not in a #MeToo way, but he carried a lot of sun cream and would always be the first offer in when it came to putting it on. A public service, if you will. You can't protect people from skin damage *and* be a creep, can you?'

'I think you can, actually. No, wait, you definitely can.'

Ottilie ignored her and flashed a Colgate smile. 'Tell me more about you. Good, bad, indifferent.'

'Wow, where to start. I have the authority of a wet flannel. The kids cheer when they know I'm taking their lessons, not because they like me, but because I'm a total pushover. I love the little gits. Our school is consistently bottom of the league tables, but I wouldn't be anywhere else. I *will* take bloody good photos for you because thanks to my newly acquired singledom, I've developed an intimate relationship with this camera,' said Poppy, pointing to her bag. 'Not like that,' she added quickly, keen to correct herself, 'but I care about my work and for the next couple of days, everything revolves around you and Will. And the booklet of corporate shots I have to take for The Mountgrave Foundation, but other than that you're my top priority.'

'You're not photographing the wedding?'

'Lola is ninety-nine per cent sure that your first choice will be here by then, so you don't need to worry,' Poppy lied. She didn't want to consider that she'd have to get through a wedding when she was trying so hard to forget her own. 'I'm entering a photography competition and my subjects are regurgitating fish guts somewhere over there,' said Poppy, pointing to the distant puffins as they dive-bombed the water.

'So that's where you're heading after Loxby?'

'Yep. Nothing like puffin growling to drown out the internal noise of an existential crisis.'

'God, the way you speak is so refreshing.'

'Is it?'

'Yeah. If you've spent more than five minutes in *their* company, you'll know what I mean,' said Ottilie.

'I couldn't say. I've met a few now. Lawrence as a brother-in-law, eh? That'll keep Christmas lively.'

Ottilie sat up and retied the strings on her bikini top. 'Oh, you have to ignore most of what he says. He and Will grew up in different homes and it isn't half obvious. He has a bad rep, but as long as you keep him at arm's length, you'll be fine. Don't tell anyone I said that. I won't win any points by spreading gossip.'

'Your secret is safe with me.'

Ottilie went to take Poppy's half-drunk glass from her. 'Oh, sorry, I thought you'd finished.'

'Mmm. Yes. Let me just...' Poppy slurped the last of the liquid and tried not to grimace as carbonated sludge slid down her throat. Ottilie took both glasses back to the fisherman's hut, locked the door, and returned wearing a straw hat with a brim so wide it flopped down to rest on her shoulders. She slipped the key into her bikini top and offered a hand to help Poppy up, her engagement ring glittering like a disco ball.

'Oh my God. Sorry, I just— How are you not sinking every time you get in the water wearing that? Is this the rock that killed the dinosaurs?' said Poppy, turning Ottilie's hand over to stare at the gargantuan gem balanced on her ring finger.

'It's a bit gauche, isn't it? I know you can resize wedding rings, but apparently not the diamond,' she shrugged. Poppy made a mental calculation about how much it had cost and hated herself for it.

Ottilie walked to the base of the stone steps and spoke to Poppy over her shoulder.

'You know how Will and I met?' Poppy shook her head. 'Teaching. Something all three of us have in common.'

'Ah, you have a propensity for masochism too?'

'Oh, it's not the horrible kind of teaching. We were in an orphanage in Vietnam, three years ago now. Bless him, he loved it there. My Will. Heart of solid gold. I wanted to bring them all home with me. The children, I mean. The locals called us Brad and Angelina. Funny, isn't it?' said Ottilie in a tone that implied she was secretly very proud of herself. Poppy didn't agree. Using neglected children as a prop for goodness left a bad taste in her mouth. 'I'd show you some pictures but I'm not on social media at the moment. That *was* a good idea Lola had, this blanket ban of posting online. When our engagement was announced, there was so much noise, I felt like I didn't have control over how people saw me. Do you know what I mean?'

'I do,' said Poppy, and she meant it.

'Will dotes on me. Really treats me like I'm the most important woman in the world.'

'Oh, I thought he'd grown out of that,' said Poppy, laughing.

'What do you mean?'

'The whole "treating like a princess" thing. He did have a bit of a reputation for it.'

'I'm not sure I follow.' Ottilie paused on the steps, her thin cotton dress almost see-through in the sunshine.

Poppy felt hot. She had overstepped a mark. Last night in the kitchens, she and Will had oscillated between awkwardness and the comfortable familiarity she remembered from their university halls. For a moment, a decade's worth of distance had disappeared. Ottilie hadn't known him then, but she knew him best now.

'I just mean that he knows how to treat people properly. He's what my dad calls a proper gent.'

'Mmm.' Ottilie twisted her hair into a lock and looked out

across the cove. 'This is such a magical time of day. I've got a beautician coming over to do a vampire facial and I don't want the evidence on camera. Do you think you could focus your shots on The Mountgrave Foundation side of things until the wedding?'

'No problem.'

As they reached a hairpin bend on the path, sticky and hot, Ottilie fell into step with Poppy and hooked an arm through her elbow. It felt strange. Lola wasn't keen on physical contact and before that, the last person she'd touched was Josh, weeks ago when they were still kidding themselves about having emotionally redundant sex. Poppy's back was slick with sweat by the time they reached the grotto. Ottilie, on the other hand, looked like she was glowing from the inside. If someone could bottle it for mass consumption, there'd be riots outside Superdrug.

'Can I ask you a favour?' said Ottilie. 'I would ask a friend, but they're not arriving for days.'

'Sure, what is it?'

'Will you have a chat with Will? Make sure he's okay?'

Poppy hesitated. This felt a lot like being a messenger, which was a role she wasn't keen to take on. 'I can, but—'

'I know you're not hugely close, but I'm just not sure he can handle all that back-slapping, ball-and-chain banter that his father's friends are so keen on. It's so old-fashioned and I don't want him to feel bullied. He's too nice for his own good, isn't he? I notice when these things take their toll before he does.'

Poppy nodded. How many more favours would she tangle herself in before her time on Loxby was finished? 'I can do that. No problem.'

'You being here is fate. I know it,' said Ottilie. Poppy stopped. She tilted her head to listen to a screeching noise in the distance, her fingers poised over her camera bag.

Ottilie stiffened, eyes wide. 'Is there a bug on my shoulder? Getitoffgetitoffgetitoff!'

Up on the terrace, shrieks and swear words carried on the breeze as gulls swooped beneath the awning. The sound of shattered glasses broke the calm serenity of the gardens. Waiters and guests jostled to retreat inside, shoulders bumping, trays clattering on the floor. Lord Mountgrave stumbled, a spattering of bird poo dripping down his left shoulder. He either didn't care or was too drunk to notice.

Poppy and Ottilie skirted round the edge of the hotel, where a flock of gulls with sharp bills and indelicate wings crash-landed on the table, each grappling at a different leg of the fetid octopus as though competing in an avian tug-of-war.

With her shoulder to the wall, Poppy tried to find a clear path back inside without colliding with a gull. Ottilie burrowed into Poppy's back and clutched her wrists from behind, using her as a human shield.

'Cover your ears!' said Lola, appearing at the French doors with a dinner gong. She clanged it with a ladle. The noise was so loud that the birds took off in a flurry of wings and squawking, leaving a mess of feathers and octopus innards strewn across the table.

'I think I'm going to be sick,' said Ottilie, ducking beneath Poppy's arm to disappear inside.

With the terrace now empty, Lola put the gong on the floor and held the door frame, her eyes wide.

'You said you wanted a distraction...' Poppy offered as a globule of seafood splattered on the patio tiles. From a first-floor window, Lawrence slid out of view, but not before Poppy saw the smirk etched squarely on his face.

Chapter Fifteen

JUNE 26TH, 2010

'Oh, wow. Lola, there are like… a shitload of people here.'

'I have no idea why you're surprised about this.'

'Because! It's a Friday night and Mungo's is doing three-for-two shots on the other side of campus, that's why.'

Lola pulled Poppy in front of her, forcing her to peer through an opening in the thick black curtains that lined the walls of the drama studio that they'd commandeered for the evening. A series of twenty portraits hung from the ceiling on thin chains, forming a meandering path that told a story of Britain's streets through Poppy's photographs. Beside each framed image, padded earphones were hooked on pegs, the interviews that Lola had conducted playing on a loop. It was the first time Poppy had ever seen her work on anything other than a laptop screen. Although her photoblog now had half a million followers, the idea of each number representing an actual real-life human was exhilarating and terrifying in equal measure. She took pride in the fact that she didn't edit her photos, but now they were poster-sized, her moments of clumsiness had no place to hide; a greasy smear as she'd grappled with her camera outside the office of a disgraced politician; her reflection in a puddle as she photographed a group of teenagers on the steps of Trafalgar Square, Greenpeace placards propped by their knees. She mentally adjusted her shots, fingers flicking through buttons and dials. Would it ever feel like the right time to let her pictures speak for themselves?

'I paid a guy called Simon twenty quid to do the sound system. He's got the mics ready. He said if we don't go out soon, he'll start singing an off-key version of "Wonderwall" until everyone's ears bleed.'

'I can't do it,' said Poppy, her mouth acrid.

'You can!'

'It's too... confronting. They won't want to listen to me. You know what students are like. If you put free snacks out, they'll come to anything.'

'Hey, it doesn't matter *why* they came, it only matters that they're here. Also, I may have said that the exhibition was heading to London after this.'

Lola interlocked her fingers with Poppy's, knowing she'd try to pull away.

'No, no, no, no. Why did you do that?!' said Poppy, her voice slipping two octaves higher than usual. She pinched her dress and tried to waft cool air down her chest, her skin prickling with heat.

'Because London is like the Emerald City for anyone who lives outside of the M25. It has clout, you know?'

'I'll give you a clout.'

'A top-tier dad joke. Speaking of which, he's here.'

'Stop.'

'Before you ask, I gave him a glass of orange juice and briefed the roving waiters to... not rove near him.'

'Good. At least I know he won't die of scurvy this week,' said Poppy, jumping from one foot to the other. Lola put a firm hand on her shoulders, one eyebrow raised. She had three pairs of false eyelashes on and a red lip so bold it was made for leaving obnoxious kisses on people's cheeks.

Lola ran her tongue along her teeth. 'I wasn't going to tell you this, but… there are some journalists here.'

'Really?'

'Mmm.' Poppy recognised that hum. It was the noise Lola made every time she was trying to downplay something huge. 'I've been keeping an eye on the big accounts that shared our posts in the last couple of months and made a list of anyone with an arms-crossed pretentious-looking profile picture, you know? Turns out that's a pretty accurate way to spot reporters.'

'They're going to expect me to say something clever and profound.'

Lola forced Poppy to look at her, chin held high with calm authority. 'Sometimes you have to ask the universe what you want and the universe provides.'

'Can the universe provide me with a bucket to throw up in?'

'No, but give me a wink and I'll cup my hands.'

'You're a good pal.'

'I know.'

Poppy took a steeling breath and pulled the curtain to one side. It was hardly like walking out at Carnegie Hall, but never before had she felt so conscious of her hands as she approached a small plinth in the middle of the exhibition, a microphone poised in the middle.

Simon switched it on and gave her a thumbs up.

'Hi, everyone. God, my fingers are sweaty.'

Nice. Of all the things to direct people's attention to, this shouldn't have been one of them. The lights in the studio dimmed, leaving a spotlight on her and Lola. Poppy was glad she couldn't make out any faces. The sense that a crowd was there at all was only noticeable from the glint of prosecco glasses.

'Firstly, thanks for coming tonight. Seriously, though, it's wild to see my photographs in one place. It's mad enough to see someone clicking through our photoblog in the library, but this is something else.' Lola took her hand for a moment and squeezed. She could do this.

Poppy slid the microphone out from its stand and felt her shoulders descend from up by her ears. 'I started *The World's Eye* as a project of necessity, I guess. I couldn't afford a studio and as much as I love nature photography, I also like being warm and being able to eat a packet of Frazzles without freaking my subjects out. I still can't afford a studio, but it doesn't matter anymore. I'm an observer. Always have been. I get caught up in the beginning of a story, but it's Lola who tugs the details out. When she started interviewing people, something clicked, didn't it?'

Lola nodded, her head tilted with pride. 'Anyway, I've learnt a lot during the past couple of years. As a photographer, sure, but it's the people who leave the greatest impression, and that's always what I aim to capture. Sometimes it's a whole life story. Sometimes it's a guy called Terry who for some reason thinks we want to know about his unusually bulbous penis.' The crowd laughed. Poppy could hear the sound of her dad's gravelly chuckle somewhere in the darkness and it made her stomach flip like a fortune-telling fish on the palm of someone's hand. 'Okay, I'll leave it there. If you want more stories, the photos do a far better job of telling them than I do.'

'Photographs are for sale,' said Lola, waving a sheet of round red stickers. 'If you have any questions for Poppy, let me know and I'll check her dance card. Thank you!' trilled Lola, switching off the microphone with a self-aware smile.

Poppy stepped off the stage and grinned as she caught eyes with her dad trying to make small talk with two of her lecturers. He nodded at her and raised a plastic cup of orange juice in her direction. Seeing him on campus was strangely comforting, like eating beans on toast after being on holiday. He was wearing his 'going out' lumberjack shirt with grey suit trousers and a pair of pointed brogues that she hadn't seen before. Historically speaking, this meant a job interview or a new girlfriend. Poppy had her fingers crossed that it was the former.

Lola pushed a glass into Poppy's hand and drained her own in three swift gulps, grimacing as the bubbles hit the back of her throat.

'Have you seen Josh?' asked Poppy.

'Nope. Your old flatmates are here, though. Two girls and a guy. You know, Will? Anyway, he's beefed up a bit since first year.'

'Really?' said Poppy, feeling flustered. 'Should I go and say hi?'

Lola placed her empty glass down on a cloth-covered table and hooked her arm through Poppy's. 'Sure, but first, I think we should rove. Drum up interest for the pieces.'

'Are you sure? I didn't realise that was part of the plan until literally just now.'

'It wasn't, but you need to take advantage of a captive audience. Besides, a punter has already asked so the ball is rolling, baby. That tall bloke has bought one – the one in the black polo. I think he's your tutor? I've already stuck a few of these around to build a sense of exclusivity,' she said, waving the sheet of round red stickers like a wad of cash. When Poppy grimaced, Lola sighed and pulled out her phone, opening an email and handing the phone over for Poppy to see.

'Go on, read it. The stars are aligned.'

'You know how I feel about horoscopes,' said Poppy.

'Yes, but we both know that you're wrong, so…'

Poppy cleared her throat and put on a cartoonish Californian accent.

'Pull a pal out of their comfort zone and it won't just be you who has success in their future.'

Lola donned a look of triumph, as though it proved her point exactly. 'See? That's you!'

'It could be *literally* anyone in this room.'

'What I'm saying is, we've got to run with the opportunity whilst we've got it. Success breeds success, as Donald Trump once claimed to say.' Lola's eyes drifted over Poppy's shoulder. She dropped her voice. 'Look sharp. He looks suitably arty to have deep pockets. Big yourself up, all right?' said Lola, squeezing her elbow before walking away.

'Joe Leibovitz,' said the man, holding out a hand. Poppy shook it.

'Poppy Pascoe. Thanks for coming along. I really didn't know what to expect.'

'Hey, it's a great show. An old colleague of mine at the *NYT* sent me your page. I'm telling you, they'd kill for half of your followers,' said Joe, his voice a measured transatlantic drawl that hit notes in three or four different accents.

'No way, really?' said Poppy. He couldn't mean the actual *New York Times*, could he? '*The World's Eye* has really grown in the past year or so. A hundred thousand new followers in the past month. I try to get out on the street every weekend, but not just London. There are so many more portraits I want to take.'

'Sounds like a busy life for a student.'

'It is, but I've never really got on with clubs and I'm about to be very unemployed, so it works for me.'

A door swung open at the back of the studio. Josh slipped inside, his jacket zipped up to his chin. He paused at the top of the stairs, hands in his pockets as he scanned the room. They'd had an argument the night before after Josh accused her of being self-centred and Poppy had retaliated by saying he was jealous of how well her photography was going. He had disappeared to the pub for the rest of the night. Despite that, the way her stomach fluttered when she saw him was involuntary. She loved seeing him before he saw her. Poppy gave a subtle wave. He caught her eye, smiled, and exhaled sharply as though he were about to run onto a football pitch.

'What do you think?' said Joe.

'Sorry, about what? Can you repeat that?' she said, her attention back on the American man before her.

'I think you should apply. For the Columbia scholarship. It's competitive, but between you and me, you've already got an established base with *The World's Eye* that any institution would love to throw weight behind. You'd be in with a decent chance.'

Poppy felt like she'd swallowed a handful of tiny and extremely energetic frogs. 'Columbia? As in, Columbia University? In New York? New York, America?' she said, searching his face for evidence of a practical joke.

'The very same,' said Joe, putting one hand in his pocket. 'You have to submit a portfolio and a letter of recommendation, but seeing as my buddy Tom has just put down four hundred on your photograph of the little old lady asleep on the Tube, I'll bet he won't take much persuading. So, what do you think?'

Poppy pinched the soft flesh between her thumb and forefinger. She'd ignored her gut instinct before, but this felt different.

'I... think I'll have to get a passport.'

Joe's face split into a crooked smile. 'Any questions, drop me an email. I'm not on the interview panel this year because I've got an assignment out in Belarus next month, but I know what they're looking for.' He handed her a matte black business card with his name embossed in silver.

'Thanks, I will.' She slipped the card into her back pocket. Was this successful networking? 'I don't have a card to give back. I should get—' Poppy stalled, wincing as the noise of feedback crackled through the speakers.

'Hi, hi. Hello, can you hear me? Ha, that wasn't as smooth as I was hoping for.' Poppy turned to the podium. Josh's voice bounced around the studio as the crowd fell quiet. His cheeks were pink in contrast to his shirt, which was straight from the packet if the crisp fold lines down his front were anything to go by. He rubbed the back of his neck and continued. 'So, yeah. Poppy knows her way around a camera, doesn't she?' Josh gave an anxious laugh.

'What's he doing?' whispered Lola, appearing by her side with a fixed smile.

'I've got *no* idea,' said Poppy, shuffling to get a better look. 'A speech?'

'Why is he so pink?'

'I don't know. He might be drunk. Or nervous. Maybe both?'

Joe nodded at Poppy and stepped away to join another man who had a similar enthusiasm for black turtlenecks and blazers.

'I saw Josh talking to your dad a second ago, so that's a sign something is off.'

Poppy pursed her lips in thought. Josh had long since lost patience with her dad. A one-to-one conversation suggested something serious. Josh raised his hand to shield his eyes from the spotlight. 'Poppy, could you come up here?'

Her heart jumped into her throat. A request like that implied that she had a choice, but it didn't feel like that. She moved before she was conscious of it, the business card poking her sharply through her back pocket. The crowd parted to let her through until she was looking up at Josh, his blue eyes wide and sincere. He gripped her hand, pulled her up to join him, and bent down to fiddle with the jacket that he'd left in a pile on the floor. The back of his hair was freshly cut, the kind of short that she liked to run her hands over. Someone in the crowd coughed and it gave her an acute awareness of where she was. If she had been out of her comfort zone before, she was catapulted into another dimension of discomfort now.

Josh stood, leant towards the microphone stand, and took her hand in his. 'Poppy, wow. I've been thinking about this for a while, but I needed a moment, right?' Josh glanced at the crowd, but Poppy was trying her best to pretend they weren't there. 'I thought, fuck it, now is as good a time as ever.' He rubbed her fingers as he spoke, like he was fiddling with Blu-Tack underneath a table. 'You're beautiful, talented, and kind. You inspire me to be a better person. I can't believe I'm saying this, but here we go.'

'Josh, you don't need to say anything,' said Poppy, desperation cracking her voice. Josh smiled, misinterpreting her request for affection. As he bent down on one knee, her dad came into view, half-tucked behind a group of students who had begun to whisper with excitement. So this was why he had ironed his trousers.

'Poppy.'

'Yep?'

She needed to get through the next minute as quickly as possible, which left her with one option.

He opened a ring box, a dainty silver band cut with a diamond that glinted in the spotlight. Josh softened, his lips parted as he readjusted his stance.

'I would be honoured – no – *ecstatic* if you'd be my wife.'

Poppy heard a collective intake of breath. If Lola was going to appear with cupped hands, the time would be right about now. The butterflies in her stomach morphed into a frenzied swarm of bees. Of all the things in her life, Josh was her constant. She didn't want to do anything that would risk it slipping away. She looked at Josh and nodded so vigorously, her head hurt. Her agreement was instinctive, her need to get off the stage equally so.

'Yes. Of course. Yes.'

Josh stood up and swung her in a tight circle, which didn't help her burbling feeling of nausea. When he kissed her, his mouth was hot and urgent as the crowd erupted with applause. He lifted a fist in triumph and the applause grew louder. 'Come on!' he yelled, rocking them both from side to side.

Poppy tucked her chin over his shoulder. She was glad he was holding her up because she wasn't sure her legs could manage it. A portrait hung on chains in the middle distance, a singular figure framed in a busy train carriage. Poppy swallowed. The elderly woman's broad chin and judgmental eyes glowered down the lens at her, a plastic rain cap tied tight under her chin.

Chapter Sixteen

THREE DAYS BEFORE THE WEDDING

'Greg, we'll skip the starters. I know the family think they're being nice by putting scallops on the menu, but if I have to look at another mollusc this side of retirement, it'll be too soon.'

'No offence to you, or your fine establishment,' added Poppy.

The barman shrugged. 'Anything else?' he said, gesturing to a staff menu in front of them.

When the island was open to the public, The Drunken Prawn was a tourist pub, but not as Poppy knew it. There wasn't a quiz machine or a white-whiskered dog snoozing beneath the bar. Poppy should know. She had spent enough time in pubs as a child, hidden in a booth with printer paper and a set of crayons as her dad shouted at the box television bracketed to the wall. They both liked horses. She drew them; he bet on them. After years of this Saturday afternoon routine, she'd learnt never to pin your hopes on something that was statistically rigged against you.

'I want something plain. Totally devoid of flavour, if possible,' said Poppy. 'I've eaten so many instant noodles recently I wince when I look at a sachet of chow mein flavouring.'

'What about an aubergine burger?' said Lola.

'An aubergine isn't a burger. It's a sad sandwich.'

'I for one am *not* having fish pie,' said Lola, her finger running down the menu. 'If the fish has touched fins with a prawn at any point in its life, I don't want to eat it.' The barman sighed.

'I'm thinking… medieval prison food,' said Poppy.

'Bread and cheese?' said Lola.

'I've only got sourdough,' offered the barman.

'Ergh. I'll cope. The cheese didn't come from a deli counter, did it?' said Lola.

'I'll dig out a mouldy slice of cheddar from the compost bin to be certain,' he said, exasperated.

'You're a good man, Greg.'

'I'll have a plate of chips with a gherkin on the side,' said Poppy. Greg nodded, then shook his head as he shuffled back to the kitchen.

'Weirdo,' said Lola. 'Who actually likes gherkins?'

'Everyone who's normal. What's the story behind your food vendetta?'

Lola yawned and dug about in her handbag, taking out a tube of concealer that she dabbed under her eyes. 'I taste test everything the kitchen staff are preparing for the Mountgrave dinners, which is fucking delicious, but it's doing a number on my digestive system. I feel like that ratty terrier my cousin saved from a roundabout off the M3. It could only stomach dog food that looked and smelt like it had already passed through a body. I was raised on mechanically removed meat, so I can relate. You can have too many nutrients, you know. Go and fetch us that bowl of peanuts from the bar.'

'They're *communal* peanuts. Are you sure?'

'I like my nuts seasoned with urine, thank you very much. Go on, I'm ingesting myself here.'

Poppy unpeeled herself from the hot leather seat, picked up the greasy bowl from the bar, and rocked back on her heels to linger at the open front door, where a cool shoreline breeze drifted into the room.

'Oh God, that's nice,' said Poppy, her back to the door, legs apart as she wafted her skirt with an exaggerated look of deep relief on her face.

'Unbelievable. Stop humping the air and bring me the goods.'

A small cough from behind made Poppy jump – more so when she realised who it was. Standing on the doorstep, Ottilie looked like a fairy from *A Midsummer Night's Dream*, all soft waves and bare feet. Will, on the other hand, clearly had stylist input when getting dressed that morning, going by the faded Vans and crumpled Joy Division T-shirt.

'Oh, hey! Peanut?' asked Poppy, holding out the bowl.

At the same time Will said yes, Ottilie said no, looking at Will as though he'd suggested licking a toilet seat.

'Ottilie, how you look so flawless with a bare face is a mystery. I *love* your anklet. Everything all right?' asked Lola.

Ottilie struck a Princess Diana smile as she reached Poppy and Lola's table. 'Could you put this somewhere?' said Ottilie. She shrugged off her crochet cardigan and handed it to Will, who draped it over the back of a chair within arm's reach of her.

'Sorry for crashing the staff quarters, Lola, but I wanted to run something by you,' said Ottilie. Will tucked his hand around her waist, but Ottilie threw him a sharp look, irritated. 'I'm too hot, can you not?' she said.

'Do you want me to make myself busy elsewhere?' said Poppy.

Will took a peanut from the bowl and nibbled it in half. 'No need, Pops. You're part of Team Bride now.'

Poppy gave him a placating smile. If ever there was a time to swallow fistfuls of rancid seafood to escape such an accolade, this was surely it.

'I'm sure this is the last thing you want to talk about,' said

Ottilie, looking at Poppy. 'You know, after everything you told me about your divorce.'

'You guys have been hanging out?' asked Will, his cheeks set with dimples.

'Poppy and I are in the heady first stages of a whirlwind friendship, aren't we? You'll have to prise her away from me at the end of the week.'

Poppy crawled back into her own seat, the leather squeaking against her thighs. Greg emerged from the kitchen and placed three plates down, one of which held Poppy's huge, singular gherkin.

'We could do this later, Ottilie. Looking at this is making me hungry.'

'Really?' she said sardonically, gesturing to the hunk of cheese on Lola's plate already marbled with sweat from the warmth that hung heavy in the air.

Poppy got out her camera and fiddled with the settings. Will caught her eye, grinned, and gave his fiancée a look as though she'd just stepped out of a Botticelli painting. Whilst Ottilie spoke, Lola nodded, but Poppy could see the series of question marks being scribbled on the notepad in Lola's lap as each request came through thick and fast.

'I want it to have the aesthetics of Meg's wedding in *Little Women*, but without the problematic undertones that swathed America at that time, you know? Ankle hemlines are great, but it feels a bit Amish, no? Not that I have a problem with the Amish. I love horses, don't I Will?'

'What?' said Will.

'Exactly. Anyway, I'm a strong believer in second chances. The concept of reincarnation is very powerful to me. My mindfulness coach, Sangmo Minghur, has a mantra about death and rebirth that I thought was so special,' said Ottilie, slipping into a drastically different accent to pronounce her teacher's name.

There's a whole bunch of Eastern philosophy behind it that I won't bore you with, but the core message is that marriage is a death of the self.'

Will barked out a laugh. 'Sounds touching, Ottie.'

'Stop it, I'm being serious. It doesn't just apply to me. We both shed our old selves and start a new cycle as a partnership. Two halves of the same coconut.'

'*Mi media naranja*,' said Poppy. Ottilie blinked at her like she was waiting for a punchline. 'It means my half-orange. Used to describe the perfect soulmate.'

'Oh, cute. Sorry, I don't speak Portuguese.'

'It's Spanish,' said Will.

'And *you're* making me feel stupid,' said Ottilie, her lips pursed.

Will placed his hands on the table, pushed back his chair, and scratched the back of his neck. 'I'm going to go… throw a stone at a wave.'

'Wait a minute, you said you wanted to be involved,' said Ottilie.

'I don't think I'm helping, am I? As long as the ceremony involves an aisle with you at the end of it, I'm a happy man.' He kissed the top of Ottilie's head, slipped a lock of hair behind her ear, and scooped a handful of peanuts before heading outside.

Poppy's heart felt like it was pressed against the sides of her ribcage. Since she had seen them together, there were things she had noticed: Ottilie's reluctance to make eye contact with Will; how he angled towards her; how she twisted away. Their friction was played out in micro-movements, the opposite of a high-school drama performance.

Ottilie lowered her voice. 'You see, this is why it's best to have these conversations without him. He has no opinion, which makes it impossible for me to have one without looking like a whiny cow. I agreed to a quiet ceremony, so long as we could do it differently.

Next thing I know, his dad's publicity team swoop in and offer us the island. How would it make me look if I said no? Now we're here, I *have* to stick my neck out otherwise I'll be walking down the aisle in a dress monogrammed with the Mountgrave Foundation logo. I'm snapping at him when I don't mean to. He makes me feel awful.'

Lola doesn't comment. Instead, she takes Ottilie's hands in her own and pumps them in the air with each annunciation. 'It. Will. Be. Fine. Okay?' Ottilie shook her head. 'It will be more than fine. It will be radiant. People will write songs about this wedding.'

Pre-Josh, back when Lola and Poppy had frequently shared a bed, Lola had karate chopped Poppy on more than one occasion for allowing an elbow to flop over to her side of the duvet. Quite simply, Lola didn't do physical contact, so she must *really* want a bonus.

'This is all *totally* normal,' she continued. 'The only thing is, I've already booked Alexandre Desplat to play your entrance music. And I'm not saying this to influence your decision in any way, but he cancelled his Southbank Centre gig to perform at the ceremony.'

Ottilie moaned with exasperation. 'Does he know the *American Beauty* soundtrack?'

Lola's pen hovered over her pad. 'I can certainly ask.'

'And the ceremony – we said the terrace, but I don't feel like it captures the same reverence as Mermaid Cove. That's where the paddleboards come in.'

'Okay...' said Lola. 'Just playing devil's advocate here, but three things spring to mind. Not impossible things, just... considerations. One, not much space for guests to sit.'

'Could we extend the decking? Put them up on a cliff?'

'Write down "binoculars", Lola,' said Poppy. Lola disguised a smile by biting her lip and nodding furiously.

'Okay, second point: it's a little trepidatious for the older guests getting up and down that path. It's a teeny bit on the steep side.'

'We could bring them round by boat?'

'We could. It'll depend on the swell that day, but… you know what, I'm sure it's doable. Last thing. Minor, really. Are you and Will going to be *on* the paddleboards?'

Ottilie drops her shoulders and leans forwards. 'No, no, no. I'll be *on* the platform with Sister Magdelina. Will is going to paddle over to join us. A break from tradition. The groom coming after the bride.'

'And he'll paddle in his suit?' said Lola, framing her question like an offhand statement.

'Well, yes. But no hat. We're not that formal. Besides, you can't wear a hat without shoes; it's creepy, don't you think?'

'Of course,' said Lola. 'And Will is up for this, is he?'

'He will be. It's paddle boarding. I'm hardly asking him to drop in from a biplane.'

'You don't want a plane, do you?' said Lola.

'No. Why, would that be easier?'

'Definitely not. Paddleboards it is. So this is it? This is what we're going with?' said Lola.

'Yes. Poppy saw the cove yesterday. It has a wonderfully ethereal energy. Very mystic. Did you sense it?'

Poppy was sure there was only one acceptable answer to this question, but *bollocks* surely wasn't it. When Lola stood on her foot with the point of her spiked heel, she employed the same feigned enthusiasm that had worked well at school when she had been trying to disguise a hangover. 'I did. Very strongly.'

Ottilie broke into a smile, her cheeks apple-pink with glee. 'I knew you would. The pictures will be amazing. I know everyone is disappointed about Christian-by-appointment-of-the-Queen-Withers not being here, but – selfishly – I hope you're still around on Saturday, Poppy.' Ottilie stood and tied the sleeves of her cardigan in a loose knot around her neck. 'It's coming together, isn't it?' said Ottilie, beaming.

'It sure is. You're almost a Mountgrave,' said Lola, wiggling her shoulders like a kitten preparing to pounce. It was such an un-Lola thing to do that Poppy half thought she'd started drinking again.

'I've already changed the name on my bank cards,' said Ottilie, her voice breathy and girlish. 'I get them out sometimes, just to have a look. Ottilie Mountgrave. Sad, isn't it? Lola, you're a star.' Ottilie tucked her hair behind her ears. 'Okay, I need to go and apologise to Will. He knows how uptight I am when I've got an idea in mind, but still. I don't mean to be so snappy. Good job I've got this,' she said, bringing her left hand up to her jaw, the diamond on her ring finger glistening in the sunshine. 'Oh, one last thing. Can you make sure the sommelier isn't serving wine from the Côtes du Rhône region tonight?'

'It's southern hemisphere only, to—'

'—remind us of the time we spent in Oz, of course. You've thought of everything. Okay, I'd best be off. I need to get ready for the wine tasting tonight. Can't wait to see what you've put together. See you soon!' Ottilie blew them both a kiss. Lola pretended to catch it, but when Ottilie drifted out of the pub like dandelion fluff caught on a breeze, Lola wiped it across her forearm.

'That's very unprofessional of me. Forget you saw anything.'

Poppy released a breath and flumped against the back of the booth. 'I honestly don't know how you do this job.'

'I'll take prima donnas over prepubescent teenagers any day. Again, don't repeat that. And stop tapping your foot – my heart rate is sitting at 152 beats per minute as it is. Good ol' high-functioning anxiety strikes again.'

Poppy bit her tongue, her restless energy waning. 'Don't you think it's weird?'

'That Ottilie thinks paddleboards are a demure way to make an entrance? Yes. It's Devon, love, not Saint-bloody-Tropez.'

'Sure, a valid point, but... her and Will. Be real, they're about as compatible as a moth and a sparrowhawk.'

'Have you ever seen a John Lewis Christmas advert? Interspecies couplings are the new gold standard of romance.'

'I don't know. She's not the kind of person I expected Will to end up with.'

'Okay, but how well do *you* really know Will? You didn't know his family owned an island. There are others, too, dotted in different continents so that they can reach a balmy twenty-eight degrees in any given month of the year.'

'He never brought it up.'

'I know the three of us used to hang out when I came to visit you in halls, but you guys weren't super chummy, were you?'

'Not after that, no.' Poppy bit into her gherkin. She tried to swallow too quickly, the vinegar juice burning her throat. Lola didn't know what had happened between them and now wasn't the time. 'I still can't get my head around it. From what I remember, his mum lives in a semi-detached in Peckham. That's a step down from unrestricted access to an island, right? Isn't she a midwife now?'

'She is. But before that she was a model. A good one, too. Look.' Lola pulled out her phone and wrote 'Carmella Deux' in a search engine. 'Stage name,' she explained. 'Real name Carmen.' The images showed an array of pyramid silhouettes, elongated legs, and a face so fierce Poppy never wanted to look in a mirror again. 'Oh, here he is. The lord himself.' Lola enlarged an image of Will's parents snapped as they stepped out of a limousine, his mum in a pleather trench coat nipped in at the waist, braids pulled over one shoulder, his father by contrast wearing a stiff shirt with an oversized collar, his skin clammy and pink. 'Perhaps mismatches run in the family,' said Lola.

'Pfft, not quite. Will definitely inherited his looks from his mum; you just can't notice it beneath the once-a-year haircut.'

'Careful, tiger. You're at risk of sounding jealous.'

'I'm not jealous!'

'Okay...'

'Don't say "okay" like that. I'm not bothered.'

'Aren't you?'

'Okay, I *am* bothered if he's getting exploited by Ottilie.'

'It's not her I'm worried about. Not that I am, because I'm professionally detached from this whole situation. But there *is* one thing I'm concerned about, and that involves...' Lola paused and ran a fingernail down her notebook, 'how to teach a nun to paddleboard before Saturday.'

'Are you going to be able to do all that?' said Poppy, pointing to the list that Lola was frantically copying into her phone.

'Mm-hmm.'

'Are you sure?'

'Yes. I have to be sure. This is the only wedding I've done where money hasn't been mentioned. Not once. If I fail, it'll be down to me not being good enough, not budget constraints. This is the career break I've spent years looking for. Next time us girls go to Center Parcs, I want to be in one of those treehouses with a hot tub and spa credits. I wasn't put on this earth to stay in economy.'

Chapter Seventeen

'Any sign, Greg?'

The barman picked up his binoculars and peered out of the window. 'No, love. There's a day boat just gone past, but I think they were chancers hoping to get into the party tonight.'

Lola drained her third pint of Pepsi and nodded. 'Security will see them off.' She turned her wrist over and set a thirty-second timer, which ticked down on a digital face. 'Pee time.'

Lola slid out of the booth and trotted past the bar, pausing to lean across the beer taps like a pin-up girl, her neck angled to peer out of the window. When she disappeared into the toilets, Poppy slipped her phone out of a hidden pouch tucked inside her camera bag. She unlocked it beneath the table and switched off 'airplane mode'. A handful of emails arrived in her inbox. A reminder to submit entries for the National Geographic Wildlife Photographer of the Year competition made her stomach flip. After two days, the best photo she'd taken featured a seagull skimming the head of a waiter who held a silver platter aloft like a shield. Poppy had refamiliarized herself with her camera, but her hands felt clunky and unfamiliar, her eye not as sharp as it once was.

The next email made her stomach flip back the other way.

From: *j.lattimer@cricklemeadacademy.sch.uk*
Subject line: *Really?*

I don't know if you've been getting my messages. I'll assume it's because of where you are rather than you changing your number, which would be an excellent way to justify victimhood to the solicitor, not that you'd be thinking of that, of course. I can see you didn't take the envelope I left on the kitchen counter, so I've attached a copy of the files here. When you have an hour, read them.

Side note: if you're trying to worry me, please don't. It was your choice to spend summer in the middle of nowhere, so being coy about it is pretty pointless. You're your own person. Start acting like one.

Poppy didn't read it twice. That kind of tactic might have worked before, but not now. Even so, her phone felt heavier, as though the email had turned into a lead weight. She deleted Josh's message and emptied her trash folder. If she read it again, her mind would race down a skittle run of consequences worrying about the mouse trap he had set for her at home. He was playing her. Even now, when she'd travelled as far south as possible, he was still playing her.

'Don't wave that around, babe. You'll get rugby tackled by Big Steve if he catches you with a phone out. He looks like Bear Grylls on steroids. Delicious.'

Poppy saluted her friend, turned her phone off, and tucked it away. Whoever invented the phrase 'out of sight, out of mind' hadn't experienced multi-platform communication. The phone burnt a hole in her pocket. Poppy gestured to Lola's jostling knee.

'What's with the twitch?'

'Oh, that's nerves and the half kilo of sugar I've consumed in Pepsi form. My teeth ache, but I've got to be allowed some sort of vice or I'll start murdering people.' Lola interlocked her hands behind her neck and pulled to relieve the tension, her chin tilted back. 'The quartet I've booked to play at the wine tasting should be arriving on the sea tractor soon. Musicians,' she said, rolling her eyes. 'They don't trust a double bass on a speedboat, apparently.'

'Sound logic,' said Poppy. Lola spread a napkin across her lap, pinched a cheese-covered jalapeño, and dropped it into her mouth. 'Ah, that's the good stuff,' she said through a mouthful. As she tore her bread up into small pieces, she gave Poppy a look that made her feel like a spotlight had been switched on above her head.

'Speaking of logic, have you put your house up for sale yet?'

'You know, I think these might be the best chips I've ever eaten,' said Poppy, holding her fork at head height. Lola sat back and crossed a leg over her knee, as though this proved her point exactly.

'Don't tell me he's still there.'

'Can you see any vinegar?'

Lola swiped the chip from Poppy's fork and bit into it. Her stern expression softened immediately. 'Shit me, these are good.'

'Told you.'

Lola swallowed and wiped her fingers on a napkin. 'Now stop avoiding the question.'

'It's not *not* up for sale,' said Poppy, mashing the end of her gherkin with the side of her fork. 'I left my details with a few estate agents a couple of months ago, but they're all so pushy. I get ten calls a day from different blokes, all called Jack or Dan. It's too much.'

'Do you know what I consider too much? Living in a house

with your ex-husband when he's been a toxic bellend for the majority of your time together.'

'Lola, I don't want to talk about it right now.'

'Then when?'

'I don't know, next week? Next month? Next millennium?'

'You avoided my calls for months. I considered driving up when you had half-term but Mum had to borrow the car. Is Josh making things difficult again? Stupid question, but seriously.'

Poppy rubbed her temples. 'Of course he is. I can't put my finger on how, but I feel totally paralysed every time I know he's in the house.'

'Not in a sex way, I hope,' said Lola, her eyes narrow.

'Nope, not anymore. We stopped shagging long after we stopped talking. In hindsight, that is weird, isn't it?'

'It served you for a time. We learn, we grow,' said Lola.

Poppy sat back in the booth and interlocked her fingers in her lap. 'I play out every possible confrontation before it happens. I'll go to make a tea, but then think about the comment he'll make when I leave the spoon on the side. Then I'll put it in the dishwasher too loudly and he'll say, "Don't be petty," and I'll get angry, then he'll call me hysterical and turn the TV up. He's unfazed. Did you know I'm still paying for Sky Sports? Me. Paying for Sky Sports.'

'What are you doing, Poppy?' said Lola, frustration and sorrow softening her voice. Poppy's throat tightened.

'I'm tired. I'm really fucking tired. At work, I pretend like everything's fine because he's going for a promotion and doesn't want any "lingering awkwardness" to affect his reputation, which – of course – ensures we have awkwardness by the bucketload. We're civilised in front of our colleagues, but I feel like the Victorian governess he's shagging on the sly. I can't socialise because he's there trying to be everyone's pal and constantly chirps the female trainees. I can't talk to Dad because he always brings it back to money. You've been busy with your career – and I love that for you. It's not a swipe. I keep busy making weird little films in the attic so that the kids at school don't take pictures of me in the Sainsbury's Local buying gin and a tub of Cadbury roses every Friday night. He hasn't changed a *thing* about his life since we split. So what does that say about me? How can he make out that I was the foundation of his fucking existence, make grand declarations of love in front of total strangers, then shrug me off when it comes to this? Like it was *me* holding *him* back for the past decade?'

Lola threw her hands up. 'Of *course* that's what he's doing! What begins with a 'j', ends with 'u' and has "Josh-is-gaslighting-you" in the middle?'

Poppy blinked. 'You can't just throw that phrase around to take down everyone you don't like.'

'Me hating Josh has nothing to do with it. I'm not that insensitive.'

'I feel like an idiot. Every *single* day. I wake up in the attic, look at the sky, and see "Poppy is a doormat" written in the clouds. You know the worst thing? I've stopped feeling happy about anything, even other people's good news. My classroom assistant got engaged last week and I wanted to scream "It's a trap!" like Admiral Ackbar in *Star Wars*.'

Lola tapped the table with her nails. 'If you can't sell the house right now, why doesn't he rent somewhere?'

'Because we can't free up funds until I've sold the house. It's a chicken and egg scenario. There's no point in us both paying rent and a mortgage.'

'This split is final, isn't it?'

'We're getting divorced, aren't we?'

'It sounds like you're still doing all the emotional labour in your relationship, so is a divorce a divorce if it looks and smells like a relationship?'

'It was my decision, so it's not a surprise that I'm also doing the heavy lifting.'

'That sounds parroted, straight up. Threaten him with the lawyer card if you need to.'

Poppy pushed her plate to the side and stood up, coordinated almost exactly with the sound of Lola's watch bleeping.

'Here we go, love. Man and a woman? They've got a chest with them,' said Greg, leaning so far out of the window that all attempts at covert surveillance were lost. 'I couldn't hear the tractor – the wind's blowing in the other direction.'

'I love it when things happen on time. There should be four. Are there four?' said Lola, swinging her bag onto her shoulder.

'Nope. Unless there's another fella in the box. They look a bit confused if I'm honest.'

'I'm on it,' said Lola, initiating battle mode.

Poppy dragged a chip along her plate to mop up the ketchup and stood up, chewing. 'I'll come with you. If you need me to, I can run a message up to the hotel on my way back.'

Lola blew her a kiss. 'You might get a hug at the end of this,' she said, grinning. They left the pub and stepped over a sun-bleached rope attached to a dinghy that had seen better days.

'If that happens, I'll pop with joy,' said Poppy, falling into stride beside her.

Chapter Eighteen

'Hi, how was the trip over? Not too bumpy, I hope?'

'I've travelled in a minibus to the arse end of England with a dicky tummy for company, so that was a breeze, love,' said the man, gesturing to the sea tractor as it performed a clunky turning circle in the shallows. He stuck his sausage fingers out to greet Lola. 'You the one who booked us?'

'Yes…' said Lola, hesitating. Poppy looked between her friend and the man. Was she? Going by the burst thread veins on his cheeks, Poppy would have guessed he was the sommelier rather than the musician.

'My wife and colleague, Crystal.' The man stood to the side, revealing a waif-like woman with hair at once so large and so blonde that Poppy made a mental note to avoid standing near her with a lit match.

'Crystal? I don't think I have a Crystal on my list,' said Lola, scrolling through her iPad.

'Stage name,' said the man. 'My name's Mike. Not so glamorous, but you can throw "Magic" in front and it works well for children's parties and hen do's. Not at the same time, mind. I've got a DBS.'

'Good to know,' said Poppy, holding a smile as she turned to Lola.

'I'll be straight with you ladies, I thought we were doing a charity gala somewhere else, but this ain't the first time the agency has given us the wrong details, is it?' said Mike, running a finger round the collar of his shirt as the sun pummelled his back.

Crystal rolled her eyes and pursed her burgundy lips. 'Oh, not half. It's why we have a broad repertoire. Give us a crowd and we'll show them a good time, any age, any gender. Just make sure we're back on the mainland by midnight so we don't get charged for the overnight car park.'

'Where are we heading?' asked Mike. 'The wife will need to change.'

Crystal waved a garment bag, her sinewy arm strained under the weight of what sounded like a heavily beaded dress. 'Got a loo I can use?'

'Uh, yes. I've set up a green room behind the ballroom.'

Crystal smacked Mike on the arm, her heavily kohled eyes wide. 'See, I told you this place looked fancy. *Ballroom.*'

'You know, I think I will wear the bowtie, love. Did you pack it?'

'Yep, underneath your emergency pants.'

'You beauty. Let's hop to it. Will one of you grab the other end of this when we reach the stairs?' he said, gesturing to the wheeled trunk. 'I don't suppose there's an escalator or something?'

'No, it's a deep breath, firm thighs sort of situation,' said Poppy, pointing to the bottom of the cliff-side path that zigzagged up towards the hotel. Lola clutched Poppy's elbow, allowing a gap to open between them and the couple ahead.

'Where are their fucking instruments?' she whispered, a deep line set in her brow.

'A good question. Perhaps they've got collapsible cellos?' Poppy offered.

'I was supposed to be getting a quartet! What do these two do? Play with a bow in each hand?'

Lola took out her iPad as they walked, brought up an email, and slowed her strides across the harbour, her heels counting the seconds with each hollow clunk on the wood.

'Who were you expecting?' asked Poppy.

'Michael, Janette, Lauren, and Oliver. Graduates of the Bristol Conservatoire.'

'Well then, who the hell are these two?'

Mike paused on the bend, a damp sweat patch blooming between his shoulder blades. 'You coming, girls?'

'Girls? Ergh,' said Poppy. 'I'm twenty-nine years old.'

'Mike!' called Lola. 'Before you go any further, can I ask you both to sign this?' She opened up a document on her iPad and turned the screen towards him.

'Wanting autographs already?' asked Mike, tugging on the lapels of his jacket.

'It's an NDA. Sign at the bottom. It means you can't tell anyone that you were here, or who you saw, and any picture, video, or audio captures could end in a lawsuit.'

'That's a bit OTT, isn't it?' said Crystal.

'Not at all,' replied Lola with authority, scrolling through her phone as she waited for them to sign.

'Stage name or government name?' said Mike.

'Whichever you'd prefer on summons papers in the event that you break the terms listed,' said Lola.

With that, Mike and Crystal signed with their index fingers.

'I've got to make a quick phone call. Poppy, would you see

them up? I'll follow you in a mo.' She gave Poppy a look that hinted at delay tactics.

'Ah, thought you'd left me to lug this up by myself. You grab that handle,' said Mike.

Poppy swung her camera onto her back and listened in to one side of a faint, but angry phone call further down the stairs. That wasn't a good sign. When they reached the top, Mike collapsed onto a bench that looked across the sea towards the mainland.

'Jesus Christ. Have you got my inhaler, Crystal?'

'Here you are, sweet,' said Crystal. She unzipped her leather bum bag to remove a blue cannister from beneath a pack of fruit polos and a box of paracetamol. 'I'll go and see where we're setting up.'

'Would you wait a minute? I think Lola needs to clear you with security—'

'You're all right, sweetheart. I've experienced it all in my time,' said the woman, her smile so gummy the diamante on her front tooth glinted in the sun. For Mountgrave-calibre entertainment, something wasn't adding up. Poppy rushed back to the cliff path, where Lola was finishing her call.

'I listened to your argument – respectfully, I might add – but there are presidential campaigns more believable than this.' She paused and held a finger up to Poppy. 'The deposit? Are you on another planet? You're not having it until you're here. That was the deal. Learn to read!' Lola hung up, her expression balanced on a tightrope somewhere between despair and rage.

'Lola, I don't know how to say this, but—'

'Magic Mike isn't an ambidextrous musician? No, no he most *definitely* is not. The fucking sea tractor picked up the wrong people; our quartet got on a boat in the opposite direction and are currently sitting by a lighthouse in Brixham wondering where the hotel is. Meanwhile, Terry ignored my very specific instruction to check for ID and didn't think to question these two, so we've got

Mike's backstreet entertainment, but I'm not entirely sure what he does or whether it involves his penis.'

'Can you get the quartet back in time?'

'The tractor isn't running anymore.'

'Speedboat?'

'Pfft, this isn't James Bond. There isn't one tucked in a lair for emergencies— Oh,' Lola's voice trailed off. Poppy gestured around them to emphasise how very likely that unlikely situation seemed to be. 'Big Steve on security can legally surpass the speed limit because he's got a special badge.'

'I assume he doesn't like it being described as his "special badge"?'

'No. He gets twitchy, but it's fun to prod the bear.'

'How long would it take for him to fetch the quartet and bring them over here?' asked Poppy.

'A couple of hours? Bit longer?'

'That's cutting it fine. Wine tasting kicks off from seven, right?' said Poppy, consulting the ring-bound itinerary that Lola had given her.

Lola chewed her lip. 'Can you sound Mike and Crystal out? See if whatever they do is appropriate to keep the Mountgrave crowd distracted?' She looked suspiciously at the couple hovering nearby, waiting for instructions. 'Sign it off with Will if you can find him. I'll go and see Big Steve. After that, I fully intend to lock you in your bedroom so no one can ask you to do any more favours. And by no one, I mean me.'

'What would you do if I wasn't here?' said Poppy, not entirely as a rhetorical question.

'I'd be sitting in a corner trying to multiply myself like an amoeba. Basically, anything it takes to make this week a success.'

The late afternoon sun dipped past a swirl of low-hanging clouds. She calculated the light levels and knew the reduced glare meant better photos of puffins diving for herring in the shallows. Poppy sighed. Yet more photos she wouldn't be able to take.

'It's a bit crass, don't you think?' said a woman with teeth so large she looked like a caricature. 'Southern hemisphere wine is what you palm off on colleagues you don't much like.'

'Don't say that to Paul Spruce; he's got stakes in Marlborough Sauvignon Blanc,' said her friend, nibbling at an onion pierced on a silver cocktail stick.

'Oh, not that he's mentioned it *once*.'

'You are bad.'

'Like his wine. You can tell he's inexperienced. By the sound of it, he has more fakes in his collection than he knows what to do with and what's worse, they're *far* nicer than the ones he produces. Are you taking the picture or not?' snapped the woman, looking at Poppy over the rim of her sunglasses.

'I thought you'd prefer me to wait until you'd stopped talking.'

'If I worked on that principle, I'd never finish a conversation,' said the woman, who simultaneously drained her martini and looked over her shoulder for another.

Poppy bit her lip and tried her best not to smirk. 'All done,' she said, clicking the shutter.

Of all the nature documentaries she had seen, there was surely nothing quite so fascinating as a room full of people who bonded over conversations about the best yacht skipper for cruising the Aegean. Poppy watched them through the viewfinder of her camera, David Attenborough narrating the scene in her mind's eye. '*Here, we see the male Homo sapiens attempting to challenge the alpha status of his peer by associating a knowledge of wine with his own virile attempts to maintain authority.*' Poppy twisted her lens and zoomed in on the path that ran alongside the hotel, but there was no sign of Lola yet.

Behind a line of perfectly spherical shrubs, Will, Ottilie, Lawrence, and Josie stood in a circle, distinct and youthful. They held an air of intentional, styled elegance, their outfits complementing one other like models on adjacent pages of *Vogue*. If Poppy stumbled across them in her normal life, she would never have assumed Will was with them. At university, he had once attended a costume party dressed as an Amazon package and used the leftover box as his laundry basket for the next six months. To call him 'unusually groomed' would be an understatement – a verdict she happily appreciated from afar.

Snap. She took a picture. Josie stood back, her grey hair combed in a heavy side-parting. Poppy squatted, framing the group in a glow of cloud-softened sunshine. Snap. Will spotted her and bent to waist level, gurning down the lens. Poppy laughed. Snap. Ottilie rolled her eyes. Snap. Lawrence slowly licked a tobacco paper. Snap, snap, snap.

Will gestured for her to join them.

'Photos! Here,' said Ottilie, interlocking her fingers as she dangled from Will's shoulder, chin down, mouth like a little duck.

'What? Oh, right,' said Will, winding his arm around her waist.

'Smile properly,' said Ottilie. Will grinned, as though he were having a school picture taken. 'Not like that.' He stuck his tongue out. 'Oh, honestly,' said Ottilie, dropping her pose. She smiled at him, a small dimple in her cheek.

'Hey, Poppy. How's your friend? I heard her yelling at the waiting staff earlier,' said Lawrence, lighting his roll-up.

'Quite right too,' said Ottilie. 'I only just got the smell of fish juice out of my kaftan.'

'She's hot when she's angry,' said Josie, her consonants soft.

Poppy laughed. 'Lola's fine. Busy working behind the scenes, you know.'

'Hey, you know what tonight is?' said Will.

'Wine tasting,' said Poppy, reaching for her itinerary. 'With a surprise, as yet unspecified. Bound to be a laugh. Speaking of which, Will, do you think the guests would be okay with something... a little out of the box? For tonight?'

Will nodded as he listened. Ottilie gave a too-quick smile. 'Sounds intriguing,' he said. 'Especially considering that it's switchover night, which means two things. One, Poppy, you're joining in. I won't take no for an answer. And two, this is when the real wedding fun starts.'

'Oh, I don't know about that. It's been mighty fun already,' said Josie sarcastically, crossing her arms over her unbuttoned waistcoat. 'Wine tasting? Old school, but okay. Although I don't imagine it appeals to you anymore, Lawrence?'

'More of a beer man?' asked Poppy.

'No, I'm a recovering alcoholic,' said Lawrence, unabashed. Silence crept into their small circle of chatter. He shrugged. 'It is what it is. Although if you say, "how admirable", I might have to push you in the sea.'

'Lawrence!' said Ottilie. 'Don't put yourself down. You've done incredibly well. You'll make poor Poppy feel awkward. Sorry about him.'

'Don't apologise,' said Poppy, impressed by Lawrence's honesty. 'What are you going to do instead?'

'Watch everyone get drunk and embarrass themselves, I expect. I might try mixing different types of squash to create a little mocktail if I really feel like pushing the boat out.' Lawrence ran a hand through his hair and put his cigarette in his mouth. 'Unless that's too embarrassing for you, Ottilie,' he said, looking at her as he flicked his lighter on.

Poppy felt a tap on her shoulder and turned to find a woman wearing a scalloped high-neck dress. Her heavily pencilled eyebrows disappeared into her curly hair as she bent towards

Poppy with the air of someone who was used to whispering discreetly.

'Hi, Lindsey Carmichael. Sommelier,' she said a touch louder. 'I'm a little confused about arrangements tonight. Would you be able to shed some light on the situation?' she said in an Australian accent.

'I'm not actually involved with the organisation,' said Poppy, 'so I'm not best placed to—'

'Only *that* man seems to think *he's* been booked as entertainment, which isn't what I was expecting, as I'm sure you can appreciate.'

'Hold on a minute. Will? Could you come with me a second?' said Poppy, panicking.

A booming voice rang out across the terrace. 'Ladies and jellyfish! If you'd like to make your way inside, the game is about to begin!'

'Oh God...' said Poppy, furiously scanning the crowd for Lola. Mike stood on a cushioned bench, arms wide like a televangelist, the corners of a sequined bowtie peeking out beneath his chin. Crystal stood beside him wearing a glittering minidress that hung from her collarbones, her hair freshly backcombed. She motioned towards the open door, a human disco ball in the face of low-angled sun and enough crystal beading to make Liberace seem modest.

'What're the logistics here?' continued Lindsey, annoyed. 'How am I supposed to work around them? I have a system, and that doesn't involve being a sidekick to... whatever he's been contracted for,' said the sommelier as the crowd were chivvied inside.

'Come on, kids! You'll be last in line for a dabber,' called Mike, walking towards them. Crystal handed a sheet of paper to a bemused-looking Lord Mountgrave and led him inside, her dress glittering as she sashayed on five-inch heels.

Assessing the situation from afar, Josie threw her arms around Ottilie and Lawrence and steered them away, giving Poppy a chance to talk to Will discreetly.

'Will, I think there's been a, er... slight booking mix-up,' she said in a low voice.

'You're telling me, sweetheart!' said Mike. 'I don't like fuss. I can work around this wine tasting malarkey, if she'll not be precious about it. I'll introduce her and all, which is something I charge extra for ordinarily. I'm a highly experienced Master of Ceremonies, if you ever need one,' he said, producing a business card from his back pocket. 'Same skills, different uniform. Crystal doesn't come with me for those ones.'

'This is *not* how I work,' said the sommelier.

'Well, we're in a pickle then, aren't we?' said Mike.

Will rubbed his chin, quietly entertained by the discussion. 'What is it you do, Mike?'

'Sorry, fella,' said Mike, holding out a hand for Will to shake. 'Mind my manners. Tonight, I'm Magic Mike and I've brought my Big Bingo Balls.'

'Bingo?' said Will. 'Seriously?'

'Will, I think Lola will be able to fix this,' said Poppy, her stomach swooping like a seabird.

'Fix what?' he said, positively lit from within. 'This is brilliant! Is Ottilie behind it? She must have been,' said Will, pumping Mike's hand with enthusiasm. 'It's a pleasure, mate! From one ex-caller to another.'

'You're... pleased?' said Poppy cautiously.

'Yeah, I used to do the calling down at the old folks' home in Stoke Gifford. I volunteered for something to do when I was waiting for an exam re-mark after everyone moved away after graduation. I *loved* it. Great banter, sociable hours, and an endless supply of biscuits. What a buzz.'

'Wow... okay!' said Poppy, clapping her hands.

Although Mike looked buoyed by Will's unexpected passion, Lindsey was slowly turning the colour of claret. Poppy scanned through her usual conflict management strategies. With students, providing two equally unsatisfactory choices usually worked, along with threats to write home to their parents. With Josh, tactical avoidance kept conflict at bay most of the time. She went with a variation of the first option. 'Could you take it in turns?' asked Poppy. 'Bingo, wine, bingo, wine, etcetera?'

'Fine by me,' said Mike, his thumbs hooked through his belt loops.

'Lindsey?'

The sommelier pinched the bridge of her nose and fluttered a smile. 'I'm sure we'll manage,' she said in a monotone.

'Come on, fella,' said Mike, putting his arm across Will's shoulders. 'If you're lucky, I'll let you call the second game.'

Chapter Nineteen

'I've seen a scorecard before, but not one like this. Excuse me. Excuse me!'

Poppy turned, still reluctant to assume any authority over a situation she had somehow helped construct. 'You all right?'

'How do you score categories on this?' said a man to her left. He flicked his card and sat back in his chair, arms crossed.

'Categories?'

'Clarity, colour, complexity. Usually, it's a round score of ten, but this one goes all the way to ninety-nine and all the bloody numbers are out of order,' he said.

'They're not categories,' said Will, bounding over to her rescue. 'They're to score bingo games. When they call a number, you dab it off on your page and if you get a line or a full house, you shout out. Nicola, you've played before, haven't you?'

'Of course I have. Don't worry, I'll set you right if you get muddled,' said Nicola, who sat across the table. 'Whenever we put a set of bingo dabbers on the shopping channel, they're a guaranteed sell-out. Oh, Will, what do we shout for a win?'

He patted his future mother-in-law's shoulder and gestured to the stage. 'Magic Mike's going to let us know in a minute.'

'Magic Mike?' she said, brightening. 'You've really pushed the boat out. I would have worn my glasses if I'd known. Can you seat me closer to the front?'

'Nicola, compose yourself,' said Ottilie's father, who joined them from the bar.

'It's not *quite* what you think,' Poppy interjected. 'I'd sit further back, if anything.' Poppy sidestepped, lifted her camera, and took a picture down the long table as guests settled into their seats, their faces a spectrum from wine-softened smiles to looks of profound confusion.

Will put an arm around Poppy's shoulder, and it felt both warm and familiar. He looked comfortable in the face of chaos, like she remembered him being when they first started university. Perhaps it was *because* Will had been born into the limbo land of privilege that he was able to tune out drama like it was a radio station he wasn't much interested in. Despite his chameleon tendencies, it seemed neither of them knew how to seamlessly end a friendship hiatus that spanned a decade.

Poppy had never been a fan of rocking the boat. She had experienced enough turbulence growing up to develop an early detection radar that constantly oscillated into adulthood. It was as though her parents had learnt the best methods of aggravation from old episodes of *EastEnders*: ripped work shirts, salty food, and dinner in the bin having all featured at some point in their relationship. So absorbed in their world of pithy comebacks, Poppy's adolescence had involved nights spent picking from a bucket of cheap chicken, taking herself to bed, and shouldering her father's dirty clothes to the laundrette. When she left home, Poppy had made a vow that the only drama she would experience in the future would come vicariously through Lola.

Seeing how happy Will was, Poppy stood a little taller. In that, little had changed. When she left home, Poppy had realised that repetitively watching *Amélie* on her own wasn't exactly conducive to making friends. Will had offered a gentle hand in the small of her back, a reassurance that she was interesting enough as she was. Being around him again, she felt exposed, like she was missing a rib and Will was the only one who knew.

The shrill sound of feedback cut through the chatter as Will stepped onto a raised platform in front of four long tables, a microphone in hand. 'Hi – is this on? It is? Cool, cool. I just wanted to come up here to say a few words.'

'The wedding's not till Saturday, William!' shouted Paul Spruce. Lord Mountgrave erupted with laughter alongside the gaggle of port-flushed faces around him. Will blushed with embarrassment. Poppy had a strong desire to punch them all in the throat.

'Dad has always found it difficult to separate family from business—'

'Buckle up, Colin! The boy's building up to a roast!' With an obnoxious air of rugby banter, a man leant over the back of his chair to slap Lord Mountgrave on the back, who pretended to bite his nails in an expression of worry.

'I'll save that for your retirement party, Dad. I do want to say thank you to the family, friends, associates, and old mates for staying on for our celebrations this week,' said Will, catching Poppy's eye. 'As a family, we've had our moments, like all families do. But we always stick a hand out for each other. There's a reason we come back to Loxby every year, and it's not just for the annual Mountgrave conference. Some of you have been solid features of my summers since I first started coming here as a teenager.' Will cleared his throat and looked across to his father, the shadow of a frown still visible. Lord Mountgrave gave him the smallest of nods. 'The Mountgrave Foundation is the sum of all the people in it. You, here today. Of the many things to celebrate, I'm so happy you're here to witness my marriage.'

Ottilie's parents began to clap, intimating that others should join in. 'Spoken like a true Chief Exec, don't you think?' said Nicola, loudly enough for it to be obvious that she wasn't concerned about being overheard.

'With that, I'd like to thank my fiancée, my light, my Ottilie.'

Ottilie paused, a glass of wine halfway to her mouth.

'They say compromise is the key to happiness, which is why I chose wine tasting for her, and she chose bingo for me.'

Poppy glanced at Ottilie, wondering if she would correct his misplaced assumption. She didn't.

'Years ago, I told Ottilie about the happy summer I spent with the best geriatrics this side of south Bristol. She remembered,' Will shook his head, joyfully surprised. 'I hope you've got your glasses full, because I can't think of a better way to kick off our celebrations. I'll hand over to Mike. Take it away, mate!'

Crystal hit play on the portable sound deck. A noise that resembled an ice cream truck remix of Tyson Fury's entrance music boomed into the dining hall. Crystal chandelier drops quivered from the ceiling bracket. Will stepped down from the platform as Mike took to the stage.

"Allo, 'allo, 'allo!' said Mike. He took the microphone out of the stand, flicked it behind his back, and caught it over his shoulder. As he passed her, Will motioned for Poppy to sit next to him near the head of the table. She poured herself a glass of wine from an ice bucket, the glass deliciously cool in her hand. Will planted a kiss on Ottilie's cheek as he sat down. She took his face in her hands and kissed him back.

'Oh, would you cop an eyeful of the betrothed! They'll be printing your faces on a teapot at this rate. Okay, who's ready to bag a full house!'

As the evening lengthened, the sun tipped the last of its

warmth inside, fuggy and thick. In a move that Poppy couldn't have predicted, Mike had successfully thawed the crowd. Snobbish scepticism was surpassed by the idea of competition, signified when Lawrence emptied an ice bucket and hustled up and down the tables for fifty-pound notes to use as prize money. Although the sommelier had tried to discuss the merits of astringent grapes during the comfort break, she gave up once the heat of the room rose to the extent that someone asked for ice cubes for their glass. When she stopped talking, no one noticed. Instead, the waiting staff distributed bottles like party bags, which only added to the commotion.

Mike's voice boomed through the room as he walked between the tables. 'Now, my usual crowd are sticklers for silence and like things done the traditional way. Oh, yes! It's not marrying your cousins and shooting pheasant for Boxing Day, but bingo *is* sacred. The game is *pure*! And a dickie bird told me that the stakes can be made that little bit higher by throwing a wager into the mix.'

Poppy scrolled through the pictures she'd taken so far that night and smiled, tapping Will on the arm to show him her screen. There were pert cheeks, dropped shoulders, and heads turned in laughter. If you squinted, they looked like a group of people who actually liked each other.

'Hey, can you take this for a while?' said Lawrence, clicking to get Poppy's attention. 'If you leave it with me, I'll spend it on one of those ridiculously large bottles of Laurent-Perrier. Taking the bullets out of the gun, etcetera, etcetera,' said Lawrence, handing her an ice bucket with a self-deprecating smile. When Poppy looked inside, she pushed it back against his chest.

'How much is in there?!' she asked.

'Not sure,' he said, looking at the notes. 'Ten grand? Twenty?'

'Bloody hell, I don't want it.'

'Why?'

'Too much responsibility.'

'If you don't take it, I'm going to blame you for the drunken relapse I'm going to have in approximately'—he checked a heavy watch on his wrist—'sixteen minutes.'

'I can't tell if you're being serious,' said Poppy.

Lawrence shrugged. 'Do you want to find out?'

'Fine. But for the record, I'm doing this for Will.'

'Oh, we're *all* doing this for Will,' said Lawrence, his voice thick.

Poppy shifted the ice bucket onto her hip. 'What do you mean?'

'There's the prize, chaps and chaparoonies!' Mike's voice boomed down the microphone. Lawrence squinted and tilted his head in a melodrama of confusion as everyone swivelled in their seats to stare at Poppy. She lifted the ice bucket above her head like a trophy and tried her best to smile, but Lawrence's words were knocking together inside her skull. What was he getting at?

'Next one to call a full house wins the lot. We haven't got a gambling licence, mind, so if it's you, note it down as a gifted donation. Preaching to the choir here, ain't I? When was the last time you filled out your expenses properly?' he said, offering the microphone to Ottilie's father. 'On second thought, don't answer that. I can't afford to go to court again.'

Josie leant forward, beckoning Poppy closer. The table corner poked her in the stomach as she looked down at Josie's messy bingo card.

'I can't keep up with this,' said Josie, leaning back in her chair. 'You take mine. Stick this in the pot too,' she said, handing Poppy a neat roll of one hundred dollar bills along with her dabber. 'It's my penalty for showing up unannounced.' Josie sucked on an e-cigarette and blew the vapour over her shoulder. 'I'm expecting a promotion soon, so y'know, I'm feeling charitable.'

With the ice bucket wedged between her knees, Poppy thought of all the things she could buy with the money that others had cast aside as loose change. A new deposit if Josh made it difficult to get her share out of the house. A DSLR camera and a dozen different lenses. A darkroom for her students.

'Eyes down. Here we go. Goodness me, number three. Get up and run, thirty-one. Up to tricks, thirty-six.'

The sound of fervour grew like microwave popcorn; initially, nothing, then frequent, overlapping eruptions of gasps and squeals as numbers disappeared and cards filled up.

'Ah, it's me!' squealed Nicola. Ottilie groaned with embarrassment. 'Bingo? Bingo! Bingo!'

Crystal hit play on 'Celebrate Good Times' by Kool & the Gang as Mike started a round of applause.

'Right, that was a warm-up round. A rubber duck for you, lovie,' he said. 'Nice if you've got a dog. All right, let's call a five-minute break. I need a sit down and you lot could do with a door open. Next round we're upping the ante. No cheating. I'll know about it!' Mike tapped the side of his nose, stepped off the stage, and shuffled towards the bathroom with a hand on his zipper.

As the room broke into chatter, Ottilie stood up and stretched. From behind, she made a show of draping her arms around Will's shoulders, but her eyes kept darting towards Lawrence. He watched her, lazily traced the lip of his glass, and went back to his conversation with Josie, ignoring Ottilie as she nestled into Will's shoulder.

'I think we can safely say that the bingo has been a success,' said Poppy, reaching across the table for a crostini. She smiled at Will. It was the first time all week that Poppy had seem him truly at ease.

'I'd say so! Thanks again,' he said, squeezing Ottilie's arm. 'Such a good surprise.'

Ottilie breezed over his comment and looked at the table behind them. 'If Mum wins, we'll never hear the end of it,' she said.

Will laughed. 'It's not like competitiveness is unusual in your family. Every Christmas, Ottilie's parents run a championship of games and the loser has to wash up after Christmas dinner.'

'Surely that's a doddle when your parents sell cleaning products for a living?' said Lawrence with an undertone of sarcasm. It went unnoticed by Will, but not Ottilie.

'Actually, they oversaw the business, then sold it off,' said Ottilie, scowling. She rolled her tongue around her mouth. 'Don't you find bingo a bit grabby? Us all sat here like we're gannets squabbling over chips.'

'Ottie is only in a sulk because she hates losing,' said Will, pulling her onto his lap.

'I do not!'

'So you hate winning?' said Lawrence.

'No, I just mean… never mind. You're putting words in my mouth.' She angled her sharp chin over her shoulder.

'Come on, Ottie,' said Lawrence, 'these are your last few nights of freedom. Lighten up.'

Poppy drummed her fingers and hummed, eager to dispel the tension that had crept across the table. Lawrence lowered his forearms and leant forward, a muscle in his neck twitching as Ottilie tried her best to ignore him. Will stroked her upper arm absentmindedly, his attention pulled away as the noise escalated around them.

'Hello, you gorgeous lot! How are we doing?' said Lola. Poppy jumped at her arrival, the ice bucket between her knees clattering to the floor. She disappeared beneath the table and scooped the scattered notes back inside, peeling a damp twenty from the leather sole of Josie's shoe. When she emerged, she was so happy to see Lola, she could have kissed her.

'What's all this about?' asked Lola, pointing to the bucket. 'That's not for the stripper, is it?'

'Don't spoil the big surprise,' said Lawrence, unbuttoning the collar of his shirt.

'No one needs to see that,' said Josie, amused. The beginning of a laugh twinged in the corner of Ottilie's mouth, but she still refused to make eye contact.

'If Ottilie's dad beats my dad at bingo, I worry that he'll be shoulder blades up in the bay by morning. Dad has got a weird alpha male thing going on this week – have you noticed?' asked Will.

'When does Dad *not* have a weird alpha male thing going on?' replied Lawrence.

'Good point,' said Josie, far more interested in the conversation now that Lola was here. She tore the crust from a dinner roll and scooped up a dollop of tapenade. 'It's why he finds *me* so intimidating. He doesn't understand that I have a masculine energy he couldn't achieve even if he bathed in Old Spice and rode a bison to the boardroom each morning.'

'I think he doesn't like you because you snogged the woman he was dating before he married Valerie,' said Lawrence.

'That woman has been my girlfriend for seven years now, so he needs to learn when to bow out. Anyway, Paul is swimming in safe waters. My brother isn't interested in merging with the Spruce business. No offence, Ottilie.'

'None taken,' she replied.

'It's the board he's trying to win over. You know they're planning on holding the vote for who's going to be the next CEO at the end of the week?'

'Really?' said Lawrence.

'Yup. You know what the market is like. Progressive CEOs are great, but you've got to make sure that no surprise skeletons are thumping at the closet door. Trust can tank, just like that,' she said, clicking her fingers. 'Apparently I don't count, since I'm permanently *out* of said closet. These two though'—she gestured to Ottilie and Will—'make Will a particularly appealing doe-eyed contender.'

'Not you too,' said Will with a groan. 'I've got no idea why Dad thinks I'd be any good. I'm not interested.'

'You're right,' said Josie. 'An office with an in-house massage therapist does sound pretty shitty.'

'If Will's in line for CEO, I might *actually* be given a division to manage rather than doing my penance as Dad's chief ball tickler,' said Lawrence.

'You tickle your dad's balls?' asked Poppy, feigning naivety.

'No, he tells me which balls to tickle and off I go, metaphorical feather in hand. I'm not a pervert. Most of the time, at least.'

Unmoved by either the news of balls or business, Will tapped the table and pushed everyone's scorecards towards them. 'Last game is starting any minute.'

'So, people are... enjoying themselves?' said Lola, scepticism underlaying her words.

'Absolutely,' replied Lawrence.

'Really? I didn't think this would be your thing,' said Will, as though he couldn't tell whether his brother was actually telling the truth.

Lawrence nodded. 'Sure. I haven't had this much fun sober since I was thirteen and Dad paid for us to have a tour of *The Fresh Prince of Bel Air* set. Although I do think that the majority of people in this room think your Magic Mike chap is a character actor as opposed to a genuine native of Skegness. I heard someone claim they'd seen him on *Live at the Apollo* earlier,' said Lawrence.

Ottilie stretched like a cat and picked up the chunky dabber. 'I guess I could give it another go.' Will grinned and kissed her on the cheek.

Poppy leant back to speak covertly with Lola. 'What's happening with the quartet?'

'We picked them up from Brixham, but by the time we got

them to the harbour here it was bloody obvious that they were off their tits on some bathtub cider that they'd picked up from a farm shop whilst they waited for us. Five quid for three litres. Objectively, a bargain, but now they haven't even got the coordination to play "Hot Cross Buns" on a recorder. Between the quartet and pound-shop Magic Mike, I didn't anticipate that classical musicians would embarrass themselves first.' Lola jerked her head, indicating that she wanted Poppy to follow her. By an open window at the edge of the room, she turned her back to the table. 'Why is Ottilie saying she organised the bingo?'

'No idea. Although I wouldn't point it out now; it'll break Will's heart. He's having the time of his life.'

The sound of heavy breathing signified Mike's return to the stage, accompanied by an unnecessary pirouette from Crystal.

'Here we go, folks! The jackpot prize game. Ooh-er. Whoever wins, just a note that we prefer tips in cash. All right, eyes down!'

'I'm going to watch from over there,' said Lawrence, tipping his glass of water into a flower arrangement as he got up. He reached the bar, or more specifically, he reached the waitress behind the bar and gestured to his empty glass with a coy smile. A hush descended in the room.

'Man alive, fifty-five.'

The soft squish of dabbers sounded around the room. Poppy sat back down and looked at the scorecard Josie had given her. One down.

'Unlucky for some, thirteen.'

Poppy dabbed again.

'You're missing them, Ottie,' whispered Will, placing two fingers on her card to mark the numbers whilst he kept up with his own.

'No more fun, thirty-one.'

Three out of three.

'Okay, okay. I think I'm winning. Am I winning?' said Ottilie, dabbing two more numbers on her card.

'I don't know, Poppy looks pretty sharp.'

Poppy missed a number, but her heart was racing. Three numbers stood between her and more money than she'd ever had in her savings. But even if she did win, she shouldn't accept it, should she? She wasn't strictly a guest. She wasn't strictly working, either. If the booked photographer arrived tomorrow and relieved her from this strange purgatory she found herself in, she couldn't do it with thousands of pounds stuffed in her hiking boots.

'Sock on the door, number four.'

Another one down. Will looked at her card, eyes wide. Chatter buzzed like sandflies hovering above the bowed heads of the guests. At the other end of the room, the gilded double doors that separated the dining hall and the atrium swung back and forth like a metronome, the back of Lawrence's head disappearing as he passed through. Ottilie slowly placed the cap on her pen and closed her eyes.

'Are you okay?' Poppy asked.

'I think I'm getting a migraine,' said Ottilie, pinching her nose.

'This is so close! Poppy, how many have you got left?' said Will.

Poppy looked down. 'One.' Her heart raced. She felt like someone had punched a shot of adrenaline straight into her chest.

'I'm going to bed,' said Ottilie. Poppy and Will caught eyes, confused. On second look, she was quite pale.

'Not yet, Ottie. You might win. You're two numbers away,' said Will, trying to listen and talk at the same time.

'I'm only going to kill the mood if I stay.'

'But—'

'Honestly, I really feel quite ill. I think… air. Some air. You stay. Have fun. Sorry.'

Josie cleared her throat as Ottilie pushed her chair back and took quick, short strides to a service door that led outside.

'Christ alive! Number five.'

Over on Lord Mountgrave's table, a slow thud built across the room as a gaggle of middle-aged men hit the table with the sides of their fists, empty wine bottles and crystal glasses tinkling with each pound.

'Up to tricks, forty-six.'

'She's got it,' said Will.

Poppy's stomach swooped. Around her, the thudding had mingled with cheers and groans of defeat. She looked at her card, but she still had one gap to fill.

'It's Ottilie. Ottilie's won! She's won!' Will stood on his chair to wave his fiancée's card in the air. When the guests saw that it was him, a handful of whoops transitioned to affectionate coos as a tinny recording of Cliff Richard's 'Congratulations' played from the portable speakers.

'Someone get champagne down here!' said Mike, pointing at Will.

Thirty-three. Poppy only needed the number thirty-three. She shivered as a salty breeze made its way into the room and settled on her clammy skin.

'Hard luck, kid,' said Josie. 'Still, who wants to deal with all that loose change?'

'Where's our winner? Come on now, I won't mention nothin' to the Chancellor!'

Will hovered in a half-stand and pointed to the scorecard. He tried to explain who it belonged to above cheers amplified by free wine, but at this stage, no one cared if his claim was legitimate.

Crystal walked hip first between the tables, grabbed a fistful of notes from the ice bucket left on Lawrence's empty chair, and threw them in the air.

'Take a picture!' shouted Lord Mountgrave, appearing at Poppy's shoulder.

'What?'

'A picture! Take one! Your job, you know?'

Poppy clumsily grappled with the lens cap in her haste to pick up her camera. By the time she lifted the viewfinder to her eye, a month's worth of wages had fluttered to the table in front of her. Poppy had an acute sense that she was entirely in the wrong place. Worse, she felt downright stupid. Stupid for feeling like she was part of this charade, stupid for smiling, stupid for the times that she'd scanned the pavement for pennies as a child to hide in an old Polly Pocket.

Poppy skirted around Will as he was led to the stage through a tunnel of back slaps and two-fingered whistles. What was she doing here, on Loxby? She had left the claustrophobia of home to give herself space to think, alone. If that was a test, she was surely failing. If she could learn to be comfortable on her own, she might not find the rest of her life so utterly terrifying. What had she proven so far? That after all this, she still didn't have the power to say no?

Poppy found Lola leaning against a pillar. They looked on as the celebration continued with a pop of champagne and an eruption of froth that saw Will standing in what was likely the most expensive puddle in England.

A jaded barman sighed and rubbed his eyes with the heel of his palm. 'I guess that leaves me to mop up. My barmaid is missing in action. Again.'

'Why, where's she gone?' said Lola. Her tight dress creaked as she stretched her arms above her head.

'She wandered off to get a crate of tonic water and took the owner's son with her. Floppy hair. Half the buttons undone on his shirt. Lawrence, is it? I would tell her not to come back tomorrow, but I can't afford to be a pair of hands down for good,' he said, tucking a blue roll under his arm.

'I guess more than one person got lucky tonight,' said Lola through a stifled yawn. 'Let's clock off. Walk me to bed, Pops? I can't feel my toes anymore and don't trust myself to get up three flights.' When they reached the marble atrium, Lola paused and took Poppy's hand. 'Hey, you did good tonight.'

'I didn't do anything. Just, sort of... pretended it was meant to be chaotic on purpose, like an immersive *Phoenix Nights* dinner experience.'

'Well, whatever you did, the result was a fucking triumph. You've saved my bacon, bish.'

Poppy knew that Lola was being sincere, but today a comment like that bounced off her forehead. She touched the ring that she wore on a long chain beneath her clothes, warm from the heat of her body. She didn't want to be a person who smarted at other people's success. She wanted to be pleased for Will. She wanted to experience second-hand excitement for the life he had with Ottilie. He deserved happiness, didn't he? But if that was the case, why had she not deserved hers?

Chapter Twenty

TWO DAYS BEFORE THE WEDDING

The open window greeted her with a glorious combination of clouds that painted the sky in broad, watercolour streaks of pastel pink and purple. Her head was heavy from the night before, so she pulled on some leggings, her trainers, and packed her camera into a compact rucksack that she'd swiped from Josh years before when a torn ligament had put an end to his fell-running career. For a moment, Poppy understood why someone would pay over five hundred pounds a night to stay in a sea view room on Loxby, even if the gulls had woken her up at five o'clock in the morning by screaming at each other from the cliff edge.

She took advantage of the quiet to slip outside undisturbed and back into an old routine, darting over the dials and buttons of her camera in a race to capture beetles and birds before they were spooked by the click of her shutter.

Poppy leant against a flint wall at the far end of the lawn and looked back at the hotel. Even though she had left the terrace house she shared with Josh, this felt like coming home. Her camera was as an anchor, thrown down to stop her from drifting further away from the person she had grown unfamiliar with. The scuffed strap that she'd picked up from a flea market sat warm and supple on the curve of her neck. After years spent lingering on the edges of town squares, city parks, and high streets, not having a camera to hand made her feel off-kilter. The further she stepped away from photography, the more she chopped up her passion to distribute amongst her students. Would she have reclaimed the title of photographer if Lola hadn't done it for her on the sea tractor? Poppy wasn't so sure.

Sea mist pulled tight around the hotel like someone had tucked it inside a blanket. She took a breath, raised her camera, and clicked. In the dawn light, Loxby was astoundingly beautiful. Poppy crouched. She sharpened her focus on the façade and clicked again. The clouds were perfectly mirrored in the second-floor windows, the rough silhouette of another early morning riser just visible behind the glass. Satisfied, she swung her camera onto her back, jogged down to the cove at the far end of the island, and back up by the avenue of palm trees that split the garden from the golf course. Her breath was sharp, her arms heavy from a burst of genuine exercise after so long spent maintaining her heart rate through constant low-key anxiety.

She paused on a platform framed by a pergola of grapevines and looked out at the sunrise as it burnt through the clouds with the promise of a hot and humid day. Over the last week, she had seen old connections forming again like lay lines after a heatwave. If she had gone to Orwell Island like she had intended, would she be feeling less like an uptight crab? Would she be ready to confront what she'd been through? Be prepared to return to half a home and the broken bits of her relationship? Attending someone else's wedding made Poppy face up to the legacy of her own. It wasn't an enviable comparison.

When a flash of white slipped out onto the terrace, Poppy's attention pulled away from the water. She wobbled on her tiptoes to look down the length of the hotel, where Ottilie skittered down stairs and across the lawn. Poppy brought her camera to her eye and twisted the lens to zoom in, but didn't click. Through the viewfinder, she saw Ottilie pinch the bridge of her nose and press the heels of her hands to her eyes. Pausing by the grotto, she dropped her head back, face tilted towards the newly broken sun, her chest heaving with jagged breaths. Poppy didn't move. If Ottilie spotted her, she'd have to explain why she was hidden in a grapevine with one leg wrapped around a pillar and a telescopic lens balanced in her palm.

Ottilie bit her lip, glanced back at the hotel, and quick-walked out of sight, disappearing down a path that led to the fisherman's hut. Working with teenagers had exposed Poppy to a jumble of unfiltered emotions, often triggered by seemingly disconnected events. It was like fusion cooking, but for feelings. Anger with elation (inter-school football leagues), jealousy with kindness (year nine girls), and hilarity with fear (sex education). What she saw in Ottilie was hard to place. Her shoulders were tight, her chin high, and her cheeks wet. With the wedding two days away, a certain level of friction was to be expected, but this seemed like something else.

Poppy hopped down from the pergola, unscrewed her lens, and tucked it away in her rucksack. Her hunger mounted. If she was quick, she'd be able to swipe a roll and a slice of pre-cut cheese from the continental breakfast bar before it reached the dining room.

As she rounded the corner, Poppy yawned. On the terrace, Will was doing the same.

'Snap,' he said, pointing at her from a distance.

'Fancy seeing you here,' said Poppy, her voice upbeat to disguise the fact that she had seen Ottilie just moments before. 'Early riser?'

'Not usually. I know a lot has changed over the past decade, but me getting up early?' Will grimaced. 'Unless there's a tennis game on in a different time zone, there's no chance.'

'Or if you never managed to go to bed in the first place?'

Will rubbed his chin and shook his head as though remembering something. 'Yeah, I remember a few of those. What was our old routine? Get to the club at nine—'

'Dance for two hours—'

'A shot of sambuca at eleven to get us through—'

'—until midnight, when we'd leave on a high, dignity intact, and get a footlong Subway on the way home, split down the middle. BBQ sauce at your end, piri-piri at mine, lettuce, sweetcorn, and black olives down the middle. Classy.'

'Oh, yeah. So classy we never did manage to verify the meat inside. Who knows what we were eating?'

Will laughed and shook his head, but his eyes were clouded. He fell quiet as they passed beneath bedroom windows. Poppy thought he might veer back towards the hotel, but he stepped down into a herb garden that she hadn't noticed before, the plants set out in ruler-straight lines with neat terracotta stakes listing the Latin names of each. Will plucked a basil leaf, scrunched it in his hand, and dropped it on the floor. Poppy could tell that he wanted to talk but didn't know how to start.

'Did you sleep well?' Poppy said.

'Not really. I've never spent so many nights alone as I have this week.'

Poppy ran her hand over a tufted head of lavender and offered a weak laugh, unsure how to gauge the tone of Will's statement. 'It's a lot, isn't it?'

Will nodded. 'She can be.'

'I meant weddings in general,' Poppy said in a rush. 'It's why honeymoons exist. Everyone thinks it's for the *romance*, but a honeymoon's base function is to put distance between you and another discussion about which gluten-free, vegan option is best for the second cousin you haven't seen since you were a kid.'

'I sussed that pretty early on. I've been doing the "nod and say yes" approach for the last couple of months. It's not like I don't care about having the mood board wedding, except...'

'You don't care?'

Will wrinkled his nose in admission. 'Yeah. I don't care. I would have been happy to elope, but Ottilie said her parents would get upset. You've met her mum?' Poppy nodded. 'Exactly. There's a reason she was the most successful salesperson on QVC. On her own, she's also quite terrifying. It doesn't end here. We're meeting up with Ottie's parents partway through the honeymoon.'

'The in-laws? On your honeymoon? Are you into sadomasochism?'

'There's a reason, but I feel like it's not going to make me sound any better. You can't judge me for the next sentence, all right?'

'Okay, hit me.'

'They have a yacht docked in Bermuda. Therefore, it would be silly not to take them up on the offer of a charter,' said Will with mock affectation.

'Oh, la-di-da! My dad has a timeshare caravan in Hemsby, so if you fancy a holiday swap at any point, just let me know.'

Will laughed and rubbed his eyes. 'It might get to that stage.' He looked exhausted, his cheek imprinted with the faint outline of a creased pillow.

'Why, what's up? Everything cool?' Poppy fiddled with the straps on her rucksack. She was secretly pleased that Will was on the verge of confiding in her. She hadn't felt useful to anyone for a long time.

'You spent some time with Ottie down at the cove the other day, didn't you?'

'Yeah. She made me a cucumber spritzer and the sight of her in a bikini left me with the creeping feeling that I should take squats more seriously.'

'And she seemed okay?'

Poppy thought back to the faces of Will's fiancée that she'd borne witness to in the past forty-eight hours. She seemed most comfortable down by the water, away from everyone else. At most, Ottilie seemed overwhelmed by the number of cogs involved in the Mountgrave machine that ticked on around her, but it wasn't as though her family were strangers to large-scale business. Perhaps Poppy had misunderstood her. When it came to this morning's sighting, Poppy held back. She didn't want to act as a go-between any more than she was already. Lola's rule was to stay out of other people's relationship drama, so that's what she would do too.

'She was fine. Nervous, but not weirdly so. I'll be honest, I didn't spend that much time with her so I'm not sure how useful my assessment is.' Poppy pulled back. 'She seemed a bit down towards the end of the bingo last night, but there might not be anything in it. Did you tell her she'd won?'

Will nodded, a brief smile on his face. 'Yeah. She loves winning. Naturally, she was fuming she'd mistimed her departure.' He put his hands in his pockets, elbows turned out. 'I don't know, I've definitely sensed a negative vibe. Something's changed.'

'If you want to offload, I'm all ears. Better to do it now than at the altar.'

Will fidgeted and pushed air into his cheeks, releasing it with a long sigh like a slowly deflating balloon.

'Okay, here's the thing. I find her *so* hard to read. I'm worried that seeing my family all in one place has been a baptism of fire and now she's freaking out about legally being part of it. When you become a Mountgrave, you get a few years on the bench and then you're pulled up to play. I didn't think about how that might affect her. It's different for me; I don't have a choice.'

'Don't you? What about Josie? She seems pretty happy commentating from the sidelines.'

Will laughed. 'If that's the impression you've got, she's put on a good performance. She's the Foundation's largest shareholder. It's *why* she doesn't have to get her hands dirty. It's also why Dad can't stand the fact that she turned up unannounced. I love Josie, but she and Dad are like either end of a pantomime horse. It's funny to watch them in the same room, but functionally it doesn't work.'

'As a person who grew up watching *The Simple Life* with Paris and Nicole, I'm pretty sure you can still maintain a job if you're an heiress. When you're that rich, everything you do is a hobby, isn't it? It's minimum pressure for maximum reward.'

'Except, where's the choice? You're not making me feel *more* positive about the future,' said Will. 'It's like those puzzles you get on the back of cereal boxes. It looks like there are loads of paths, but only one actually ends up at the pot of gold.'

'Who cares if there's no choice; it's a pot of gold.'

Will sighed and rubbed the back of his neck.

'Sorry! I didn't mean it like that. I guess I'm still struggling to see you as a multi-millionaire international businessman.'

'That's probably because I'm not. This lifestyle agrees with Ottilie far better than it does me. It was different when we first got together. I met her in London – Lawrence introduced us – and right after that we were chasing summer around the world, volunteering and remote working. I don't want to go into too much detail because it's not my story to tell, but she's not had it easy in life, despite what everyone thinks. Since we came back from Laos, it's like the world has shifted on an axis even though we haven't moved. I know this is a proper "tiny violin" moment, but Dad hasn't exactly let me figure out what I want to do. I told him years ago that I don't have a business head, but he's pulling me into 'informal chats' with his colleagues almost every other day and I leave worrying that I've let him down, even though I'm not sure what I was supposed to be doing in the first place. Ottilie has been so busy preparing for the wedding that I've barely seen her. Oh, and apparently we feature in dodgy tabloid articles now, which my mates send me links to thinking it's hilarious.'

'Not the Sidebar of Shame?' asked Poppy.

'Yes, the Sidebar of Shame,' said Will.

'I bet no one reads them except for saddos with no purpose in their life.' Poppy visited such websites at least once a day, but would never admit to it.

Will ran both hands through his hair, his curls bouncy in the damp morning air. 'I get photographed nowadays. Not in a cool *The World's Eye* way, but in a middle-aged-man-hiding-behind-your-recycling-bin kind of way.'

'That's insane,' said Poppy. 'I had no idea this was the world you came from when we were at university. I'm guessing you don't like the attention.'

'Would you?'

'My students once made a TikTok of me topping up my deodorant in the store cupboard and that was a bleak few months of internet fame. I can't imagine what it's like when strangers make up gossip columns about you.'

'I have no idea what they get out of it. I try to absorb all the stress to stop Ottilie from feeling it. Maybe it comes across as being overly laid-back, but it's only because I'm acting as a buffer to protect her. I don't know, I feel like it's not enough sometimes. I feel like *I'm* not enough sometimes.' Will sat on a low wall, pulled a rosemary sprig from the border, and plucked its leaves off one by one. If you swapped the balloon sleeves for a crumpled T-shirt, Will looked like a lovelorn Regency hero.

'Did you ever feel like that? With Josh? Don't answer if you don't want to.'

'No, it's fine.' Poppy sat opposite him and leant forward. 'I did and I didn't. I put him on a pedestal, for sure. You remember what he was like, right?'

'Josh? Oh, yeah. I remember,' he said, a sarcastic undertone to his voice. Poppy found a basal defensiveness rippling below the surface. She pushed it to the side.

'Whatever way you look at it, I always craved stability,' she said. 'I craved not being the one making decisions all the time. I never had that in my life. He was overprotective and that felt like a compliment. Over time, he swallowed me up vertebra by vertebra until I didn't have a backbone. And I barely resisted.'

Will softened. 'That surprises me. You were always self-assured at uni. Like, intimidatingly so.'

'A few people have said that. I still don't really know what it means.'

They fell into a comfortable silence, the waves lapping the cliffs on the other side of the fence. 'Did you ever bring it up with him? Josh?'

'I used to, but he was so good at arguing that somehow we'd end a conversation having both accepted blame for something he did.'

Will shook his head. 'You see, Ottilie and I... we don't argue. That's not her style. She grows pensive and distant. I think that can be worse. I'm wracking my brains over whether I've done something to annoy her, but even if I had, she wouldn't tell me, so I'm stuck.'

'Why wouldn't she tell you?'

'She likes to claim that everything is fine and then she'll text me a picture of our unmade bed a few days later with no context. I love her, but it can be a bit confusing. I don't know. I can be *too* chill. She keeps me on my toes.'

'Yeah, I'll say. Have you tried having a direct conversation? You know, on a day when you *have* made the bed, so she hasn't got one hand on the shotgun.'

'I tried that. Whenever I bring up anything that sounds like criticism, she lashes out and blames it on being a Gemini. I looked it up online and the thing that sticks out is that ninety-seven per cent of the world's dictators are also Gemini. In hindsight, I should have anticipated how that would be misinterpreted when I brought it up with her.'

'Linking her personality to Hitler isn't a great way to initiate domestic reparations, I'll give you that.'

Will exhaled sharply, his mouth tight. 'I'm not explaining myself very well. It's not like we've got this *big* relationship problem to solve. I worship that girl. But...'

'But?'

'I don't know how to finish that sentence.'

Poppy bit her lip and looked out to sea, which had slowly come into view as though dials on the horizon had been twisted into focus. Poppy wondered whether now was the right time to bring up her sighting of Ottilie. Did a right time exist? Would Will feel better or worse knowing that she'd seen his fiancée so upset?

Will looked so dejected, Poppy couldn't help but reach over to squeeze his arm. He looked at her hand and smiled.

'Hey, take it from me, the longer you leave awkward conversations, the harder they are to have,' she said.

He nodded. 'Thanks, I will. I'm probably overthinking everything, aren't I?'

'There you go. I'm sure there's nothing to worry about.'

Will rubbed his eyes and stretched. 'God, I wish there was a Subway on the island.'

'Me too,' said Poppy, thoughts drifting back to food.

'Fancy raiding the kitchens? I think there's a leftover tiramisu.'

'For breakfast? Absolutely.'

Chapter Twenty-One

'I f you could tuck your shirt in on the left?'

'My what?'

'Your shirt. I can see a bit of your stomach.'

Will disguised a laugh and rubbed his jaw, relaxing the pose he held.

'Ah, blast. It's one of those awful Balenciaga shirts. Not worth their weight in gold, not since they moved production to Indonesia. What does a man have to do for Italian tailoring made in Italy, hmm?' Lord Mountgrave jabbed at his shirt, tugged his blazer straight, and ran a spit-coated finger across his eyebrows. 'What about the boy? Is he all right?'

'Oh, he's fine.' Poppy smiled at Will from behind the camera as he groaned at his father. 'If you could chat whilst I move around you, that would be great. The lighting is so good, it's doing my job for me.'

'Did Julia give you the brief?'

'Yes,' said Poppy, although the neatly typed document she had been handed earlier was wish fulfilment more than anything else.

Poppy raised the viewfinder to her eye and shifted to the left to line up a golden ring of bokeh between the two men. As far as candid corporate shots went, she wasn't sure what message these were sending. Lord Mountgrave's arm was stiff around Will's shoulder, crumpling his linen suit with a sweaty palm. Will was lithe, tall, and broad-shouldered, a contrast to his stout and deep-jowled father.

'I think we need to try something else...' said Poppy, tapping her flip-flop against the terracotta tiles.

'Shall I get him to sit down?' asked Lord Mountgrave. Will's lips twitched with a wry smile.

'We could do that, but how about if *you* sit down? Lean forward, elbows on knees? Will could stand to the side. It would give me great angles – and present a kinship between the two of you. Quiet, but powerful.'

'No, no. Better if Will sits. I don't want to look like I'm ailing. It sends the wrong message.'

Will perched on the edge of a flower bed and winced. 'I can't sit here for long. I'm getting penetrated by a shard of flint.'

Poppy stood back and crouched beside a Greek pot so large she could safely climb inside. She fell into a rhythm, clicking and twisting. For someone who observed so much, this was a job that appealed to her natural instincts, the good and the bad. You could tell a lot about a person by the way they reacted when the shutter sounded. Her father scowled and told her to sod off. Lola sucked herself in and up, her curves accentuated by a waspish waist. Lord Mountgrave barely flinched, but Will constantly fidgeted, self-consciousness colouring his cheeks.

Lord Mountgrave tilted his head and lowered his voice, but not quietly enough to stop Poppy from hearing.

'Try to keep a lid on this business with Lawrence, will you?'

Will maintained a neutral expression. 'There is no business.'

'There are lots of people here, son.'

'Mm. I'm aware.' He glanced in Poppy's direction. She stayed behind the camera, thighs screaming from the squatted stance she held to avoid a purple flowered cactus protruding from the rockery behind her.

'I don't want it to look like we're at each other's throats as a family,' said Lord Mountgrave.

'Have you given Josie that memo?'

'That's different. You have to handle Lawrence with a little more care. He's a good talker. There's a lot you can learn from him, you know. He can get an investor to sign over seed funds between sets at the French Open. Extraordinary. He has a chip on his shoulder, mind, and he can royally piss someone off if the mood takes him. I say the same to him, you know. He can learn from you. As much as he tries to convince us otherwise, he's not an idiot. He knows how much money I've spent on keeping him on the straight and narrow, and out of the papers.'

'Do you think that might be the problem?'

'Not at all. He's grateful. Who else is going to give him something to do, eh? This is a big moment for our family. For the company. On Sunday I'm going to announce my decision as to who will succeed me as CEO, but we both know it's not going to be him. Are you marking me, Will? The board want to see a fresh face behind the desk. Someone in the family who isn't a loose cannon. We need to avoid unnecessary squabbles. Timing is everything.'

'I'd say so. We *are* here for my wedding after all. Last night was supposed to be transition day,' said Will, speaking with careful articulation.

'Yes, well,' muttered his father, as though he hadn't heard. He took a deep breath, his shirt straining to reveal a fuzz of white hair between his buttonholes. 'When you're settled in the company, you'll know what I mean. Weddings *are* business, if done right. I think the world of Ottilie. She's exceptionally good for you, like your mother was for me.'

'I'm not sure Mum shares that opinion.'

'Don't play us off against each other – it's not a good look. Is she still planning on coming?'

'Yes, obviously. Not until Saturday morning, though.'

Lord Mountgrave nodded sagely but made no further comment. 'Are we done?' he said, tapping his thigh. Poppy stood, her ears burning. She flicked through the photographs and noted the tightness in Will's jaw, the cavalier expression on his father's face as he casually berated his son.

'Just a few more. How about the two of you looking over the railing out to sea?'

They readjusted, Will reluctantly so.

'Look, I know Ottilie is a feisty girl, but don't do what I did and imagine your problems away. Wrangle some control back into your court. There's more than one way to fuck up a marriage. I should know. I've fucked up three.' He scoffed, a short exhale from the back of his throat. 'Here's some advice,' Lord Mountgrave said, his voice soft. He sounded on the verge of sincerity. Will leant in to listen. 'There are two things worth investing in: newspapers and partners.'

Will held his hands up. 'Ah, here we go.'

'No, hear me out. One's there to keep your name out of the mud and the other dusts you off when you've taken a good shafting and need to be put to bed.'

'I've got no idea what you're talking about, Dad. It sounds a lot like you've been going to illegal sex parties.'

Lord Mountgrave fumbled and glanced back at Poppy. She busied herself with the dials on her camera.

'What am I trying to say?' He tapped his signet ring on the metal banister.

'I haven't got a clue, Dad.'

Lord Mountgrave clicked his fingers. 'Don't fuck it up, son.

Ottilie is your best chance. Your best PR. I was good at getting them, just not keeping them. I sat on the wrong eggs.'

'I'm marrying Ottilie, not trying to hatch her,' said Will, rubbing his face. He didn't sound angry, more exasperated.

'Speaking of good PR.' Lord Mountgrave readjusted his pocket square as his publicist walked towards them, her steps purposeful and cat-like as though someone had smacked each hip with a horse whip.

'The Spruces want a word with you, Colin,' she said, blinking behind thick-rimmed orange glasses.

'Right you are.' Lord Mountgrave sniffed deeply. 'Julia. Crumb check.' The publicist lowered her glasses and flicked a singular speck from the padded shoulders of his jacket. 'Right. Off we go. Will, I'll debrief with you afterwards.'

'You don't have to, Dad.'

'Nonsense. You need to start listening to the cogs in the machine. Tick tock.'

Lord Mountgrave trotted down the steps like a fluffed-up pigeon, chest out, chin tucked.

Will sighed.

'I'm not sure I was meant to hear any of that,' said Poppy.

'Probably not. I'm kind of glad you did, though. I've been convincing myself otherwise, but now I'm more sure than ever that when I told Dad I didn't want to work for him, he heard "I desperately want to head the company one day."'

Poppy removed the lens of her camera with a satisfying clunk and nestled it inside its padded bag. 'I'd actually go one step further and say you're already working for him.'

Will made a noise that verged on a growl and scratched his neck. He unbuttoned his cuffs and pushed his sleeves up to the elbow, exposing his muscled forearms. 'I need to get out of my head. I've got an idea. If you disappear for a couple of hours, Lola won't come and yell at me, will she?'

'No. Lola posts an itinerary under the bedroom door before my alarm goes off each morning and there's nothing on there for the next few hours except "independent free time". I feel like I'm on a really weird school trip. I get told when to eat, what to do, and where to do it. In a way, I like being overscheduled. It doesn't give me any time to think.'

'That's what I need. Less thinking. How do you feel about going... off plan?'

Poppy put her hands in her pockets and swayed from side to side. 'Does it involve wearing trousers specific to a sport? Because we might need to build up to that,' she said.

'No trousers at all, actually,' said Will. Poppy raised her eyebrows. 'How do you feel about surfing?'

Chapter Twenty-Two

'Where is this from, the children's section?' said Poppy. She pulled at the arms of the wetsuit, but the crotch stayed resolutely between her knees. 'I feel like a banana being shoved through a keyhole.'

'Do you need some help?'

'Unless you can stuff me inside this thing, I'm not sure how much help you'll be.'

Will gave her a bashful smile as he pulled at a cord between his shoulder blades, zipping his wetsuit up to the neck in one graceful arc. Poppy listened back to herself, cheeks increasingly hot.

'Give me a minute. Don't look. This isn't very dignified.' She wiggled the suit up from her ankles inch by inch, her nails slipping on the well-worn neoprene.

'Ready?'

'No! Don't look!'

'I'm not!'

After a few well-placed karate jabs, her fingers appeared wriggling at the end of the sleeves. 'Can you zip me? If I bend at the waist, I may pass out.'

Will tugged at the cord, his fingertips warm against her skin as his thumb ran along the inside of her collar. Poppy took a sharp intake of breath.

'Ah, sorry,' he said, standing back.

'What?'

'This *is* a junior wetsuit. I've just seen the label.'

'I knew there was a reason I couldn't fill my lungs to capacity,' said Poppy, tugging her hair out from the rubber seal around her neck. 'Well, I'm not taking it off now. You'll have to cut me out if it comes to it.'

Will bit his bottom lip, his cheeks dimpled. It triggered a jolt in Poppy's stomach that she hadn't expected. 'I'll carry your board to make up for it,' he said, hoisting the surfboard under his arm.

The sand was warm in the shallows as they paddled out into the bay, each stroke awakening Poppy's muscle memory. A flipbook of her pre-teen summers in Devon flashed behind her eyes: her borrowed, battered surfboard by the caravan steps, lunch made up from other people's leftover chips, licking Calippo juice from her wrist, hair stiff with salt crystals, the hurt when her parents didn't think to ask what time they should expect her home.

Will sculled to face the shore and straddled his board with well-practised dexterity. Poppy did the same, her suit squeaking as she strained to get her leg over.

'Looks like we scared the waves off,' he said.

'Shame they're a prerequisite for surfing.' Poppy used one hand to try and subtly loosen the material around her crotch.

'I'm not bothered if you're not. It's nice to be out on the water.' A gentle swell passed beneath them. Their boards bumped noses.

'What was going on up there?' asked Poppy, nodding towards the island.

'What, with Dad?' Will rubbed the back of his head with his knuckles. 'It's what it looks like, I guess. I figure he wants me to be the next CEO of the company. It wouldn't happen right away, but still. He has this idea to put me through an intensive five-year training programme so I can step up when he steps out. Thing is, I haven't earnt it and I'm not interested. I want to do something that makes me happy. I don't want to be responsible for the livelihoods of thousands of people. There are *Macbeth* levels of in-house scheming at The Mountgrave Foundation.'

'I don't remember that play having a happy ending.'

'No shit. Everyone dies.'

'Right,' said Poppy, clicking her fingers.

'I know the company's success comes from Dad's total obsessive focus. It's basically a job requirement. But me?'

Poppy sculled, turning her board around to face him. 'Knowing you at eighteen, I wouldn't say that obsessive focus came to you naturally, unless it was *Mario Kart*.'

'Exactly! Oh, here's one.'

Poppy looked at the wave that rushed towards their feet. She rocked down onto her stomach, but before she could get to her knees, the power died and slipped beneath her board. Will paddled back to meet her, water dripping from his angular chin. For a moment, Poppy couldn't feel the painfully cold water against her bare feet. She broke eye contact, pushing her hair back over her shoulders.

'Would working with your dad be *that* bad?' she asked.

'This is the thing. It's not exactly following him down the mines, is it? It's so privileged to be offered a job like that on a plate, but it's not what I want to do. One, I'd be shit at his job, and two, I'd hate myself for doing it.'

'You need to tell him,' said Poppy, her voice soft.

'I don't know how I'm going to convince him. I do ad hoc research for climate charities, but Dad thinks it's a power move to piss him off. The explanation is never enough. He wants proof that I've found something better than what he can offer me.'

'You don't owe him one. You know what he told you about "wrangling control back", well here you go. You'd be doing what he's been *encouraging* you to do this whole time.'

'He's literally a world leader in negotiation. It makes arguments pretty fucking impossible.'

'Well then, he can't give you that kind of advice and then dictate how you use it. I know it's as appealing as snogging a dead octopus, but I think you need to tell him you don't want to be CEO, now or ever.'

Will gripped the sides of his surfboard until his knuckles grew pale. 'That's so far from the dynamics of how we work as a family. You've probably figured out by now that our relationship is still fairly new. I've seen him more in the past year than I have my whole life. Growing up, Mum would have flight details sent through by one of his secretaries so I could see him for a weekend, albeit in between meetings. I'd get odd, expensive Christmas presents that I never wanted to open in front of Mum. I've always gone along with it. Done what he wanted. It's better than nothing, isn't it?'

'Why? Does it have to be that black and white? Everyone gets to piss their dad off a little bit, especially when you're a teenager.'

'Did you?'

Poppy scooped the water beside her knees and let it drain through her fingers, the sun glistening through each droplet. 'Not really. Never had a chance. The parent–child relationship in our house sort of… flipped when Mum left. Dad's been trying to balance the scales ever since I became an adult, which complicates things even more.'

Will lay back on his board and closed his eyes, arms tucked under his head. 'It's not just him. Ottilie thinks I should take up the offer. Show some more enthusiasm. Even if I did want to be CEO one day, it has to be approved by the board and she doesn't think they take me seriously as it is. I'm still figuring out what I want to do. Ottie thinks I'm being stubborn, but I'm not. Dad's got a big press conference planned the day after the wedding and won't tell me what it involves, so that's more than a little terrifying.'

'I'll agree that the timing could be better,' said Poppy, 'but if you don't want to have this hanging over your head on Saturday whilst you're trying to remember your vows, I'd say something now.'

Will opened one eye, his lips slightly parted. 'Since when did you get so wise?'

'I always was,' said Poppy, snorting a laugh. 'Saying that, there is a difference between giving advice and acting on it. I talk a big talk, but as soon as I'm faced with any sort of confrontation, I go all flimsy like damp cardboard.'

'I don't believe that. This coming from the woman who organised an occupation when the campus staff wouldn't call an exterminator to deal with the rats in our building?'

'It takes a lot of energy to remind yourself who you are after taking so many tiny steps away from it.'

Will sat up. 'Wow. Deep.'

'Is it? I thought it was quite shallow around here,' said Poppy, leaning over the side of her board to look down at the seabed below.

'Ha. Good one.' Will groaned, reached above his head, and stretched his neck one way, then the other. 'I'll try and speak to Dad tonight. Let's hope it's not another conversation that's bound to blow up in my face.'

'I'm guessing that chat with Ottilie didn't go too well?'

Will's voice slipped into a higher octave. 'Yeah, you could say that. She said I was having a beta-male moment and I needed to think about the big picture.'

'What's the big picture?'

'I'm not sure. She used a lot of hand gestures, like she was conjuring a tornado. I didn't press for an explanation.'

'If it's any consolation, a beta male is not a bad thing. Josh called himself a "natural alpha" on more than one occasion. He had a massive tattoo of a howling wolf on his forearm that he used to call his she-wolf. So at least you're leagues below him on the Leader Board of Toxic Masculinity.'

'True. Besides, it's not just for me, is it? If I get straight with Dad, it might help my case with Ottilie. She gets wound up by how limp-wristed I can be around him. She gets wound up by a lot of what I do at the moment. But hey, one problem at a time, right?' Will scrubbed the back of his head with his knuckles..

Behind her, Poppy heard water surging towards them. 'Here we go, this is it!' she said. Before she was able to kick herself away from Will's board, he clasped her hand and ran his thumb across her knuckles. Warmth unfurled in her chest like a cat turning over on a sunny windowsill. Poppy's mind raced. What was he doing? The water rushing in her ears suggested this wasn't the time to think about it.

Realising too late, they leant forward and began to paddle furiously, pushing off their boards as the wave broke and tripped over itself. She popped up to a standing position, knees bent, hurtling forwards as the water roared beneath her feet. In her head, she was tracing a line in a barrel wave, her legs long and lean, hair pushed back from her face as beachcombers looked on in awe. The reality was quite different.

Poppy's suit was so tight it felt like a resistance band had been stretched between her knees. With one foot stuck on the edge, her board swerved and dipped, her control over its direction entirely futile. She slammed onto her elbows, hip bruised, a curtain of wet hair stuck to her face as Will careered towards her. The wave lost momentum as Will's board rode up and over the tip of hers, bringing them both to a stop as they tumbled into waist-high water. Poppy's fall was cushioned by Will's stomach; he took the full impact of her knees when the strap around her ankle tightened as her board tugged at the end of its cord. She untangled herself and rolled onto her back, pulling Will with her. He pushed himself up, one hand by her shoulder, the other by her waist. She felt the pressure of his chest against hers, the wispy clouds obscured as he dripped saltwater into her eyes.

'It looked a lot easier in *Point Break*,' said Will, his voice raw.

Poppy nodded in agreement, momentarily distracted by a droplet of water that hung from Will's lower lip.

'We can put this down as training for the fifty-year storm,' she said. Will laughed. The droplet fell and landed on her nose.

A cough from the shore made them jump. Will bolted upright, leaving two imprints in the sand where his hands had been. His expression hardened as he staggered to his feet, offering Poppy a hand. She was glad of it. The ability to bend her knees was severely in question.

'Um, hi,' said Ottilie. She held a length of hair behind her ear to keep it from whipping across her face.

'Hey!' replied Poppy, instantly annoyed at how quickly she'd switched into a tone of voice that made her sound culpable in something she wasn't. Ottilie didn't return her smile.

'Are you heading back up?' said Ottilie.

'Who, me?' asked Poppy.

'Either, both...' said Ottilie, her mouth a thin line, eyes wide as she looked between Poppy and Will.

'Yeah, sure. Poppy, you go ahead. I'll sort the kit out,' said Will, nodding towards the mess of cord tangled at their feet. 'Is everything all right, Ottie?'

'Sure, sure, it's good. I'm just worried, that's all. Will and I are acutely aware that we've asked you to sacrifice a lot to be here, Poppy, and I just wanted to say thank you, for everything. First the photos, and now Will is convincing you to jump into the English Channel when I'm sure you'd rather be elsewhere.'

'No, it's fine. I'm used to the sea. I spent summers—'

'It looks like Christian is on his way,' interrupted Ottilie. 'The photographer. The real one. He should arrive sometime in the next twenty-four hours, at which point, you're off the hook.'

Poppy nodded and gave a too-quick smile. It was one thing changing her plans to be here, but to be dismissed so casually felt worse, like she was surplus to requirement. One side of her wanted to witness her old friend expand his bubble of joy as he crept closer to his wedding day, but the other side knew that she'd be watching through her fingers with a lump in her throat.

'Isn't that great, Will?' prompted Ottilie.

'Yeah, yeah. Although…'

'What?'

'Poppy *can* stay, if she wants to. I'm sure Lola wouldn't mind you bunking with her. Why don't you stay for the wedding?' said Will.

'Perhaps Poppy doesn't want to? You shouldn't feel obliged, I mean. I'm sure you'd rather be off with your puffins. That is *why* you came to the south coast, isn't it?' This wasn't so much a question as a retrieval of evidence.

Poppy rubbed her hand across her collarbone, her chest unusually flat and box-like under the tight wetsuit. 'I'm glad I was able to help you guys out. If you need me to stay, go, whatever, it's all good.'

'You've already gone above and beyond, Pops,' said Will. 'But please think about whether you'd like to come to the wedding.'

'All right, don't pressure the poor girl. You'll have her complaining to Lola and we don't want to add to *that* burden.'

'What do you mean by that?' said Poppy.

'She's getting a little hollow-eyed. I don't want her to burn out before Saturday. The ceremony is finely tuned, what with the floating pontoon and paddleboards. I don't want to worry about whether the tide will rush in at the wrong time.'

'It's really heart-warming to see you so invested in the wellbeing of my friend,' said Poppy, her voice level. Ottilie blinked, taken aback. She could cope with being dismissed, but she wouldn't let Ottilie talk badly about Lola when she'd seen first-hand how much energy she had poured into the whims of a budgetless bride.

'I've got to say, Ottie. I'm with Poppy on this one,' said Will. 'You've overstepped a line there.'

For a few seconds, they stood in awkward silence. Ottilie ran her tongue across her teeth. 'You know what, you're right. I'm being unfair. Actually, I wondered if you'd walk back up to the hotel with me, Poppy? There's something I'm keen to talk over.'

Poppy nodded. She went to change behind the shack, loosening the Velcro from around her ankle to peel off the wetsuit, which was a far easier task than it had been to get into. She left it draped over a chair and pulled her sundress over her head, which stuck uncomfortably to her tacky, salt-licked skin.

Ottilie sat on the steps that curved away from the beach, a haughty look on her face. Despite the fact that she was younger than Poppy, Ottilie had 'middle-class mum waiting for a late Waitrose delivery' energy that seemed at odds with an environment so serene.

When Poppy emerged, Will waved to her from the shallows, his wetsuit pulled down to the waist.

'I want to discuss shots for Saturday,' said Ottilie, her eyes fixed on Will.

'Saturday?' Poppy was confused. Unless she was mistaken, Ottilie had made it quite clear that she wasn't keen to have her on the island for much longer.

'The ceremony?' said Ottilie. She gripped Poppy's wrist and pulled her behind a rocky overhang.

'Woah, what are you doing?' said Poppy.

'I need to ask you something.'

'Okay…'

'Can I come to your room tonight?'

'It's not my room really. When Christian Withers turns up, I'll have to bunk with Lola but hold on – I'm a bit confused about whether you want me here or not. You said the photographer was on the way? The *real* one,' she added, somewhat pettily.

'No, he is. But that's not the reason.' Ottilie's eyes were glassy, her lips bee-sting full. 'I don't want to sound dramatic, but if I don't speak to you tonight, I may not be here tomorrow. I'll come to your room. Don't tell anyone I'm there and make sure you're alone.'

'What's going on? You're freaking me out.'

'Shh, just tell me if you can or not. Please. I don't know who else I can trust.'

A headache pressed at Poppy's temples. The face slap of water combined with Ottilie's guilt-inducing doe eyes had caught her off guard. Was this something to do with Will? If Ottilie opened up to her, perhaps she could mediate a conversation between them?

'Okay, but if you've murdered someone, I'm not paddling the body out to sea. It's terrible for the environment.'

Chapter Twenty-Three

JUNE 14TH, 2011

Poppy clenched the pillow as Josh moved beneath the cover, her wedding band digging into her skin as she gripped the sheets. A swallow cheeped and trilled outside their balcony, the sound of a noisy market stall and Greek haggling drifting in through the open doors. Above the open window, a bow of pink flowers softened the sunlight that crept towards them. Heat from their entwined bodies hung in the air, air that Poppy gasped for as Josh pushed her knees towards her chest.

She gulped as though she were submerged in water, drowning in waves of overlapping pleasure until she thought she might burst. Poppy grappled for the back of Josh's head, pulling him up to her, legs hooked around his back. As her heartbeat dropped to a steady thrum in her chest, Josh slipped his arm under her head and dropped down onto the pillow with a self-satisfied groan.

'You look pleased with yourself,' said Poppy.

'As do you,' Josh replied. He kissed her shoulder and kicked the duvet to the floor, his leg settling between her knees. After three days on the island of Kefalonia, Poppy and Josh had slipped into a routine that ping-ponged between cooling swims in the

Ionian Sea, eating copious amounts of hummus, and frequently tangled bedsheets.

Josh pushed himself up and reached for the bedside table, where Poppy had left a paper bag of fresh fruit from the market earlier that day. His stomach muscles tensed as he fished inside with one hand and picked out a fig. After shuffling close to her, Josh pushed his thumbs into the flesh, and split it in two, handing half to Poppy before biting into his own. She grinned at her husband.

Although now entirely at ease, Poppy had been nervous about leaving for their honeymoon after a wedding that wasn't short of drama. Her aunt had been bullish, her drunk father had been put in a taxi by nine o'clock, and Lola had spent an hour in the toilets with Josh's mum, who was bawling over the bridesmaids' hemlines not matching. It had taken nearly ten days for the lingering anxiety to recede. Through it all, Josh had been steadfast and attentive, smoothing out her worries with inexhaustive reassurances that nothing else would fall apart when they left for their honeymoon. He even drove to her father's house with a boot full of batch-cooked dinners after Poppy worried that Tony Pascoe would forget to cook for himself, having slipped into a reclusive period as he so often did after big family events.

Josh pulled Poppy onto his chest and slowly ran a finger up the back of her neck as they listened to the burble filter in from outside. When a knock at the door fractured their stupor, Josh groaned.

'Did you order room service?' asked Poppy.

'Nope,' said Josh, shrugging.

'Will you get it?' she said.

'You get it.'

'I'm very naked.'

'So am I.'

'I have two bits to cover up. You have one,' said Poppy.

'Free the nipple,' he said, rolling Poppy over. He kissed a line from her thigh to her throat, his breath forming goosebumps on her skin.

'Absolutely,' she said. 'But not my nipples and not today. Go on.'

A look that verged on irritation flashed across Josh's face. He swung his legs over the side of the bed and pulled on a pair of boxers, the elastic snapping as he unlatched the door. Poppy dragged the sheet back onto the mattress and tucked it under her armpits.

A man spoke, his voice gentle and warm. 'This arrived via email for you at reception. Enjoy, Mr and Mrs Lattimer.'

'Thanks, mate,' said Josh, taking an envelope from the concierge. He closed the door and lifted the flap as he walked back towards the bed, turning the card over as he reached Poppy. She pushed her hair to one side and leant over to read.

To the new Mr and Mrs Lattimer,
If my timing is correct, I'd make an assumption that right about now you'll be needing a break from the shag fest of your hotel room, so here's something to get you outside. Poppy, if you can take a photo of Josh on said donkey, I'll die happy.
Yours, from a predictably rainy England,
Lola

'Lola?' said Josh. He smirked and walked to the bathroom.

'What's she saying about a donkey?' said Poppy, unfolding the sheet of paper underneath. She read the page and laughed. 'You'll never guess.'

'What? Lola's chosen the menu for our next meal out? Booked herself a flight to join us?' Josh loaded his toothbrush and started brushing, his bicep flexing as he leant against the doorframe. Poppy rolled her eyes and threw him a playful smile.

'It's our wedding present from her. Ha! She's organised a donkey trek across the mountains. Oh, cool. We're going to do palm reading. Apparently, this woman's a ninth-generation mystic. Ninth!'

Josh turned, spat in the sink, and splashed water on his face. 'So Lola paid for our wine on the first night we were here, had pastries ordered to our room yesterday, and now she's hijacked another day of our honeymoon? Not sure how I feel about that.'

Josh and Lola didn't have the smoothest of friendships, but recently he had been particularly vocal about what he called Lola's 'overinvolvement in their lives'. Poppy tucked her hair behind her ears. Whatever puncture had burst the bubble they had been in moments before, Poppy was keen to repair it.

'What do you mean? This sounds like a laugh,' said Poppy. 'To be fair, we haven't really travelled very far since we've been here. Let's go to Eleanor's fortune-telling farm.'

'Why would anyone want to spend half a day with a mountain woman who scams people with woo-woo bullshit?'

Poppy bristled. 'Is it because you're worried the poor donkey won't be able to houff you up the mountain path? I'll see if there's a disclaimer in the small print that protects the donkeys from carrying anyone prone to an excessive consumption of protein shakes,' said Poppy, unfolding the printout.

'Really funny, Poppy,' said Josh, his ears red.

Poppy held her hands out. 'I'm joking, obviously. This woman sounds like a legend. To be honest, I don't care if she makes it all up on the spot. I bet she's got some stories to tell. I wonder if she'd be up for having her photo taken? You know, I've been thinking about restarting *The World's Eye*,' said Poppy. She reached for her camera bag, unzipped the side pocket, and checked to see if she'd packed spare memory cards. 'If I rebooted the page, I could start uploading portraits and interviews from abroad. *The World's Eye*, with a real global scope.

Think of all the stories I could showcase from different countries.'

Josh flicked a towel over his shoulder and sprayed deodorant under each arm. 'Do you think your obsession with collecting people could maybe take a break whilst we're on honeymoon?' he said.

Just like that, Poppy's excitement rolled to the base of her stomach like a marble in a bath. 'What do you mean?'

'This is what you used to do. When you were out doing your street photography three times a week and stuck in your room the rest of the time, editing and typing up interviews. That page dominated your life. I never got to see you.'

Poppy pushed her camera bag away. 'There's a reason that page did so well. I poured everything into it.'

'Exactly. Everything.' Josh knelt on the bed and slipped a hand around her waist, his chin propped on her shoulder. She resisted when he tugged her towards him. 'Come on. Would you rather I didn't give a shit about spending time with you?'

'That's not the problem. I feel like we were talking about a donkey trek one minute and now I'm choosing between photography and you.'

Josh grinned and gave her a quick kiss. 'You already chose me.'

Poppy kissed back, but by the time she realised what he'd said, her throat felt tight with the threat of tears. Was that how he saw it? She twisted the wedding band on her finger as Josh went back to the bathroom. He couldn't have meant it like that, not when he knew the scale of what she had turned down to start a life with him in England just a year before. Poppy took a few measured breaths. By the time Josh came back, Poppy had tidied her swell of frustration into a recessed pocket of her mind. She'd come back to it later when she wasn't at risk of ruining their honeymoon.

'So... what are we doing? Is the donkey trek a goer or are we going to have to pass on hearing about our unwritten future?

Come on, don't tell me you're not curious,' she said, not meeting his eye.

Josh emerged from the bathroom, his chest still bare. He pulled a pair of running shorts out of their suitcase and wriggled his fingers through fluorescent yellow sweat bands, glancing up at Poppy as she sat on the bed, still wrapped in the sheet that had covered them both. 'Go on ahead,' he said. 'If you want to stink like a donkey all afternoon in thirty-two-degree heat, be my guest. I'll catch you at dinner. I could do with the extra training. I haven't been for a run in five days. I feel like a blob,' said Josh, pinching a non-existent roll of fat. He opened his running app and filled up a bottle of water from a jug in their mini-fridge.

'Oh,' said Poppy, fiddling with a button on the duvet cover. 'Because when you said you wanted to spend time together, I thought you meant... never mind.'

'You take things so literally. See you later, wife.' Josh bent down, kissed Poppy on the forehead, and left.

Chapter Twenty-Four

TWO DAYS BEFORE THE WEDDING

Poppy smiled at a waiter who placed a jar on the table, a tealight flickering inside. It was early evening, the darkness accelerated by thick clouds that hugged the coastline. Between 6 and 8pm, little happened on Loxby Island. Business was finished, mid-afternoon hangovers were slept off, and the staff were setting up for dinner service, laying out strangely specific cutlery, like lobster crackers and silver prongs that looked as though they could double up as surgical tools should the need arise.

'This place must be worth millions, right?' said Poppy, lifting the jar to eye level. 'And you're telling me they're running jam jars through the dishwasher to make rustic centrepieces?'

'No,' said Lola, reaching over to tap the glass with a long acrylic nail. It tinkled sweetly. 'It's crystal. There's a whole offshoot of homeware you can buy that replicates crap objects in expensive materials. Yesterday I was talking to a stockbroker who told me he'd paid someone to give his kitchen a "stripped-back French château aesthetic". The decorator literally threw acid at his cupboard doors. And got paid for it.'

'I'm in the wrong business,' said Poppy.

'You *are* in the wrong business,' said Lola, giving her a knowing look. 'Take teaching. It was never your dream – it was Josh's.'

'You told me that years ago.'

'Yeah, and you didn't listen to me. Before you say anything, I know you don't like dwelling on the whole what-could-have-been narrative, but your photography is fucking good. After that exhibition, I fully thought we were going to make *so* much money together,' said Lola, her index finger trailing a figure of eight in the thick linen tablecloth. 'New York. Milan. Tokyo. I even bookmarked the luggage set I was planning to buy. No knock-offs in sight.'

'Speaking of knock-offs, did I tell you I found an online shop selling inkjet prints of my photos from *The World's Eye*? I reported it for plagiarism, obviously, but I still see those pictures popping up all over the internet, so it's basically impossible to prove I'm the original artist.'

Lola grinned. 'See. An *artist*. That's what you should be calling yourself.'

'Maybe I was. Not anymore.'

'You sound like an actor who can't get an invite to the Met Gala anymore. You're only twenty-nine.'

'I've lived a life, all right?' said Poppy, smiling as she swigged her gin and tonic. She fished out a wedge of cucumber and bit into it. It's not that she didn't want to talk about how directionless she felt, but it felt like diving into a canyon so deep she couldn't see the bottom.

'Nelson Mandela lived a life. Virginia Woolf lived a life. Anne Lister lived a life. You married your first boyfriend. So have *most* women throughout history. The difference is, you chose to leave, which was the right thing to do. Don't tell me you're regretting it,' said Lola with genuine reproach.

'No, it's not that. I hate being a divorce statistic. It makes me feel haggard and old.'

'Are you serious? Getting divorced young is the coolest thing ever. It gives you an air of intrigue. You can make casual references to your *ex-husband* at dinner parties. It helps if you touch your clavicle at the same time, like this,' said Lola, demonstrating with a faraway look in her eye. 'And then you never elaborate or give context. Instant cool points.'

Poppy laughed and shook her head, her thoughts cloudy.

'Trust me, when half the people our age are going through the same thing in ten years' time, they'll all wish they were you.'

Poppy batted a moth away as it dipped too close to the flame. 'What about Will and Ottilie?'

'I cannot pass judgment on my clients until they're safely past the altar,' said Lola, a knowing quirk in her eyebrow. 'Mainly because that's when the second half of my payment comes through. Now, onto other matters. Please let me plan a divorce party for you.'

'No way. What the hell would that involve? Tearing up my wedding dress and performing a sad macarena?'

'Well, you have to do *something* to celebrate this rebirth. Poppy 2.0. Go on a pilgrimage. Re-ignite *The World's Eye*. Get a fringe.'

'I just left one commitment. I don't need another, especially not a fringe.'

'Girl, you have talent. You had a window of opportunity when Columbia offered you a scholarship, but that shit is in the past. You have to find a new way to get your work out there.'

'I have. Nature photography. I like being tied to an animal's schedule. It's outdoors, it's straightforward, and I don't have to spend hours transcribing the interviews. Take puffins. Who doesn't like puffins?'

Lola tipped an ice cube into her mouth and crunched it. 'Puffins are safe. Puffins are the pandas of the bird world. No one knows if they contribute anything to the ecosystem other than looking cute. Don't be a puffin.'

'Well in that case, I don't know what I'm going to do with my life. The thought of going back to school is making me feel a bit sick. Josh is moving to senior management, so he'll be coming in to observe me. Setting targets. Living the megalomaniac life of his dreams.'

A look of horror passed over Lola's face. 'That's proper fucked up. Why didn't you get out of there when you had the chance?'

'I've only been thinking ahead one month at a time. Anything else makes me feel weak and useless.'

'You know what will help provide you with some clarity?' said Lola, nodding decisively.

'What? No, no, no.'

'Yes. Wait here.'

Lola pushed her chair back and trotted towards the hotel, her heels clacking on the paving slabs. In her absence, Poppy tuned in to the crickets whirring in the darkness and the gentle breeze that carried laughter from the open windows. After five minutes, Lola returned with a deck of cards and a velvet bag that she placed on the table with a clunk.

'You *know* I think tarot cards are bullshit,' groaned Poppy.

'Because you're uneducated and shrouded by modern life's insistence for clean, lateral logic. Embrace it. Serious face, okay?'

Poppy sighed and straightened up. Lola took Poppy's hands and flattened them on the table, palms facing the sky.

'Now. Important question. Would you like to hold a crystal?'

Poppy burst out laughing, the exertion of surfing having settled painfully in her underused muscles.

'Fine. You don't deserve one. Okay, here we go.' Lola cut, shuffled, and restacked the deck. She took Poppy's hand and dangled it over the top, nodding as though this confirmed something. Next, she laid down three cards, each one placed on the table slowly and deliberately.

'How long have you been doing this?' asked Poppy. 'Be honest, did you buy a course on Groupon?'

'Shh! You'll put me out of alignment. Okay. This one represents the past,' said Lola, turning a card over.

Poppy angled her head to read it upside down. 'Oh, great,' she said. 'Death. Really?'

'No, this is good!' said Lola, pushing the card towards her.

'"Death" doesn't *sound* good,' said Poppy, pointing at the card. 'The knight is literally a skeleton riding a horse with red eyes.'

'It means rebirth. Change, you know? Which you've had.'

'In abundance.'

'Did you turn it around? Because it means something different if it's flipped the other way. Stagnancy and resistance. Ring any bells?'

Poppy ignored her. 'What's the next one, oh Grand Mystique?'

'The present. You, where you are now.' Lola paused, her hand flat on the card to ensure Poppy was paying attention before she continued. Poppy rolled her eyes, laughed, and gave Lola a thumbs up. Lola flipped over another card. 'Oh, ma chérie!' Lola gasped, red fingernails held at lip level. 'The Fool!'

'It gets better and better,' said Poppy, rolling her eyes.

'Now, the Fool can be bad, *but* I don't feel like that applies to you,' pondered Lola, resting her chin on her hand. 'The fool is on a journey, sometimes wise, sometimes mad, sometimes both.'

'That sounds exhausting. Are you sure it doesn't involve a nap and a family bag of minstrels?'

Lola made a pinch gesture in the air to stop Poppy talking. 'You move towards the edge of the mountain, planting your feet, taking a risk, you know? You have a choice to make.'

'Wasn't the last one about making choices?

'No, the last one was about... hmm. Hang on, I forgot.' Lola pulled out her phone and began to tap on the screen.

Poppy jumped when her camera bag vibrated. 'Did you just send me a text?'

'No. Fuck, don't let anyone see your phone,' said Lola, her voice dropping to a whisper.

'It's in a flap at the bottom of my camera bag. I can't reach it,' said Poppy, ducking below the table. 'My strap is caught around your chair leg.'

Lola grappled with the buckle and pulled out Poppy's battered iPhone. They stayed under the table as a member of kitchen staff wheeled a trolley along the terrace, the silverware rattling as it passed over uneven tiles.

'Who is it?' said Poppy, bumping heads with Lola as she tried to look at the screen.

'It's an unknown number, but a Bath location. I'll answer it. Security won't get fussy if it's me, I'm taking calls all the time.'

'No, it's okay, I'm sure it's just a PPI thing, or—'

'Hello?' said Lola, leaning back in her seat. 'Yep, Poppy speaking.'

'Lola, don't worry, it's—' Lola held a finger up and rolled her tongue around the inside of her cheek, her neatly outlined brows furrowed.

'Sorry, he's done what?' said Lola, glancing at Poppy.

'Give the phone to me.'

Lola shooed her away and sat back in her chair. 'This has not been arranged with my consent. No, you listen to me. That is *my* property and *you* need permission from the homeowner to arrange viewings.' Lola held the phone to her chest and blinked in shock. 'That fucker! He's trying to sell your house!'

'Lola, pass it here and I can—'

'In future, anything relating to the house should be directed to me via my solicitor.' Lola blocked the microphone with her hand to address Poppy. 'You do have a solicitor, don't you?'

'No,' said Poppy, her stomach tight.

'Why the fuck not?!'

'I haven't got round to it.'

'Jesus.' Lola uncovered the mouthpiece. 'I'll forward you a name and email address tomorrow.' Poppy rapped the table and gestured for Lola to give her the phone, panic rising. She stood up, the metal seat sticking to her clammy legs as she reached over the table. Lola took a step back, her voice less brash as she spoke down the line. 'No, I've been on a work assignment. Very exclusive. Barely any phone signal.' Poppy could hear the caller from where she sat, but the words were indistinct. This time, Lola didn't interrupt. 'Sorry, how long ago?' She looked at Poppy. 'Right. Like I said, I'll be in touch.'

She ended the call and passed the phone over, fixing Poppy with a cold stare.

'Who was that?' said Poppy, despite knowing exactly who it was.

'An estate agent. They seem to think you're selling your house.'

'It was inevitable, I suppose.'

'Poppy, this is *your* house. I just went all-guns-blazing on that poor woman thinking that Josh had organised it without telling you.'

'He said he was thinking about it,' said Poppy, angry at how small her voice became when she was forced to talk about him.

'You broke up with him. Just because he's hurt doesn't mean you can let him treat you like this. How do you know he's not going to use this as a chance to get back at you?'

'Because he wouldn't.'

'He *could*, which means he will.'

'I'll sort it, don't worry.'

222

'I'm not worried about me. I'm worried about you. That estate agent said that you've been ignoring her emails and calls. Do you even want to sell the house? Move somewhere else, start afresh?'

'I do, but I haven't had time. You need a PhD to understand the paperwork. I don't trust that—'

'You'll go through with it?'

Lola broke eye contact. Up at the hotel, the receptionist waved at them both and pointed to a man next to her who wore a linen jacket with a silken scarf bundled underneath his chin.

'Christian is here!' she called. 'The photographer!'

Lola put the phone behind her back and waved in return. 'I'll come and meet him!'

Poppy picked up her camera bag and opened the flap for Lola to put the phone inside. 'Looks like you'll get to see your puffins before the end of the week,' she said, the shadow of their previous conversation momentarily forgotten. She raised her eyebrows, as though trying to make a point. 'I'll catch up with you later.' Lola clacked up the terracotta stairs, switching into the professional, exuberant persona she adopted for guests at Loxby.

When Poppy pushed her chair in, she noticed a lone tarot card face down on the floor. She pinched their empty glasses with one hand and picked it up. A jester looked back at her, one knee angled as he danced on the edge of a cliff, a white rose in hand.

'Thanks a lot,' she said, her stomach sloshing with anxiety as she slid the card inside her bra.

Chapter Twenty-Five

Poppy was used to being the refuge of students who wanted a legitimate excuse to stay off the playground at lunchtime. For some reason, she attracted the kids who listened to old Belle and Sebastian albums and still used Tumblr, which were two things that seemed stuck in a time warp from when she was a teenager herself. They spent their lunch hours making collages with blunt scissors and talked at length about friendship groups that shifted with the force and devastation that usually came with living on a fault line. Consciously or not, Poppy often found herself as the reluctant keeper of confessions, but something about Ottilie's hot and cold treatment made her suspect that there was something bigger at stake.

When a soft tap sounded on Lola's door at midnight, she got out from the duck-down cover she'd just climbed under, having dismissed Ottilie's insistence of a clandestine meeting as a temporary reaction to stress. Poppy opened the door, her eye mask caught in a matted lock of hair, and blinked in the bright hallway light. Ottilie blinked back. Without a word, she slipped inside before Poppy had a chance to greet her.

'You're going to have no nails left at this rate,' said Poppy as Ottilie sat on a wicker sofa by the window.

She pulled her heels in, eyes wide like a cat in a carry cage. 'Does anyone know I'm here?' Ottilie asked.

'I don't know – do they?' said Poppy, registering the nervous energy that hummed around Ottilie like a force field.

'Not unless you've told someone. No Lola?'

'No, she said she'd be back late.' Poppy rubbed her eyes. 'I thought you wanted to talk about shots for Saturday, but since Christian showed up, I figured you'd be having that conversation with him.'

'Did you really think I wanted to talk about photography? God, no. That's the furthest thing from my mind. This *place*. I never know whether the conversation I'm having is the conversation I'm having. Do you know what I mean?'

Poppy lifted the duvet to find the robe that she had swiped from the pool house earlier and pulled it on like a cocoon. She had to try and find a way to stuff it into her rucksack before she left.

'I can trust you, can't I?'

'I'll be honest, you're freaking me out a little bit. Has something happened? Is Will okay?' asked Poppy.

'Will? He's fine. His cousins have flown in from North America and want the whole "British" experience, so they've gone off to shoot something wearing tweed, which is ridiculous. Tweed is for winter. When my dad learnt that he stopped wearing ordinary clothes from November through to February.'

Poppy tightened the belt on her robe and took a tentative step forward. 'Do you have friends coming over? I'd use it as an excuse to watch *Bride Wars* and eat my weight in brie, but I can't speak for everyone.'

'My girlfriends aren't arriving until Saturday afternoon. Reception only.'

'Really? That seems unfair. So, it's only your mum and dad for the ceremony?'

'Yep. The actual ceremony is small and intimate, but still, I overheard Will's dad talking about how my friends "would make it feel like Ibiza in low season" so I don't need to think too hard about why the capacity has been capped until after the formal proceedings are over. We're going to throw another party back in London. I haven't told Will yet, but you know, that's the plan.'

'Two celebrations? Like Kim and Kanye?'

'No,' said Ottilie, revulsion passing across her face at the thought. 'We're not having half as many roses.'

'Mmm. Five thousand is enough when you think about it.'

Ottilie stood up, fingers spread to emphasise her point. 'I don't think you're taking this seriously.'

Poppy laughed. 'I would, but you haven't actually told me *why* you're here. I'm only really qualified to talk about photography. How helpful I'll be outside of that, I don't know.'

Ottilie took a deep breath. 'I need to lie in a bath.'

'Sorry?'

'I find it much easier to talk when I'm surrounded by a body of water.'

Poppy would have laughed if it weren't for how anxious Ottilie looked.

'How long are you going to be? If I'm leaving tomorrow, I need to check when the sea tractor is running.'

'Someone will do that for you,' said Ottilie, waving her hand in dismissal as she walked past Poppy to the bathroom.

She heard the taps run and glanced at the clock. She couldn't get used to the way so many of Will's family treated time like a commodity that they deserved more of than other people. Resentment built up in her chest, as it had done all week. Each request from Lola, Ottilie, and Lord Mountgrave stacked higher and higher like a Jenga tower, one movement away from toppling over.

'Come in here. I've made you a nest of towels, see?' Poppy heard Ottilie slip into the water. She walked to the bathroom with her eyes closed, hand outstretched until she reached the doorframe. 'Sorry, I always forget that some people aren't as comfortable with nakedness as I am,' said Ottilie.

'It's not a big deal; I'll face the wall,' said Poppy, squatting to the floor. Ottilie turned over, but not before Poppy saw a tattoo that stretched down her spine. A half-moon curved between her shoulder blades above a trail of stars dotted between each nook of her vertebra. Ottilie caught her eye.

'Oh, God. Don't look at that. I'm getting it covered up. It's huge, isn't it? I forget it's there most of the time, but it's a bit loud. I blame my late teens. I never understood the concept of moderation at that age, even when it came to tattoos. I've slowed down since then. Got some perspective. I've swapped cocktail bars for church groups, can you imagine? I didn't realise how much I need philanthropy to maintain any semblance of a normal life. It's not like that here. Loxby is a bubble. A toxic bubble most of the time.'

Poppy shuffled so that her back was resting against the side of the bath. She stifled a yawn, not yet sufficiently alert for Ottilie's verbal memoir.

'Is that where you met Lawrence?'

Ottilie paused, thrown by Poppy's interjection. 'What?'

'At a church group? Is that where you met Lawrence?'

She paused. 'Yes. An *Alcoholics Anonymous* group used the hall. Lawrence must have mentioned that he had some issues getting sober? I used to volunteer there – helped source catering, made coffee, you know? Super rewarding. It's indirectly how I met Will, actually. Lawrence introduced us, then I went to Laos as part of an outreach programme run by the church and he was booked into the same hostel. After that, I stopped going out four times a week and figured out what I want instead. Will grounds me like that. We didn't come back to England for three years and by the time we did, we were engaged. I only had a faint idea about all of this,' said Ottilie, gesticulating at the marble-clad bathroom they were in.

'It's not a horrible surprise, is it?' said Poppy.

Ottilie exhaled audibly. 'No, but you've seen what it's like. I feel like a fish trying to climb a tree. Every time they change our plans without telling me, it's like I'm the problem.'

Poppy nodded without realising. She knew what that was like.

'That's why I wanted to come to you. Will trusts you and I know you want the best for him. He told me a bit about you and your ex-husband. Josh, was it?' Poppy hadn't heard him described in the past tense before. They weren't officially divorced yet, but what difference did that make?

'Did Josh's family ever do that? Make you feel like you couldn't breathe?'

'Yeah, but it stemmed from him I suppose. In his mother's eyes, Josh was the golden boy. He was… very good at rewiring my thoughts. I wanted so badly to be good enough for him that I forgot to be good enough for myself.'

Ottilie put a damp hand on her shoulder. Rather than being annoyed at Will for telling Ottilie about her relationship, Poppy was comforted to know that it wasn't all in her head. The feelings she frequently pushed down came gurgling up to the surface. Regret. Shame. Embarrassment. Will had seen the cracks in her fledgling relationship, as had Lola, and to a lesser extent, her dad. Why hadn't she?

'Josh was very good at manipulating situations to ensure I'd say or do something in a certain way. Weekend trips to London after an argument, antique camera reels from specialist auctions, explosions of love that felt filmlike and swoon-worthy. I won't even get started on his proposal. He made it look like it was all for me, when it was actually all for him.'

Ottilie sat up a little and pushed her wet hair back from her face, her skin less pink and blotchy than before. 'That's how I feel.'

'In that case, what is it about Will that you love?' asked Poppy.

Ottilie slipped deeper into the water. 'He walks three miles to buy my favourite coffee beans on a Saturday. When I had the flu and said I missed the park, he brought a potted tree up to our apartment balcony. He's kind to his mum. And he adores me. I love him. So much. Despite everything he's attached to, I love him. It's his family that are the problem. I know you've not had the best experience with marriage – I hope you don't mind me saying that – but I like the idea of knowing that Will and I have each other's backs. We're each other's best defence against whatever his family throws at us.'

'Wouldn't that be the case anyway, married or not?'

'Yes, but… that's not what I mean. I know it's gauche to admit it, but I *like* grand gestures. I like symbolism and ceremony, being part of a legacy, but doing it our way. Will is infuriatingly loyal. I want to do something that shows how serious I am about our life together, because he deserves that from me. I've never doubted his integrity, not once. I'm sure you've noticed what he's like – pouring himself into his relationships, friends, family, and everyone in between.'

Poppy nodded. Had she forgotten how easily won Will's loyalty was? She thought their friendship had picked up from where it had been abruptly cut short, but maybe there wasn't anything special about it after all. Perhaps he really was like that with everyone.

'It's me who wants this wedding more than him,' said Ottilie. 'He should be at the centre of a proper celebration, and not just because he might get voted in as the next CEO. Just because of who he is. The thing is, every time I try to make a mark on the wedding, his family change it to something they want instead. Will is the foundation I want to build my life on. I'm not easy to be around, but he cares for me just the same. What more could I ask for? We have stress as a couple, sure, but after this, when it's just us, I know everything will be fine.'

'You know, marriage isn't like being programmed. You don't experience a factory reboot after you've signed a piece of paper. The problems you have now will still tick along afterwards, just below the surface.'

'Oh, I know. But a wedding is a milestone. A solid jumping-off point. Wherever you go, whatever culture, everyone understands a marriage. I know things have changed for you since, but how did you feel in the run-up to your wedding?'

Poppy tilted her head to one side. 'It felt bohemian. We were young and barely out of university. Some people thought we were cool, which was a first for me. My dad hated Josh and made no secret of it. He's a great judge of character, but drank a lot so I never knew what exactly to sprinkle a pinch of salt on.'

'So it was other people who caused your problems?'

'Oh, to begin with, sure. Josh's mum broke into a happy neurosis when we told her we were engaged, but Josh's opinion took precedence when it came to the day itself. We were so caught up in wedding planning that I didn't pause to think about whether we were rushing things.'

Ottilie scooped the steaming bath water and ran it through her hair. 'I want to do something that represents *us*, but now we have a corporate audience thanks to this bizarre business conference I didn't know was happening and the fifty or so friends that Colin invited to our celebration. That's fifty people I was told we didn't have capacity for. I grew up with Mum and Dad spending every waking hour on their business, so I understand the pressure, but there comes a point where you need to have a separate life. It's partly why I came off social media. I worry that I'm losing a grip on my own story.'

'That surprises me. You have the yogi sun-kissed personal aesthetic of dreams *and* access to half the country's glossy magazines. You have a platform. Surely you can do what you want with it.'

'I have no control. Colin drives the narratives. I've seen paparazzi pictures of myself in magazines that *he* owns. How does that happen? What about my independence? If Will was in there steering the boat it would be better for both of us, but he's so stubborn that he won't even consider taking over from his dad.' Ottilie was on the threshold of tears, one manicured hand covering her eyes. 'I'm done with it,' she said between clogged lawnmower sobs. 'I need to get off this island. I can't think straight. You're leaving, aren't you?' she said, hooking her arms over the side of the bath. 'I wish Will and I could leave too.' Ottilie swallowed. Her eyes scanned the room, her face brighter than before. 'What if we did it? Left together? Me, you, and Will? We could say that we were going on a pre-wedding photoshoot back on the mainland. If we got away, we'd have the freedom to move into the next stage of our relationship, on our terms.'

In the time before her teacher training year had started, she had cobbled together work from a number of freelance clients and covered everything from pregnancy shoots to newborns, corporate headshots, and school year pictures. Pre-wedding was new to her, especially the kind that involved smuggling the bride and groom back to the mainland, never to return for the actual ceremony. Ottilie clearly wasn't as superficial as she thought. She wanted Will to be happy. If Poppy had the power to do anything, helping them was surely the right thing to do.

'How does Will feel?' asked Poppy, nervous of her answer.

'Will is just as conflicted as I am, but he's trying to please everyone. You should see the legal pack Colin's lawyer had us sign. I feel like a company that the Mountgraves are buying. Will is so torn about the whole situation. You know Lawrence is given a personal living allowance every month, right? He's not on any inheritance plan, not after he had his episode a few years ago. Too risky for the stakeholders knowing that he could piss it away in a weekend. I didn't sign up for this level of scrutiny. Neither did Will.' She sounded panicked now, as though someone might be listening at the door, ready to smash it down, throw a sack over her head, and toss her in the back of a van.

'This is a big decision, Ottilie. Do you and Will really want to go? Without telling anyone? Do you think this could just be the stress talking?'

'I know what he'll say. He wants to do what's right for both of us.'

Poppy knelt on the towels and looked at Ottilie, square on. 'I hear you, I do. But Lola… this is the biggest job she's had in her career. I understand why you feel like there's no other option, but I think you owe her a heads-up at the very least.'

'It may be her job, but it's my *life*. If Colin or his awful PR woman get wind of any plan, they'll make it impossible for us to leave, and then what? If you had your time again, wouldn't you want to have this conversation before your wedding passed you by?'

Poppy slipped down into the towels, the back of her head pressed against the bath. She knew the answer to that question more than she was ready to admit. If she helped someone avoid an event that would dictate the rest of their lives, was it worth the risk? Then again, dramatic feelings weren't solved by dramatic solutions.

'I understand what you're saying,' said Poppy. 'But would you at least sleep on it? This might not be the only solution. It's nearly one o'clock. There's nothing you can do until tomorrow. In the meantime, speak to Will. If you guys decide that leaving is the only option, I'll talk to Lola, okay?'

Ottilie nodded in earnest. 'I'll make sure her fee is covered, no matter what happens. This won't affect her. You understand, don't you? Why we need to do this.' Ottilie swallowed and bit her thumbnail. 'If not for me, for Will.'

Poppy uncrossed her legs and tied her hair back, her chin high. 'I understand, but look... I doubt it'll be easy. If I can help, I will, but when you both have some distance from here, I'll have to bow out. I've got too many of my own problems to fix. If it's roles we're assuming, I'm not the Kim Kardashian to your Paris Hilton.' Poppy stood up and handed Ottilie a towel. 'I work with children. I can't afford to do a sex tape.'

Ottilie laughed, nodding. Her eyelashes were damp and dark, highlighting the youth she had tried to disguise with sharp contour lines and an austere expression. 'I can cope with that.'

Chapter Twenty-Six

THE DAY BEFORE THE WEDDING

When Poppy stepped outside that morning, the tiles were damp and warm from the overnight rain that had woken her up in the early hours. The humidity stuck to her skin and the waiters were beaded with sweat as they laid the breakfast table with toast racks, platters of smoked salmon, and sliced figs.

Poppy's stomach protested, caught between hunger and worry. By the time she went to sleep, she had replayed Ottilie's conversation over and over in her head, to the point where she'd recalibrated the meaning twelve different ways. She didn't know Ottilie well enough to rule out the idea that she might be melodramatic by nature. Was the threat to flee a façade? Was Poppy an unwilling audience member for Ottilie's one-woman show? Sure enough, as Poppy loitered by the French doors, Ottilie was at the table outside, Will's arm draped across her shoulders, Lawrence sat opposite slowly turning the pages of a newspaper. Ottilie kissed Will on the cheek and ran her hand up the back of his neck as he leant in to her touch. For a couple on the cusp of fleeing their own wedding, they seemed incredibly laid-back.

Poppy lifted her camera and clicked, if only to distract herself from the pang of envy that twanged in her chest.

Ottilie and Will turned when they heard her shutter. He pushed his chair back to stand, but Ottilie ran her arm down Will's leg and nestled into his chest, keeping him in his seat. Lawrence glanced up from his newspaper, looked at Ottilie, and flicked the pages straight.

'I wondered if you were sticking around,' said Will.

'I was wondering that myself, but I can't find Lola to ask if I'm clear to leave.'

'No worries, you can check in with me,' said Will, brightening. Ottilie looked at her from beneath a lock of sea-curled hair, her diamond-sharp eyes disguising fragility beneath an air of buoyant ease.

At the other end of the table, Lord Mountgrave was deep in conversation with Nicola, her eyes hidden behind large sunglasses. Beside her, Josie spoke with Paul, his scalp the same colour as the salmon-pink shirt he wore. Josie pulled her ankle onto her knee and pushed her hair to one side, cool and demure despite the heat.

'Oh, no pictures this morning,' said Lord Mountgrave, wafting his hand in the air when he saw what Poppy was holding.

'Hang on, you're telling me you're *not* George Clooney shooting an espresso advert?' said Poppy, putting the lens cap back on her camera. 'Dammit. I was going to make my fortune.' Lord Mountgrave softened when he realised she was being sarcastic.

'Ah, very good. Anyhoo, I've arranged a gathering – business, strictly speaking – whilst the youngsters are out partying tonight. Very informal, but there's a lot to do, so I don't want to contend with bloody click, click, clicking all day,' said Lord Mountgrave, his face contorting as he pretended to take pictures. 'Christian is taking over the photography for the ceremony, isn't that what your wedding person said? Lola? Purple hair? Frightening?'

'Poppy was going to stay as a guest,' said Will, forking a piece of salmon from the platter.

'I don't think Poppy has decided yet,' said Ottilie. 'Besides, I doubt she wants to waste her holiday with us. Make sure you let me know when you leave.'

Will pulled back from her. 'Ottie, Poppy and I are friends.'

'Is that why she didn't get an invite?'

Lawrence took a sharp intake of breath, teeth clenched.

'Ouch,' said Poppy. She tried to disguise her hurt by laughing and flicking a dial on her camera to keep her hands busy. Based on their conversation the night before, Poppy understood Ottilie's need to play it cool in public, but that felt like a particularly low blow. Will stared at his fiancée like an alien had slipped under her skin. Clearly, Ottilie was yet to share her wedding anxieties with him, like she had promised she would.

'Well, this has become uncomfortable. I did think a little turbulence was overdue,' said Josie, biting into a green apple.

Lord Mountgrave gestured to a nearby waiter for another coffee. 'If you want to leave, that's what you ought to do,' he said. 'But make sure you see Lola before you go. There are certain things you'll need to be cleared on. Security, first and foremost.'

'Oh, of course,' said Josie. 'It's compulsory that all outgoing visitors are probed upon departure, just to make sure you aren't squirrelling silverware up your ass.'

'I only went for the teaspoons,' said Poppy. A dribble of orange juice ran down Will's chin as he spluttered with laughter. If he was disguising a covert departure, he was doing incredibly well.

'You know, this one's funny,' said Josie, pointing at Poppy. 'I'm surprised you two never had a thing at college.' Will continued laughing, harder.

'Oh dear, how have we got here?' said Nicola, glancing up with concern.

'What?' exclaimed Josie, holding up her hands. 'We're all

adults here. After all, Poppy's not the one with the ring, right?'

Lord Mountgrave pushed his chair back sharply. 'Poppy, a quiet word?'

'Dad, come on. You don't need to do the cloak and dagger routine,' said Lawrence, lowering his sunglasses. 'We're having a nice, relaxed breakfast. Poor Nicola hasn't had a chance to open her book,' said Lawrence, flicking open a hefty paperback that sat in front of Ottilie's mum.

'Fine,' said Lord Mountgrave holding his hands up. 'This concerns all of you, really. Nicola and Paul, you're off the hook, naturally.' The couple sank back into their chairs. 'Poppy, you've been involved in the event planning and are the anomaly here, so I'm mainly angling this at you. Professional feedback, if you will. I'm aware the bingo business was a bit of fun. I'm no stranger to a laugh when it's appropriate.' Poppy doubted this was true. 'But the silliness stops now. This is serious. You can have your japes in your own time, but there are some incredibly important people here and we can't afford any more slip-ups.'

Lawrence snorted. 'Hear that, Will? You can't have fun at your wedding because Dad *cannot afford it*,' he said, imitating his father's voice.

Will shifted in his seat, uncomfortable. Poppy held the back of a chair whilst she mulled over a thought. 'What about the bingo? I believe Ottilie was the organiser, to great success,' said Poppy, steeling her resolve. She wasn't going to be made into the scapegoat here.

'She knows me so well,' said Will.

'Well, what can I say?' said Ottilie.

Poppy sat down, unfolded a linen napkin, and laid it across her lap. If Ottilie and Will decided to leave Loxby early, or swallow through a ceremony they didn't want, Poppy was at least going to eat her fill of fresh patisserie before she had to rely on the granola bars she'd shoved into her rucksack.

'To her credit, the bingo did help remove a few rods from a few proverbial arseholes,' said Lawrence.

'No need to be crass,' said Lord Mountgrave. 'Ah, here she is.'

Coming from the hotel, Lola handed an envelope to a woman in a corporate dress, her arms already laden as she skipped on a half-step to maintain pace with Lola's stilettoed stride. She gave her a final instruction and turned to face the table.

'Morning, campers! How are we?'

'Having a wonderful breakfast, thanks,' said Josie. 'We haven't had a bird dive-bomb us for the fish, which is a small miracle. Did you instruct someone to shoot the seagulls?'

'No, but the harrier falcon we have looking for drones might have scared them off,' said Lola, her breezy disposition a balm for the prickly tension that had crept around the table.

'Lola, if my theory about girls with purple hair is correct, you're the type who checks their horoscope. Correct?' said Lawrence, shuffling forward in his chair.

Lola pursed her lips. 'I dabble,' she said.

'That's an understatement,' said Poppy. 'Lola is my personal mystic. I always win between five and ten pounds on the Euromillions. It's a tidy earner, but keeps me grounded,' said Poppy. 'I'd be a terrible millionaire.'

Lola never took up a hobby without becoming totally obsessed by it. Poppy thought back to the brief but intense *Twilight* phase she went through in the late-noughties and winced. She had talked Lola down from having two puncture marks tattooed on her neck, which if anything was Poppy's greatest achievement to date.

Lawrence opened his arms to the table. 'Help us with a deduction. This book. Is it, or is it not, total bollocks?' he asked, holding up Nicola's paperback.

'Is that the 1994 edition of *A Synthesis of World Astrology*?' said Lola.

'The very same,' said Nicola with a proud smile. 'I use it like an almanac. We've recently taken on a raft of interns – young people, Ottilie's age or thereabouts – and astrology is their water cooler talk. It stops me being the scary boss when I can recite a star chart by heart.'

'Lola's tempted to flick through, I can tell,' said Lawrence, running his thumb along the pages. Lord Mountgrave yielded to the positive change in tone and gestured for Lola to join them.

'Five minutes. But then I've got to talk to you about your departure plans,' said Lola, tapping Poppy on the arm as she tucked her skirt beneath her to sit down. Poppy's heart quickened. She felt like she had been pulled into a reluctant espionage plot, unsure of everyone around her, wondering who knew about Ottilie's confession, and whether she was being scrutinised for changes in behaviour. 'I've seen this on eBay; they go for a fortune.' Lola took the book from Lawrence. 'Let's look up… Will. Date of birth?'

'February 24th, 1989.'

'Here we go,' said Lola, cracking the book's spine. 'Always the most handsome and popular person in the room by virtue of their natural charm. Pretentious folk envy their ease.' Lola gave Will a thumbs up. He performed an aw-shucks face in return.

'Hold on, let me see that,' said Lawrence, turning the book to face him. 'I will add that the next sentence reads: "Wonder abounds at how this simple-looking person can have such appeal." Yeah, that sounds about right,' he said, winking at his brother.

'Someone do me,' said Ottilie, leaning forward. She slid the book towards Poppy, her interest piqued. 'May 30th, 1992.'

'Okay.' Poppy ran her finger down the birth chart. 'That makes you a Gemini.'

Ottilie nodded eagerly. 'I think it's something to do with being good fun.'

Poppy skim-read the page, but struggled to find a passage that was particularly complimentary. 'How about this? A Gemini is an insistent demander of affection and loves nothing more than… than a— I've lost my place,' lied Poppy.

'Spotlight,' said Will, reading over her shoulder. 'This person can be exhausting to the often sedate people they pull close to their side.' Will pretended to loosen his collar. 'No comment.'

'Oh, *lovely*. Thanks a lot.' Ottilie folded her arms and pulled her head away from where the others crowded the book.

'Is there anything in there about being sensitive to criticism?' said Lawrence, taking an elongated slurp of his orange juice.

'Don't worry, it's all bollocks really,' said Poppy.

'Let me do the honours,' said Josie, holding her hand out. 'Brother, you're not exempt from this character analysis.'

'Ha! I get enough of that in the left-wing press. Did you know that *The New Yorker* did a twelve-page spread on me a few months ago? Some spine-curled cretin on his laptop made good money from my hard work. And they call *us* unethical,' he said with an overtone of pride.

'It's too early for this,' said Will, pushing on the plunger of a cafetière.

Josie balanced the book on her knee and cleared her throat. 'April 3rd. 1955. I didn't have you down as an Aries man.'

Lord Mountgrave shrugged. 'I haven't a clue what that means.'

Lola grimaced at Poppy, and demurely folded her hands in her lap.

'Remember, this is *all* fallacy,' said Josie, her eyes scanning the page. She looked up to check everyone was listening. 'Aries often suffers from a superiority complex.'

Poppy caught herself partway through a laugh. She was quickly joined by others, who snorted into their hands, Ottilie's parents included.

'Come on now, read from the bloody page,' said Lord Mountgrave.

'I am! See?' Josie turned the book to face him. 'It's not all bad. It says here that you're a bit of a heartbreaker. "His easy dispatch in romance sees a rolodex of partners who fall for their open attractiveness and candid confessions of love".'

'So was it Will's mother or mine who'—Lawrence cocked his head to check the book—'"Inspired guilt for avoiding time with family"? Or was it your "demand for uncritical attention" that made them bow out? Hypothetically speaking.'

'Have you been drinking?' said Lord Mountgrave, his gaze cold. Poppy felt the warmth sucked from the air as laughter died on their lips. 'Apologies, everyone.' Lord Mountgrave stood up and smoothed his shirt down. 'Lawrence has a difficult past that he struggles to keep a handle on. Is this some sort of vendetta? Hmm? What is it you're after?'

Lawrence gave an ugly laugh, but she could tell he hadn't anticipated this response as colour flushed his cheeks.

'Have you been missing your appointments? You know, for up here.' Lord Mountgrave rapped the side of his head with his knuckles.

Lawrence stood, pocketed his cufflinks, and rolled his sleeves up to the elbow. 'As fucking delightful as this was, I've had colonics that I've enjoyed more, so for that reason I shall depart. Enjoy.'

'For Christ's sake, Lawrence!' shouted Lord Mountgrave. He slammed his hand on the table. The crockery jumped, tinkling as a crystal glass hit the floor with a smash. 'Sit down and eat your eggs!'

'Dad!' said Will, moving between them.

Ottilie pushed her chair back, skirted around the broken glass, and walked away, yanking open a side door to disappear inside. Lola sighed and followed her, leaving Poppy to retreat by a twisted grapevine. A wasp landed on her shoulder. She didn't want to draw attention to herself by swatting it away, so kept as still as possible as it crawled across her skin.

'Paul, let's go. I'll ask the caddy to bring our clubs round,' announced Lord Mountgrave.

The two fathers walked away. Josie tracked them as they passed the table, her eyebrows raised in simple disbelief. 'What the fuck was that about?' she muttered when they were out of earshot.

'I'm really sorry,' said Will, turning to Poppy. He noticed the wasp and flicked it away.

'Hey, don't apologise, it's—'

'Not okay.' He shook his head, his shoulders round with embarrassment. 'I thought we might get through a whole meal in peace. Just one, you know? Before the wedding.'

'I value your ambition, Will,' said Josie with a shrug. 'Naïvely placed, though it be.'

'It was only supposed to be a bit of fun.' Nicola splayed her hands across an open page of the book that had been discarded on the table.

'You can't win them all, Mrs Spruce. Ironic, isn't it? That my brother's refusal to accept his quick temper resulted in… a disproportionately quick temper.'

Seeking a lifeline, Poppy listened for the sound of Lola's clacking heels as she returned, her forefingers pressed to her temple. 'Ottilie's in the ladies' loo. She's asked for you.'

'Thanks,' said Will, turning to leave.

'No, she wants Poppy.'

'Me?'

'Yep,' said Lola. 'Try and win her over, will you?'

'I'll do my best,' said Poppy as she stepped over the broken glass.

Chapter Twenty-Seven

The smell of fresh linen filled the atrium as Poppy stepped inside, cool marble abating the heat. She walked towards the nearest bathroom, not entirely sure which one Ottilie had locked herself in.

'Poppy?' asked a receptionist. 'There's a call for you.'

She hesitated before turning around. Apart from the people already on the island, no one knew she was here.

'Are you sure?' she asked. 'I get all sorts at Starbucks. Polly, Piper, and once Peter, weirdly enough.'

'Poppy Pascoe?'

'Ah. That is categorically me. Is it urgent? Only I've got a situation...'

'He sounded quite concerned. Your husband?'

Poppy paused, light-headed. 'My husband has called?'

'I can have the call put through to the housekeeper's office if you like? It's a little more private. Through here,' she said, opening the door to a small room containing a large desk that sat below old-fashioned service bells on the wall behind.

'Thanks,' said Poppy, her heart racing. The receptionist left the door open and gave her a sympathetic smile. Whatever Josh said had clearly endeared him to her. How that was possible from so many miles away, she didn't know.

She picked up the receiver but couldn't bring herself to talk.

'Poppy? You there?'

She nodded.

'Poppy? I can hear you breathing.'

'Sorry, I'm here,' she said, immediately angry with herself. Even though he was so far away, her first instinct was to apologise. She had to stop doing that.

'What are you playing at? Loxby? I thought you were going somewhere off the coast of Wales. Are you trying to get my attention? Fussing about getting your money from the house? Why? So you can spend it with him? How you're managing to afford that place is a fucking mystery. I know how much you've got in your account.'

'Firstly, I'm not paying for this. Secondly, what do you know about my money?'

'We have a shared bank account, Poppy. But of course, you're *independent* now, aren't you?' he said, his tone mocking. 'About fucking time. I've had enough of being held back by you.'

'Good. At least we're on the same page.'

Josh didn't retort immediately. She heard him breathe sharply down the phone. 'Is he the new guy? Is that what your fake trip has been disguising?'

'What are you on about?'

'Will? I thought I recognised him. Rekindled your relationship now that his family finances are public knowledge? Honestly, I thought better of you. I've seen it in the paper.'

Poppy looked over her shoulder, worried that someone might hear Josh's voice through the receiver. If there was a picture, why had no one mentioned it? Unless they hadn't seen it yet? 'Will's here, yeah. By coincidence.'

'So you went surfing in a spray-on wetsuit by accident?'

Surfing. There must have been a photographer on a boat further out in the bay, when they had both been barrel-rolled by waves, boards tangled on the shore. 'It was a child's wetsuit.'

'Fucking hell. You *are* there with him.'

'It's *his* wedding. It's nothing to do with me,' she said, her voice hushed, but urgent. Why was she explaining herself to him?

'Do you realise how embarrassing this is? One of our colleagues sent me the link, you know. You're not named, but it's pretty fucking obvious. I denied it was you, so... you're welcome. Now, is this some plan of yours? Splitting up wasn't enough for you, so now you're trying to prove you can move on faster than me?'

Poppy's head swam. She swallowed, but her throat was tight. The interrogation came thick and fast, barely giving her time to process a response before the next question came. She let him talk, and talk, and talk, his words more cutting the longer she went without responding. At first, his insults hit her like a slap, but she held fast until it didn't hurt anymore.

That silence was an option hadn't occurred to her before. The more he goaded, the less she cared. The weight of his words filled each gap and hollow of her chest until it felt like her ribcage would burst. What was this for? Why was she still allowing Josh to decide when he could snip her into pieces like a paper doll with neat pigtails?

Poppy clutched the wall with one hand and looked out of the window, her eyes fixed on the horizon.

'So what's it to be? Are you going to stop embarrassing me and start acting like a grown-up? I've let you have space. I've respected your choice. We're split, separated, whatever you want to fucking call it. But I won't be made to look like an idiot on a national fucking scale. You owe me that much.'

'Josh...' she said, acid rising in her throat. Her nails scraped the wall, but if she let go, she wasn't sure she'd have the resolve to follow through. 'I am not your responsibility anymore and you are not mine. There is nothing to talk about. I'll speak to you, but it'll be letters and they won't be coming from me, they'll be from my solicitor.'

'Are you joking?'

'Don't call again.'

Poppy put down the phone and took three slow, steeling breaths. She left the office and turned to press her forehead against the door, closing it with a click.

'That sounded intense...' said Will, who stood in the corridor.

Poppy jumped and ran the pad of her thumb under each eye, tears threatening to spill over. She wasn't ready for anyone else to see, or comment on the conversation she'd just had. 'Rubbish mascara. Keeps smearing...'

'And there was me thinking you had an uncomplicated life.'

'Does anyone? I think that's just adulthood. A Groundhog Day of people saying "things will slow down soon" until one of you slips into a coma.'

Will laughed, but his smile was sympathetic. He gestured to the closed door. 'What was that about?'

'Nothing. Nothing worth worrying about, anyway,' she said. The adrenaline dissipated, leaving her heady and disorientated. She wanted a distraction. After many years, cutting contact with Josh needed time to settle. It had taken so much willpower to initiate the split that she hadn't considered how the energy would go on draining her in the months that followed.

Poppy folded her arms and nodded towards the atrium. 'How's Ottilie doing?'

Will filled his cheeks and exhaled slowly, hands on his hips. 'I tried to go in, but she's locked the door. Hint taken.'

'It's all become a bit much,' she said, referring to her own situation as much as anyone else's. She made to leave, but Will stayed rooted to the spot, one hand clutching the back of his neck like he was being lowered into a police car.

'Are you okay?' said Poppy.

He didn't speak, only shook his head.

'Talk to me if you want to,' said Poppy, happy not to be discussing her own problems.

Will closed his eyes, lashes grazing his cheeks. Poppy leant against the wall and waited until he was ready to talk. Eventually, he mirrored Poppy on the opposite wall. They both slid down the wall until they were sitting on the carpet, ankles touching in the middle of the corridor. She pushed her finger into the plush hallway runner and bumped Will's foot with her own. He looked up.

'I don't know what's happened since we've been here. Ottilie is hot and cold, sometimes five times in the same day. My family, well… you saw that. Sorry, again.'

'Hey, you're lucky you never met my dad when he was at his worst. It can't help, though. Having to manage your family as well as Ottilie.'

'I manage my family *for* Ottilie. I feel like an idiot. I genuinely thought Dad was doing this grand gesture. You know, giving us the island for the week, hosting the wedding, showing an interest. It was *never* for me. It's all a power move. If he convinces everyone to vote me in as the successive CEO, it's still him that wins. I can't believe I didn't see that before.'

'It's a testament to how much trust you have in people,' said Poppy.

'That's exactly what Mum warned me about. She always said that Dad used goodwill to cash in later.'

'Then get away. If it's not the right time, there's an alternative, right?' She held her hands in front of her, like she was a magician revealing a magic trick. 'Don't. Get. Married. Not tomorrow, anyway.'

'But... Dad is pinning so much on this. If I pull back and stall the wedding, I won't be able to keep up the pretence that I'm happy with becoming CEO one day.'

'Let him deal with it on his own. You don't owe him for something you never asked for.'

Will shook his head. 'I can't do that. I know he doesn't deserve my sympathy, but he's made it clear that this week is about business just as much as anything else and I can't be the reason the company crashes. I never had him growing up and I don't want to lose him now. More than that, I'll be letting Ottilie down. But... this week hasn't played out how I thought it would.'

Poppy felt like someone had flicked a walnut at her stomach with a catapult. She knew it wasn't her place to make sweeping judgments on Will's family, or Ottilie, especially not now. He needed someone to listen, and that was something she could do.

'I think you'll find that Ottilie is on the same page,' said Poppy. 'She wants to marry you, but it seems like you've both lost your heads with everything that's going on here. Talk to each other, then decide what to do.'

'She won't talk to me.'

'I'll have a quick word first, if you like?'

'Are you sure? I know you said you were keen to leave. I don't want to delay you.' Will lifted his knee and draped his arm across it, his face awash with tiredness. It felt different and yet the same as when they'd sat like this in their student kitchen, the oven whirring as beige freezer food cooked, the events of their lives dissected over mugs of tea and slow-onset headaches.

'I'm sure.' Poppy stood up, her knees clicking as she straightened. 'Even though I feel like an old lady.'

Will smiled and pushed himself back up the wall. He scooped her in a one-armed hug. She could hear his heartbeat.

'Don't worry. I'm on your team, okay?' said Poppy.

'Okay,' said Will, releasing her.

Will followed Poppy into the atrium and down a side passage that linked the reception with the ballroom. When they reached the bathroom door, she paused, confused. Unless Ottilie was sobbing in the company of a frat house, the chanting was coming from elsewhere.

Before she could investigate, a group of men burst through the ballroom doors wearing gorilla costumes, their height and universally broad shoulders a sign that they'd grown up eating American beef. They chanted Will's name and ignored his piqued expression, taking it in turns to jump on him, whilst ignoring Poppy entirely.

'You ready, big guy?' called one of the men, a floppy gorilla mask under his arm. 'Your bachelor party starts in T minus fifteen minutes.'

Will broke into a smile. 'When did you guys land?'

'About three hours ago. Ryan has been drinking since we took off from JFK, so you better get this on or he'll pass out before we reach the mainland.' The speaker gestured to a jelly-legged man at the back of the group, his frog smile and red eyes a sign that he wouldn't last long. Will was handed a yellow suit and instructed to put it on. Whilst his cousins jostled around him in a happy haze of testosterone, Poppy shouted across the noise.

'Give me two minutes and I'll make sure you get to speak with Ottilie before you go.'

Poppy opened the door to a bathroom lined with green subway tiles and clunky, sharp sinks that matched the Art Deco style that ran throughout the hotel. The last cubicle door was pulled closed, the lock set to 'occupied'.

'Ottilie?'

'What?'

'It's me.'

'Who?'

'Poppy.'

The lock clicked open. Ottilie appeared in the crack of the door, her face puffy and pink. When she spoke, her voice broke. 'I've decided. If you can get me off the island tonight, I can meet Will on the mainland tomorrow. I want to marry him, but not here. Not like this.'

'Better catch him quick. His cousins have just started manhandling him into a banana costume,' said Poppy.

'Okay.' Ottilie splashed some water on her face and retied the shirt she wore over her crochet dress. 'And you can help us?'

Poppy bit the nail of her little finger and paced across the tiles. 'Give me some time, but I'll do what I can.'

Ottilie gave Poppy a strained smile, her hand on the door handle. 'One more thing. If anyone suspects that something is up, will you let me know? I don't want to cause more drama than necessary.'

Poppy nodded. 'Sure, but before I do anything else, there's someone I need to speak to.'

Chapter Twenty-Eight

DECEMBER 31ST, 2017

Lola. 8:41pm.

> *Have faith, Poppy. You are strong. If you need me, I can be round*
> *in twenty minutes.*
> *I'll see you tomorrow, okay?*
> *L x*

Poppy slipped her phone into a clutch bag. Every time she thought about what she was about to do, a wave of nerves washed over her. She had practised her conversation opener like a bizarre mantra in the mirror each morning before work and each night after she washed her face, skin pink from unnecessarily vigorous scrubbing. *I don't think we should be together. I need to be alone. I don't think we should be together. I need to be alone.*

After months of thinking about it, a few near misses, and long, exhaustive conversations with Lola in the attic, Poppy had realised there would never be a good time to break up with Josh. All this was true, yet Poppy hadn't considered how being dressed as a 1920s flapper girl might make it more difficult. The New

Year's Eve party they had been invited to was *The Great Gatsby* themed, but if the night turned out the way she predicted, Poppy would be seeing in the new year alone. It was why she couldn't leave the conversation until tomorrow. The thought of Jools Holland counting down from ten to one like a tiny human trumpet was too much, especially if Josh turned to her for a kiss she couldn't return when the party poppers burst. Besides, she wasn't in the party mood – not that you could tell from the glittery kohl around her eyes and dark purple lipstick.

Josh only paid attention to her mood when it directly impacted something he wanted to do. Living with it was a minefield. When it suited him, he was an attentive, all-consuming feature in her life, but when it didn't, he was distant and cold. Poppy was suffering from the long-term effects of emotional whiplash. She loved Josh, but she didn't like him anymore.

Pitbull played as Josh got changed, the double doors of their wardrobe open as he combed his hair back with gel. Pitbull made music for people who didn't like music, which was why it suited Josh.

'Can you draw me a tash?' he asked, angling a trilby hat on his head.

'A tash?'

'Yeah. Like Marlon Brando.'

Poppy's heart thumped in her chest as she pulled the lid off her liquid eyeliner. Josh sat at her dressing table. 'Are you sure?' she asked, unable to give him the real reason why this was a bad idea. You couldn't break up with someone when they looked like the Doritos logo. You just couldn't.

'If I'm going as *The Godfather*, I've got to look like *The Godfather*.'

'There's isn't a godfather in *Gatsby*.'

'It's pretty much the same thing.'

Poppy held her breath, coloured in a sparse moustache, and snapped the lid back on. 'There.'

'Thanks.' Josh ran a hand up her leg and squeezed the inside of her thigh. When she tensed, he frowned at her. 'What's up?'

'Can we go for a walk?' she asked, the words tumbling out before she could haul them back.

'What, now? We've got to leave in twenty minutes. You know what it's like at these things; everyone gets pissed too early and I won't be able to talk to Caroline and Stu.'

'Who?'

'God, Poppy. You really need to listen more in staff briefings. Caroline and Stu. The new deputy heads? I've got to show initiative. You know, get in with them early.'

'Surely that applies to work meetings, not fancy-dress parties in a colleague's new kitchen-cum-living room extension?'

'And that thinking is why I'm going to get the promotion.'

Poppy felt her throat tighten. She knew her muscle memory would try and convince her to stop, but she resisted. 'Please, can we go for a walk? Just a quick one. It's important.'

Josh slowed the buttoning of his collar, alert. He nodded.

Outside, the night was unseasonably warm for mid-winter. They walked behind a row of red-brick Victorian terraces and through a set of wrought-iron gates that led into a graveyard. Broken tombstones lit up with blooms of purple and red as teenagers lit cheap fireworks in the park.

'What did you want to talk about?' asked Josh, rubbing his bottom lip.

Poppy looked at him as they walked. He was brooding, wide-shouldered in a suit borrowed from his grandfather, hands pushed deep in his pockets. Poppy knew what she had to say, she just needed to say it.

'I don't know if you've noticed, but I've not been myself recently.'

Josh put his arm around Poppy's shoulder and squeezed. Her phone buzzed in her pocket. She glanced at the screen. It was Lola again.

I believe in you. Hold fast! L x

It was like her friend could sense her hesitation rising, the panic catching in her throat.

'I have noticed you've been a bit off,' said Josh. 'You're barely eating. I wondered... no. You go on.'

'You wondered what?'

Josh half laughed, half coughed. 'I wondered if you might be pregnant.'

Poppy's nerves took a swan dive. She hadn't considered this in her rehearsals. 'No. Oh, no that's not what I was implying.'

Confusion flickered across Josh's face. What had Lola told her to do? When you say it, just say it. Don't do a run-up. A punch in the gut hurts more if you can see someone walking towards you with a boxing glove. *Straight out with it, babe.*

'Before I go on, I just want you to know that I've thought about this properly and I don't want to hurt you. That's never what I wanted to do.'

Shit. Somehow, she'd done it anyway.

'Yeah, you're freaking me out now,' said Josh, his face pale as they walked under a streetlight. Poppy pinched herself so hard her eyes began to water. She turned back on herself, forcing them both to stop.

'I don't think we should be together anymore,' said Poppy, her eyes wide with insistence.

After a moment, Josh spoke, his voice neutral. 'Why?'

'When I'm around you, I don't recognise who I am. Sometimes you speak to me like you actually profoundly dislike me and it's making me not like myself either. We're different people now,' said Poppy, rushing her words as anger flashed across Josh's face. She was kidding herself if she thought this might be easy.

When Josh spoke, it was in a whisper. 'Of course we aren't the fucking same now. We're six years older. We've got jobs.'

Poppy remembered her next line, despite the blood rushing in her ears. 'I think I need to be on my own.'

'Yeah, yeah… because fucking off is always something you're an inch away from doing, isn't it?' Josh shook his head, furious. 'Every time things get tough, it's what you want to do. It was the same with New York, it was the same for your mum, and now history is repeating itself. Why am I not surprised? You can't blame me for every anxious feeling you have, however terrible the patriarchy is.'

'What?! This is *only* about us. You don't have to bring my fucking mum into it,' said Poppy, her worry morphing into anger that forked out of her mouth, hot and sharp.

'Don't you dare,' said Josh, pointing at her with a finger raised like a gun. 'If it's parents we're playing around with, you haven't won Top Trumps. My dad fucked off too. I would never do that. I do everything right by you. You don't *have* to be alone, not with me. Isn't that what you want?'

'You can't tell me you haven't noticed how things have been. We're ghosts in each other's lives. Be honest!'

'You want some hard truths? Here's one: you're selfish and manipulative. Listen to yourself.'

Poppy felt her throat close. She tried flexing her hands, but she couldn't feel her fingers. Talking was useless. Like a tablespoon of Alphabetti spaghetti, all meaning was lost in a jumble of incomprehensible letters. Panic rose inside, dominating her with one singular thought. *Make it stop.*

'I… I…' Poppy gulped and closed her eyes.

'I what?' said Josh, flicking open his jacket.

She couldn't do it. She'd been so close to starting again and yet, she couldn't do it.

'I think we need some time apart.'

'Yeah, we do, because you're not making sense,' said Josh, as though he were in a rush. 'I'm going to go to this party. There are people I want to talk to. *You* can do what you want. If it's independence you're after, there you fucking go. If you still want to talk about it tomorrow, fine, but *I'll* say when. You can't spring this shit on me when I'm not prepared for it, okay? People are staring. Come on, I'll walk you home.'

The following morning Poppy didn't speak to Josh. Her resolve had entirely failed. She met Lola for brunch as promised, her eyes hooded, her heart hollow.

A bell above the café door tinkled when she pushed it open. From a corner, half-hidden behind the fronds of a palm fern, Lola waved, slurped a mug of tea, and tidied a messy stack of documents into her handbag.

'Sorry about the papers,' said Lola, snapping the lid on a highlighter. 'I'm having a nightmare with the venue for that wedding I told you about. Essentially, I know it's a hotel near the sea, but they won't say where exactly "until necessary" for legal reasons. Madness.' Poppy scanned through previous conversations she'd had with Lola. If it was the wedding she only ever referred to as The Big One, Lola had been annoyingly vague. However, it could well be the case that she *had* told Poppy, but the details had bounced off her forehead, distracted as Poppy was from Lola's excited monologues by a constant murmuring of dread.

Lola pushed her cat-eye glasses into her loose purple hair. 'You look like shit, if you don't mind me saying.'

'I feel like it.'

'How did he take it?' said Lola, chin propped on her hands.

'He...'

'I don't *hope* that he's devastated, but he fucking well should be. Do you think he knew it was coming?'

'No, he didn't. He had a huge suit on and a fake cigar in his pocket,' said Poppy, building up to her admittance of failure. Her head ached from a lack of sleep, her memory fuggy and incoherent.

'Well, that sounds like it was made easier,' said Lola. 'Did you stay there last night? How are you feeling? Fuck, I'm *so* proud of you. Total champion. When you didn't text me back, I nearly drove round, but he's a good talker, isn't he? I assumed you'd be at it for hours. That's the worst bit done, I promise. You know you can stay with me, right? If he has the audacity to make this difficult for you. We should get you a glass of prosecco. Not for me, obviously. Oh, babe. This is the start of something. I promise you.'

Lola sat back in her chair, cheeks dimpled with pride. Poppy's heart sank. She loosened her scarf and tapped her foot with restless energy. She couldn't bring herself to look Lola in the eye, because as soon as she did, Lola would know.

'Oh, babe. It's a bit overwhelming, isn't it? Don't worry about the practical stuff. I can always head back to yours and pack a bag if you don't want to go. I'll borrow my Uncle Kev's rottweiler to keep Josh out for a while. He's got a pet ASBO. Excellent guard dog.'

'I didn't do it,' said Poppy, stealing a glance at Lola. The awkward silence that fell between them was cut through by a barista steaming a jug of milk. By the time it stopped, Poppy felt tears prickling behind her eyes.

'What do you mean you didn't do it?' said Lola.

'I didn't go through with it. Or, I did. I tried to. I said

everything I'd written down, one way or another, but it didn't work.'

'You either broke up with him or you didn't, babe. Which is it?'

'I don't know how literally he took it, but I did explain how I feel,' Poppy rubbed her eyes, her skin hot and sore from anxious tears. 'Maybe I jumped the gun. If I'd spoken to him more when we had a chance to fix things it might be different.' Poppy replayed her conversation with Josh until the image of his crestfallen, moustachioed face was etched on the inside of her skull. Lola didn't understand how hard it was to break up with someone who refused to be broken up with.

'When will it be bad enough to leave?' said Lola, her voice strained.

'Please don't be upset.' Poppy clutched her friend's hand, panicked. Lola calmy and carefully extracted her fingers and pooled them loosely in her lap.

'We've been here before,' said Lola, scratching her nose with her little finger. 'What did he say this time to make you change your mind?'

'It wasn't him. You know, I don't think I've been honest either. I keep saying he's made no effort with me, but that's not true. Last week, he asked me to go bouldering with him.'

'Did you want to go bouldering?'

'Well, not particularly, but it shows something, doesn't it? He's not a monster.'

'If you don't mind me saying, that's a low fucking bar.'

'Can you stop talking about him like that?' said Poppy. 'I know you hate him, but I've been with Josh for eight years.'

'Fine, fine. I know you don't want to stay with him, whatever you're telling yourself now, but I can't force you to be ready when you're not. At the end of the day, nothing I say will make a difference until you decide yourself,' said Lola.

'I know.' Poppy nodded, her chin heavy and childlike. She

brushed away a fat tear, exhausted. She couldn't bring herself to say it aloud, but Lola was right.

'I really want you to listen to me now,' said Lola. 'I'm not going to do this again. If you're deciding to stay with Josh, that's on you. But his behaviour isn't just affecting you anymore. I have a fledgling business. Every time you say you're ready to leave him, I'm there. This was the last time, okay? When you call me next, it has to be because you're ready to move on, and not before.'

'I don't want to hurt him,' she said.

'Why are you not maintaining that same standard for yourself?'

'Lola—' said Poppy, her hands flat on the table.

'What?'

'I love you. Don't think I take you for granted. I don't, truly.'

'I love you too. That's why I'm putting this boundary in place. Do you get me?'

'Not really,' said Poppy. She squashed the feeling of freefall that prickled in her chest.

'You will, eventually. Now, can you please buy us a flapjack? You look so sad they might give us an extra slice for free.'

'It didn't work last time.' Poppy gave Lola a fleeting smile, which she returned, exhaling through her nose. As she walked away, Lola caught her wrist and pulled her into a hug, arms encircling her waist.

'I'll be strong enough. I will. Just not today,' said Poppy into Lola's hair.

'I know, darling. I know.'

Chapter Twenty-Nine

THE DAY BEFORE THE WEDDING

Poppy scanned the expansive dining room before spotting Lola. In the corner, a hundred glass jars pinned a linen tablecloth down, all at various states of upcycling. Lola swore as she attempted to tie a bow with her stiletto nails, roughly pulled the knot loose, and dropped the lace over the back of a chair adorned with pre-cut lengths of twine.

'Hey, I need to talk to you,' said Poppy.

Lola looked up, a chunky chalk pen now in her hands.

'Has someone died? Who is it? I have a contingency plan for this, but it depends on the age,' said Lola. She put the cap back on the pen and propped it on an easel that displayed a partially complete seating plan.

'Everyone is alive, as far as I'm aware. It's something else.'

'Oh.' Lola pursed her lips. 'Disappointing. I'd been waiting for a good time to test drive my mortality manoeuvres. What's up?'

'Can we go somewhere else? Somewhere a bit more private?' said Poppy. She dropped her voice, conscious of being overheard by the bar staff who lived off gossip like it was a rapidly depleting life source. She'd worked as a silver-service waitress at university, so she knew what it took to make it through a ten-hour shift with the minimum government-sanctioned breaks.

'Will we be long?'

'I don't know. It depends on your reaction.'

'All right, but I've got fifty thousand things to do. Ottilie wants the "homemade wedding" look but doesn't want to pick up a glue gun, so yours truly spent last night learning squiggly calligraphy. If the photos from this wedding aren't all over Pinterest the moment we leave this island, I'll have failed.'

Poppy picked at a hangnail and nodded at the army of jam jars double stacked on the table. 'It looks brilliantly shabby chic, but—'

'I know,' said Lola dreamily, stepping back to admire her work. 'I could add another two hundred quid to my fee for this. FYI, I can't sit down. I'm breaking Ottilie's wedding shoes in.' Lola pointed to her feet. She wore a pair of fluffy slipper socks tucked into plastic sandwich bags, which were in turn stuffed into sky-blue satin ballet shoes, complete with ribbons loosely criss-crossed at the ankle. 'She has wide feet and doesn't want blisters. I don't want to sweat into her shoes. It's a paradox for which I've found a genius solution.'

'Isn't that the kind of task that she should be undertaking?'

'From now on, I am following the path of least resistance and saying yes to everything Ottilie requests. She doesn't remember most of it, so if she's happy, I can get on with organising everything else behind the scenes. By extension, Will is happy, and as long as he continues to trot around in a haze of pre-marital love, the Mountgraves are happy, which means I'm happy and still within shot of a bonus. Win-win!'

'Uh, about that. Let's talk.'

Lola beckoned Poppy to follow her into the kitchens, but when they pushed the chain-link curtain back, they found Tamiko hunched over a steel workbench, slicing carrots so quickly he sounded like a woodpecker on speed.

'Jesus, it's hot in here,' she said.

Tamiko sighed, as though this wasn't the first time the kitchen had been used for a meeting of the privy council. He nodded towards a broad stainless-steel door. 'There's a walk-in freezer over there. Cool off if you like. I'll pretend I didn't see you, or we'll lose a hygiene star.'

Before Poppy could object, Lola had slipped out of Ottilie's wedding shoes, propped them on a high shelf, and heaved open the door of the freezer. The rush of cool air was soothing, like someone had placed a cold flannel across the back of Poppy's neck. Lola sighed as she stepped from one pink foot to the other.

'Wedge that lamb leg in the door jamb; I've seen *Jurassic Park* more than fifteen times. Even velociraptors can't grapple their way out of an industrial freezer when the door slams shut. Right, what's up?' said Lola.

Poppy shook her hands in front of her. 'All right, I don't know how to say this delicately, so I'm just going to go for it.'

'Unlike you, but okay.'

Poppy turned towards her friend, hands clenched in anxious fists.

'I don't think this wedding should go ahead.'

Lola tilted her head to the side and slid her tongue over her teeth. 'And your reasoning for that is…?'

'I have it on good authority that Will and Ottilie don't want to go through with it. Not right now, anyway.'

'What is this bollocks? Are you undercover with *Heat* magazine?' said Lola, laughing.

'I'm serious. Haven't you noticed?'

'Noticed what?'

'That this whole wedding seems a bit… off?'

'Take the tin hat off, Popster. Of course it seems off – the Mountgraves aren't a normal family. It's like walking into Harrods and thinking it's a bit off that they don't sell Dairylea Lunchables. This lot don't *do* ordinary.'

'But not Will, right? I know we haven't been in each other's lives for a few years, but I think he's trying to be too many things to too many people. I'm worried about him. This wedding has seen them chugging along a train track that neither can disembark from without causing a fatal disaster.'

'Wow, thanks for the vote of confidence, Poppy. I didn't realise this wedding was traumatic to the point of making people question the whole basis of their relationship.'

'That's not what I'm saying at all. I don't know *how* to explain it without sounding bitter or overbearing.'

'Try your best.'

'Ottilie is planning on leaving before the wedding. She wants my help and I think we should at least consider what she's asking, objectively.'

'Poppy, I'm going to be as measured about this as humanly possible. You really – and I mean *really* – should have opened with that bit of information. When did she tell you this?'

'This morning. Well, technically last night, but I thought she might have been exaggerating. I was telling her about *my* wedding. About how I'd spent the day looking for reasons to lock myself in a toilet cubicle—'

'Oh, great. You told my bride about *your* terrible wedding and now you're wondering why she's freaked out and wants to bail?'

'No, no it wasn't like that. Will thinks something is wrong too. This week has been the tipping point, not just with the wedding. His dad is trying to manhandle him into a job he doesn't want. He's been sent a load of pre-written responses to interviews that Lord Mountgrave's publicist has organised. Ottilie has been staying down at the fisherman's hut on her own and everyone thinks she's a diva for wanting to change the ceremony. In reality, she feels like she's lost herself. You know what? I *know* how that feels. If she doesn't feel comfortable going through with it, she shouldn't.'

Lola measured the weight of each word as she spoke. 'You know when I said "make sure the bride is busy, happy, and calm"? Yeah, the small print should have read "distracted and blissfully naïve". My job is to make sure she gets to the altar without worrying about anything, if that wasn't painfully obvious.'

'I can't lie to her.'

'What are you talking about? Of course you can.'

'You can't be serious. On a fundamental level, I don't understand how *anyone* could look at them as almost-newlyweds and think, yep, those two are living their dream! Come on, you must see it too.'

'And you're saying this after being in their company for… what, three days?'

'I'm saying it objectively.'

'Pfft, no you're not.' Lola crossed her arms.

'I am. Will and I used to be close—'

'Tell me more about that. Used to be close? Was this before or after you moved out of the same flat? Unless you have something else to tell me?'

'I'm trying to be sincere,' said Poppy, charging on. 'Will *always* hated confrontation. He never wants to put anyone out. From what Ottilie has told me, he doesn't know how to slow things down without causing a publicity shitstorm.'

'You've got this wrong, babe. I don't think Will is the reason you're trying to convince me to stop this wedding. I think your *total* inability to face up to your own failed marriage is why you've been bitter and cynical since the moment you stepped foot on Loxby.'

Poppy coughed, incredulous. '*You* asked *me* to come here!'

'As a favour! For my job!'

'I'm supposed to be taking some time for myself, on an island half a mile that way,' said Poppy, jerking her thumb towards a box of langoustines. 'I've wasted the best part of the week here when I should be *there*, on my own, untouched by other people's drama.'

'Really? Do you still think that's where you're *supposed* to be? Alone in the middle of the ocean so you can really hunker down behind that mental barricade you've constructed to stop yourself from actually moving on?'

'Josh hasn't made it easy,' said Poppy, her initial adrenaline wearing off. She clutched her elbows, shivering uncontrollably. Whilst Poppy made herself smaller, Lola did the opposite.

'Don't even start,' said Lola. 'I *know* he's a bellend. Colonel Twatface. The Almighty Arsehole. He's a fucking gaslighter. Manipulative, and clever with it too. I know that turning him into a human dartboard was what you needed to push through the divorce. But you can't lie to me anymore. I saw the email on your phone. He's not the one holding things up. *You* are. Why haven't you signed your divorce papers?'

'It's not that I haven't signed them, it's just—'

'Has he signed them?'

'Yes.'

'Have you signed them?'

'No, but—'

'But what! You either want to divorce him or you don't. You either want to stay married or you don't. This isn't the Middle Ages. You're not going to be dragged through the streets with a rope around your waist for divorcing your shit husband.'

Poppy coughed, incredulous. 'That's low. Really fucking low.'

'Why should you care! You're divorcing him! Good fucking riddance!'

'You don't need to be so brutal,' said Poppy, her throat tight.

'Don't I? I *want* you to react. If I'm making you feel angry, good! About fucking time! In all the years you've been with Josh, you've always defended him, just a little. Don't you think that's ab-fucking-normal considering the circumstances?'

'Not particularly. I'm not a cut-and-dried kind of person.'

'You were when I first met you. You wouldn't take shit from anyone.'

Poppy shifted, her mouth tight. 'And there was me thinking that losing your temper was a bad thing.'

'It beats being stoic, silent, and bitter. He made you feel scared, Poppy!' said Lola. 'He made you give up everything you enjoyed! I didn't see you for months – total radio silence. Do you know how worried I've been? What happened to your opinions? Your thoughts? Your social life?'

'Look, you have no idea how hard this has been, all right? I know I instigated the split, but following through has been a very different thing. The separation— I've had to deal with it on my own,' said Poppy, panic clawing at her throat. She didn't want to lose anyone else.

'Oh, no, no, no. Don't pretend that no one was there. I offered, but you pushed me away. You know what? I've gone through some shit in the past few years too. I nearly relapsed,' she said, an invisible inch between her thumb and forefinger. 'I was *this* close. But I didn't say anything because you were in the thick of it with Josh.'

'I didn't know… Are you okay—?'

'Yes, I'm fine,' snapped Lola. 'I didn't burden you with it because I knew you wouldn't be able to cope, not with the tunnel vision you've had.'

'If you're so good at predicting what I can and can't handle, you shouldn't have asked me to come here.'

'You would have taken it personally if I hadn't.'

Poppy pondered the thought. 'All right, maybe. But it's not exactly easy to be all *woohoo, weddings, together forever babes!* when you can see through the fantasy with crystal bloody clear accuracy.'

Lola threw her hands up in protest. 'You know everything that's happened here? It's not about you! I know that your relationship is *long* overdue for some unpacking, but you have to stop seeing the details in someone else's life as directly relating to your own.' Poppy opened her mouth to retort, but the sentiment died on her lips. 'This is my job. Career-wise, it's make or break for me. Should Ottilie and Will be getting married right now? I honestly haven't given it a moment's thought. Plenty of couples don't showcase their best selves in the week of their wedding. Am I going to do my best to deliver them what they want, even if it means folding origami swans in my sleep? Yes. That's it for me. That's where it ends.'

'But Will is our friend.'

'He *was your* friend; he's *my* client. That's all I can afford for him to be right now.'

Poppy tried to rub warmth back into her arms. 'I can't do nothing. If Will keeps going through the motions, he'll be miserable for years to come. Loyalty comes into it, surely?'

'Exactly,' said Lola, folding her arms close to her chest. She trapped Poppy in an unwavering gaze. 'You took the words right out of my mouth.'

Poppy shuddered. Like always, she broke eye contact first. There was a surge in the pit of her stomach that felt partway between nausea and flame-licked rage. If Lola walked away, Poppy knew she would cry, but her friend was too dignified to shiver, too stubborn to leave. Now that her adrenal glands had stopped pumping quite so hard, she realised just how cold she was. Poppy let her gaze fall to her legs, which were covered in corned beef blotches. 'Do you want me to leave Loxby?'

'Do what you need to do. I'm not ordering you about. If you want to give Will some moral support, stay for Will. If you want to help me out by talking Ottilie off the ledge, I'd welcome it. I really would. Basically, I want to do my job without it being jeopardised. But if you can't separate your feelings from this situation, I don't think you should be here.'

Poppy's eyelids felt hot. If Lola could get through this conversation without crying, Poppy could too, putting to one side that there was every chance her tears would form into ice crystals before they reached the end of her chin. She measured her voice before she spoke, testing each word for cracks.

'I'll go. I've had a half-packed bag since I got here, so... yeah, I'll go.'

'Okay,' said Lola, nodding. 'The proper photographer is here, so we'll cope without you.'

That stung. 'Will I see you next week? At the cottage?'

'I don't have the capacity to think about that right now.'

'Of course.'

'I'll tell Will and Ottilie that you've gone, if you don't have time to find them,' said Lola, more as a statement than speculation. Poppy scratched her arm, irritated.

'Oh, I see. You're pushing me out through the back door.'

'I'm just trying to be helpful,' said Lola, fatigue underlying her words.

Poppy hugged herself as shivers ran deep into her core. She felt spiteful and immature, her mind throwing out revenge acts reminiscent of grapples at the peg rack in primary school: stamping on Lola's foot, flicking her ear, tugging on a lock of hair. She took pleasure from seeing Lola's feet tinged blue against the icy tiles.

Poppy couldn't even be insulted with dignity.

'Bye then,' said Lola, her voice cut with sarcasm.

'Bye.' Poppy turned to leave, her heel heavy on the wet tiles. She slipped and lunged for something to hold onto, hand closing around the girthy end of a whole frozen salmon. She recoiled, and split into laughter, but Lola didn't join in. Instead, she held the gaze of a pig carcass that was strung from the ceiling on a butcher's hook. Poppy cleared her throat, silence emboldening the awkwardness between them. 'Do you want me to leave the lamb leg in the door?'

'Yes. I'll come out in a minute,' Lola snapped.

Poppy stepped over the slowly thawing meat, the heat of the kitchen enveloping her as she sidestepped behind chefs who moved with choreographed precision between workstations.

Outside, the sea air cut sharply in her throat. In all the years they'd been friends, the only arguments they'd experienced were ones that had involved Lola trying to start a fight with someone who had shouldered their way in front of her at a bar. It was Poppy's job to deescalate, always.

The further she got from the freezer, the more Poppy recognised how bitterness had built up in both of them. It wasn't just today. She could see it in Lola's tight jaw, her impatience, her nails as they dug into her forearm. She resented her, just like Josh had over the years. By the time Poppy had reached the hot terracotta tiles outside, her feet throbbed with pain as his voice replayed in her head: 'Look at the things you've screwed up in your life, eh? What's the common denominator? You.'

Chapter Thirty

'Extra cheese, please.'

'It's already got cheese on it.'

'I know, but I want extra cheese. Like, as much cheese as you'd normally put on, but then all of that again.'

'That's a lot of cheese.'

'I'm aware.'

'Almost half a block.'

'Excellent.'

The barman slowly shook his head, scribbled down her request, and walked it over to the kitchen hatch. The chef ducked to look at the order slip, then at Poppy, who leant against the bar. Poppy saluted him.

With just over twenty-four hours to go until the wedding, activity down at the harbour was limited to deliveries and dignitaries. Poppy waited for her food and watched as small boats with polished hulls glided up to dock, their passengers quaffed, pressed, and polished in ways that Poppy had only ever seen in the pages of *Vanity Fair* shoots. If Josh were here, he'd speculate on how they kept the lines in their trousers so crisp. The thought made a lump bubble in her throat, but she didn't know why. Josh had a fierce love for Sweden, not for IKEA, but for 'their appreciation of the utilitarian form'. Naturally, this was a conversation killer at dinner parties.

From the kitchen, the sound of oil crackling made her stomach tighten with hunger. She'd eaten more thumb-sized slices of fish since being on Loxby than she would ever likely see again, but now was the time for stodge, and lots of it. Poppy pulled her camera out of her bag, clicked the memory card out, and pushed it into her laptop.

The pictures she'd taken over the last few days appeared on her screen like stills from a film. Was it possible for light to look expensive? It certainly did here. Poppy scrolled back to the photographs she'd taken at dawn, the sky filled with candy floss clouds, the long tables in the ballroom, the curve of Will's neck as Josie leant up to whisper something in his ear. Overall, there were far more of Will than there were of Ottilie, but his bride had spent most of the week on the other side of the room, as though she and Will were the opposing ends of a magnet.

The more photographs she flicked through, the more confused she was about the feelings that stirred in her chest. Poppy noticed things she hadn't seen when sitting in front of Will, the small signs of ageing that gave his softness an edge, made his jaw a little sharper, his eyes a little creased, his back a little straighter.

She clicked through her memory card until Will's broad back morphed into Josh's slight footballer's frame from six years previous. When she used to go on shoots for *The World's Eye*, Poppy would take a thousand photos in a day. Her meticulous organisation of raw files had slipped over the years. The memory card she had used must be an old one. Poppy flicked onto a picture of Josh, taken as he walked through a cobbled courtyard in Crete, a small tub of vanilla ice cream in one hand and a thick guidebook in the other. The next was on the balcony of a hotel they had stayed in, the concrete walls bleached by Mediterranean sun. Josh gripped the railings, his tongue stuck out towards the camera, skin dewy from the heat. She'd forgotten how he so often had a laugh pinched between his teeth.

'Chips with cheese, cheese, and more cheese.' Greg placed a bowl on the table. 'Let me know if you need us to charge up the defibrillator.'

Poppy thanked him, shut her laptop, and wiggled it back into her bag between tightly rolled clothes. She took her chips out into the afternoon sun and immediately regretted not spraying her inner thighs with antiperspirant as she all but squeaked with each step. When she emerged by the concrete slipway, she stopped. Sitting in the sunshine, sleeves rolled up to the elbow, was Lawrence.

'Oh.'

'Oh yourself.'

'Didn't fancy joining the others for golf?'

Lawrence snorted. 'I have some standards.'

'You do know this is technically staff quarters,' said Poppy.

'Indeed. It's why I'm fairly sure no one will bother me. Except you, obviously.'

Poppy leant her bag against the stone wall of the pub and squatted to join Lawrence, who sat with his legs dangling inches above the water. He used a duffle bag as a pillow, the chocolate-brown print and YSL monogram recognisable from the knock-off markets Poppy used to attend at the greyhound track with her dad.

'Are you hiding?'

'Not as such,' he replied, closing his eyes in the sunshine.

Poppy crossed her legs and balanced her bowl in the hollow. She was devoid of concern for anything other than the string of cheese that dangled from a chip as she lowered it into her mouth.

'That's disgusting,' said Lawrence.

Poppy wiped her lip and swallowed. 'Go on, admit it. You're a little bit jealous.'

Lawrence pulled his glasses down and squinted at her in the sunshine. 'You know, I take it back. You're quite hot when you eat. In a way that makes me feel uncomfortable. I could be into it.'

Poppy swallowed and frog-smiled, oil smeared across her chin. 'Not a chance, mate.' She wiped her fingers on a wooden post and rearranged her dress to form a buffer between her bare skin and the hot stone she was sitting on. 'You're off, are you? Day before your brother's wedding? Classy.'

'So it would seem.'

'I'm not having a dig at you. It's a solid decision.'

'No sarcasm? You disappoint me. I did have the distinct feeling that you – how should I put it – would happily stamp on my disembowelled entrails?'

'I would phrase it as "strong feelings of *disdain* towards your guts", but I don't hate you. I don't hate anyone.'

'Really? It's my neutral stance.'

'Is that why you've been trying your best to screw things up for your brother all week?'

'I haven't got a clue what you're talking about,' he said, each word slow and decisive.

Poppy swallowed a clod of hot chip mush and rolled her eyes. 'Swapping names at lunch the other day? Poking the angry badger that is your dad? Disappearing from family events with a waitress? This isn't a soap; you can't go around doing things like that.'

'Oh, *that's* what you're referring to? Come on, lighten up.'

'You need to... un-lighten up.'

'Is that your best fighting talk?'

'You're infuriating.'

'I get that a lot.'

They let the noise of the water take over as it splashed against the sagging sides of a sun-bleached dinghy.

'You don't fancy it, then?'

'What?'

'A shag.'

'Oh, Christ no. At least offer to buy me a lemonade first.'

'I would, but I don't carry money and I don't really want to run anything up on the family tab right now.'

'Why, are you running away?'

'I'm not a teenager with daddy issues.'

'You're not?'

'I'm an adult with daddy issues. Very different.'

Poppy laughed and shook her head.

'So what's going on with you? Why are you leaving?' said Lawrence.

'Do you *really* want to know or are you being polite? Because you don't need to bother.'

'You know what? I'm feeling rather tired. Wake me up in ten, will you? I've got a boat coming,' said Lawrence. He crossed his arms over his chest and shuffled into a comfier position.

'I'm being a dick,' said Poppy. 'Sorry.'

'So am I. Glad we got that out of the way. Now, why are *you* leaving? Did you shag the waitress too?'

'No. The photographer arrived.'

'I thought you *were* the photographer.'

'Not the real one. It's that Christian guy. The one who has a fat address book of magazine editors. That way, Will and Ottilie can feature in the six-page wedding spread of their dreams.'

'Meow.'

Poppy rubbed her eyes with the heel of her hand. 'I have, as they say, stopped swimming upstream.'

'Well, I for one need to offer you congratulations. You lasted –

what was it? – five days in the company of my family? That's my personal best, and I'm *obliged* to spend time with my father.'

'What do you mean? Legitimately ducking out of family events is one of the best things about being an adult.'

'Yes, but I'm also required to make an appearance at things like this, otherwise I'd have to find a proper job and my CV leaves rather a lot to be desired.'

'I forgot, you still get pocket money, don't you?'

'Don't say it like it's a dirty word.'

'Okay, so that's a yes. Does Will?'

'God, no.' Lawrence turned onto his side and propped his chin in his hand. 'I have a contract. Don't scoff – I'm being truthful. I've been a bit naughty in the past, so it's part of the deal.'

'What does "naughty" constitute in your book? Not turning up to the country club with the right coloured trousers?'

'I wrapped a car around a tree in southern Italy whilst off my tits on a pretty potent cocktail of alcohol and whatever I could find in the medicine cabinet.'

'Shitting hell. Really?'

'Yeah. It caused a bit of an uproar. I was told all of this second-hand, of course. I can't remember a thing. I tell you what, waking up after a coma is bad, but not quite as bad as waking up in the midst of an enforced period of cold turkey.'

'Was anyone hurt?'

'Other than me? No. Well, the olive tree didn't fare too well. Turns out it was ancient – the oldest one for three hundred miles. The locals held a funeral for it. In terms of sympathy, that fucking tree muscled me out big time.'

'So that's why you don't drink?'

'Mmm. I thought it would make me less of an arsehole, but some things are inherited. Dad likes to keep an eye on me from afar. Emphasis on "afar".' Lawrence pushed his hair back and twisted the signet ring on his little finger. 'No, let me be specific. Dad's PR woman, Julia, likes to keep an eye on me, but there's very little maternal about that. Will was the one who pulled through when it came down to it, but everyone's patience has a breaking point. Essentially, our father throws money at a problem, but you can wager he'll cash it in later down the line. If I'd had my wits about me, I'd have asked someone to lock me in a toilet for three weeks instead. Perhaps that would have been easier for everyone.'

'That sounds pretty heartless.'

'If I hadn't gone to rehab, I wouldn't have met Ottilie, which by extension means that I'd have kept her from meeting Will and we wouldn't be sitting on this dock preparing to flee a wedding destined for a very public divorce. It's funny how things turn out, isn't it?'

Poppy's bowl fell between her knees and clattered on the pebble-dash floor.

'Wait, wait, wait. You met Ottilie in rehab? Are you sure?'

'Quite. It's about the only thing I *am* sure about, considering it was the first time I'd been sober in about nine years.'

'Congratulations, by the way. For being sober. I mean it.'

'Hey, thanks. That's good of you to say. Seriously. It feels odd being sincere, but yeah… Anyway, they give you a commemorative coin for each milestone, but I lost mine in a game of blackjack.'

Poppy did a double take and bit into a chip.

'Joking! I'm joking, obviously.'

Poppy rolled her eyes. 'So, Ottilie. You met her at rehab? Was she volunteering?'

Lawrence laughed so much he had to sit up to stop himself from spluttering. 'Yeah, volunteering. Good one. Can you imagine Ottie leading art therapy? Or taking a genuine interest in other people's problems, for that matter?'

'I don't know, the way she says it had me thinking she was a serial philanthropist. Maybe?'

'It's not her thing.'

'So, she was *in* rehab? With you?'

'I can tell you're finding this hard to grasp. Let me paint the picture. She was a big name on the Chelsea scene a few years ago. She'd throw these big fucking parties, but you'd see her for five minutes and then she'd disappear, like Gatsby. She went into rehab before me, but we overlapped by a month. A few of the old gang ended up in The Priory. The party moved location, so to speak. Less cocaine, more cocoa.'

'Ottilie told me you met whilst she was volunteering at a church group.'

'Church? Well, I guess that's not wholly untrue. The AA group we both went to took place in a church.'

'Hey, no judgment from me, I'm just curious as to why she'd lie about it. Maybe she's worried about how it would look now that there's so much attention on her and Will? In a way, I get it. I don't think it's been particularly easy for Ottilie to find her place in your family.'

'Don't feel too bad for her. We've all got our shit going on. Will is a glutton for punishment. He's the kind of guy who goes for a walk with the sole intention of finding an abandoned kitten to look after. Sure, Ottilie is fun, when she's getting her own way. She's hot. Ordinarily, she's great at dealing with The Grand Puppeteer that is our father, but that's a red flag if ever I saw one. If you notice the strings, it's because you're skilled at the craft yourself.'

'But she's not just marrying Will, is she? She's marrying into *The Mountgrave Foundation*. It's so public! Has she been given any support with that? Has Will? He hasn't grown up around your dad in the same way you have.'

'Exactly. Lucky him.'

Poppy stretched her legs and sighed. 'I feel sorry for her and Will. Everyone here seems to have an opinion to do with their wedding. I've not come out unscathed either. I've only been here for a few days and I've never felt worse about myself.'

'Oh, welcome to The Mountgrave Experience. It's like one of our theme parks, but the adrenaline comes from never quite knowing when someone's going to screw you over.'

'Your lot makes my family seem incredibly tame in comparison. I only witnessed extramarital affairs and the premature death of my mum. Normal stuff, you know?'

'You shouldn't joke about that,' said Lawrence.

'Why? That's not how it works. *You* can't make jokes about my family, but I can. My mum died. It is what it is. *Dick & Dom in da Bungalow* proved to be worthy babysitters on Saturday mornings. It wasn't all bad.'

'Is that why you got married when you were fifteen?' said Lawrence.

'Fuck off, fifteen! I was twenty-two!'

'That's basically fifteen.'

'I knew what I was doing. I can't let myself regret it. It's been too long and it wasn't terrible, not all of the time.'

'Has anyone approached you about being a spokesperson for long-term monogamy?'

Poppy laughed. It felt good. Her verbal filter was on holiday, encouraged by Lawrence, who Poppy could safely assume hadn't had one to begin with.

'That's fucking rough, though. About your mum. No one should have to deal with that, no matter what kind of person they are. Hey, if I've learnt anything, it's that you can't expect anyone to look after you in the way you can look after yourself.'

Poppy nodded slowly and bit her lip. 'I know. I'm working on that.'

'So what's your reason for getting out of the viper's nest?' asked Lawrence.

'Lola needed me, then I sort of… got passed around until I served my purpose and people started to wonder why I hadn't left. Then we had a huge argument, which is a first. I was never supposed to be here, so I don't really deserve to feel upset about it. Basically, my presence has ultimately caused more problems than it has solved. As such, I'm bowing out. I'm not going to linger where I'm not wanted.'

'Oh, darling. You can't take it personally. This is a rite of passage. You're one of us now.'

'How has Will avoided getting macerated by the machine?'

'He hasn't, but he's not clever enough to notice. It's his best asset. It protects him. He's malleable enough to be excellent PR. Good-looking, oblivious, and unquestioning. Like Forrest Gump with a bachelor's degree.'

'Has anyone ever told you that you're quite obnoxious?'

'Of course they have. It's why I get away with it.'

Poppy wiped her bowl with a fat chip, ate it, and licked her fingers. From the other side of the pub, Poppy could hear the chug of the sea tractor pulling into the dock.

'You coming?' said Poppy.

Lawrence licked his thumb and wiped a scuff mark from his shoe. 'On that thing? Absolutely not. I'd rather remove my foot with a cheese knife than get the sea tractor. I've got a boat coming in approximately… seven minutes.'

'You mean, you *don't* like inhaling illegal levels of diesel fumes whilst you travel?'

Lawrence laughed.

Poppy wondered whether the detached bravado Lawrence performed was *his* version of self-protection. It was why she was so readily willing to give herself the label of failed photographer. If she did it first, it blunted the knife for the next person.

Poppy stood up and held out a hand to Lawrence. 'It was... an experience meeting you,' she said. Lawrence shook it, his palm cool despite the heat.

'Likewise. I doubt our paths will cross again.'

From a window that peeked through to the front of the pub, Poppy saw a familiar cascade of blonde hair. The sound of light footsteps reached them before Ottilie did. A moment later, she appeared round the corner with a leather rucksack slung over one shoulder. She beamed at Poppy, but her face fell when her eyes drifted down to Lawrence. He cleared his throat.

'What are you doing here?' said Ottilie.

'What it looks like. Scuba diving,' said Lawrence, readjusting his silver belt buckle.

'You're leaving?'

'Indeed.'

'Together?' said Ottilie. Poppy didn't appreciate the incredulity that slipped into Ottilie's voice, but whether this came from reproach or confusion, she wasn't sure.

'No, not *together*,' said Poppy. 'I am, in fact, the only one who *should* be legitimately leaving this island.'

Ottilie folded her arms. 'I didn't think you were leaving so soon. We had plans.' Ottilie glanced at Lawrence. 'Poppy promised to take me... on a hike,' she said, saying the last word as though she'd coughed it up from the back of her throat. Poppy credited her quick thinking.

'It seems like Poppy is all hiked out,' said Lawrence. He flicked his sunglasses down and checked his watch.

Ottilie squatted next to Poppy. 'We had a plan. For the hike. There's another harbour on the south side – great view. I should take you there. To say thank you for jumping in to help out this week. I'm sure we can figure out the details of how you're going to leave later,' she said, her voice unwaveringly cool and full of hidden meaning. Ottilie's chest heaved as she took shallow breaths, her gaze fixed on Poppy in a way that emphasised how very much she was trying to extract her from Lawrence. Was this why Ottilie had followed her down to the harbour? Did she think Poppy was still going to help her with a getaway plan? After her argument with Lola, Poppy had done as requested and left without entangling herself in other people's problems. But was she too entangled already?

'You know, I never promised I'd go on... the hike,' said Poppy. 'I've got my own trip to get back to. Talk to Lola. Maybe she'll be able to help.'

Poppy refused to offer a more detailed solution than that. She wasn't going to allow other people to dictate her movements anymore.

'You can't pull out now. We had an agreement.'

'Sorry. Things have changed.'

A tap on the glass made all three turn towards the window. Greg pulled the frame up and pushed his head outside. 'Poppy? There's a call for you. You're wanted up at the hotel. It sounded urgent.'

Chapter Thirty-One

L ord Mountgrave sat at a table set in a recess of the atrium, hidden from the main corridor by a well-placed staircase, framed by panoramic views of the bay. He lowered his espresso cup as the buckles of Poppy's bag clanked against the polished floor.

'Good, you're here,' said Lord Mountgrave, uncrossing his legs.

Poppy clutched a stitch in her side and leant against a marble pillar. 'Has something happened? Reception said... Eurgh, I can't catch my breath. They said it was urgent. Can I have some of that?'

Lord Mountgrave gestured to the table, his ringmaster guise far less insistent than the tone of his message had implied. Poppy poured herself a glass of iced water and drank it in fish gulps.

'Has something happened?'

'Yes, as it goes.'

Poppy's neck prickled with unease. She had spent years shirking the feeling that things went wrong when she disappeared. The burden of this settled under her skin, soothing and cumbersome as a weighted blanket. As a thirteen-year-old, her fears had been confirmed by missing suitcases and stale beer that she scrubbed out of the carpet before school. Fears weren't irrational when they proved themselves to be true.

Lord Mountgrave nodded towards Poppy's bag. 'The photographs. Correct me if I'm wrong, but I'd say that supplying the images after you've taken them is an integral part of being a photographer, no?' He wore a wry smile, thumbs in his pockets as he waited for Poppy to answer. Her relief made way for irritation that prickled at the centre of her chest.

'I was planning on sending them to you when I reached the mainland,' she said, covering up the fact that she hadn't given a thought to this at all.

'No problem. See, I had fibre optic broadband installed the year before last, so if it's on a digital cloud – whatever you call it – you can do the transfer here. You know, we were the first establishment in the South West to have the lines installed? Hugely expensive, but it takes someone to lay the tracks first, doesn't it? Hello?' said Lord Mountgrave, bending to recapture Poppy's attention after she became distracted by the sight of Ottilie walking past the window, hair gleaming in the sunshine as she side-eyed Poppy before quickening her pace with long, bounding steps. *She's not my problem, she's not my problem, she's not my problem.*

'Sorry. Photos. Yep. I can get those to you.'

'Wonderful. Now, any chance you've seen my boy?'

'Which one?'

Lord Mountgrave paused, as though remembering he had more than one choice. 'Lawrence.'

'He was at the harbour ten minutes ago, but he'll have left by now.'

Lord Mountgrave considered this, but it didn't bother him as much as Poppy had assumed it would. 'Right, right. Look, about earlier. You'll have to forgive me for all that nonsense. I apologise if I came across as ungrateful, stepping in as you have done.' He spoke with caution, eyes trained on the entrances and exits of the room like he was assessing how best to defend himself from an incoming mob armed only with a blunt pâté knife and a series of quick remarks. 'It's all of us cooped up here, isn't it? Bound to scratch at one another's throats sooner or later.'

'Try a caravan in Torquay with a set of pyrotechnic cousins.'

Lord Mountgrave snorted a singular laugh, hands in his pockets. 'Quite. No matter. It's heading north from here on out. Tell you what, don't have your children raised in different countries. Will is a good boy, but Lawrence ducks and dives like a rabbit on a bungee cord. And he wonders why he's not given *more* responsibility. Not like Will. He needs to have the spotlight this weekend. I'm glad Lawrence has taken himself off. It's for the best. He's incredibly sensitive, you know.'

Poppy felt a twinge of sympathy for Will's brother. She was no stranger to inconsistent parenting, but at least she didn't have any siblings to be pitched against.

'This is a big weekend. *Really* big,' continued Lord Mountgrave, pronouncing the word with one more syllable than it needed. 'The focus is all on Will. I can't express how important this is.'

'Right! It's not every weekend your son gets married.'

'Married? Yes! Quite, quite. Will's cousins arrived this morning – did you see them? They've bundled him off for a stag. I did say it's a little dicey the night before the wedding, but it's what we did in my day. Ordinarily, we do stags quite literally, up at the estate in Scotland. Good fun. Carve up the carcass right there on the moor. Here, I'll show you mine.'

Lord Mountgrave buttoned his jacket with one hand, opened a side door, and trotted up a discreet spiral staircase. Poppy assumed he wanted her to follow him, so she tucked her bag out of the way and tripped on her flip-flop in her haste to keep up, hoping that her cooperation would ensure she could make a swift exit.

'There he is. Right between the eyes,' said Lord Mountgrave, pointing to a stag head mounted at one end of a wood-panelled wall dotted with busts in various states of deterioration. 'Didn't know what hit him. I tell you, a bullet in the skull is far more humane than getting hit by a Volvo on the A303.' He looked at Poppy, an almost reverential look in his eye. 'Before I pulled the trigger, he looked right at me. Beautiful.' He paused, a deep groove set between his brows. 'And more importantly, my stag is bigger than my father's. Spiteful man. Good riddance.'

'I think they're more beautiful alive. The deer, I mean.'

'Ah. You're one of them. Alas, William prefers clay. A waste of crockery, in my opinion.'

Poppy clapped, her patience waning. 'These photos. There are hundreds of files, so the earliest I can transfer them to you is maybe... three hours from now? But I can't do it here; I need to leave.'

Lord Mountgrave blinked, perplexed. 'That won't do, I'm afraid'

'That may be the case, but I have to leave tonight. There's somewhere else I need to be.'

'Oh? Well that settles it,' said Lord Mountgrave, clapping his thighs. 'The tractors will have stopped by now. What is it, five o'clock?'

'Five-thirty,' replied Poppy, her voice quiet. Her stomach knotted like tights in a tumble drier.

'Mmm. We're within twenty-four hours of the wedding, so no more sea tractors. I've got a private boat, but I'm afraid that's only for emergency use. You can't be too careful. The things people will do to crash the party... it beggars belief.'

Poppy's voice dropped. 'So I can't get back to the mainland?'

'Not unless you swim,' he said, followed by a singular snort. Poppy bit the inside of her cheek, worry mottling her pink chest. She couldn't stay here for another night, not now she'd made the decision to leave. She had no bed, for one. Where was she supposed to sleep?

Poppy took a breath, counted to ten, and thought about where she'd most like to have a cry. She could pull the double sleeping bag that Josh had given her as a wedding gift over her head. Cosy, but soul crushing. Or, she could find a toilet stall, but there were too many polished surfaces in the bathrooms at Loxby. She'd rather not see a reflection of herself at this moment.

'Look, I'm sure we can make something work.' Lord Mountgrave scratched his chin. 'I need those pictures as soon as possible. I'm hosting a dinner tonight and if I don't have a slideshow to go with the speech I've prepared, I'm going to look bloody ridiculous, aren't I? I'd ask Julia, but she's stuck on a call, Eastern time. There are important people in attendance. Fat pockets. This will be of benefit to you as well. There are plenty of photographers who would give their right arm for a chance to show their work in front of benefactors like these.'

Poppy shook her head. 'I can't stay for another night.'

'Is something the matter? Do we owe you money? Lola can take care of that. It'll be in arrears.'

'What? No, that's not it. I… I made a promise to a friend, which means I can't be here.'

'We're in a pickle then, aren't we? I need something from you and you need something from me. You need to get back to the mainland and I have a private boat. You have pictures and I need a visual. See where I'm going with this?'

'No, not quite.' Poppy thought it sounded like the basis of a legal case she'd rather avoid, if possible.

'Wait there,' said Lord Mountgrave, gesturing to a set of French doors that opened onto a large balcony shaded by the winding boughs of a wisteria, the petals sun-baked and crisp. He left the room and came back with a chrome laptop tucked under his armpit, placing it on a table outside. 'I'm really arse-tweaked for time. If you could bend your no doubt important plans and give me the pictures now, I'll ensure that you're back on the mainland by supper.'

Poppy recognised the cool glint in his eye, the pout, the subtle realignment of his posture to take up more space. He had played the silverback card, but so could she.

'How do I know you're going to follow through? Because so far, my experience of favours here is like belly-flopping off the side of a cliff. You think it won't hurt but eventually you smack arse-first into the sea.'

'Your friend. Lola.' He said her name with a lazy air and wiped a sheen of sweat from his top lip. 'If I was offering my services as a consultant, I would say hers was a fledgling business. Do you know what that means?'

'Yes, but I'm not sure if we're talking at cross purposes here, because—'

'It means it would only take *one* phone call. That's it. Do you know which papers I own?'

Poppy shook her head. Anger built in her chest, but her words were stuck in her throat.

'Nearly all of them. We're not the easiest clients to deal with – I know that – but I've hardly noticed she's here, which means she's doing a bloody good job. Of course, a good word goes a long way, but that's the problem with reviews, isn't it? Bad ones are harder to shake off. Impossible, some would say. Now, back to you. I don't do this techy, computer-whizz stuff. My dinner guests will be up here in ten minutes. Old business friends. If you hand over the pictures, jazz up the presentation, and click through the slides when I give you a nod, I'll have the boat brought round so you

287

can get to… wherever it is you need to get to. How about it? Ah, speak of the devil.'

'Good things, I hope,' said Lola, appearing by the stairs.

'I'll leave you to mull that over, Poppy,' said Lord Mountgrave, his eyes cast down as he straightened his cuffs and left.

Lola folded her arms, waiting until he was out of earshot. 'I thought you were leaving.'

'I was.'

'So…' Lola inspected her nails.

'Lord Mountgrave wants my photographs for a speech he's doing tonight.'

'He's doing a speech?' said Lola. She blinked slowly. 'That's news to me. But after all, aren't you the oracle of all matters nowadays?' Lola paused. Poppy knew her friend was capable of sarcasm that soured the air with vinegar, but she'd never been on the receiving end of it before. Lola took a pin from her hair and held it in her teeth. 'What's up?' she asked, speaking from one side of her mouth. 'You're not saying much.'

Poppy stepped back as a parade of waiters walked out onto the balcony with vases stuffed with frothy gypsophila. 'I'll be gone soon. I'm not going to interfere.'

She took the memory card out of her camera and slid it into her back pocket, trying to quash the feeling that she had made the wrong decision. Did Lord Mountgrave count this as genuinely urgent, or had she been deceived? The more she allowed herself to be involved, the less she understood why she was doing it. Was it for Lola? Was it for herself? When would she recognise the difference between helping someone out and allowing herself to be walked over? The boundaries she'd tacked around herself were paper thin and flopped down with the slightest breeze.

She hadn't thought about what happened next. Somehow, the idea of leaving Loxby for solitude on an even smaller island had morphed from a reward to a test of emotional stability that she was now sure she would fail.

This was Lola's job. She had pulled Poppy out of countless crippling situations in the past. The least she could do was help her now.

A chef Poppy recognised from a few days before stepped onto the balcony, a soggy tea towel in his hands. 'Lola?'

'Mm-hmm?' she uttered with tight lips.

'We've had an issue with one of the fridges. Something has gnawed through the cable at the back so the whole thing switched off a few hours ago. We're down to five courses rather than seven.'

Lola breathed so slowly it turned sinister, then faced the chef with a fixed smile. 'Fabulous. I'll find a paper guillotine so we can slice off the bottom of the menu, shall I? Go on, show me the damage.' If Lola had returned to sarcastically chastising the staff, she couldn't feel as bad as Poppy did. Before Lola disappeared, she turned back.

'Hey, I'll… I'll speak with you in a minute.' Lola squeezed Poppy's forearm and followed the chef out. When Lord Mountgrave returned with a spritzer in hand, her stomach turned steely.

'Nice girl. Big future ahead of her, don't you think? So. What's the verdict?'

Poppy clutched her elbows and gave an almost imperceptible nod. 'All right. I'll do it. But I need to be gone straight afterwards. That's a given, right?'

'I'll make the call now,' said Lord Mountgrave, sliding an iPhone from his paisley-lined blazer.

Chapter Thirty-Two

Lola once held Poppy's hair back whilst she vomited six blue WKDs into a shower tray whilst doing the same herself, so Poppy shouldn't have been surprised by her ability to solve a food crisis and source a projector at the same time.

By the time she'd plugged everything in and opened the presentation Lord Mountgrave intended to use, she heard Lola outside, directing guests upstairs in her best ringmaster voice.

'Have you found one yet?' said Lord Mountgrave, hovering behind her with his hands in his pockets.

'There's a great picture of you and Will here,' said Poppy, opening a file.

'Good, good. Open with that, but I want to feature the hotel for the grand finale. Long distance. Bit of scenery. Regal, you know?'

'Right… how about this?' Poppy opened a photograph that she'd taken at dawn the previous morning before she had bumped into Will. She cropped out the black slugs that criss-crossed the dewy lawn, allowing the lilac sky to dominate the landscape with pink and purple streaks that bounced off the Art Deco windows.

'Ah, there she is. What a beauty. Get it in. Slide five.'

'I can sharpen it up, if you like? Bring the colours out more?' asked Poppy. She may be editing under duress, but she wouldn't let a photo of hers go on display as anything less than perfect.

'Sure, as long as you're quick. I've got a soundtrack to go with it. A bit of atmosphere. Gorgeous song. Reminds me of my dear old mum. It'll play automatically when we get to the end. I'll raise a glass, everyone drinks, blah blah blah, family values, done.'

Poppy nodded. She didn't think it was any use mentioning that he needed speakers for the song to play, but she could solve that problem herself. At least it would keep her away from the balcony for a few minutes. She needed a distraction from thoughts of Will and his crocodile smile. Poppy's mum had once told her that she had an 'addiction to smoothing out rough edges,' which had been a real kick in the teeth. She'd grown up with eggshells underfoot, always feeling like it was her job to act as an emotional windsock. It was just her and her dad: two people stuck on the wrong side of adulthood. Was it any wonder that Poppy had turned out the way she had?

After she'd dragged two stand-alone subwoofers to the balcony doors and linked them up to the laptop, Poppy stood back to wait for her cue, hidden from the terrace. She listened to the scraping of chairs, the chatter, the tinkle of silver on ceramic as the balcony filled up. The night before her own wedding, she had inexplicably made Josh's mum cry for politely declining her 'something blue' gift, thus ensuring a public display of sobbing on the patio of a Toby Carvery, which had somewhat soured the occasion. Whichever way you looked at it, there was something grossly Freudian about wearing your mother-in-law's garter, yet Poppy's reaction to second-hand hosiery was what had been considered tasteless.

Lola appeared in the hallway and paused in front of Poppy, a crate of table favours held tight to her chest like a shield.

'Hey. Look, I heard about the mess-up with the transport. I'm sorry about that,' said Lola, her mouth tight.

'It's fine. I've sorted it.' Poppy folded her arms and waited until the silence became painful. 'What are those?'

'Pre-wedding favours for the wedding guests. Dried chamomile, lavender, valerian root… and rose-quartz crystals. They've been charged under a full moon to encourage a good sleep.'

'They've been what?'

'Charged. Under a harvest moon, specifically.'

'Right.' Poppy was desperate to make a joke. Crystal healing was one of their top three topics of friendly ridicule, alongside expressive hula-hooping and spotting Instagram boyfriends in real life.

This was ridiculous. Over the course of their friendship, they had weathered far worse than this. She wouldn't take back everything she'd said earlier, but by the same effort she couldn't deny that her old insecurities had needled their way in, packing more force behind her words than she had intended. Poppy cleared her throat, but it was Lola who spoke first.

'I think it would be good for us to have a bit of space from each other.'

Poppy flinched. This was not what she had expected. Space? Poppy hadn't seen Lola for months. Luckily, she had perfected the art of disguising hurt. Poppy swallowed, shrugged, and cleaned the muck from under her nail. 'Sure. Seems obvious.'

Without Josh, she was relieved. Since being on Loxby, the past decade had been brought into sharp focus and it was only now that she realised quite how far she had drifted from the person she recognised. Will had reminded her of who she used to be; how she could laugh and smile, what she used to love. If he disappeared from her life again, it would be painful, but she would cope. But no Lola? Without her, she was bereft.

'I think you're needed.'

'What?'

Lola jerked her head towards the balcony. She pushed open the door with her hip and reached back inside to twist a dimmer switch.

The balcony sunk into darkness. Lord Mountgrave tapped his glass with a dessert spoon as Poppy slipped outside and squatted beside Josie, who sat nearest the laptop.

Poppy reached up and hovered over the laptop's trackpad, the terracotta patio tiles radiating the day's warmth beneath her shins. Josie bent down, her white silky shirt luminescent in the darkness. 'If you get bored during the speech, you can join my drinking game. One sip every time my brother uses Latin when regular English would do.' Josie winked and sat back, filling her glass to the brim. The guests fell quiet.

Poppy clicked the first slide. The Mountgrave Foundation logo beamed onto the wall, garishly purple and bright.

'Thank you, thank you,' said Lord Mountgrave. 'Paul, careful where you point that glass – you'll send it over the side. Ha! All right, all right. Thanks everyone. I know it's not traditional to do a speech the night before a wedding, but I've never liked rules and it's my bloody island.' His laugh echoed around the horseshoe table, parroted by those who sat around it.

Opposite, Lola finished handing out favours and leant against the railings, avoiding eye contact. Now that she was over the initial shock, Poppy allowed a blanket of sadness to pull tightly around her chest. Her friend was pretending she didn't exist.

'I want to pay homage to a few of those who couldn't be here tonight. Those who have made Loxby. Those who made The Mountgrave Foundation. Those who will make *more* Mountgraves!' Will's father spoke with more purpose than affection, like a politician at a party conference, safe in front of a home crowd. 'Will is a good sort. Always has been,' he said, nodding to Poppy. She clicked the slide. On the wall, a picture of Will as a toddler came into focus, the sleeves of his tiny dressing gown rolled up four times over. Next to him, a former Prime Minister was caught mid-speech, his polka dot socks the only signifier of personality. How had she lived with Will for a year and not known this about him? 'He carries the family values that Mountgraves have fiercely commanded for years: arbitrium, fide, fiducia. Determination, loyalty, and trust.'

Josie nudged her back, winked, and raised a glass. 'Twenty seconds. That's a record,' she whispered, licking red wine from her top lip.

'The Mountgraves have built kinship on this island that goes back centuries. And drunk enough Bordeaux to flood the channel.'

'Hear, hear!'

Lord Mountgrave pinched his chin and resettled his features as the laughter died down. 'On a more serious note, Will and Ottilie's celebrations mark not only a new chapter in their lives, but a fresh dawn for all of us gathered here today. I've admired the Spruces from afar. We've done business for longer, but in this modern age, they do it best. I'm not too proud to admit it. After all, legacy is important to me. Why? Because it was important to my mother. She was widowed at twenty-three yet gave up the easy life to build on the foundations that she first established here, with my father. Loxby is steadfast in more ways than one. We have little reason to employ duplicitous tactics, in life *or* in business. We're a "what you see is what you get" kind of family and we don't apologise for it. Mother taught us that. I like to think she's proud of what we've achieved and will be equally proud of this union, with Will at the helm.'

'Are we chartering a boat?' said Josie, leaning forward with her elbows on the table.

'A helpful contribution, as always, sister,' said Lord

Mountgrave, his jowls quivering. 'If we could raise our glasses, please?'

The fizz of rapidly refilled champagne flutes trickled like a water feature. 'Mother, this one is for you.'

Lord Mountgrave gave her a thumbs up at waist height. She clicked through to the next slide, which triggered the opening piano medley from Elton John's 'A Candle in the Wind' to play through the speakers.

Gasps of appreciation burst from the guests as the image she'd taken of the hotel at dawn was projected on the wall. Poppy allowed half a second of pride to wash over her before her stomach sank with such velocity, she thought she might be sick. In the top right-hand window of the photograph, naked back pressed against the glass, was a woman. More specifically, a blonde woman with the tanned skin of someone who could afford to live in a perpetual summer across three continents. Ottilie. Embarrassing, sure, but not cataclysmic. That would be if her knees weren't pinned to her sides like a butterfly caught in a sliding door. Behind her, head down, but with the unmistakable fop of sandy hair that came with a fee-paying school, was Lawrence. Poppy couldn't believe she hadn't noticed. That said, she hadn't seen the image as a fifteen-foot projection before.

If her mind was a web browser, she had the equivalent of twenty open tabs, each one trying to fix the problem before her. She wasn't sure of anything, but she knew she had to get the image down before anyone else noticed what she had.

Poppy tugged at the projector cable, but it was jammed at an angle in the socket. The more she pulled, the less it moved. Shaky with panic, she slammed the screen shut. The laptop fan stopped whirring, but the projection continued to beam onto the hotel's whitewashed wall. As a last resort, she sprang to her feet and pressed her body as physically close to the beaming lens as possible, plunging the balcony into semi-darkness.

'I love this one! Isn't it great!' shouted Poppy, shimmying so aggressively it made her regret not packing a sports bra. Elton crooned into the night sky as Poppy whooped herself in the midst of an audience stunned into silence.

Lola marched towards her, the sound of her heels hollow on the tiles. Poppy lunged for her hands, but Lola leant back, the whites of her eyes sharp with wariness.

'What the *fuck* are you doing?' she hissed.

'Dance with me. Please, don't question it. You have to trust me. Distract them,' Poppy whispered.

She hooked her arm through Lola's and pulled her into the beam of projector light, the image distorted as it split between their bodies and the wall behind. Poppy had to keep the guests' attention absolutely *anywhere* else until Ottilie's splayed knees and Lawrence's orgasm face were wiped from their periphery.

'Tuuuuuune!' bellowed Poppy, desperately trying to fill the void between melancholy choruses entirely out of sync with her movements. On their next rotation, her friend's mouth dropped. Lola had noticed it too.

'Oh, fuck!' whispered Lola, her dancing more erratic. She jabbed her hands into the air as all the energy from her face sank into the tips of her fingers.

'Keep moving until we figure how to get it off the wall!' uttered Poppy, her words tucked behind a manic smile. 'We need to cut the electric. Or... smash the projector,' hissed Poppy.

Lord Mountgrave stepped closer and raised his voice. 'This is extremely off-colour you know!'

'Colin, I know you find it hard to spice up a speech, but backing dancers?' said Josie, pushing back her chair with unbridled delight. 'I underestimated you!'

'These two seem a little... addled, wouldn't you say?' said Ottilie's mum. 'Reminds me of Ibiza in the 90s.'

The guests froze in a shocked tableau, as though any

movement might signal their affiliation with Poppy and Lola. The exception was Josie, who shoulder-danced in her seat. Slowly, the guests began to laugh. This was a good sign. Josie was a heat-seeking missile for attention. If *she* hadn't noticed the soft porn on the wall, there was a fair chance no one else had either.

Lord Mountgrave leant so close that Poppy caught the scent of cognac on his breath. 'Cut it out. *Cut it out,*' he hissed. 'I don't know what kind of stunt you're pulling here, but it stops now,' he barked.

'No, it's just... it's just... wow, what a voice!' said Poppy, blindly jabbing buttons on the projector. Lola slipped away as Poppy's soul slipped from her body.

She gripped the projector with both hands and closed her eyes to avoid the threat of eye contact. Whatever she was doing, Lola needed to be quick. The bulb was hot and her dress was polyester. At least if she set herself on fire, she'd legitimately be able to swan dive off the balcony and into the sea, dragging the projector with her.

The song cut, replaced by the noise of sea birds that squawked like sirens.

'Did you forget to pay the bills, mate?' asked Paul.

Poppy cooled her burning cheeks with the backs of her clammy hands. The scent of satsuma oil told Poppy that Lola was standing behind her.

'Grab the laptop and meet me upstairs,' she hissed.

Chapter Thirty-Three

'How can she have an arse like that when I've only ever seen her eat breadsticks and hummus measured by the teaspoon?' said Lola.

'That's the thing we're focused on right now?' replied Poppy.

'I pay two hundred quid a month for a German woman to scream at me in the park every Saturday and I don't look like that.'

Poppy flipped the display on her camera and zoomed in to the photograph until the two contorted bodies filled the screen. 'Woah, close enough. Your telescopic lens really does pick up the detail, huh? Is... is that his shaft?' said Lola.

'No... I think it's a weird reflection from the—' They tilted their heads and leant in towards the screen. 'Yeah, that's definitely his shaft.'

Lola gagged. 'I think I'm going to be sick.'

'It *is* a weird shape.'

'Not the penis. More *where* the penis is going.'

Poppy dropped her camera on the duck-down duvet and

groaned with exasperation. 'I knew something was up, but not *this*.'

'Up? As in, erect? Because I love a pun as much as the next woman, but in this moment?' Lola shook her head. She reached behind her, tugged her zip down, and stepped out of her dress, leaving it in a pool on the floor.

'What are you doing?'

'I can't wear clothes when I'm stressed.'

'I've never seen you do that before.'

'I've never been this stressed. It's probably why I slipped Big Steve my phone number yesterday. That's how bad it is. I don't *do* subtle hints and now I've asked *him* to call *me*?'

'How horribly heteronormative of you,' said Poppy.

'Don't,' she said, shaking the thought from her head. Lola paced lines in the thick carpet, her hands interlocked below her chin.

'Is there a chance this *isn't* Ottilie? Could it be the waitress? From the other night?' asked Poppy.

Lola arched an eyebrow and nodded. 'We've got to check. Rule out all possible alternatives.'

'Ah, I know!' Poppy clicked the zoom button with her thumbnail. 'Ottilie has a tattoo. On her back, see? I saw it the other night in the bath.'

'I'm sorry, what?'

'Long story.'

'You know… you're right.' Lola squatted and rifled through the folds of her dress. When she found her phone, she opened an image, and dropped it where Poppy sat cross-legged at the end of the bed. Lola resumed pacing in her underwear. A picture of Ottilie filled the screen, taken in the fitting room of a bridal boutique dated six months before. In it, she looked over her shoulder, the low plunge of her dress coming to a tapered end at the small of her back. Half-hidden beneath a swoop of messy blonde hair, the same tattoo was clearly visible: a half-moon with a string of stars dotted down each vertebra of her spine.

'Well, that's that,' said Poppy, her arms heavy. 'This must be why she wanted to leave. I can't *believe* it. I haven't felt this betrayed since Mel B left the Spice Girls. This plan of hers to run away before the wedding... do you *ever* think she intended to run away *with* Will?'

Lola bit her lip and shrugged. 'I doubt it. He's not exactly hard to read, is he? I saw him as he was getting in a boat with his cousins and at most, he was a smidge subdued, but he'd just had a double shot of vodka forced into his hand by a fella called Brett, so it could have been that.'

'And what about Ottilie? Do you think she'll still try to flee on her own?'

'I don't know how she could without drawing attention to herself. Last time I saw her, she asked three or four times if everyone was okay, then after word went round that Lawrence had left, she stopped being so on edge. I thought it was the normal breaking point when a bride mellows out and starts enjoying themselves, but clearly not. Maybe she thought that with Lawrence fucking off, she was in the clear?'

Poppy bit her thumbnail and nodded. 'We need to do something.'

'I'm not sure we *should* do anything, you know. This isn't straightforward,' said Lola, agitated. Lola kicked her dress across the floor and reached for the clasp of her bra. 'You have no idea how much money has been put into this. The videographer I booked has won four MTV music video awards. *Four*. She's flying in from LA. As of this second, she'll be somewhere over the Atlantic.'

Poppy switched her camera off. She'd been staring at the picture for so long now that the silhouette of Ottilie and Lawrence was scored on the back of her eyelids, possibly for eternity. 'I understand that you've spent the last year planning this wedding, but staying out of their relationship is surely no longer an option we can sit with. If you care about them as individuals, it's obvious, right? Even without Shaftgate, I can tell Will has reservations, but he won't admit to them. We've got to tell him.'

'Mmm. So, if I take away the extra serving staff, the photographer, the food, the people who have flown in from every continent, the musicians, the DJ, the horse handler—'

'Horse handler?'

'Don't ask. If I take away all that – oh, and the second half of my fee along with the most sought-after testimonial in the wedding industry this year – if I take away *all* that, what should we do?' asked Lola, a pained look on her face. 'I honestly don't know. I don't get involved in the personal lives of my clients. It's not part of my job.'

'You're their wedding planner!'

'Yes,' said Lola, exasperated. 'I plan the *wedding*. That's it. But this isn't just about Will and Ottilie.'

'The family...' said Poppy. 'The way the Mountgraves interact with each other? They need a flotilla of therapists to wade through their problems. I understand why you're not exactly keen to be the first volunteer when it comes to peeling back a layer of the trauma onion. Will is only normal because he spent most of his childhood saving up pocket money for phone credit like the rest of us.'

Lola wiped her lipstick off with a damp flannel and peeled off her fake eyelashes. 'Look, what if we delete the picture? Pretend we never saw it?' She put her hands on her hips and tapped her scarlet painted toes. Lola gauged Poppy's less than enthusiastic reaction and shrugged. 'Okay, stupid idea. But you asked me to think objectively, so now you have to do the same.'

Her belly fluttered. 'What do you mean?'

'I've looked at the angle of your camera lens, babe. If you put your feelings for Will aside, what would *you* do?'

Poppy plucked at a loose thread on the duvet cover and glanced around the room uneasily. 'Like, friend feelings?'

'You know what I'm talking about. You being mates at uni – it didn't just fizzle out, did it? Something happened. What?'

'It's been years since I last spoke to Will.'

'Not the question I asked.'

Poppy swallowed hard. 'We had an argument at that very first club night you hosted. Totally out of the blue. He was needling me about why I was with Josh and then told me if we couldn't be together, it would be too painful for us to be friends. I thought he was being dramatic, but... look where we are now.'

Lola tilted her head to the side, her mouth hung open. 'Which Shakespeare tragedy did he fall asleep reading? Jesus *Christ*. So, to complicate things further, in the week of his wedding, I've unknowingly presented him with the former subject of his unrequited love?'

'No, it's not been like that. I... I think we need to focus on the problem at hand.'

'I respectfully disagree.' Lola pouted and waited for Poppy to speak. 'Do you like him?'

'Well, I mean... I care about Will in the same way I'd care about anyone in a situation like this.'

'You're giving me a lot of preamble for a straightforward question. Unless it's not straightforward?' Lola quirked an eyebrow.

'Well, yeah. I think he has a right to know that his fiancée is shagging his brother.'

'Shhhhh!'

'Sorry, sorry! Yes, he *should* know. But I don't want that to be the reason he bails on the ceremony tomorrow. He shouldn't marry Ottilie because she's not right for him, not by a long stretch. And before you say anything, it's not because I would be any better. God, I've got more than enough work to do on my own relationship hang-ups before I could even consider—'

'Getting off with him?'

'No... no!' said Poppy, swinging an overstuffed pillow at Lola's knees. 'What do I think? I think Will should get as far away from Ottilie and this island as possible, at least until he figures out how to put some rock-solid brick-wall boundaries up. The Mountgraves have no idea how to maintain anything that resembles healthy family dynamics, not outside of the weird Christmas calendar photoshoots that seem to have become a priority. Yeah, they're rich, but the rest is textbook toxic family. I should know; I'm still training myself to remember that it's not my job to manage everyone else's emotional equilibrium. That's exactly what Will is trying to do.'

Lola kicked her bra across the floor. 'Okay, so we need to tell him. Of course we do. At the same time, these people aren't like us. There's a whole publicity campaign built around this wedding, not to mention the huge fuck-off CEO announcement that Lord Mountgrave is getting his balls in a twist about.'

Poppy groaned. 'Remember at graduation, when you told my flatmate that you'd seen her boyfriend snogging someone else in the disabled loo at Lizard Lounge?'

'Do I ever. She dumped him, sobbed on me in the club toilet every Friday, then took him back in time for interrailing around Eastern Europe before he shagged someone else on a bunk bed in Bratislava. Never heard from her again.'

'Exactly. That situation was messy, but this could be a far messier and more expensive mistake for Will, so we've got to act now,' said Poppy.

'Lord Mountgrave has already told me that the company stock value fluctuates depending on what news coverage they've had. It's why he's kept Lawrence so close to his side for the past year. When he pissed up the wall of the British Embassy in Paris, share prices went down. When he went to rehab, they shot up, so fuck knows what'll happen if everyone finds out he's the reason this wedding is cancelled,' said Lola.

'Do you think it's why Will's dad is forcing him into the CEO role?'

Lola nodded. '*Fuck.* That's another thing we'd prematurely expose if it all came out.'

'What if I call Lawrence? Try and get him to come back and take some responsibility? He's probably on a yacht in Cannes by now, but we've got to try,' said Poppy.

'This is a Mount Vesuvius level of disaster.'

'I know, but we need to initiate some kind of damage control.'

Lola nodded, her eyes pink. Poppy couldn't swallow past the lump that had formed in her throat. She hadn't admitted everything to Lola. As much as she tried to convince herself otherwise, she *did* like Will, however irrational or misplaced. He made her feel like she was enough. Telling him about Ottilie's affair was a risk. If Poppy was the messenger who brought his world down, he might not want her in his life afterwards. She had to be okay with that.

She was, wasn't she?

Chapter Thirty-Four

'Wait, wait, sorry, I ran to catch you, but… God, there are a lot of stairs in this place, aren't there?' Poppy clutched the marble-topped reception desk, her chest heaving.

'I was just about to close up,' said the woman behind the counter. She switched off her computer screen, picked up a cloth, and gestured for Poppy to remove her hand. 'It's nearly midnight.'

'I know, I know, but this is an emergency.'

'An emergency?' she said, rubbing at the fingerprints Poppy had left behind. 'If it's a blue-light sort of emergency, that's a whole stack of paperwork I've got to do.'

'No, not like that. I need a phone number for someone who was staying here.'

'We don't do that. You're not the first to ask, not even this week,' she said, picking up her handbag from below the desk.

'Could you make an exception? I wouldn't ask unless I was absolutely desperate,' said Poppy.

'No way. I'm on triple wage this week. I can't risk my job. There's someone monitoring CCTV and there's a camera over there,' she said, nodding behind Poppy. She turned around. Sure enough, a beetle-eyed camera lens protruded from a corner of the atrium, trained in their direction.

Poppy paced in front of the desk. 'I don't suppose you know Lawrence? He's the son of Lord Mountgrave?'

'Lawrence?' said the receptionist, her head tilted to the side. 'Oh, I know him. If I were less professional, I'd tell you about the off-menu room service he's tried to order in the past. He's gone, hasn't he? I sent someone to service his room a few hours ago.'

'I need to speak to him. Urgently.'

'He got to you too, did he? Trust me, he's not worth chasing,' said the receptionist, squatting behind the counter to swap her heels for ballet pumps.

'Not me, someone else.'

'Lola? The wedding planner?'

'No. I can't say. But it's bad.'

The receptionist narrowed her eyes and glanced at the CCTV camera. 'If you're gonna give him a metaphorical bruising like he's done to some of the people who've worked here...'

'It's on the cards, yep,' said Poppy, eying the clock.

'My work husband, Giorgio, quit because of Lawrence. He broke his heart, properly brutal, like. Lawrence ghosted him, in real life. Fully ignored him in the corridors like he was a servant on *Downton Abbey*.' She shook her head, flicked her screen back on, and scribbled on the inside of a concierge card, slipping it underneath the mouse mat. 'Use the reception phone,' she said, her back to Poppy.

'Thanks,' whispered Poppy, gratitude flooding her cheeks with warmth.

'Tear him a new one for me,' she said, opening a door that led to the staff accommodation.

Poppy slipped behind the counter, lowering the chair until she sat below the eyeline of the camera on the wall. She picked up the receiver of an old-fashioned handset and dialled the number that had been left for her. The phone rang as Poppy's heartbeat thrummed in her throat. Laughter from a late-night gathering in the smoking lounge echoed through the atrium. She hadn't thought ahead to what she might say or do if Lawrence *didn't* pick up. After the fifth ring, the call clicked through, and Poppy considered putting the phone down herself.

'Hi, Cat. Did I leave my jacket with the dry cleaner again?'

'You *un*believable shit.'

'Steady on. I don't normally take sex calls in transit.'

'It's Poppy.'

'Even better. Shall I go somewhere private?'

'Gross, no. I don't know how much time I have, so I'll cut to the chase. I know why you left early.'

'You'll have to be a little more specific. I know it seems like I left early, but for me this is perfectly on time.'

'Ottilie?' said Poppy in a hushed voice, scanning the atrium.

'Oh. That.'

'I know what you did and so does Lola.'

'Hold on, *what* do you know? Whatever you're thinking, there are a few details to iron out.'

'There's a picture.'

'Of…'

'Let's just say it doesn't leave much to the imagination. If you're going to have an affair, doing it against a window is pretty short-sighted. They're literally fucking see-through.'

'Who took the picture?'

'I did.'

'Pervert.'

'Not on purpose! You're incredibly lucky. Do you know that? That picture was projected in front of your entire family *and* your father's business associates. I nearly singed my dress trying to block it from view. It's a wonder no one else noticed.'

'If you're planning on selling the picture, you'll get enough for a decent holiday in the Maldives at the very least. Dad's papers pay the most, but they won't buy it, obviously. Something to consider.'

'What? I'm not going to sell it. Are you remotely bothered? I thought this was why you left early?'

Lawrence breathed in through his teeth. 'Can you give me a minute? Please.'

Poppy jiggled her knee, impatience making her restless. After some rustling and a muffled conversation, Lawrence came back on the line, his ordinary bravado slipped like a wonky picture frame.

'I thought I'd have a bit more time than this.'

'Time for what? Because if it's an explanation for Will, I would argue that you're in the wrong place to deliver it.'

'I owe someone honesty, so you may as well have it. I've totally and royally fucked up. It's not the first time my mistakes have been photographed, but that hardly matters now. Ottilie and I have a... history, of sorts. Before they got together, we convinced each other that rehab was a waste of time. It's no wonder that a handful of our relapses overlapped. Boozy brunches, pills, whatever else. Not all of it was secret. Will knows we had a thing back before they got together.'

'I can pretty safely say that he's not aware you and Ottilie have *still* got a thing. He's marrying her! Are you seriously going to let him go ahead with this?'

'I couldn't bring myself to tell him. I know that puts me at amoeba level in the hierarchy of lifeforms, but it's the truth. He put me up when I came out of rehab and refused to tell Dad where I was, no questions asked. What have I done in return? Solidly screwed up every decent relationship I've allowed to take root in my life. I'll accept that this is bad, even for me, but I've closed the door on it. What Will does tomorrow is *his* choice, although I expect his decision will depend on how much you choose to tell him.'

'Me? No. This is one hundred per cent *your* problem. You need to come and fix it.'

'What do you want me to do? I can't un-shag Ottilie.'

Poppy held her hand over the receiver as an older man pushed open the swing doors from the smoking room, clutching his wife's arm. As he approached the desk, Poppy muttered down the phone. 'Wait a minute.'

'Towels. They haven't been replaced in my room,' he said, tapping the counter.

Poppy held the receiver to her chest. 'Yes, I'm sure I can sort this for you...'

He looked at her expectantly. 'Behind you. In the airing cupboard. See, Aine? This place isn't what it once was.'

Poppy propped the phone on the desk, where it rocked like an upturned banana. She scurried into a cupboard, lunged for the nearest shelf, and pushed a towel towards the man's chest whilst grappling for the phone again. He threw her a disgruntled look as they stepped into the lift. Poppy waited until she saw the floor counter tick up to first before speaking again.

'Are you moonlighting on reception?' said Lawrence.

'No. Don't change the subject. None of this is Will's fault. He can't see what's going on around him.'

'He's an adult. Look, I know everyone thinks I crawled out of the sea from the discarded shell of a crab, but that comes with the Mountgrave territory. Some dads teach their kids to ride a bike. Some dads let their sons fire a long-standing employee as a gift for their eighteenth birthday. Will didn't have that experience, I did. Will is a nice person, I'm not.'

'That sounds like a massive cop-out if you ask me.'

'It is. I'm being a twat because I deserve to be treated like one.'

'So come back and face up to it. It can be a fully immersive experience for you, like seeing Avatar for the first time in 3D, but with a higher chance of someone kicking you in the dick.'

'I can't. It's happened and that was the last time. I know it's a cliché, but it really was. Before this week, Ottilie and I hadn't hooked up in months. I'm not interested, but... I don't know, I can't explain it. If you're angry at anyone, she's equal parts to blame here. I told her I'd blow the lid on what we'd done, but it was an empty threat. I wanted her to sweat, maybe tell Will herself, but I guess that hasn't happened. What I do know is that I can't face him. I can't face any of them. I told him to break up with her when she cheated on him the first time.'

'She's done it before?'

'Indeed, a few years back. The only thing I can offer now is the pretence that I don't exist.'

'You're the only one who benefits from that arrangement. How is Will supposed to understand what happened if all I can show him is this picture? It's brutal. You've forced him to do this with an audience poking their heads around every corner.'

'I'm not pretending otherwise. I'm a piece of shit. Feel free to communicate the same to Will—'

'And a coward,' added Poppy.

'Yeah, and a coward. A fucked up shitty coward. Trust me, it's better for everyone that I'm not there. I thought Ottilie and I would fade out. Become a joke we'd laugh about on New Year's Eve in twenty years whilst Dad hosts a party in a suit that's too tight. Ottilie's a good laugh when she wants to be, although she's done her best to prove otherwise. With a fair wind, she and Will would have been good for each other, but I guess something changed.'

'Yeah, I wonder what.' Poppy's heart felt heavy. As the call ticked on, she was more and more certain that the responsibility of telling Will the truth would fall to her. He would hate her for it. How would she cope with that?

'So, you're prepared for this to roll on?' said Poppy, her head in her hands.

'I've scheduled in some silent self-loathing. I have a question for you, though. A few hours ago, you were sitting on the dock with me ready to jack it all in and save yourself. What's changed?'

Poppy paused. Anguish that had once popped and spat had cooled into a pool of resentment.

'You should be here,' she said, her voice weak.

'And you shouldn't, arguably.'

Poppy nodded. He had her there.

'I've got to go. I won't be able to hear you in a second. I'm on the runway,' he said.

'Where are you going?'

'Nice try. I know I deserve retribution, but I'm not going to sharpen the pitchforks and start handing them out. I'll be... somewhere the news is in a different language. Look, I was planning on messaging Will when I landed, but if you're there—'

'Are you seriously about to ask me for a favour?'

'I'm giving you some information. Do what you want with it. I wrote him a letter. It's in his suit jacket. It's not an explanation because I don't have one, but it's something. Call it an admission, a confession, whatever will help. Make sure he finds it, will you? I really do have to go now.'

'Stay classy, Lawrence,' she said sarcastically. The line went dead. Poppy's numbness solidified and morphed into a strong desire to smash the phone against the wall, but that would draw attention to herself. This wasn't about her. This was about Will.

Chapter Thirty-Five

MARCH 5TH, 2017

'What's the deal with gin nowadays? I don't know whether to drink it or spray it on myself,' said Poppy, leaning over the bar to read the labels on a row of cut-glass bottles that sparkled on a lit shelf. She shrugged and pulled her purse out. 'I don't fancy booze tonight. Soda water, please. With cucumber, a couple of olives, and a lemon wedge. Oh, and a drop of cordial. Elderflower. Thanks.'

'What the hell did you just order?' said Lola, looking at Poppy with mild disgust. 'We're not at a salad bar, babe.'

'It costs the same as a regular G&T and there's one of my five-a-day in that glass. Who's laughing?'

'I've drunk some weird shit in my time, but that's a monstrosity,' said Lola as the barmaid slid the glass between a row of beer taps and held out a card reader.

'One sec, Lola, what are you having?'

'Fat coke, please.'

Poppy paused. 'What?'

'Coke. Of the cola variety. With all the sugar.'

'Okay…' said Poppy. 'Wow, is this it?'

'Mmm. This is it. No more booze. Don't make a big deal out of it though. I'm trying to keep it chill otherwise my brain will fire off the alarm bells and you'll find me lying under a keg with my mouth open by the end of the night.'

'Sure, whatever helps. Still, I'm proud of you.'

Lola folded her arms and nodded. Poppy gave her a small smile. She tried to temper her reaction, but she was so happy for her friend she wanted to burst a number of party poppers at close proximity to celebrate.

Lola huffed and adopted a look of bleak resignation. 'That's me cancelled as a wedding reception guest. You know what it's like. Everyone invites a wild card so they've got some decent gossip for the start of their wholesome married lives together. I *am* that wild card.'

'All those groomsmen that will remain unsnogged...' said Poppy, trying to keep the tone light. 'When does your mourning period start?'

'Oh, immediately. I've signed up for seven dating apps in the past week. I thought I might shag my way out of it.' Lola picked up her glass, took a sip, and emitted a satisfied 'Ah!'

Three months ago, Poppy had opened her front door on a Sunday to find Lola passed out in the front garden despite the fact that she'd gone to a club in a city forty miles away. Over a plate consisting entirely of hash browns and a swimming pool of ketchup, she had told Poppy that she was going sober, but that she wouldn't make the switch unless she could do it 'properly'. Today must be the day.

'I've started eating family buckets of fried chicken in the KFC car park at night. One vice swapped for another. Linda McCartney would be spinning, I tell you.'

Poppy felt the edges of her anxiety crystalise like limescale. She was selfishly pleased for Lola. She needed something to distract her from the prickling tension that had crept between her and Josh.

Poppy nudged Lola's arm, scooped an olive out of her glass, and dropped it in her mouth as they sashayed between tables. 'Right, who's here?' asked Poppy as they turned towards the pub garden. Lola pushed the door open with her hip.

'Kirsty just arrived – she's positioned herself next to Omari because he's newly single with extra muscles from a sad gym routine – Hannah's here, as is Prab – bad haircut, pretend you haven't seen it – and Luke and Joel, who arrived at the same time I did. They just got engaged, so make sure you say congratulations unless you want him wafting his knuckles in your face for the next hour.'

Poppy nodded, glad that Lola had an encyclopaedic knowledge of friendship groups and the dynamics that made them tick.

'Josh has been acting off since he stepped foot in the place,' she added, speaking out of the corner of her mouth as she waved to their group on the other side of the patio.

'Has he?' said Poppy, pulling her jacket tight against the cool spring air.

'Yeah. He's cracked a few genuinely good jokes, so naturally I'm suspicious. Why did he arrive before you, anyway?'

'He had triathlon training round the corner.'

'Of course he did. Hey! Look who I found!' Lola announced as they reached the table. She sat on a corner, leaving Poppy to squeeze onto a picnic bench that was too small for six grown adults. Josh swigged his lager as she squeezed her bag under the table.

'Good session?' she asked Josh.

'Shit,' he replied. 'I twisted my knee during transition two.'

Poppy grimaced in sympathy. That would mean an evening

spent in terse silence as Josh timed himself getting in and out of his wetsuit.

'How's school, Poppy?' asked Omari.

'Oh, you know. Too much marking, not enough time.'

'You should have done PE. Getting paid to tell kids which way to kick a ball sounds like a good deal.' Omari nudged Josh in the ribs. He rolled his eyes and smirked.

'I tell kids which way to point a camera, which is easier if anything,' she said, well-practised in the art of dodging jibes about how easy teaching apparently was.

'Still, schools have great maternity leave, don't they?' said Hannah.

Poppy spluttered on an olive, her throat stinging with brine. 'So I've heard.'

Prab put both palms on the table, her excitement barely contained. 'I *always* wondered who would be the first of us to have babies.'

'Why, is someone pregnant?' said Poppy.

'I don't know, are they?' Prab winked from beneath her thick fringe.

'Is there a reason you're looking at me?' said Poppy.

Prab's smile faltered. She glanced at Josh, her head tilted to one side.

'Well, yeah. It's on the list, isn't it?' he said.

'Ah! I knew we forgot "small infant" in the weekly shop,' said Poppy.

Lola laughed, but she was the only one who did.

'You guys have been together for an age,' said Luke, his hand on Joel's knee. 'I can't wait until we're making decisions like that. Did I tell you I proposed to—'

'Woah, woah, woah. Decisions? I didn't know there had been any,' said Poppy, her brow furrowed.

'Hang on, I thought you *were* already pregnant,' said Omari, leaning across the table. 'I just didn't want to say anything. Not that you look it. You look great.'

Hannah leant away from him, her chin tucked. 'Take a second to listen back to that.'

Omari faltered. 'Ah, shit.'

'My womb has never felt so popular,' said Poppy, her skin hot and irritated. 'Back in a minute. Feel free to discuss the status of my fallopian tubes whilst I'm away.'

Poppy used Omari's shoulder to help lever herself off the bench and quick-walked inside. As she pushed on the women's bathroom door, she heard scuffed footsteps behind her.

'Poppy—'

'Why did you say that?' she snapped, turning with such speed her ponytail whipped her across the face. Josh scratched his chin with his little finger.

'Because I know you're lying to me.'

'About…?' Poppy asked the question, but she knew the answer.

'You tell me.'

'Stop testing me, Josh, I genuinely don't know.'

'Your pill.' He waited for the penny to drop, but Poppy was still thinking. 'I found three packets in the bin.'

'They're old ones,' she said.

'Don't lie to me, Poppy.'

'They are, they're'—Poppy scanned the mirrored corridor, but she wasn't sure what she was looking for—'I never said I wanted to have a baby, like… *now*.'

'Are you having me on?'

'Yes! Why the hell are you going through the bins? Am I under surveillance now?'

'We've been married for nearly six years. We've got a *really* fucking good life. What do you think happens next?' he said, his consonants sharp.

'I don't want to talk about this now. When you're aggressive, my mind doesn't jump to the thought of procreation, surprisingly.'

'Aggressive? That's how you're labelling me?' He bit his bottom lip and cradled his fists. 'You're an embarrassment. There's *nothing* wrong with me. It's *you* reacting like I've just asked you to be my fucking handmaiden.'

Poppy recoiled, her eyes wide. He'd said this kind of thing before at home, but never in public.

'I never said that children were high on my priority list.'

This wasn't entirely true. Poppy had an idea that children would feature in her life at some point, but recently the noise that had once been a loud ringing in her head had grown dull, like she was listening to it through a wall.

'What bumped it down? Too much of a sacrifice, is it? I'd be making sacrifices too, or had you not realised that? At the end of the day, I'm not the one who pushed this topic to begin with.'

'You are.'

'I'm not!' said Josh, his voice husky with anger. A barmaid looked up from the tap she was cleaning. Josh noticed her make eye contact with Poppy and moved to block her view. He lowered his voice. 'I'm *not*. We've spoken about this.'

'Yeah, in the same way we've spoken about going to New Zealand and investing in a drinks cart. I wasn't aware a baby was something we were *actively* seeking,' she said. As the words left her mouth, she knew they didn't suit her. At this point, raising a child with Josh would be like asking a swimmer to catch a cannonball when they needed a life ring.

'You *told* me you'd stopped taking your pill.'

'I *told* you I was thinking about it. Even if I had, you can't go announcing it to everyone. Now every time we go out, to a BBQ or whatever, they'll watch what I drink and make endless comments about it.'

'They won't. They're our friends, not the fertility police.'

'You *know* that's not true. Why? Because you let them believe I'm pregnant.'

'Poppy, lower your voice, for Christ's sake. You might not realise it, but you sound hysterical. That's not you.'

'Maybe it is. Maybe I've felt *hysterical* for months. Is it hysterical to want to maintain some semblance of privacy over my own body?'

'It's *our* baby,' said Josh, catching himself as the words left his mouth. 'It *would* be our baby.'

'Yeah, and it *would* be my body. I control it, so I also have the right to an opinion on how it's spoken about.'

Josh smirked and shook his head, his tongue pushed against the inside of his bottom lip. 'I knew you'd turn this into a feminist thing.'

'Well, thanks to your wonderful Day of the Girl assembly, I'm all clued up on feminism. Speaking of which, thanks for taking my ideas, putting them on a shit PowerPoint, and passing them off as yours. No one uses fucking Comic Sans anymore.'

'No, I'm drawing a line there. Comic Sans is the easiest font to read. Besides, you can't claim equal rights as "yours". Feminism is a movement, not a monopoly.'

'You know what women really like? Having their own rights explained back to them. With caveats.'

'I'm the Equal Opportunities representative at school. I *had* to deliver that assembly. You know I'm going for the Deputy job, or do you not want more income coming through the house?'

'It's *wild* to me that you can't see a hint of irony here. Progressive ideas shouldn't be used for career opportunities.'

'Yeah, well, you wouldn't know much about that, would you?'

Poppy coughed, incredulous. Josh leant against the wall and massaged his palm with his thumb, refusing to make eye contact.

He knew he'd dealt a low blow, but was too stubborn to backpedal.

'If we're taking a trip down memory lane, should we talk about what I gave up to be with you? A master's in New York? The chance to be a fully professional photographer?'

Josh held his hands up, his mouth small and mean. 'You strung out a list of reasons why you didn't want to go. You didn't like flying; it was too expensive; you needed to keep an eye on your dad,' said Josh, ticking them off his fingers. 'You claimed you didn't need the exposure of an academy in New York. You were good enough on your own. Is that what you're saying now? That you don't need me?'

'No. I'm saying that I'm slowly suffocating.'

Josh went cold, his eyes glazed with indifference. 'I'm sorry that being married to me has been so painful for you.'

'You're twisting my words.'

'Poppy, I didn't force you to stay here when that creep with the goatee offered you a scholarship.'

'He wasn't a creep! You proposed to me at my first public exhibition. What was I supposed to do, say yes and fuck off to America for a year? Everyone would have hated me. *You* would have hated me,' she said. Poppy felt light-headed, like a valve inside her had disintegrated over time and finally blown. Josh flexed his fingers, his breathing staggered. 'Be honest with me, would you have waited?'

'Would you have wanted me to?'

She paused. Josh pressed his temples and shook his head. 'I can't believe this. Did it ever cross your mind that whatever... issue that's affecting our relationship should have been brought up earlier, back when we could have done something about it? Why now? Take some fucking responsibility; you can't come out with shit like this without having an end goal in mind.'

'I don't know. I think I know, but—'

Josh elbowed the wood panelling beside him, the force rattling a pendant that hung from a glass wall light. 'Which is it?'

Poppy stepped back. In the gap that had opened between them, a man opened the bathroom door, fiddling with his trouser zip. Poppy and Josh turned to look at him. 'Sorry,' he mumbled, side stepping behind Josh.

'Every decision we've made as a couple has swung solidly in your favour,' said Poppy, her voice quiet.

Josh rolled his eyes. 'We live in a townhouse – your choice. Yes, you put down the deposit, but I've spaffed money doing it up because *you* don't like new builds.'

'We live ten minutes away from your mum. Whose choice was that?'

'She lives alone.'

'So does my dad.'

'You don't even like him.'

'You don't get to say that!'

Josh exhaled through his nose, as though it took every ounce of willpower for him not to punch the wall.

'Wow. Honestly, I don't think I know you anymore. Six years. Six *fucking* years and now you're acting as though you've swallowed Simone de Beauvoir's backlist? You're my wife.'

'What does that even *mean*, really?'

Josh wiped his face. There was a small part of her that felt a thrill of excitement when he got angry. At some point in the future, she would spend a lot of money unpacking this particular reaction, but not now.

'I hold my hands up. Is this about what I said out there, or is there something else going on with you? You've not been right for weeks. Months, even. It's not just me who thinks so.'

'Oh? I'm not Princess Diana. I don't think anyone else analyses my behaviour with that much interest.'

'The head has mentioned it at school. Said your last lesson

320

observation was... what was the phrase he used? Frantic? Which is odd because you're a brick-wall level of boring at home. Every time I try and get a rise out of you, there's nothing there.'

'That's because I can't have a conversation with you anymore without doubting myself fifty times a minute. I don't know what my opinions are anymore. I tell you I'm worried, you tell me I'm catastrophising. I tell you I'm excited, you tell me to calm down. I tell you I don't feel much at all and you say I'm being distant. Is it any wonder I don't know what to fucking say?'

Josh hooked his arm around her waist, pulled her close, and laid his forehead on her shoulder. He smelt good, which annoyed her. It would have looked intimate if it wasn't for the strain in his neck and the press of his fingers against her hip bones, a little too hard. 'Pops, listen to me. Don't you think a baby would be good for us? Give us something to focus on, you know?'

Poppy slipped underneath his arm, her heartbeat pulsing in her throat. 'Remind me what century you're living in? Babies aren't correctional tools, Josh.'

He nodded, as though she'd fallen beautifully short of his expectations. 'This is what we're doing now, is it? I feel like you're about to call me a misogynist.'

Poppy performed a slow clap. Exasperation had made her eyelids heavy and her tongue loose. 'Bra-fucking-vo.'

'I am not going stand here and listen to this. You can tell everyone why I've left without saying goodbye because that's what you deserve. Let me know when you're ready to have an adult conversation.' Josh's voice cracked as he spoke, his eyes pink with anger or sadness – Poppy couldn't tell. He rocked on his heels, chin aloft as though he were waiting for an apology.

Lola appeared behind him. 'Jesus, Josh. Have you had a few too many E-numbers tonight? We can hear you from outside. Poppy, what's going on?' asked Lola, her voice light, her eyes narrow.

'Lola, this has got *nothing* to do with you,' said Josh.

'If you're upsetting my friend, I think it bloody well does. Poppy, do you want to go?' said Lola, her tone insistent. Poppy nodded. 'Right, come on then.' Lola held out her hand. Poppy knew with singular focus that taking it was the only way she would have the courage to leave. This was her life raft. She needed to climb on.

Chapter Thirty-Six

THE WEDDING DAY

Poppy pushed herself off the floor, wincing, her neck stiff and sore from spending the night with her ear pressed against the thick carpet. Lola's room was above the suite that Will would ordinarily be sharing with Ottilie if she weren't still hiding out in the fisherman's hut. After hearing a group of men failing to shush each other quietly in the early hours of the morning, she had been listening for the moment that Will was finally in his room alone.

Whilst waiting for signs of life downstairs, Lola had channelled her stress into backcombing and hair pinning that bordered on sadomasochism, resulting in a gravity-defying beehive that had distracted her until they heard a window open on the floor below. Eventually, Lola had gone to investigate. A few minutes later, Poppy heard a keycard being inserted into the door, signalling Lola's return.

'Is he there?' asked Poppy.

'He's there,' she said, fanning herself with her hand. 'You were right; his cousins crashed in there with him. I kicked them out on the pretence that we had wedding timings to discuss, but I panicked when Will looked so worried and said that the dried rose petals had arrived but were blush pink, not fuchsia. All in all, I don't think I bought much time. Do you still want to tell him on your own?'

Poppy nodded. She got to her feet and tried to rub the carpet grooves out of her cheek. 'I don't want it to come across as an intervention.'

'Good thinking,' said Lola, smoothing down her satin dress. 'I know this is selfish, but I've got to pretend that I don't know what's happened. There are ten places I need to be this morning and I can't call anything off before I know what Will wants to do.'

'Okay, you keep busy. I don't think anyone will be looking for me since Christian arrived to take over, so leave the awkward conversations to me. Is there any chance Ottilie will turn up early?'

'Doubt it. I'm walking hair and make-up over to the fisherman's hut in... thirty minutes,' said Lola, checking her watch. 'So she'll be out of the way until the ceremony. In theory.'

'Right.' Poppy pressed her knuckles into her eye sockets, the pressure alleviating the tension that had built up. 'This is not how I thought the week would end.'

'You're telling me. I'm still not sure about this. If Lawrence left a letter for him, do we really need to get involved? I don't think this will go down quietly. People love a wedding, but you know what gets more headlines? A public jilting.'

'I doubt he's going to walk around in his wedding suit for the next thirty years. Anyway, I thought you said the media was being carefully controlled?' asked Poppy.

'It is, but I've heard people talking. As much as this feels like *Big Brother*, Will's dad can't control everything. Lord Mountgrave is trying to direct noise towards the wedding, but there's enough bad blood here to fill a swimming pool. If it's a "source close to the couple" we're thinking about, there are some strong contenders here who would happily use it as an opportunity to see the Mountgraves with muddy knees. Inappropriate wording, but you get me, right?'

'I know, I know.' Poppy was hot. She opened a window and took a deep breath, looking down at the stark white walls of the hotel. On the floor below, Will's window was also pushed open. Her stomach twanged as she heard him singing every other line of Al Green's 'Love and Happiness', the music tinny, as though he'd put his phone in a fruit bowl like they used to do at university when no one had a speaker to hand. He can't have found the letter yet. That was if Lawrence was being truthful about the letter at all.

'I can't let Will go in blind,' she said, turning from the window.

Lola's phone rang. She glanced at the number and tapped her teeth with the end of her nail. 'I've got to go and brief the arrivals team. Metaphorically speaking, before we jump out of the plane, are you sure about this?'

'I am. But I also feel a lot of other things. Bad for you, mainly. This was supposed to be your big career break.'

Lola smiled, resigned to the idea. 'The only bad publicity is no publicity, right? I've got some decent pictures for the website, thanks to you, and I've mentioned my business name in every conversation I've had this week. Subliminal messaging, except... not so subliminal.'

Poppy exhaled sharply. 'If something drastic happens, I'll let you know, but not before. Ignorance is bliss and all that.'

'Hydraulic ejection into a different country is bliss, more like.' Lola enveloped her in a hug, her arms birdlike and stiff. 'I could get used to this whole affection thing,' she said, her voice muffled by Poppy's hair.

'We'll work on it.' She interlocked her little finger with Lola's and squeezed.

'For someone who has avoided drama for the past decade, you do seem to be making up for lost time,' said Lola.

Poppy stood outside Will and Ottilie's suite, glanced down the corridor, and knocked before she had a chance to retreat. A silver domed food cart trundled behind her, pushed by a waiter with a linen tea towel flicked across his shoulder. The smell of cooked eggs and warm butter hung heavy in the air as Poppy stumbled forwards, the door clicking open. Will caught her elbow, his other hand adjusting the navy silk tie that he'd partially pulled through his collar.

'Hey! I didn't know whether you'd left yesterday. Does this mean you're staying for today?'

'Today, er... Yeah. I actually came to talk to you about that. Can I come in?'

Will pulled the door wide and gestured for Poppy to follow him, finishing the knot of his tie. He kicked the door shut with his heel, smiling. 'Are you doing "getting ready" photos? You're a bit early. Dad's been down already, but the guys are showering up. It probably wasn't the best idea to eat Pop Tarts and play Uno when we got in last night, but it's not every day you get married.'

Poppy faltered, her feet rooted to the floor. 'Will, I need a word.'

'Where's your camera?' he asked, looking at himself in an antique mirror so large it was like the room had been built around it.

Poppy wandered further into the room, unused to leaving without her lens bag strapped around her waist like a cowboy's holster. Will caught her eye in his reflection, jawline smooth and boyishly buffed. Had he picked out a new aftershave? One that would capture memories of today? Taken more time to shave?

Thought about the first moment he'd be alone with Ottilie after the guests had locked themselves back in their rooms with sore feet and cloudy heads?

'Are you all right?' asked Will. 'I thought it was me who was supposed to be wobbly. I can't seem to do this bloody tie,' he said, shaking his head as he pulled it loose again.

'I'm not all right. Look, I need to tell you something.'

Will turned, still for the first time since she'd come into the room. He scanned her face, looking for evidence that she was building up to a joke. When it was clear she wasn't, he put his hands in his pockets, his chin dipped. 'What do you want to tell me?' he asked, his voice quiet.

'I'm going to jump straight to it because there's no way of saying this nicely. Ottilie and Lawrence slept together a few days ago. Here, at the hotel. I know it's happened before too.'

At first, Poppy didn't think Will had heard her. He blinked, immobile except for his foot, which tapped on the carpet.

'I'm so sorry. I know this is horrible timing, but I couldn't leave without saying something. She doesn't think anyone knows.'

Will ran a hand down his neck and let out a deep, low groan.

'Will, I—'

'Give me a minute.' He held the heel of each hand against his eyes, his shoulders quivering.

Poppy pinched her thumb, the pain distracting her from the instinct to comfort him. After all, she'd had a head start on the landmine of information that Will was experiencing for the first time.

'This isn't happening,' said Will, his voice quiet. 'She told me... she said... are you sure? You wouldn't tell me if you weren't sure, would you?' His voice caught in his throat as he brushed his eyes with the heel of his hand.

Poppy nodded. 'I'm sure.'

He turned to face her, cheeks damp, gaze wandering around the room without settling on anything. 'Lawrence?' he said.

'Yes.'

'You're sure?'

'There's a photo. I didn't realise until I saw it on a screen. They were in the window, the other morning, before I bumped into you. You can see them both, but his—'

'I don't need the details, please.' Will rubbed his chin, his eyes wild. 'I'm going to kill him. Where is he?'

Poppy spoke in a rush as Will stalked the room, one shoe in his hand as he looked for the other. 'Not here. He left last night. I managed to get him on the phone when I found out, but he wouldn't tell me where he was going.' Will dropped the shoe and collapsed onto the end of a stiff chaise longue.

'I want to punch something.'

'Understandable.'

'Is Ottilie coming here? Back up to the hotel?'

'No, Lola said she'll be at the fisherman's hut until the ceremony.'

'Of course. This makes sense now. Why she's been down there so much, only seeing me when it's got something to do with wedding arrangements. I'm an idiot. I bet everyone's been thinking it. Stupid, wet-behind-the-ears Will.'

'No, that's not true.'

'It's been so much worse than I've let myself believe. Ottie and me. I thought that once we were on our own, it would be different. Less like we're kids putting on a show for our family to stop them arguing for five minutes. I think, I… I knew it in the back of my head,' he sighed, rubbing his scalp with his knuckles. 'That something was wrong. But not this.'

Will wiped his face and pinched his lips, his eyes glassy. 'I don't want to end up like my dad.'

'You're nothing like him. I know I've only been around you

both for a few days, but you're kind and genuine in a way I can't recognise in him.'

'Then what's wrong with me?'

'There's nothing wrong with you.'

'That's not true. It *can't* be true. I wouldn't have a fiancée who fucks my brother seventy-two hours before our wedding if there wasn't a sign on my back that says, "total imbecile, treat as you fucking well like".'

Poppy winced. 'I think Ottilie's taken advantage of you, but that's not your problem. It's hers.'

'Really? I feel like this *is* my problem. An acute, needle of a problem that's repeatedly stabbing me between the ribs.' Will sat up straight and tried to breathe, his hands on his knees. 'I think I'm about to have a heart attack,' he said. He did look unsteady, his forehead beaded with sweat as he grappled with his top button, the other hand pressed against his chest as he gulped for air. Poppy knelt beside him.

'Breathe, Will,' she said. 'Like this.' She took his hands and forced him to look at her, rounding her lips to slow her breath. 'Like you're blowing through a straw.' He copied her, his breath ragged, interspersed by sharp gasps. 'And again, slow, slow, slow. You're safe. Your body is telling you you're not, but you are. Flex your hands, get the blood back. That's it.' Poppy continued to guide Will through each breath until his shoulders dropped. 'Stay still. I'll get you something to drink.'

She went to his palatial en suite and filled a glass with tepid water.

'Thanks,' he said, taking the glass. He sipped it, his hand shaking.

'No problem. I've had a few choice moments in the art cupboard at work. Panic attacks are fucking awful.'

A few minutes later, his breathing had slowed. 'That's never happened to me before. Sorry.'

'Don't apologise, please.'

He squeezed her hand and let go. 'Is there anything else I don't know?'

'I don't want you to pass out, but Lawrence did say he left a note in your suit jacket. Am I right in thinking you haven't read it?'

Will shook his head and tapped his knee. 'I haven't taken it off the hanger yet.'

'Do you want me to do it?'

'No. It needs to be me.' He shook his head, his mouth partly open as he looked towards the mahogany wardrobe.

'Don't stand up too quickly,' said Poppy, helping him to his feet. He pulled open the doors, unhooked his jacket, and laid it on the bed.

'Did he say which pocket?' said Will, scrunching creases into the pressed linen lapels as he flipped the jacket over.

'No, just that he put it there himself.'

Will put his hands on his hips. 'There's nothing here.'

Poppy joined him, double checking each stitch and seam with less frantic hands. 'There's a serious pocket deficit in women's clothing. But you're right. There's nothing here. He wouldn't have said it as a joke, would he?'

Will shook his head. 'I don't think so. He's spineless, but he doesn't have the patience for delayed gratification, even if he was sadistic enough to enjoy it.'

'Maybe someone took it? A cleaner or something?' offered Poppy, although it was a weak theory.

Outside, Poppy could see three members of staff moving along the path that led down to the cove, a string of bunting trailing behind them.

Will rubbed his lip. 'I need to think. You know the ridge that looks out to the bay by the harbour? Not above The Drunken Prawn, but near the surfing hut? There's a gorse bush that hides an overhang. Can you meet me there in an hour? If I have to stay in this room for a second longer, I'll lose it. There's too much of her here.'

'Not that I want to rush you, but the ceremony is supposed to start in under two hours,' said Poppy, her heart thrumming.

Will pulled his shoes on, his eyes wide. 'I know. I've got a decision to make.'

Chapter Thirty-Seven

An hour later, Poppy leant in the curve of an overhang, tucked out of sight from anyone walking on the coastal path that lapped the island. The small bay that she and Will had surfed in two days before rolled below, the waves frothing as they crashed towards the beach. Will paced in front of her, his curls buffeted by the wind.

'Are you sure?' said Poppy.

'Don't ask me any more questions. Sorry, my head is a mess as it is. If I spend more than thirty seconds thinking about it, I doubt I'll answer the same way. I'm *not* sure. I'm about to walk out on my wedding. There are dozens of people there already.'

'And a drone.'

'And a fucking drone!' Will never swore. He was like a Sunday afternoon stand-up in that sense: harmless and often complaining about the etiquette of queuing. Panic had sunk behind his eyes and made his mouth tight.

'Look, you don't have control over any of that. Unless you want to fake your own death and live in Cuba for the next fifty years, you've only got two options. One, go and tell Ottilie that you're not going through with it and stay, or two, go and tell Ottilie you're not going through with it and leave.'

'And there's definitely no situation in which I can punch Lawrence in the face?'

'In the future, perhaps, but not today. I'm sure he's on the other side of the world by now.'

'What's the time?'

Poppy checked her watch. 'Just gone twelve.'

'Shit! I'm supposed to be walking down the aisle in twenty minutes. This is a waking fucking nightmare,' he said, clenching and flexing his fists. Poppy nodded as Will walked back and forth, his once polished brogues dull from the dust clouds he kicked up.

'I can't just leave.'

'It's *one* of the options. I know that most people in your situation wouldn't think twice before inflicting pain in the other direction, especially after what Ottilie did. Your family too—'

'Why not chalk them all up, sure,' said Will, rubbing his throat. 'My mum is here. I can't believe I brought her back to somewhere she hates for *this*.'

'I'm not trying to make you feel worse, I promise. Even after what you just went through, it's not in your nature to deadbolt the barn door and set it on fire after. Think about waking up tomorrow. If you leave now and say nothing, you'll still be in the blast zone. The pain will cling to you, follow you around. Other people will be impacted if you don't deal with it now.' Will nodded, his eyes closed. Poppy didn't think it was appropriate to mention that she'd almost directly lifted this line from a documentary about Chernobyl.

Will kicked a pebble, unclasped his cufflinks, and threw them over the cliff side. Or at least that was the intention. In reality, they tinkled against a nearby rock, the result far less dramatic than Will had no doubt hoped for.

'If you leave now, you'll give Ottilie time to spin the story and that will double the awkward conversations waiting for you when you come back.'

Will held his hands out in front of him. 'How is it possible for her to cheat and still come out on top?'

'I don't know. Have you *heard* of the royal family?'

Will resumed pacing. 'Ottilie doesn't deserve an explanation. *I* do. *She* should have to tell them what's happened.'

'Be honest, if she hadn't been with Lawrence, how would you feel about going through with this today?' Poppy's heart raced.

Will paused. His bitter energy was palpable as he stood on an incline in front of her. 'I don't know. That's what's killing me. Ottilie and I... I can't trust how I felt then, because the version of her I loved doesn't exist. I'm not like my dad. I never wanted to be the kind of person who bailed as soon as relationships got difficult. If I'm brutally honest with myself, I felt ripples of... something that wasn't right. If that was instinct, then why did I ignore it? Why am I standing here with this tiny bouquet pinned to my chest?' said Will, flicking the taffeta-wound buttonhole pinned to his lapel.

'Maybe you felt like you owed her something? Maybe it was harder to pull out knowing all the questions you would have been asked?' Poppy stepped in front of Will, forcing him to stop pacing. When he met her gaze, his brow softened. 'Consider me a veteran in this game,' she said.

'We've had a conversation like this before. Do you remember?'

Of course Poppy remembered. Since being on Loxby, she'd assumed she was the only one who did. 'If it's the one I'm thinking of, yeah, I do.'

'I understood why it was too late for me, but I never understood why you thought it was too late for you. I do now.'

Poppy bit her lip and nodded. 'It's hard, isn't it? I'm not trying to turn you on to my way of thinking, not really. I don't want to draw parallels between our situations, but it's taken me this long to realise why I held onto Josh. I thought if *I* was good enough, if *I* kept bending and caring and putting him first, I'd be rewarded with consistent love in return. That's not how it works. The only reason I've become as bitter and cynical as I am is *because* I was kidding myself for so long about Josh. I don't want you to end up like me.'

Poppy's pulse thumped in her chest. These thoughts had been burrowed in the back of her mind for so long now, she hadn't realised how freeing it would be to let them fly.

'Be real,' said Poppy. 'We can talk about your relationship until this time next week, but the reality of it is that your dad booked out the family island and turned your wedding into a springboard for his business, not to mention that he's manipulating you into a job that you don't want. That's a huge amount of pressure! At least I only spent nine hundred quid on M&S party food and a DJ that wouldn't play anything produced after 1986.'

Will laughed, his expression hard. He cleared his throat and traced the corners of his mouth. When he looked at Poppy, his eyes were set with resolve. 'Right, I'm going to do this.'

'Okay.'

'It's the right thing to do.'

'It is.'

'And whatever happens next, it won't be as bad as being legally bound to a woman who thought I was the second-best option.'

'You were never the second-best option. Always the first.' Poppy put her hands on Will's shoulders and squeezed. He placed a hand over her own and squeezed back, his taut brow easing into a look of heavy fatigue. 'I'll be right behind you,' she said.

Chapter Thirty-Eight

The path down to Mermaid Cove had been decorated with prayer flags that zigzagged around each hairpin bend, taking them closer to the burble of chatter that echoed in the natural amphitheatre of the cove. Ottilie's vision for a new-age, bohemian, spiritual-but-not-religious ceremony had somehow been expertly pieced together by Lola and what Poppy assumed was a small army of assistants borrowed from the hotel. Artfully frayed bunting hung above rows of wooden chairs, each decorated with sprigs of eucalyptus and gypsophila.

The guests were already in their seats, each curved row facing the podium-cum-altar that sat proud on the water. In the front row and wearing a sleek green jumpsuit, Josie stretched her legs. Beside her sat a woman with the self-contained poise of someone who knew her angles, a sharp-shouldered suit jacket accentuating her slender frame. Unmistakably, this had to be Will's mum, Carmen. Across the aisle, the feathered fascinator of Nicola Spruce quivered in the breeze as she beamed at her daughter. As promised, Ottilie had followed through with her shirking of tradition and was already standing on the podium, reversing the role of a late-arriving bride.

When Will reached the point where he'd become visible to those gathered below, he paused and took a breath as though he were about to step out onto an Olympic diving platform. Poppy didn't want to follow straight away. Instead, she squatted behind a tuft of pampas grass to watch.

A cheer built momentum as the guests spotted Will. Whilst they were distracted, Poppy slunk down the last few steps and traced the bottom of the cliff until she reached Lola, having spotted her voluminous beehive by the fisherman's hut. With a Britney Spears-style radio mic taped to her cheek, Lola clapped overenthusiastically as she glanced between her watch, Will's colourless face, and Ottilie.

Will's bride had perfectly captured a look partway between a *Vanity Fair* centrefold and a quirky adaptation of *A Midsummer Night's Dream*. Her dress hung from her shoulders on spaghetti straps, heavy lace draped below a plunging backline and enough fresh flowers to tempt a swarm of bees. She tapped her bare foot, readjusting herself when the harpist plucked the opening notes of Bruno Mars's 'Marry You'. Across the water, Ottilie turned to face them, her expression doleful and demure.

Poppy skimmed behind a stack of folded deck chairs until she reached Lola, who bent her microphone out of range.

'What's going on?' she said, speaking through a fixed smile. 'I didn't know what to do, so I made an announcement that the groom was running late. We've run out of ice and if we don't shift things along soon, the nun is going to get sunstroke and keel over.'

'The nun? What nun?'

'There.' Lola pointed to the podium, where an elderly woman stood in a fuchsia-pink habit. 'Well, she's not a proper nun. Not anymore. Ex-communicated. She's freelance now.'

'She's ancient.'

'I know.'

'How did you get her onto the podium?'

'We rowed her over.'

'Oh God.'

'What?'

'Will is doing it now.'

'Seriously?!' said Lola, peeking from behind her hand. Will picked up an oar and stepped onto the paddleboard, his face scrunched with concentration. He looked at the podium and tentatively pushed off the side. 'And he couldn't have managed this earlier, before I gathered everyone for the ceremony?'

'It's been a complicated morning.'

'You're telling me!' said Lola. 'This lot... they're going to know I had something to do with it.'

'Why?'

'Because of you!' she hissed, tilting her head to smile in mock affection as a nearby couple craned backwards to look at them.

'I've only been paid half my fee,' said Lola. Poppy smarted, ready to launch into a manifesto on the importance of doing what was right. Before she opened her mouth, Lola put a finger on Poppy's lips. 'I know, I know.'

'What do you know?' she said, her voice muffled.

'You haven't said it, but I know what you're thinking and you're right. Will doesn't deserve to be punished for something his twatty brother did. I can't force him. It would be Victorian levels of marital coercion. Eurgh, can you just give me a minute,' said Lola.

'We really need to—'

'Thirty seconds.' Lola closed her eyes, the highlighter on her cheekbones radiating in the sunshine.

'What are you doing?'

'Mentally spending all the money I would have earnt off the

back of this wedding. Bali. Mojitos. A silk kimono. It's mindfulness, Poppy.'

'Can we do the mindfulness later? When Will isn't about to break up with his fiancée? We're squatting over a grenade here.'

A splash drew their attention to the pool, where Will had dropped to his knees on the paddleboard, an oar tickling the water as he missed the podium where Ottilie stood. A gasp leapt from the guests as the paddleboard spun and bumped against a boulder in the cove, causing Will to wobble. Ottilie waited for him like an earth-bound angel, her boho waves dancing in the breeze as the affectionate burble of chatter crept towards awkward silence. The whole incident made Poppy want to deep-throat her own fist.

'Oh, he's doing it *now*, now,' said Lola.

The photographer who Poppy assumed was Christian lay on the floor, his camera angled on the waterline.

A peacock feather quivered in Lola's hair. 'I think I might pass out,' she whispered. 'What's his plan?'

'I honestly don't know. He hasn't thought that far ahead.'

'We can't be here when it all kicks off,' said Lola.

'It might *not* kick off. Ottilie might try and save face.'

'I can see why she'd try to avoid a public jilting, but I honestly don't think she considered that Will might find out. She must really want access to that Harrods gift list…'

Poppy dug a nail into her palm. Would it have been better to do the same a decade ago when she still had her twenties in front of her? It wouldn't have drowned out the humming voice in the back of her head; the one that told her the only way to maintain a stable life was to keep your expectations low.

They watched as Will gripped the pontoon, his knees on the board, his torso wiggling as he tried to protect his expensive Italian suit.

'I need to get closer,' said Poppy, craning on her tiptoes.

'You go ahead; I'll make some calls,' said Lola.

Poppy made her way back to the stairs that led out of the cove.

By standing on the first step, Poppy had an overview of the cove. Fifty feet above, a drone whirred, capturing footage. By the time Will leapt onto the podium beside Ottilie, the suit of his trouser leg was damp from where it had slipped into the water. He stood, Ottilie smiled, and the nun turned the first page of her order of service. From a pocket in her habit, she handed Will a microphone, but he refused to take it.

Lola caught her eye. 'What the fuck is he doing?' she mouthed.

What *was* Will doing? Ottilie looked... happy? Camera shutters clicked in quick succession. The nun dabbed her forehead and began to address the guests, but Ottilie swatted the air to dismiss her. From where she stood, Poppy could only see Will's back. He took Ottilie's hands in his own and held them. Poppy swallowed hard. He was going to go through with the ceremony. After a morning spent pacing tracks around the hotel to help him make up his mind, Will had crumbled.

Poppy clutched her head and turned to Lola, who put down her phone. 'I can't sit through this. He's making a mistake.'

'I don't think you'll have to,' said Lola, her stiletto nails pinching Poppy's skin as they looked towards the cove.

Chapter Thirty-Nine

'How *fucking* dare you?' screeched Ottilie, her smile slipping into a sneer of Greek theatre proportions. 'Really? You're doing this *now*?'

Will's knee jerked like a broken matchstick as he stepped backwards, his heel slipping off the platform. Ottilie pinned her bouquet under her armpit and slow clapped, her tongue sliding across the inside of her teeth. 'Well done. No, seriously. Well fucking done.'

'What's going on?' asked Lord Mountgrave, struggling out of his chair.

Newly aware of her surroundings, Ottilie looked across the water where the guests sat in varying degrees of bemusement. Beside her, Lola spoke furiously into her microphone from behind a cupped hand.

'Well?' said Ottilie. 'Are you going to do this? To me? To your family? Or might there be a *tiny* chance we can discuss this *later*, like adults.'

Will ran a hand down his face and pulled at his lower lip. Ottilie tried to take his hand, but he pulled it back.

'Don't. *Don't* do that.'

'Sorry, who are you?' said Ottilie, a sardonic edge slipping into her voice.

'Who am I? Who are *you*? Do you want to tell everyone? Because I didn't come here to publicly shame you. You've shamed yourself and if Lawrence were here, I'd say the same thing to him. You can't twist this.'

'Lawrence isn't here?' said Lord Mountgrave, with faux surprise. He unbuttoned his jacket with one hand and pretended to think. 'He must be, uh… do we think this conversation could take place back up at the hotel?' He raised his voice and addressed the guests, who had started to mutter. 'They've got the jitters – totally understandable – we can push back by a couple of hours. Lucky this isn't a registry office, eh? Ladies and gents, if you wouldn't mind holding on for a moment, I'll have some more drinks brought round.'

'Dad, would you please stop with this charade. I'm not doing it anymore!' shouted Will.

'Can someone get me a glass of water?' asked the nun, her voice small. Everyone ignored her.

Will loosened his tie. 'I'm not marrying you, Ottie. Not today, not tomorrow, not in a parallel universe.'

Ottilie turned away from the guests, but her voice carried on the breeze, quick and insistent. 'You know what I've been through. You know how much pressure comes with being part of all *this*,' said Ottilie, thumbing towards the shore. Her resolve was waning. Poppy recognised it well. Anger and self-loathing circled each other like a dog snapping at its own tail. 'We can sort ourselves out. Let's not be silly. *I* can sort myself out—'

'I don't want you to. I never asked for you to be *anything* other than who you already were, but you've not done the same with me. On my own, I've never been enough for you. The past three years… I've been thinking about them for a while now. How much of it was genuine? You always found reasons to be around my family. Half of them, anyway. The whole time we've been together, how often have you met my mum?'

Carmen stood up, her self-assured stance commanding attention with minimal effort. If it wasn't clear before that she had been famous in her modelling days, it was now. She ignored everyone and focused solely on her son.

'Will, come on—' said Ottilie.

'How many times?' he interrupted.

When Ottilie remained silent, Carmen raised her voice. 'Twice.'

Ottilie spluttered, as though this claim was unreasonable. 'You're guilt tripping me. She lives in a really awkward place.'

'It's south east London, Ottilie.' Will fiddled with the flapping cuffs on his shirt. There was a strength in him that lifted his chin and hardened his gaze. 'Look, all I ever wanted was you. I loved you. I did. I know it makes me sound stupid, but what does it matter now? I deserve to be enough. If not for you, for someone else.'

'Why are you being so melodramatic, talking in the past tense like that?'

'Don't patronise me anymore. I'm leaving. Don't follow.'

Lola took a tentative step forward, the silver tray in her hands quivering with tall glasses of straw-coloured fizz. 'Would anyone like a cucumber and elderflower spritz? No?'

The nun raised a wobbly hand.

'Oh, this is typical. *Absolutely* typical,' said Ottilie, ugly with anger.

Will shook his head. 'I don't want to turn this into a tit for tat. If you want to tell them what happened with Lawrence, please, knock yourself out. Don't push me into doing it for you.'

Lord Mountgrave patted his forehead with a silk pocket square and stepped towards the water. 'Will, be reasonable now. The past is the past. Besides, this charade is classic behaviour from

Lawrence. Classic. Don't let him taint what this is. The boy has a reputation for it, you know that. Always has.'

'What do you mean? You knew about them?' said Will, his shoulders rounding from the weight of the week.

'We all have a bit of a rogue phase. Families are... complicated tapestries of life, and ours has quite a lot of colour in it. Siblings, eh? Josie and I have—'

'Woah, woah, woah. Don't even start, Colin. I've got a folder on you *this thick* that I could pull out in a second,' said Josie with a snap of her fingers.

'I can second that,' said Will's mother, folding her arms.

Will scratched behind his ear like a dog trying to dislodge a grass seed. During a lull in their argument, Poppy walked towards the water's edge as the guests talked in loud and conspicuous voices.

'What has she done?' asked an elderly woman whose hat brim was so large she had to lift it to peer out.

'I think there's been an affair...' replied the person sitting next to her.

Lola hurried two waiters out of the fisherman's hut with trays of cut-crystal glasses, but Poppy could see how futile distraction techniques would be now that confusion had morphed into disbelief on one side and outright hostility on the other.

A seagull swerved away from the overhead drone, screeching as it barrel-rolled. The only person still seated in the front row was Josie, who leant forward, her elbows on her knees as Ottilie's parents berated Will from afar. Chatter burbled behind Poppy as she tried to catch Will's attention by waving.

'Black sheep,' someone said. 'There's one in every family, you can count on it.'

'At a wedding? Awful business.'

'Awful *for* business,' said a woman with a Swedish accent,

nodding towards Lord Mountgrave, whose neck was mottled pink.

'What's wrong with you?' said Poppy, glancing between her and the platform, where Will stood. 'He can hear you.'

Dried petals from a display of confetti cones caught on the wind, scattering themselves across the water. From the same direction, Lola joined Poppy at the water's edge. 'We need to get him out of here,' she said.

Poppy did a mental calculation of the escape route. 'Will! Come on!' she yelled.

Will scraped Ottilie's hand from his arm, pushed the paddleboard away with his toes, and launched himself onto it headfirst as though he were going down a slip 'n' slide. The momentum worked. When the nose of his board bumped against the rock, Poppy and Lola hooked him at the elbow and slid him onto the jetty. Marooned in the middle of the cove, Ottilie shouted for Will, the podium wobbling as her toes curled over the edge. The nun gripped her beaded waistband for stability as water flooded across Ottilie's train, the lace heavy as she struggled to kick her feet out from underneath.

'You can't leave me to deal with them on my own!' she called.

Will pushed himself into a seated position. Poppy took his chin in her hands and gently turned him to face her. 'Leave her to it, Will. This isn't the Middle Ages. No one's going to pull out burning torches for a pyre.'

'Oh God, oh God, oh God,' said Lola, as Lord Mountgrave sidestepped away from Ottilie's parents. He reached them in a few broad strides and crouched to their level, but stood when a stitch in his suit twanged like broken spaghetti.

'My boy, we'll do whatever we need to do *after* the ceremony. Give it time. I know a cracking marriage counsellor. Very discreet. You can both see her next week. She really knows her stuff.'

'You've been married four times!'

'That's not the point.'

'Dad, I know you think that wedding certificates accrue points like a loyalty card, but that's not me.'

'Son, don't let Lawrence spoil things for you. Look, he is who he is. There's nothing we can do about that now. He's shown remorse, which is more than he's done before.'

'How do you know?'

'Well, I... I, uh... I can tell, you see—'

Will shook his head in disbelief. 'The letter. You took it. Did you think it would stop me from finding out? I can't believe you were going to let me go through with this. Wow. That's... really fucked up, even for you.'

'Now, hold on a moment. How *dare* you speak to me like that?'

'Like what?' said Carmen, who stepped between her son and Lord Mountgrave, a vintage Chanel handbag tucked under her arm. 'I warned him about pinning too much hope on you. He had twelve years of Christmas cards in someone else's handwriting, and nothing in between. "Too busy" were you? How do you expect a child to understand that?'

'I think you'll find that running a corporation does, in fact, make one fairly busy.'

'I'm sorry, that wasn't an invitation to speak,' said Carmen, holding up a slender hand. She slowly shook her head. 'I didn't want him to turn into a snob. I wish that was the worst of it. With you, it's never something for nothing.'

'Dad, face it,' said Will. 'You've used me, like everything and everyone else in your life.'

Lord Mountgrave put his hands in his pockets as though they might betray him by reaching out to comfort his son. He dropped his voice and spoke in a monotone.

'You're not making sense.'

'Yes, he is,' Poppy heard herself say. She tugged Will to his feet, her heartbeat thumping. She couldn't believe Lord

Mountgrave had once intimidated her when he was as pathetic as this.

'Do you understand what you're walking away from?' he said. 'I'm lining you up for a job that most men would lop off their left testicle to have a chance at. CEO. On a plate.' Poppy winced. It was hardly an appealing image, but she didn't need to explain that to Will.

'I don't need your job,' said Will.

'Don't be stupid. If it's pressure you're worried about, I won't throw you in at the deep end right away.'

'Colin, listen to your son. He doesn't want it,' said Josie, who had slipped into the semi-circle they had formed around Will. In the distance, Ottilie was reaching for an oar that floated just out of arm's reach. 'Everyone here knows it too,' continued Josie, 'including the board.'

'I wouldn't be so sure,' said Lord Mountgrave. 'Where do you get off, flying in to tell me how to run the business I've spent my entire adult life building?'

'Building? You inherited it!' Josie pushed her hands in her pockets and squinted with a hard smile. 'Profits are down. There's no expansion. You've produced a nice publicity image, but no one believes it. Even if Will wanted the job, he's not going to get it. I am. It was always going to be me. You'll run this business into the ground if you insist on using your children as puppets. No offence, Will, but if you took the job, you'd have a fucking horrible time, with or without that girl on your arm,' said Josie, gesturing to Ottilie behind them.

'This is outrageous,' said Lord Mountgrave.

'It may be, but it's the truth. I have the board's word that they'll vote me in as CEO when it's officially proposed tomorrow. There have been whispers about it all week, but you were too busy trying to put on your happy-family campaign to notice. The more you resist this, the more damage you'll do. See? I'm not a total asshole. In a way, I'm protecting your assets.' Josie cupped her ear, as though she were listening for something. 'What's that? Oh, you're welcome.'

Lord Mountgrave's cheeks drained of colour, his hair damp at the nape of his neck. 'Will, ignore her. She's filling your head with nonsense.'

'Business. It's a bitch, am I right?' said Josie.

Behind them, Ottilie's father unknotted a rowboat and threw the line to his daughter, who caught it with the reactions of someone who had played competitive lacrosse at school. Josie nudged Will with her foot, her eyes insistent. When Poppy followed her line of sight, she noticed it too. The steps leading out of the cove were clear. Will kissed his mum on the cheek and nodded.

'Will, come on,' said Poppy. 'Let's get you out of here.'

Chapter Forty

'**O**nce more and I think we've got it!'

Poppy's heel slipped in the base of the dinghy as she tried to catch her footing. Her arm felt clumsy and slow, but urgency took over as she coordinated her tugs with Will and Lola. On the fifth pull, the engine puttered to life with all the enthusiasm of a slug on a hot tile. Poppy tipped the engine into the water as Ottilie appeared beneath the swinging sign of The Drunken Prawn.

'I can confirm that she's angry, Will. Severe, acute anger,' said Poppy, eyes fixed on his jilted bride as she shouted for them to stop.

'I'd like to go. Now,' he said, his eyes wide with fear.

'Got it.'

Poppy twisted the throttle a little too enthusiastically, the force sending them slipping onto their backs.

The knowledge Poppy had of seafaring was entirely contained within the running time of *Point Break*: useful for recalling surf-based one-liners, less so for practical methods of captaining an ancient dinghy. Poppy grappled for the waxy rope by her side and dragged herself up, looking out beyond the harbour through wind-whipped hair. She twisted the throttle again. At first, they lurched forwards at a pace that surprised her, the dinghy smacking the surface of each wave. After a few seconds, the engine ticked over and dropped to a bass thrum as they swerved to the left. Although she had a firm grip on the tiller, Poppy couldn't figure out how to keep the boat straight.

'No, shove it that way!' cried Lola, jerking her chin towards the mainland as they circled back towards the island. Considering the crowd of wedding guests now assembled by the harbour, the situation was less than ideal.

'What's going on?' shouted Lola above the noise of the rattling engine.

'I think the rudder must be broken!' said Poppy.

Poppy pushed her hair off her face and groaned as they swerved towards the very spot they had left moments before. Lola used her hand as a sun visor and squinted at the dock, her eyes wide. 'What the hell is she doing?' she said. On the dockside, Ottilie appeared to be unlacing her shoes.

'I can't turn the engine off. If I do, I won't get it started again.' Poppy pushed the tiller until the handle pressed into the dinghy's inflatable side. A boat-length away from the shore, Poppy, Will, and Lola tried their best to evenly distribute their weight in the boat, which performed one tight circle after the other, their speed slowing to a crawl.

'Will! Will, please. Let me come with you so we can talk,' shouted Ottilie, ignoring her mother's protests as she lowered herself down the barnacle-studded ladder.

'Surely she's not going to try and swim in that dress?' said Poppy.

'I wouldn't be so sure,' said Will.

Ottilie reached a rung slick with seaweed. When the boat

closed yet another circle, she dropped from the ladder. Although shallow, the water was well above her waist.

Will and Lola leant backwards as Ottilie waded towards the boat. She hooked her elbows between sun-bleached fenders that dangled over the dinghy's side, her shoulders covered in goosebumps, skirt floating around her like an ethereal jellyfish.

'Will! Please, we just need to talk this through,' spluttered Ottilie. She gulped, caught between crocodile tears. 'They're your family. You know what they're like. I can't fix this on my own. I need you. You understand— I didn't mean what I said before— My head is a mess.'

Poppy took her hand off the throttle. She would help Will with an escape plan, but drew the line at testifying in court if Ottilie drowned because her wedding dress got caught in the propeller.

Will commando-crawled over to Ottilie, his face slick with sea spray. By this point, they were at a standstill, gentle waves nudging them back to shore. Poppy had the familiar feeling that she might lose him again. The difference this time, almost ten years later, was that she knew she wouldn't lose herself. She had a strength that was no longer buried. Whatever happened now, she could weather the storm.

Poppy and Lola locked eyes from either side of the boat, Will stretched between them. Her friend knew what she was thinking without her needing to say a word. Lola scooted forward, the boat wobbling as she sat in a puddle that had risen around their ankles.

'Shall we... shall we pull her in?' Lola asked

Ottilie clutched a length of sun-bleached rope, her knuckles white. Will didn't take a moment to think about it. He unhooked her hands and held them, like he had at the altar. Ottilie broke into a smile, her yoga-toned forearms taut as she reached up to kiss him.

'Go!' shouted Will.

'What?'

He let go of her hands and Ottilie slid back into the water as Will slipped to the floor from the thrust of their feeble engine, his forehead pressed against Poppy's knee.

'Is she okay?' he said, shouting into the wind.

Poppy followed their wake back to shore, where Ottilie had pulled herself up onto a barnacle-encrusted rock, her dress sodden. 'She's fine, but, er… *we* might not be.'

'What's wrong with the boat?' asked Lola, panicked. The sides had sagged, the puddle at the bottom rapidly expanding as they bumped over each wave.

'There's a hole!' shouted Will. Lola followed his gaze, where a small tear flapped in the hull. She shoved her thumb inside it to plug the gap. 'I can't guarantee my nails didn't cause this to begin with,' she said, smudging her thick eyeliner as she wiped sea spray from her face.

'Will, get a paddle and help me out!'

Will unhooked the spare oar and wielded it like a lance over the side, his tie flapping over one shoulder.

'How's it looking?' asked Poppy, trying to judge the distance between them and the mainland.

'I think we have… a minute. Maybe two before we sink. Can everyone swim?' said Will.

'I have a silver medal for under-18s synchronised swimming,' said Lola. 'But I'm useless without a nose clip.'

'Useful to know, thanks.'

'Quick, take off your shoe and start scooping.'

Will hesitated, his eyes steadfastly fixed on hers. He blinked salt water out of his eyes and lurched towards Poppy as the dinghy bumped up and over yet another wave. Cold water slapped her face as a seagull flew overhead, its squawk shrill. Were gulls like vultures? Could they anticipate the likelihood of death at sea?

Will pulled at the lace of his shoe. 'I've never been more

thankful to have size-twelve feet.' As he reached over the side of the dinghy, Will paused and put his hand on Poppy's knee, his touch comforting despite the bitter English sea. 'Hey. Thanks,' he said, a sad smile pulling at the corners of his mouth. 'For the rescue effort. If anyone was going to pull through, it was you. It was always you. That's the truth.'

'You're not dehydrated, are you?'

'Promise.'

'Hold that thought,' said Poppy, her chest blooming with warmth. 'We're not on dry land yet.'

Epilogue

THREE MONTHS LATER

'What the hell is that supposed to be?'

'It's a puffin,' said Poppy, as she turned her half-painted mug over in her hands.

'More like a fat penguin,' Lola snorted.

'Don't shame me for *actually* attempting to paint something rather than getting huffy and giving up.'

'I have *not* given up. It's Jackson Pollock inspired,' said Lola, loading up a paintbrush.

'Jackson Bollocks.'

'Oi!' Lola flicked purple paint at Poppy, who laughed and shielded her mug with a curtain of hair.

'I did not pay twenty quid to leave without a bloody puffin mug,' said Poppy.

'Fat penguin.'

'It's a puffin! It's supposed to be commemorative.' Poppy squinted at her painting. It really *did* look like a fat penguin, but she'd committed to it now.

'You guys are going to have us kicked out,' said Will, who squinted at his own design, his tongue stuck out in concentration.

'I'm ruining your date, aren't I?' said Lola. She looked between Poppy and Will like a proud parent. Poppy rolled her eyes, her cheeks smarting. Lola was many things, but subtle was not one of them.

'It's not a date, it's a celebration. You've reached a milestone too.'

'Exactly. That's what you don't understand about my design,' said Lola. 'It's an artistic representation of my time on Loxby, see? Each splatter captures the gradual demise of my nervous constitution.'

In Lola's words, the three of them were only allowed to congregate in a location that guaranteed a lack of excitement or drama, which was why they'd ended up in a paint-your-own-pottery café on the outskirts of Bath. Poppy's half-term break marked the beginning of bitter weather, in stark contrast to the thirty-degree heat they had experienced the last time they were in one place together. Will wore a deep-red turtleneck sweater, which Poppy suspected he had chosen for two reasons. One, it sharpened his jawline, which was now hidden beneath a short beard. Two, if someone recognised him, he could pull it past his cheekbones and claim he was someone else.

Although it had been months since the short but intense furore caused by The Most Exclusive Wedding That Never Happened, Will still avoided passing newsstands. On the other hand, Lola had secretly collected every issue that featured leaked shots of Loxby, especially if they showcased the table settings that she had spent hours designing but never managed to use.

Three weeks to the day after they left the island, a stream of articles from The Sidebar of Shame still filled Poppy's notification feed, each one featuring a photograph of Ottilie in a highly lit studio, her best 'scorned woman' pose filling the screen with sharp elbows and barrel curls. The timing wasn't a coincidence. It would have been the last day of Will and Ottilie's honeymoon.

Seeing as half the country's tabloids were bankrolled by the Mountgraves, Ottilie ensured she appeared in the other half.

'Personally, I'm quite offended that no one has noticed my masterpiece,' said Will, finishing a crude outline of a seagull with a flick of his wrist.

Poppy and Lola leant in. Will had painted the three of them in a dinghy, their expressions dabbed in crude black paint: Poppy's steely look of determination, Will's exertion as he pulled on the boat's oars, and Lola's open-mouthed scream, outlined with her signature red lipstick.

'Why am I the only one who looks terrified when I distinctly recall being the first to make it to shore?' said Lola.

'The first to make it to shore with the most articulate backstroke I have ever seen in a time of crisis,' said Poppy.

'I *told* you I used to be a synchronised swimming champion.'

'Do you think they'll send a robot submarine down to inspect the wreckage in a hundred years' time, like they did for the *Titanic*?' asked Will.

'I don't think it will inspire a £500m-pound film, despite how determined you were to row us to safety. Do you remember the state of the thing by the time we bailed? It was like balancing on a deflated balloon,' said Poppy. 'My poor camera.'

'Your poor camera? My poor thumb, more like. I felt like I was giving the boat a pessary,' said Lola.

Poppy laughed and shook her head in disbelief, even though she knew it was the truth. By the time they had staggered up the beach between family picnics and children with buckets swinging from their arms, they had gathered quite a crowd. Thanks to a credit card that Lola had slipped in her bra cup, they had been able to buy T-shirts from a tacky tourist shop before figuring out how to get as far away as possible in the shortest amount of time. Poppy still wore "My sister went to Devon and all I got was this lousy T-shirt" emblazoned across her chest in bed.

'Did you ever get your memory card back?' asked Lola.

'No. Will's dad has it in a safe somewhere,' replied Poppy.

Will leant back in his chair and frowned. 'I couldn't say where it is now. We're still not talking. I only get updates through Josie, but she's not great at keeping in touch.'

'I guess she's pretty busy now, what with the new job?' asked Poppy, pretending she didn't know the answer. She didn't want Lola to feel left out, even though she'd heard all the headlines from Will during snatched phone calls.

'Yeah, she is,' said Will. 'I owe her one, regardless. Dad made it pretty difficult for me to sell my shares, so Josie cut through the red tape for me. That's it. I'm not attached to The Mountgrave Foundation anymore, except by name.' Lola gave Will an opera clap.

'Is it a bit like having access to Monopoly money?' asked Poppy.

'Give me some and I'll let you know,' said Lola, nudging Will.

He laughed. Under the table, his thumb stroked the length of Poppy's little finger, lighting sparks in her stomach. 'I keep asking Poppy to let me invest in her studio, but she won't have it,' said Will, his mouth crinkling with a smile.

'My girl is independent now, what can I say?' said Lola, bumping her shoulder. 'How's the new pad holding up? Do you smoke French cigarettes on the balcony? Stretch canvases whilst listening to obscure jazz records from the thirties?'

'Yes, all of the above,' said Poppy, nodding sagely. The one-bedroom flat she had bought in a building that backed onto an overflow canal wasn't exactly Montmartre, but it did come with a studio in the eaves that was flooded with light at three o'clock every afternoon. She loved it so much she had dragged her bed up there, difficult though it had been to pull a mattress up a spiral staircase. In a strange way, it reminded her of the attic she had shared with Josh, with one big difference: that she actually wanted to be there. It had taken a chunk of the money she had received from the sale of their house, but she needed to keep some back. Her work application for a transfer to a nearby college had been accepted, meaning that from next week, her hours – and pay – would drop by half. Still, she didn't have to worry about bumping into Josh, which was priceless.

'Is Josh still being a twat about the whole thing?' asked Lola.

'Yes and no. He got his solicitor to send over yet another list of items he wanted to keep. Power plays, like always. I told him he could keep his horrible sofa suite, but I want the retail cost, plus ten per cent for the inconvenience. He agreed.'

'Where did this hard baller come from?' asked Lola, impressed.

'I think it was spending a week in the company of Will's family. I've developed a ruthless streak. Speaking of which, where's Loxby?' asked Poppy, inspecting Will's plate.

'I'm pretending it doesn't exist,' said Will.

'Final point – consider it a constructive critique… you're not as muscly as that,' said Lola, pointing to the miniature Will painted on his plate.

'A self-portrait can be whatever you want it to be. Isn't that right, Poppy?'

'Well…' said Poppy, her voice high. 'I guess it's a bit different with photography.'

'In the culture of fairness, here's one for you, Lola. What's this blob?' said Will, pointing to a clumsy heart near the lip of Lola's mug.

'You know I'm unsentimental at the best of times, so that shows my love of funerals.'

Will leant over to Poppy and spoke near her ear in mock secrecy. The warmth of his breath on her neck made her skin tingle. 'Is she being serious?'

'Deadly,' said Poppy.

'Do you miss wedding planning?' he asked.

Lola tipped back her third espresso and wiped lipstick from the rim of her cup. 'Absolutely not. Funeral coordination is much better. When all is said and done, it gives me a better quality of life. I get my weekends, the client doesn't talk back, and you find just as many drunks crying in the loos, so I had a set of transferable skills without even realising. I'm booked up, day in, day out. Weird, when you can't really plan for a funeral, but hey, that's why I moved to London. It's basic business economics. Big place, more proverbial buckets kicked, endless bookings for me.' She pointed her paintbrush at Will. 'Your lot put me off weddings for life.'

'That's understandable,' he said, inspecting his mug. 'I'm finished.'

'Me too,' said Poppy.

'Thank fuck you're better at taking pictures of birds than you are of painting them,' said Lola.

'Excuse me,' said a woman, tapping Lola on the shoulder, 'but would you mind your language? We brought my mother here for her eightieth birthday and it's somewhat polluting the occasion.'

'Polluting?' said Lola, hooking her arm over the back of the chair to look at the group. Poppy lowered her eyes. This woman didn't know who she was dealing with. 'Point taken. I'll pipe down. How old did you say your mother is?'

'Eighty.'

'In good health, is she?'

'Thereabouts.'

'Hmm. Well, if anything changes...' Lola plopped a satchel onto her lap, slipped out a business card, and closed the woman's hand around it. When she squinted to read it, Lola leant back and gave a thumbs up to a sour-faced elderly woman who by all observations was having a horrible time. 'Happy birthday!'

'Really subtle marketing techniques you've got there,' said Poppy.

'You've got to hustle where you can. Do you want this?' asked Lola, pointing to the splattered mug.

'Not really.'

'Will?'

He looked up, brightening. 'Seriously?'

'It's yours. Order me a matcha latte to go, will you? I need to counterbalance the caffeine. Be back in a hot minute; I've got to change.'

Lola shouldered her bag and disappeared, her sharp heels echoing down the hallway.

Will pulled his ankle onto his knee and shifted his chair an inch towards Poppy's. He dropped his paintbrush on the oil cloth, leant towards her and breathed as though he had just stepped outside after too long indoors. Poppy's stomach fizzed, increasing to a swoop of warmth as Will kissed her collarbone.

'Don't let Lola catch you doing that – she'll start screaming,' said Poppy. She could feel her heartbeat in the soft part of her neck, between her jaw and earlobe.

'When are you going to tell her?' said Will.

'I'm not sure. Not yet.'

Poppy felt Will nod. Beneath the table, she interlocked her fingers with his, their palms pressed together.

'I haven't got any meetings on Friday,' he said. 'You know what that means?'

'What?'

'I can drive up. Spend a few days together. If you want to.'

Poppy shook her head. 'I can't. I'm in Manchester this weekend. There's an urban riding school that's just opened and I'm going up to photograph the place. Well, I will be during the six hours I'm not on a train. I didn't fancy staying over. Unless you want to come? Make a weekend of it?'

'So long as it doesn't involve a boat, I'm there,' said Will, smiling.

'Hey, I got you a present,' said Poppy.

'You did?'

Poppy lifted the flap of her backpack and wiggled a photo album free. She handed it to Will, who weighed it in his hands.

'Have you slipped a gold bullion down the spine?'

She laughed. 'Open it.'

The album creaked as he lifted the cover, the pages musky from years spent in an antiques shop. On the inside cover, Poppy had collaged Will and Ottilie's wedding invites, given to her by Lola. The letters read:

We invite you to celebrate: Will Mountgrave

'When did you do this?' he said, tracing the words with his finger.

'Whilst you were in New York working through stuff with Josie. I was packing the house up and found a box of stuff in the attic that I'm pretty sure hasn't been opened since we left that grotty student flat. There were unopened pots of garlic pizza sauce that went out of date in 2009, which I'm pretty sure is a nuclear disaster waiting to happen.' Poppy was conscious that she was rambling. She only ever rambled when she was nervous. 'It didn't take me long.' She paused. 'Okay, it took me ages, but that doesn't mean you have to like it.'

In her newly empty living room, Poppy had spent more hours cutting and sticking than she had during the two years of her art GCSE, back when every project book was covered in sticky-back plastic and images of plump lips torn from the pages of *Vogue* magazine.

Will turned a leaf. Poppy had transformed each photograph into a miniature work of art, laser-cut paper and comedy motifs interspersed between the pages. The photos drifted through the years, the first page dominated by their first night living away from home, eighteen years old, their flatmates pointing at Will, who had two bottles of cheap cider stuck to his hands with duct tape. Edward Ciderhands – the pinnacle of campus-based drinking games. In the next image, the flash of a club photographer illuminated the neon paint dabbed down the bridge of Will's nose as he looked at someone with soft beer-drunk eyes, a dimple in each cheek. Up until last week, she hadn't noticed it was the back of her head in the image, that it was her he had been looking at the whole time.

'Is it weird? It's weird, isn't it?' said Poppy, reaching over to take the album back.

'Are you kidding?' He turned another page. 'It's amazing. I can't believe you managed to do all this. It must have taken ages.'

'Not that much time. An ordinary amount of time,' lied Poppy.

Will flicked to the last printed photograph. It was sharp and monochrome, emphasising the markings of a black and white puffin, eyes looking directly down her lens. One foot of its bowling-pin body slid down the front of Will's beanie hat as he squinted in the sunshine. It was the most comfortable she had ever felt behind a camera.

'Poppy—'

'What?'

She held her breath. They hadn't quite figured out what speed they worked best at. Their university friendship had had a lack of boundaries, and it hadn't served either of them well. So much time had passed since they had swigged from the same carton of orange juice, swapped jumpers, fallen asleep on the floor of each other's rooms. The next time she saw him, he had been marrying someone else. A decade had passed and they were stitching the bookends of their lives together.

'I don't believe in fate,' said Will.

'Good, because it's bollocks,' she agreed.

'But if I did, I'd say that the photographer catching norovirus is a pretty good example of it.'

'They'll print that inside a Valentine's Day card one day.'

Will sat back in his chair. He lifted his chin and looked at her as though she had said something profound.

'Oh, I forgot. There's a theme to this.' Poppy took the album from Will and placed it on the table. 'Something old.' She pointed to the cracked leather cover. 'Something new.' Poppy flicked to the most recent picture – a day trip to London during which they'd seen no landmarks at all and sat in the back room of a pub, talking for hours. 'Something borrowed.' She tapped a beer mat pinched from The Drunken Prawn. 'And something blue.'

Poppy bit her lip, nerves bubbling in her chest. She placed a blue envelope on the table. He looked from the page to Poppy, and back again. 'Is this for me?' asked Will.

'Not really. I just thought you might want to see it. It's a bit of a moment. For me, anyway. I feel like I need to do jazz hands or something.'

'Okay... I can cope with weird, but y'know, within reason,' said Will. He slipped his finger underneath the envelope flap.

'No, wait,' she added hastily, clutching her forehead.

'I won't look at... whatever this is if you're not ready for me to. That's not a loaded statement, I really mean it.'

Poppy took the envelope back and gathered herself. 'Before you read this, I just wanted to say that it *is* a gift, but it's for me.'

'Right...'

'What I mean is, as brilliant as you are—'

'You forgot very handsome and cool.'

'—And as handsome and cool as you are, I would have done this anyway,' she said, sliding a thick wodge of paper out of the envelope. 'I wasn't ready to sign my name to anything when I first arrived at Loxby, even though I'd split with Josh months before. I was being stubborn, sure, but there was more going on. Dark stuff. It felt like a splinter lodged in my head.' Poppy took a deep breath and removed her hands from the front page.

Will took the papers from her and wobbled them in his hands. 'Wow. Do you think they use a special stapler to get through a stack this big?'

'Not quite what I thought your attention would be drawn to...'

'What? Oh.' Will fell quiet as he scanned the page. She'd seen a similar look before in her students when they first opened exam papers. Poppy bit her thumbnail and glanced down the corridor, half-hoping that Lola would come back immediately and at the same time, not for another hour at least.

'Like I said, I'm not trying to make out that this is a gift. I just wanted you to see it.'

Will put her signed divorce papers down on the table. He ran his thumb up the back of Poppy's hairline and pulled her towards him. His gaze was urgent, his bottom lip swollen as though he'd been biting it. He stopped, an inch from her lips.

'I'm proud of you. I'd be proud of you even if I didn't feel the way I do.'

'And how's that?'

'Like I want to throw you over my shoulder and book a room in the nearest Travelodge.' He released a strained breath. 'That's if I had the strength to perform a manoeuvre like that. Either way, I'd give it a good go.'

'A Travelodge? Have you forgotten I've been on your *actual* island? And you're offering me a Travelodge?' Poppy grinned. Will mirrored her.

'Hey,' he said.

'Mmm?'

'Come here.'

He lifted Poppy's chin. Her elbow slipped on her divorce papers, the kiss more urgent and quite possibly toothier than she had intended.

'Oooh!' Lola's sing-song voice boomed from behind a chutney display. 'I knew it! I bloody knew it!'

'You didn't!' said Poppy.

'I did. Let me tell you now, if it comes to it, you'd best elope. And you can forget about calling me to be a witness. My Mountgrave wedding days are *done*. I'll come to your wake and nothing before, d'you hear?'

Poppy laughed and closed the photo album, the last few pages ready to be filled with photographs that didn't yet exist.

Acknowledgments

Wahey, we're here again! I have a pint of tea on the go, so buckle in.

I can measure the pain of the writing process, quite literally, with how many times I've kicked the sofa. I am proud to say that *The Wedding Crasher* caused just one kick. Hooray! I honestly had a blast writing this book and spent many joyful lockdown hours with Poppy, Lola, and the Mountgraves. Years ago, someone once told me that I was rotting my brain by watching numerous reality TV shows involving wealthy people making bad choices, but ha! Look where we are now!

Thank you to Joe, for all the walks I dragged you on to help me brainstorm ideas. Your patience helped tease the seed into a sapling. Also, thank you for delivering tea to my desk. And wine.

To my agent, Hayley Steed, for being the best sounding board and champion. I owe you multiple glasses of bubbles in a room where there are many sequins and we are wearing most of them. Thank you to Elinor Davies for your ever lovely emails and sharing your thoughts on my first draft when I had a wobble. A big squeeze to everyone at Team Madeleine Milburn!

To Tilda McDonald, who didn't blink twice at my idea for opening the novel with a deflating dinghy scene. Thank you for your funny, insightful thoughts and my early, often messy, plot questions. You will always be my first!

To Jennie Rothwell, my wonderful editor, for your sharp eye and unwavering enthusiasm, especially when wrestling with the many legged octopus that was my first draft. It's such a joy to know that you understand my sense of humour – and when it has gone too far! The fact that you love Lawrence as much as I do says it all.

To Lydia Mason for your keen copy editing eyes – you worked wonders on that tricky timeline, thank you!

To Charlotte Ledger and everyone at One More Chapter who put their heads together to publish great books, thank you for everything you do behind the scenes.

So much of novel writing involves sitting in a room on your own whilst characters squabble in your head, so when Sara Roberts holds out a digital hand to pull you into the fun world for a while, you take it. Thank you for jumping in with fantastic ideas and supporting the weirder ones I have, you social whizz, you!

The reason I write about bone-deep friendships so often is no doubt because I am in the orbit of pals who are the best bunch of people I know. Endless thanks to my Norfolk Girls who answer my odd questions via WhatsApp and bat 'What if' ideas around with me. One of my greatest regrets in life is that we never filmed our amateur version of *Pride and Prejudice* as twelve-year-olds. One day this wrong will be righted.

Thanks to Emily and especially to the woman who keeps us both in line: Tonya Harding's mum.

To Mum, Dad, Linford and Rachael, who are always the best cheerleaders. Also to Cassidy, who is my favourite toddler to FaceTime. Sorry there aren't enough dinosaurs in my books.

To the McKibbens, human and animal, for being so lovely

during the chaotic midst of a pandemic, book writing, and flat buying.

Showing up every day is half the battle with writing and London Writer's Salon makes that a happy obligation. Who knew that sharing space with two hundred writers every morning is the best way to keep your chin up and your fingers typing? Thanks to Matt, Parul, and the LWS team for hosting Writer's Hour, to Portia Holdsworth for our solo writing sessions with big chats and even bigger cups of tea, and Holly McCulloch and Mary Hargreaves for the voice notes and voices of reason.

Finally, but most importantly, to my readers. If you've ever shouted about a book of mine, reviewed it, pushed it onto friends, or loved it quietly, thank you. It means the world. You are the very goodest of eggs.

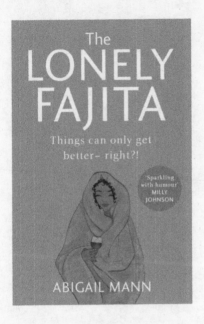

The
LONELY
FAJITA

Things can only get
better– right?!

'Sparkling
with humour'
MILLY
JOHNSON

ABIGAIL MANN

It's Elissa's birthday, and she's accidentally booked a cervical
smear instead of a celebration… Great. The icing on the cake? Her
boyfriend is kicking her out of their houseshare.

So when she's offered the chance to live with a pensioner rent-free,
Elissa knows she needs to impress Annie, who turned down the
last twenty-two applicants. Somehow, even after Elissa goes on
about 'definitely not being an axe-murderer', Annie chooses her.

And just like Elissa, prickly, sweary, big-hearted Annie could use a
friend. Elissa may have nowhere else to go, but is she just where
she needs to be?

Available now in ebook, audio and paperback

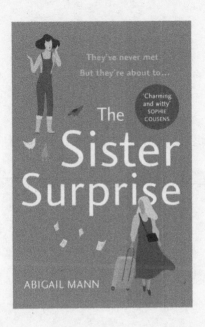

They've never met.
But they're about to...

'Charming
and witty'
SOPHIE
COUSENS

The
Sister
Surprise

ABIGAIL MANN

Journalist Ava takes a DNA test hoping to discover her roots. Instead, she finds out she has a half-sister ... whilst on a live stream watched by 100,000 people. Her boss thinks it's the perfect click-bait story. Ava just wants to go to Moira's tiny Scottish village and meet her.

But when Ava arrives undercover as a volunteer farmhand, she realises Moira – who's her pig-wrestling, chatterbox polar opposite – might not be delighted by the news. And the longer Ava stays in Kilroch, with its inappropriately attractive minister and ties to her hidden family past, the more complicated this surprise is going to get...

Available now in ebook and paperback